THE TRINITY EFFECT

by

Eleanor!
Thanks for your
support. Hope
you like it!
Mark

MARK GEIGER

www.TrinityNovel.com

FOREWORD

During my 25 plus years as a lawyer, practicing mostly criminal law, I have learned a lot about psychology and the dynamics of how people relate to one another. Why is it that people, who I believe are basically good, can be evil? Can any of us, when pushed too far, or in the face of extreme injustice, do something "bad" that somehow seems right at the time?

I started writing creatively in the late 1990s. I was inspired by authors such as Dan Brown, Harlan Coben, Clive Cussler, James Rollins and Stephen King.

I was raised Catholic but ended up spending more time in a Presbyterian church when my then wife's decision to convert away from Catholicism opened my eyes to the inconsistencies and intellectual dishonesty of the religion I grew up with. However, I didn't find the Presbyterian religion to be any different than Catholicism. The primary problem with both religions was their failure to encourage, much less allow, freedom of thought. I was taught as a Catholic not to read the Bible because it was "too confusing." I was told to listen to the priests because they will lead you.

I'm not sure what draws me to religious thrillers—perhaps it is the notion that so many of us are indoctrinated into religion at an early age and what we are taught tends to bring both comfort and then confusion, as we grow older.

The questions that motivated me to write this novel include: Can the end ever justify the means? Would/should a Deity, whether it is God, Buddha, Mohamed, etc., permit humanity to kill in their name? While we all know of examples throughout history of this happening, what is the price we all pay for these decisions? Are we so far gone as a society that we can only be saved by a prophet, or is salvation always in our own hands?

Through The Trinity Effect, I hope to motive readers to ask questions, and to seek answers. One of my goals is to persuade those who blindly believe to use their intellect to analyze what they are being taught and choose for themselves. In so doing, my hope is that each individual will create their own relationship with God as THEY see God.

ACKNOWLEDGMENTS

I am very thankful to my wife, Pam, and my dogs and cats for putting up with my crazy life. Pam has been an incredibly loving and supportive partner as I continue my journey to develop my craft as a writer, and juggle my career as an attorney. It is something that I greatly appreciate.

Prior to 2006 I had written two novels and had tried to get published. I was not having much luck. I attended the Maui Writers Conference and Retreat at that time, and since I love movies, I chose to take a screenwriting course being offered. That is where I met Michael Andres Palmieri, the Director of the Screenwriting Program.

I worked with Michael privately, and through his coaching, I was able to produce several screenplays, and then put to use what I learned in screenwriting back into my books. One of the key elements of Michael's coaching was that he was able to give me insight into myself as a creative person. In so doing, he empowered me to get beyond my own self-imposed limitations. The end result was that I became, and continue to become a better storyteller. He is a valuable colleague and friend.

Last, I am also grateful for my editor, Christine Dubios.

CHAPTER I

In the beginning was the Word, and the Word was with
God, and the Word was God (John 1:1).

Jesus said to Judas, "Step away from the rest of [the disciples] and I shall
tell you the mysteries of the kingdom" (Judas Gospel, 24). "[I]t is the Lord,
the Lord of the universe who commands, [not the priests]. . . the Lord com-
mands, 'On the last day they will be put to shame' (Judas Gospel, 41).

SOMEWHERE IN NAPLES, ITALY

Five men, dressed in dark, cotton pants and heavy-duty, black military shirts stood next to a large, well-used van inside a hulking warehouse, checking their Glock 19s. One man–- middle-Eastern looking, just like the others—chambered a round and shoved the gun into a shoulder holster. He opened the driver's door and climbed in. The others entered on the passenger side. No one spoke. Their movements were deliberate and purposeful. Their leader had preached to them about the need for their actions, the dire state of the world, the rampant sin. Some were sure he was right, but others had doubts. The believers felt that doing nothing was worse than what might come. It wasn't a sure thing, this solution their leader came up with, but if he was right, not many would make it.

The driver started the engine, pushed the automatic garage door button and waited for the huge aluminum door to open. Before they left the warehouse, the driver turned around and glanced behind him at the enclosed, concrete death chamber, with one sealed door and a small window. Near the chamber, on a table, was a small nebulizer, with a tube running to a small inlet on the wall of the room. On the floor, nestled next to the table, stood a small refrigerator containing the deadly virus. Fifteen to twenty other men rolled out a huge piece of thick plastic, which would eventually hang from ceiling to floor, cutting the warehouse in half. Piles of HAZMAT suits were stacked on a table near the concrete room.

Gustav, the group's leader, sat in the passenger seat, certain that what they were doing was right but uncertain if it would work. What if the virus wasn't as effective as they thought? What if their scientists hadn't properly replicated it? Failure wouldn't be condoned.

They all belonged to an underground Christian sect known as Trinity. It had been in existence since WWII. Never had they undertaken something this drastic. People believed that they were responsible for a myriad of terrorist attacks around the world —from abortion clinics to the burning of a Klan building in Mississippi that killed fifty of the misguided fools. No one would argue that they didn't get what they deserved.

And yet, no one could prove that Trinity was responsible. Gustav's great uncle would have been disgusted with how they had perverted the reason he and others founded Trinity. Originally, it was a secret, Vatican-based group of resistance fighters dedicated to ousting the Nazi's from Italy. While the Pope signed a treaty with Hitler, and chose not to decry the horrors of Nazi concentration camps and the occupation, there were those inside the Vatican who would not–could not–condone what they did. And so, Trinity was born.

But there was more to it than that. Pope Pius XII had never decried the Nazi atrocities the way one would expect of a Christian leader of his importance. He was one of the first to sign a treaty with Germany. He never spoke out against a German roundup of Jews in Rome in October of 1943, which could have been seen from the Vatican's windows. Later, the Vatican did save Jews from the Nazis, but it was the failure to recognize the Nazi threat that drove many of Trinity's members to form the secret organization. Sitting back and doing nothing was not an option. They had to act. That many of the members were Vatican-based made it easier to hide their organization.

They assisted the French resistance and the Italian resistance with terrorist-like bombing runs and guerilla assaults against Nazi strongholds. But unlike other resistance groups, they survived the war, if only to move from physical resistance to intellectual resistance. They became a group of disgruntled religious leaders and thinkers who were dissatisfied with much of Christianity. That they finally had the resolve to take matters into their own hands warmed Gustav like a shot of whiskey. They would take back the world and turn it into something their God would be proud of.

But Gustav had some misgivings. He didn't doubt, he just wasn't sure. And they had to be sure. The deadly virus –with a 100 percent kill rate within six-ten hours of exposure—was frightening. Orfeo, Trinity's leader, had no doubts, or so he said.

"Only the faithful will survive," Orfeo proclaimed. Gustav had faith, as did Trinity's members. But that amounted only to several hundred people. Was their version of faith the same as most Christians or Buddhists or whoever believed in a deity? But then that was the point. There weren't many that deserved to survive. And the world was a cesspool of sin, greed and evil, a message that had been preached to them for years. Orfeo was convinced that they couldn't wait for the Second Coming, or anything else that might result in an overall cleansing that the world hadn't seen since Sodom and Gomorrah.

As they drove through the warehouse door and headed for the coastline, Gustav felt a small pang of guilt for what he was about to do. But it didn't last long.

SOMEWHERE ON THE COAST OF NAPLES, ITALY

The tourist bus was jammed in between a long line of traffic, unmoving, waiting for the moment when it could continue its journey along the Amalfi coast. The road clung to the side of a very steep hill, curving around the contours of the rocky, steep landscape, impossibly narrow and nearly impassible for two-way traffic. Houses were nestled here and there along the road, where it passed small towns. Some of the houses were perched on the side of the hill in such a fashion that one wondered how they managed to avoid falling into the ocean below. Cars and tourist buses moved along at the posted speed only to get jammed up around a particularly narrow curve or busy area. It was a journey that amazed, dazzled and frustrated locals and tourists alike.

Inside the tourist bus, Amy Fredericks impatiently glanced at her watch. Her sister, Melissa, looked out the window. Across from them, an old couple seemed content with whatever happened. The temperature-controlled interior was relatively comfortable, but outside, the mid-July temperatures were hot and humid. Everyone, with the exception of Amy, was dressed for the heat. The man noticed that Amy wore long pants and what his wife would call an old lady blouse. Her sister, younger and with an air of confidence that Amy had too but in a different way, wore shorts that showed off her nice legs and a tight, bright, sunshine-colored t-shirt, with a plunging neckline. Hanging in the "plunge" was a crucifix medallion, something that Amy had given Melissa for her 10th birthday. She'd worn it ever since.

Melissa had tried to get her to dress like her that day but Amy talked about not having the body for it. "It's hot and humid and we're going to be hiking in Tuscany by the end of the day," she'd said. "You look like an old woman," Melissa told her. But she knew that Amy had tried to hide behind academia her entire adult life. And she was good at it.

"Relax, sis. We'll get there," said Melissa.

Amy looked up. "In whose lifetime? We'll never be able to see everything and get back to the ship by five."

Amy subconsciously fingered the crucifix hanging around her neck. Melissa looked squarely at her sister, feeling the need to change her focus.

"He won't help you. You have to help you. Just relax. This is our vacation. You're not on a timetable now."

Amy, as if to make her point, defiantly opened a book, written by Father Frank Thomas, entitled "The Ancient Languages of Jesus: A New Translation," and pretended to read. Frustrated, Melissa shook her head.

Melissa remembered when they were young teenagers, waiting in the hospital for news about their mother. She had contracted a deadly infection and wasn't expected to live. Their father was his typical, stoic self but Melissa and Amy were a mess. They went to church, praying with their priest. But their mom got worse. The doctor told them that she may not survive the night. Desperate, they went to a friend who suggested they talk to her pastor, the leader of a non-denominational

Christian church. After spending some time with him, they went back to the hospital, expecting the worse. But the doctor had good news. Their mother would be fine. It was a shocking recovery from a deadly infection that the doctor could not explain.

Amy and Melissa knew what had happened. It was then that they bought each other matching crucifixes. They wore them wherever they went.

"Look around, Sis. This is gorgeous. The coast, the ocean, this amazing and crazy road taking us to an ancient city with churches and history and…"

Amy continued to read her book, trying to ignore her sister. Melissa's brow furrowed and her face turned red. She grabbed the book and yanked it out of Amy's hands.

Amy's head jerked up. "Hey, what the heck—"

"You're going to have a good time if I have to bribe you," said Melissa, her voice louder than she intended. To make her point, Melissa allowed the book to slip down, toward Amy's feet. The old couple sitting across the aisle glared at Amy, who sat in the aisle seat and then at Melissa, as if to admonish the sisters for invading their privacy. Amy grinned like she had just been caught cheating and mouthed, "Sorry," as she turned to Melissa, and whispered, "Keep your voice down. You're making a scene."

Amy cocked her head to the side, indicating that Melissa should look across the aisle. She glanced around Amy at the man who was still giving them the stink eye.

Keeping her voice down, Melissa said, "Sorry. You're just so exasperating."

"You know how important my work is."

"Look, you're intelligent, you've got an amazing resume—I get that. But there's a time when you have to enjoy yourself. That's why we're here, remember? For a vacation. Just the two of us. "

Amy didn't say anything. She knew that Melissa was right. But Amy reached for the book, not wanting to admit her fears. Once inside its pages, she knew she would feel peace, almost at ease. She brushed the hair back from her face, but it didn't yield; it seemed to have a life of its own, a tangled web of deceit designed to cover and hide the Amy that she wanted to be but didn't know how.

Melissa watched her carefully, wondering if she would open the book again or put it away. And for a moment, Amy considered doing just that, but instead, she surprised herself and put the book down. She felt momentarily exposed, a pang of fear coursing through her body. But she looked out the window at the scenery and realized that her sister was right; it WAS spectacular. It hit her like a rip tide and made her feel alive. She hadn't expected to feel that.

Amy leaned across Melissa and opened the window, allowing the smell of sea air and flowers to enter the cabin. For a moment, Amy allowed herself to take it all in, but deep in the recesses of her mind, pangs of guilt crept in.

Melissa saw something different in Amy's face and placed her left hand on top of Amy's right hand. They smiled at each other and Amy continued to take in the scenery.

"It's nice," she said.

Melissa started to respond and then stopped herself. She knew that whatever she said, she'd be fighting against a rising wave, one that would be propelled forward no matter the forces used to keep it back. This was Amy, her sister, a great person, brilliant but socially inept. Melissa wanted her to get some counseling but Amy had resisted, not wanting to talk about the thing that ate at her and pushed her into isolation. It was their father. The general, Amy called him. To his credit, he supported them no matter what they did. But he had driven them so hard. Melissa just took it in stride. Not Amy, who took the "pushes," as Melissa referred to them, as goading, criticism. In fact, Amy told Melissa on many occasions that their father expected her to be perfect, that if she failed at anything, she would BE a failure. This was, in part, how she became a brilliant scientist but it was also the reason she had very few friends and rarely dated.

Melissa and Amy would escape to church when they were young. They grew up Catholic but by the time they'd reached their middle teens, both started to question their priest about things that didn't make sense. Amy had asked about the devil and whether he was real. The priest gave a rather odd answer that she couldn't remember but the tone of it was that the devil was more of a representative of evil. Melissa never forgot the priest's shocked look when Amy wondered how that could be the case when the Catholic religion exercised demons and the "devil."

It was that incident, plus their mother's survival, that motivated both of them to move away from mainstream, organized religion. They gravitated to non-denominational religion. Interestingly, neither their mom nor dad endorsed any form of faith. They knew their mom wanted to but seemed reluctant. At least getting involved in such things got them away from their dad for a while, which was welcome.

As they got older, Amy tended to use science and knowledge to appease their father's demands for success. Melissa volunteered at an animal shelter in high school and then studied veterinary medicine in college.

Melissa hoped that this trip might pull her sister out of the social funk she was in. They'd had a good time since they got to Italy but Amy still couldn't let go. She looked at Amy and couldn't help but wonder if she was fighting a losing battle.

The couple across the aisle–both retired and in their mid 60s–satisfied that the two young sisters had worked out whatever was bugging them, looked lovingly at each other. The man, sitting on the aisle, leaned in closer to his wife.

"She needs a good man."

"Which one, dear?"

"Oh, you know, the good looking one."

The woman looked around him at Melissa. "You must mean the younger of the two."

"No, I don't. The one across from me. She's beautiful. Look at her face."

The woman stared at her, trying to look past the un-kept hair, the fuddy-duddy pants, the loose-fitting blouse. She could see real beauty there, hidden beneath an exterior designed to scare men away. She nodded in agreement.

"Leave it to you to notice."

"Of course, I have you, don't I?"

She smiled and tugged lovingly at his arm. "Having a good time?"

"As long as I'm with you, I am."

She playfully punched him in the arm. "Oh, stop it. You sound like a cheap romance novel."

The woman kissed her husband on the cheek and then noticed Amy grabbing her stomach.

"Oh, no, not that again," said the old woman.

Her husband followed her gaze. Melissa saw Amy grimace. Amy's stomach rumbled and she felt it inside, whatever she ate, wanting to come out once again.

"It's coming back, isn't it?" asked Melissa.

Amy nodded. "Shit. I'm going to have to go again."

Melissa rose and maneuvered past Amy to the front of the bus, where the tour director was speaking, in Italian, with the bus driver. She stopped when she saw Melissa approach.

"Yes, can I help you?"

"Sorry. It's my sister again."

The tour guide tried not to indicate her disgust but Melissa could see it in her face. "When we get out of this traffic . . ."

The guide turned to the bus driver, who looked at her with a quizzical expression. "*Mio Dio, e lei un' altra volta!*" (My God, it's her again!) said the tour guide.

The bus driver shook his head, trying to remember where they could get off the road. Just then, the traffic started to move and he pointed ahead. "*E' vicino, un kilometro.*" The bus finally moved forward and the tourists let out a quiet cheer.

The tour guide turned to face Melissa. "Tell her there's a rest stop about a kilometer ahead."

Melissa nodded her thanks and walked back to her seat. As she passed by the other passengers, most of them gave her dirty looks, having guessed what was coming next. The tour guide grabbed the microphone and turned it on.

"We have a slight detour ahead. Restroom stop."

There was a collective groan among the passengers. A young couple in the seat in front of Melissa and Amy half turned around, giving Amy a dirty look. But she clutched her stomach, hoping she could hold it and trying not to notice the people staring disapprovingly at her.

The van carrying Trinity pulled in and waited at a rest stop just off the coastal highway. They didn't have a plan to grab anyone in particular; the first tourist bus that stopped was adequate for their purposes. Buses inundated this area of the coast. Sooner or later, they'd have their target.

Not more than ten minutes after they parked, a tour bus stopped in the parking lot and a young woman left the bus and hurried for the rest room. Gustav gave his nod of approval and he and two of his men got out of the van and walked, slowly and with confidence, toward the tour bus.

Inside the bus, both the tour guide and bus driver stared at the men. Something wasn't right about them – they wore black and they were expressionless, very serious. The driver turned to the tour guide, and said, "*Ho un brutto presentimento.*" (I've got a bad feeling about this.)

Gustav put his hand under his coat and fingered his Glock. He and the others stopped at the bus' door, his men behind him, waiting for the driver to let them in. Gustav smiled and gestured for the driver to open the door. The driver hesitated but then saw something that changed his mind: Gustav's crucifix hanging around his neck. He let out a sigh of relief and flipped the door lever.

Gustav stood aside while one of his men entered the bus, drew his silenced Glock and immediately shot the driver through the forehead. Brain matter and blood sprayed the window behind him. The thug pulled the driver from his seat and threw him out the door.

Some tourists sprung to their feet, their faces etched with controlled fear; others were frozen, staring at the scene playing out before them, unable to express any emotion. Several tourists stifled screams. The tour guide stood to the side, stricken with shock. Gustav walked slowly down the aisle, his index finger to his mouth, and then he turned around and headed back to the front of the bus. In his other hand, he held his Glock, which, for the moment, he pointed at the ground.

When he got to the front of the bus, Gustav pulled a plastic bag from his pocket, opened it and gave it to the stunned tour guide. "All valuables in the bag, please. That's wallets, watches, passports, cameras, cell phones, iPads, computers."

The tour guide, in a daze, complied and then handed the bag to the other passengers. One of the other thugs used a towel to clean the window off and then sat in the driver's seat. He closed the door and started the engine. Gustav pointed to the body outside the bus and without saying anything, one of his men retrieved him and pulled him into the bus, tossing him on one of the seats at the front of the bus.

Melissa glanced at the restroom, wondering what they were going to do with Amy. But as they drove away, the van followed. She was safe.

Inside the restroom, Amy finished her business, relieved that, hopefully, this was the last stop. She popped another Imodium and washed it down with a couple handfuls of water, wondering if she should be drinking the water at all. After checking herself in the mirror, she turned around, opened the door and stepped outside. She took a couple of steps and stopped dead in her tracks. Where's the bus? She replayed in her mind the layout of the parking lot when she entered. There was a van or bus or something there. What about a car? No car. Just the bus and something else, like a van. She couldn't imagine why they left her there. Melissa wouldn't stand for it. Since they were both gone, she reasoned that their absence was related. Or maybe not. Maybe the van left first, then the bus. If they left at the same time, did that mean that the van took the bus? That didn't seem likely but it was worth considering.

She reached for her cell phone, but her pocket was empty. Did she drop it in the stall? She checked her fanny pack; not there. Before she turned to check the bathroom, she remembered that the phone was in her bag, inside the bus. She paced back and forth, playing the options through her mind. She could walk down the highway, back to the coast, where there were a lot of people. But that was over a kilometer away. If she stayed there, someone would come. She ran through the parking lot to the road and stood there, anxious, worried about Melissa.

Inside the bus, the elderly couple stared blankly at the gunmen and at each other. The woman whispered to her husband, "What do they want?"

He shrugged his shoulders and leaned into her. "Couldn't be money. Probably terrorists."

"So they'll hold us for ransom?"

Another couple in front of them turned around. "You think they're Muslim?"

The old man shook his head. "Look at that one's neck," he said, pointing. "He's wearing a cross–a Christian symbol."

Gustav heard the whispering and looked back at them. "No talking." It was easy to imagine how scared these people must be but frankly, neither he nor any of his men cared. If they were worthy, they would survive. Some wondered if they would find any in this group with what it took to survive.

As they drove to the warehouse, Gustav wondered if any of them had any idea what was in store for them. Most, if not all, would die a grizzly death, some time in the next 10 hours. It would prove their point–that Trinity was not a fringe group with a bizarre agenda but an organized force to be dealt with.

Near the old man and his wife, Julie and her young husband, Matt, huddled next to each other, their fingers entwined, as if that would save them. Julie was so scared she trembled. All she could think about was that these were terrorists and they would torture them. She didn't notice the cross so she incorrectly wondered if they were Muslim or Al-Qaeda, intent on making some political point by torturing and then killing them. Matt could only think about how he was going to get out of there and save himself. It was a good thing that Julie didn't know the selfish thoughts coursing through his brain, not that she could do anything about it. He wanted to live–the hell with the rest of them, even his new bride. He could find someone else once he got out of the bus. He wondered if he should approach the terrorists and offer them money. His family was quite wealthy. But he quickly dismissed the thought when he realized that his true intentions would be made known to everyone, a very embarrassing situation. He'd have to play it more coyly than that.

Nearby, another young couple just clung to each other, saying over and over that they loved each other. They assumed, like most of the passengers, that they would die today.

Melissa watched the terrorists carefully, looking for weaknesses. She never thought about the odds being against her; in fact, she didn't care. She knew some karate and tae kwan do, courses she took with Amy several years ago, and was sure she could take several of them out. But how could she take them here, in the bus? It was smart of them to hijack a bus, she realized. It would have to be later, when they got off. But she needed help. When she glanced around the bus, all she saw were terrified people, no one who apparently had the guts to go after these guys. If Amy was here, they'd be hatching a plan right now.

WAREHOUSE, NAPLES

Melissa sat in the bus, staring at the seat in front of her, trying not to think about how mad she was that she couldn't stop these guys, trying to deny another emotion that was getting worse: fear. The driver had stopped in front of a warehouse in a remote section of what she thought was Naples. He waited for the van in front of them to open the garage door. This couldn't be good.

The people around her literally trembled with fear. She heard whispers. They wanted to know why these people had taken them; most thought they were terrorists, but they didn't look like terrorists. What could they possibly want with them? Would they kill them?

Finally, the warehouse door opened and the van pulled inside, followed by their bus. Melissa and the others looked around, trying to see what was inside, but it was dark. Holding their weapons, Gustav and the driver ordered the passengers off the bus.

Melissa could see fear and horror in the faces of the people as they reluctantly left the relative safety of the bus. The old woman across the aisle from her stopped in front of Gustav.

"Please, don't kill us." He pushed her forward, shaking his head in disgust. Her eyes adjusted to the light, Melissa quickly scanned the warehouse and was drawn immediately to a dozen or so Trinity members hanging large, floor-to-ceiling, wall-to-wall plastic sheeting that cut the warehouse roughly in half. She couldn't make out what was on the other side, as the sheeting was thick and cloudy. But she could see a lot of activity—people walking around wearing what looked like full body containment suits. On the far wall were three large circles intersecting–two circles side-by-side with a third ring slightly above and in the exact middle of the other two. Known as Borromean rings, they are a Christian symbol of the Holy Trinity. That was puzzling. Why would they have such a symbol on the wall?

It seemed highly unlikely that the people who wanted to kidnap them would be a religious organization and possibly Christians.

Melissa saw the other tourists staring at the rings. Curious, she did a quick head count. There were 19 of them. She noticed a young couple, wearing very expensive, designer clothing, approach Gustav. The young man had a cocky, over-confident air about him.

"My father is very wealthy. He'll pay whatever you want if you release us," said the young man.

"We are not after money, young man. You are what we are trying to eradicate. Selfish, money-hungry sinners who have polluted our world."

The two looked shocked, as if they did not understand how any-one would turn down money. The young man looked at his wife and then back at Gustav.

"We don't belong here! What's wrong with you! We can pay what-ever you want!"

His wife, Julie, took Gustav by the arm, trembling with fear. "We didn't DO anything! There must be a mistake!" The others murmured restlessly. Before Gustav could say anything, the young woman ran for the door. Her husband, Matt, started after her but another pas-senger restrained him.

"NO! JULIE!" yelled Matt.

From behind, a large man stepped forward, drew a 9mm Sig Sauer from his coat and fired two shots into the woman's back. The force of the shots catapulted her forward. She hit the ground. Not moving. Dead.

"JULIE!", Matt yelled as he raced to her side. He held her head in his hands, tears running down his face. His eyes darted around the room, pleading for help, a miracle–something to save his wife. The rest of the group huddled together.

The man who fired the shot turned to the group. Melissa stepped in front of him, her face tight with anger. "You son-of-a-bitch! You shot her in the back!"

He stared at Melissa, his expression a strange mixture of cold, unrelenting power and something else, something akin to grace. She couldn't help but take a step back. He was disarming.

"Young lady, you may be correct. But in the end, this is necessary to prove our point. You are simply a casualty."

The man turned to Gustav. "Get them into the room. Let's get it done," said Gustav.

Gustav and four armed thugs pushed the tourists through the plastic sheeting. Inside the makeshift room, the workers had removed their containment helmets, as if whatever they were afraid of had been neutralized. Empty containers were stacked all around; to the left of the concrete room stood wheelbarrows and unused bags of concrete and concrete blocks.

As they were led to the room, Melissa noticed that the open door was at least two inches thick, made of what appeared to be solid steel and with heavy seals around the doorjamb. A wireless video camera was perched on the wall, inside the concrete room, near the ceiling. It fed directly to a laptop where several Trinity soldiers sat.

After the last captive entered the room, the armed thugs backed out and closed the door. Melissa noticed that there was no way to open the door from the inside. She looked around, on the walls and the ceiling. She noticed the old man looking up at the wall where it met the ceiling. There were two vents; one on the ceiling and one on the wall, about 7 feet off the ground and close to the video feed attached to the outside wall. She felt some air movement.

The old man pointed toward the vents. "What are those for?"

Melissa heard the dread in his voice, as if he knew the answer but needed to ask, just to hear someone disagree with what he was thinking. Melissa said, "Looks like air vents. You notice the door? You can't open it from the inside."

His voice trembling, the old man said, "What's the point of the air vents if they don't want money? What do they want with us?"

The man's wife grabbed her husband by the arm with one hand and the put the other on Melissa's arm. "It'll be all right. I have a feeling that we'll get out of here."

Melissa glanced at her and then at the old man, who absentmindedly scratched his head and looked around, as if he didn't believe her. Melissa didn't share her optimism, either.

"It could be a video feed. Why record us unless they need a video of what happens in here?" said Melissa.

A middle-aged man and his wife glanced at the vent and then, their faces wrought with worry, looked soothingly into each other's eyes, trying to make it go away. Others hung onto their loved ones, trying to hide what they knew to be the case. Others muttered to themselves. One woman started praying. Another man recited the 23rd Psalm. One young man and his wife clung to each other, crying on each other's shoulders. The fear of death hung in the concrete death chamber. It was impossible to escape the inevitability of it all.

Several thugs stared at them through the window. The middle-aged man began pounding on the window, his voice quivering with emotion.

"Please, don't kill us. We can help you. What do you want?."

The thugs turned away, while the middle-aged couple stood at the window, screaming and imploring them not to kill them. The rest of the group stayed close to one another in the stark room. The elderly couple hugged each other. Melissa tried to comfort them.

"My sister is out there. She'll help us. She won't let this happen to us."

A large group of Trinity soldiers gathered near the concrete death chamber and bowed their heads as Orfeo led them in a prayer. "We are here, engaged in your work, brother Judas. With the administration of the gift you gave us, we will give the World a new beginning, as we will cast out the unbelievers and challenge humanity to believe in your teachings."

Orfeo reached inside his coat pocket and withdrew a small book, "The Judas Gospel," opened it and started reading. "Jesus said to them, 'Those you have seen receiving the offerings at the altar that is who you are. That is the God you serve, and you are those twelve men you have seen. The cattle you have seen brought for sacrifice are the many people you lead astray before that altar. God has received your sacrifice from the hands of a priest–that is, a minister of error.' "

Orfeo made the sign of the cross, followed by the rest of the group. "We will repair the error of those going before us and will create a new generation of priests who worship correctly. It is a new beginning we create. Go forth, one and all."

Inside the concrete room, Melissa and the others stared in disbelief at the prayer circle. "They're praying?" she said.

"Before they kill us," commented the old man. The group looked on, baffled at the sight of men praying before a ruthless killing.

One of the scientists stepped away from the group, put his containment helmet back on and then carefully opened the small refrigerator. The door opened with the "pop" of something under pressure. He withdrew a small vial. The prisoners inside the chamber noticed that all the other Trinity soldiers had left the room and were standing on the outside of the plastic sheeting.

He took the vial to a small container several feet from the concrete room's outer wall. He slipped the vial into the container, carefully closed the lid and then pushed a lever down that was perched on the container's top. He backed up and walked to the concrete room's only window and stared inside. He waited.

Inside, everyone stared at him, knowing that the vial held something he was afraid of. They turned their attention to the small, steel mesh vent, on the wall above them. Melissa thought she heard something. A hissing noise. It was coming out of the vent. And there it was. A mist. Death.

Everyone in the room saw it. As if some long dormant survival instinct had kicked in, there was a collective knowing that caused universal panic. Many pounded on the window, screaming for help. Others held loved ones and cried, wailing and begging for mercy. The elderly couple snuggled next to each other on the floor, the old woman trying not to show how scared she was. The old man wasn't afraid to die–he'd led a long, full life. But he had hoped that he could approach the end on his own terms. He never envisioned dying like this. He was relatively certain that they were being subjected to a deadly gas. Why would these people want to harm a group of strangers? It didn't make sense. If they didn't want money, then why do this?

Melissa looked at her watch and then slumped down on the floor, wondering how long she had.

ATHLETIC CLUB, COLUMBIA UNIVERSITY

Jacob Mathews hit the racquetball with all that he had, trying for a kill shot down the forehand wall. At 40, he could still move like a man ten years his junior, but Father Thomas, his playing partner, defied what anyone would think a man in his early 50s was capable of doing. He ran around the court like a 20-year-old, smashing anything near him, getting balls Jacob could only dream of.

Jacob watched the ball hit the front wall, a foot or so from the floor and for a moment, Jacob relaxed. He was one point from beating him. For the first time in years. True to form, Father Thomas, in the wrong strategic position but in the perfect position for that shot, somehow managed to get his racket on the ball as it rocketed off the front wall. He hit it back at the wall but when Jacob saw–or more accurately, heard–the ball skip, he relaxed for a moment, picked up the ball and returned to the service box. They were tied and Father Thomas had been serving and if that shot hadn't skipped, the game was over.

Jacob stood in the service box, bouncing the ball but Father Thomas looked at him with a quizzical expression.

"What?" asked Jacob.

"Game's over, bud."

"Over? What are you talking about? Your shot skipped."

"No way."

"You're blind. It skipped."

"I may be old but not blind, at least not yet."

Father Thomas moved toward the back of the court to apparently accept service. For a moment, Jacob thought he was screwing with him. But instead of getting ready to accept the serve, he left the court, grabbed a towel and sat down in a chair just outside the glass-walled enclosure and wiped the sweat from his forehead, face and arms.

Jacob stared at him through the back wall, shaking his head from side-to-side. The old fart was cheating. Priests don't cheat. Of course, Jacob knew better. Father Thomas was an incorrigible cheater, which really irritated Jacob because he didn't need to cheat. Jacob often wondered if he did this to goad him. He had to realize that Jacob knew what he was doing.

Jacob sauntered out of the court and sat next to Father Thomas, who handed him a towel. Jacob wiped the sweat from his face.

"No breaks. It skipped. Game wasn't over. Therefore, I win," said Jacob, still looking straight ahead. "I mean, you forfeited. You left before I could serve."

Father Thomas draped the towel over his legs and leaned forward. He glanced sideways at Jacob.

"Bull."

"Bull? Priests don't curse."

"That's not cursing."

"It's short for bullshit."

"Bullshit is cursing. Bull is not."

Jacob playfully threw his towel at Father Thomas. It hit him in the face but Father Thomas never flinched. "OK, you win," said Father Thomas.

Jacob stared at him. "Literally?"

Father Thomas got up. "Time for a shower."

Jacob winced, knowing this wasn't over and followed Father Thomas to the locker room. He had to hand it to him–Father Thomas did everything he could to be a regular guy. Over all the years they'd known each other, Father Thomas never used his beliefs or his job to lord over Jacob.

After showering, the two walked together outside the athletic club. Jacob noticed Father Thomas adjusting his clerical collar, as if he were making a point. He stared at it for a moment, hoping that Father Thomas would notice. He did.

"What?" said Father Thomas.

Jacob gestured toward the collar. "And that's supposed to persuade me?"

Father Thomas raised his eyebrows and stopped. He eyed Jacob. "No, Jacob, I know that nothing the Church does impresses you."

"That would be true. But of course, I was talking about your skipped shot. "

Father Thomas tried to deflect Jacob's comment by ignoring it. The two started walking again. "How about double or nothing?" asked Father Thomas. Jacob gave Father Thomas a surprised look and then laughed.

"You are an old fart. I'll play you again only if you promise to have your eyes checked."

"Yeah, well, I can still spot a tit on a fly at 50 feet."

"I didn't know flies had tits."

Father Thomas tried to control his ever-increasing inclination to laugh but couldn't. He chuckled and clapped Jacob on the back.

"You just can't stand to lose," said Jacob.

Father Thomas thought for a moment. "Maybe. But even a fool, when he holds his peace, is wise. He that is quiet is a man of understanding."

"So, does that scripture describe you or me?"

Father Thomas thought for a moment and then realized that Jacob was right. "You're a lot smarter than you look."

"And I'm about to whip your ass in the debate."

"You can try."

Jacob put his arm around Father Thomas' shoulder and then withdrew it as the two walked toward the auditorium. Jacob knew that at best, it would be a draw. He couldn't help but wonder if Father Thomas, as bright as he was, would be able to intelligently respond to the innovative argument he was about to make.

POLICE STATION, NAPLES ITALY

Amy paced back and forth in the lobby of the police station, waiting for someone from the U.S. Embassy to help her. She had a bad feeling about what had happened to Melissa and didn't think that officials were telling her everything they knew. They tried to make it sound like nothing, when the hijacking would alarm any reasonable person. She wanted answers and so far, the cops treated her with no respect, as if she was somehow bothering them with her tale of how the van had taken the tourist bus. She told them that this was the only possible explanation but they acted as though she was wasting their time. They said that they couldn't do anything until the bus had been missing longer or until a ransom demand was made. One of the cops actually suggested that she had left the tourist bus because of an argument.

All of this got her tuned up, ready for a fight. They didn't know whom they were dealing with, she thought. She would pound them into the ground before she allowed them to treat her like a factory worker. Her body tensed like a fighter.

As she readied herself for another confrontation, David Miller, the American Embassy representative, walked reluctantly into the lobby. He didn't know much about her other than her story about being abandoned at the rest stop. The police commissioner told him that she was convinced the bus had been kidnapped, that her sister and all the occupants were in danger. Miller heard that she was an emotional mess, and that she was insistent and unwilling to listen. He sure as hell didn't want to deal with her but, it was his job.

When he entered the lobby, Amy lit into him immediately. "You're from the Embassy?"

Miller retreated, his face registering surprise. He looked past her. "Yes. And you are—"

Amy got in Miller's face. "Amy Fredericks. What the hell are you doing about my sister? These assholes think I'm either crazy or just an emotional woman who hasn't taken her medication. I've got several PhDs, one in ancient languages, the other in archeology. I will not be taken lightly. Understand?"

Miller maintained his ground, wondering if she was nuts or if she really had all those degrees. "Yes, I understand. Tell me . . ."

"The bus stopped for me to use the restroom. When I came out, the bus was gone. The tour company has no idea where it is," she said, interrupting him.

"I understand the police are stumped as well."

"I haven't gotten anywhere with them. They suggested that maybe I left on my own, that I had an argument with my sister or something ridiculous like that."

"No calls, nothing? No ransom demands?"

Amy shook her head in disgust. Just then, detective Costini of the *Polizia di Stato*, walked in. She'd been waiting for a "supervisor," as she had demanded. This must be the guy. He wore a cheap, blue suit and a tie with too much yellow in it. But he was impeccably groomed.

Costini looked at Miller, trying to ignore Amy. He could see the anger and fear in her eyes so it was paramount that he maintain his composure.

In a quiet voice, Costini said, "I am detective Costini. I'm sorry to report that although we are doing everything we can, we don't have any information yet."

Amy pushed in front of Miller and stared at Costini. "You don't have any information? Isn't that what I gave you, information?" The words flew out of her mouth, with as much sarcasm as she could muster.

"What are you waiting for? A bus full of dead bodies? You guys are pitiful. How long has it been? Two, three hours and you know zip."

Costini nervously scratched his head, something he did when he tried to maintain his composure. He nodded slightly and softened his expression. "I understand that you're upset, madam. But we're doing everything we can."

Amy pushed her face into his, her face glistening with anger and fear. "That's not good enough! I want her found, do you understand?" She choked back tears, glaring at him.

"I'm sure it's nothing. They probably . . . " implored Costini.

Amy wagged her index finger in his face. "You're not listening. A bus does not disappear. My sister would NEVER leave me like that."

Trying to hold in his impatience, Costini said, "I told you, we're doing the best we can."

Miller took Amy gently by the arm, trying to move her away from Costini. "C'mon, let's go."

Amy dug in her heels. "I'm not moving until you start doing your job."

Costini glanced at Miller. Amy followed his gaze, suddenly realizing why he was there. "Oh, so that's why you're here? To get rid of the crazy woman?"

Miller moved her gently toward the door, but she pulled back, glaring at him. She turned back to Costini but slowly allowed Miller to direct her movements. No one that knew her would have recognized the normally controlled, unemotional Amy. Part of her knew this and it pushed her forward, wherever Miller told her to go.

Miller whispered in her ear as he directed her to the elevator. "You have to give them time to do their job. I'll take you back to your hotel."

Amy tried to stand her ground, but she knew that for the moment, she'd lost. So she backed out, still staring at Costini, her eyes conveying anger and pain. Costini couldn't help but let out a sigh of relief when she left.

WAREHOUSE IN NAPLES

The thugs stood outside the concrete room, their containment suits in a pile on the floor; some watched the dying tourists through the small window, others worked on computers, tracking the progress of the disease. It had been only several hours since the initial exposure.

The leader and Gustav watched a video monitor, unflinching, uncaring, focused on one thing and one thing alone: the progress of the disease. Gustav never would have guessed that they would find an ancient virus to accomplish their goals, one, ironically, belonging to their inspiration: Judas. THE Judas. Through a series of amazing ironies, Trinity came across Judas' ossuary and discovered an ancient, deadly virus inside that would be resistant to any serums that man could throw at it.

That they were relying on the Judas Gospel as their Bible made the circle complete. It all made sense. Once they decided to use the Gospel and then discovered the means to accomplish their ends through their prophet, Judas, most Trinity members were sure they were doing the right thing.

Gustav remembered what their leader had said, in their secret meeting place, right under the noses of organized religion. It was only several months ago that he had spoken to a gathering of Trinity members about the plan to disseminate the virus. Standing in front of them, on a platform, his black cassock a strange contrast to his message of death, he spoke.

"We are anointed to bring the world to the precipice, to take all of us to a New World, where faith in ourselves, in the message of Judas, in what Jesus was really here for, will flourish. It cannot flourish without challenging the faithless to prove they are worthy of Judas and his message. We have seen many religions, including our own Catholic religion, rocked with sexual abuse allegations, financial wrong doings, lies and mismanagement. Not enough has been done to deal with our leaders who have perpetuated these wrongs. It is up to us to right these wrongs. Our plan will draw them into a web that will destroy those who believe blindly.

I know that some of you fear that we are acting too drastically. But in this world of decadence, of faithless people who have lost the ability to listen and understand the Word, unspoiled by those who have perverted its true message, it is the only thing that will cleanse the world. Judas, like us, was the only disciple who understood who Jesus really was and that he had to sacrifice him to the Romans to help him leave his earthly body. We are doing the same thing for the human race. The world is an evil place that Jesus needed to escape. And Judas helped him as we are helping humanity."

"Some of you have been talking about how our actions are a slap in the face of Christianity. I don't disagree. The Church has been falling apart for years. The lying and cover-ups have finally caught up to them. First, we hear about priests abusing young men and the Church's blatant denial that this was occurring. Then recently, it's revealed that they did know but kept things quiet. That cost the Church millions and affected many."

"This kind of bad judgment is not new. We all know that Trinity was formed as a reaction to the Vatican's apparent support of Nazi Germany during the Holocaust. Recently, there are stories about Vatican corruption, including questions about the Curia. It is time to bring them down. It is time to strike a blow to Christianity, to show all religions that they have forgotten their way. It is Gnosticism that will give us answers and set the world on the correct course. Your actions today are the first of many that will lead us to enlightenment."

It was a good speech, and in theory, if the tourists had the same degree of faith in Judas that Trinity had, they would survive the virus. That was the theory, anyway. But as the leader continued to watch the poor souls, he realized that they didn't have faith. They were all sick. They would be dead in a matter of hours. If only they knew how simple it was. If only they knew how much institutionalized religion deserved what it was going to get –its duplicity, thrown in its face. The leader knew that the ultimate test for any religion was when its faith was challenged. The cataclysmic virus would throw Catholics, Judaists, Protestants, Lutherans—all religions—into a tailspin that would expose them for who they were. Religion's self-serving reaction was predictable and was the kind of groupthink the Vatican professed was anti-Christian. Finally, he would expose them for who they were.

Inside their concrete casket, Melissa leaned against the wall, coughing. She spit up a large amount of blood. Blood ran out of her mouth and down her shirt. Using her shirt bottom, she wiped some of the blood from her mouth. She felt the heat of the fever consuming her body, sapping her of strength.

Melissa tried to summon the will power to fight off the blitzing virus, defiant and intent on beating it, but it was too powerful, sapping her of strength and resolve, as it proceeded toward death. She was disgusted with herself for giving in to the disease, unable to resist its progression any longer. She slumped to the floor, her back against the concrete wall. Everyone else in the room was on the floor, dead or nearly dead.

She thought about Amy, her incredible intellect, the need for love in her life, the good times they'd had. She wished that Amy could learn to give in a little, to enjoy life instead of attacking it, to have a life outside of her work. She knew it was her father's fault. He pushed both of them hard, but he was much harder on Amy. Melissa was sure that it had enabled Amy to become the brilliant scientist that she was. If only she could learn to trust men and not to view them as drill sergeants. Melissa and Amy had gone out together with other friends from time to time, but that stopped when they all got boyfriends, all except for Amy. Melissa knew of a couple of men she'd dated, but it never lasted more than a couple of weeks. She'd bury herself in her work and that was the end of it. Even so near to death, she worried about her. Their parents had died in a tragic accident so they only had each other. She couldn't bear the thought that she wouldn't be there for her.

Next to her was the old couple, in a heap, the blood draining from their mouths, ears and noses. Everyone around her was in similar shape. The speed of the disease was like nothing Melissa had ever seen.

In between coughs, she said to the old lady, "Why are they doing this?"

The old lady coughed and wiped the blood from her mouth. "I can't imagine."

Without looking at her, her husband asked her, "What? You can't imagine what?"

"That we're going to be alive much longer."

Melissa noticed the young man whose wife was killed, huddling by himself on the far wall. He looked so alone, ready to die with no one to comfort him. She got up enough strength to move across to the room to him. She tried to lower herself to the floor but she flopped over, losing her balance. Once she righted herself, she noticed that he was too far-gone to notice her. When she took his hand in hers, he whispered, "We're going to die, aren't we?" As if that wasn't painfully obvious.

CHAPTER II

It is finished (John 19:30). Not by water only, but by water and blood (I John 5:6).

'[Your] star has led you astray....No person of mortal birth is worthy to enter the house you have seen, for that place is reserved for the holy' (Judas Gospel, 78).

WAREHOUSE, NAPLES – 10 HOURS LATER

Most of them were dead inside the concrete room. But there was a fighter among them, someone who wouldn't succumb to the disease. The leader couldn't help but be impressed by her resolve. He stared at her through the window. Gustav came up behind him.

"Time?" asked the leader.

"Ten hours."

"It's faster than we thought."

Gustav nodded and then saw Melissa still moving. "I thought you said they were dead."

"All except for her."

Melissa sensed that someone was watching her and tried to stare him down. She could barely open her eyes. It was hard to see anything. Her eyes weren't focusing right. Everything was shrouded. But she had enough left to recognize one of the jerks that brought them here to watch them die in agony.

What little brain function was left focused on what Amy would do to them. They had no idea who they were dealing with. She wanted to say something to them but she didn't have enough energy to speak.

She heard a sound, like someone gasping for air. No one around her was alive, or so it appeared. Who was doing that? Oh, she thought . . .

it's me. Just then, she thought she could see a bright light, then a face. Was it Amy? Trembling, she reached her hand out to touch the face and then, just as suddenly as it appeared, it was gone. Her arm hit the floor. She was so weak . . .

Melissa closed her eyes. And then she did the strangest thing. She smiled.

"She smiles at death?" asked Gustav, staring at her via the video.

"Yes, she is strong."

"But no faith."

Inside the room, Melissa had one, final thought. Slowly, using the life force still lingering inside of her, she flipped them the bird. She smiled. And then she went into the light.

The leader turned around and motioned to one of his men. The thug removed the DVD from the recorder, put it in a DVD sleeve and ran to a waiting van. He handed it to one of the thugs sitting on the passenger side.

"The world is soon to learn who we are, Gustav. And they will live only if they have faith."

Gustav nodded unconvincingly. He checked his pocket for ammo and joined other Trinity members in the van. If their leader knew about his concern, he'd probably kill him. It wasn't as though he didn't have faith. He didn't know if he could trust that it was strong enough to save him from the powerful disease that ravaged those poor souls and that could send the world over the edge. What if their scientists were wrong? What if the virus killed everyone?

ART RESORT GALLERIA UMBERTO, NAPLES

While Amy paced in her room, Miller sat across from her in a recliner, his index finger producing a staccato-like sound on the table next to him, as he thumped it, waiting, hoping. For the third time, he picked up the empty coffee cup next to his hand and set it down before he placed the rim on his lips, seemingly unable to remember that he'd drained the cup 15 minutes ago. He quickly glanced at his watch and then at Amy. Also on the table was the phone, the one they'd been waiting to ring for several hours.

The phone rang. Amy leapt for it, but Miller got there first.

"Yes?" asked Miller.

Amy could barely contain herself, hoping for the best, fearing the worst. She wanted to rip the phone from his grasp and demand answers, but she managed to control herself.

"Is she alive?" she asked. But Miller listened, seemingly ignoring her.

It was Costini on the phone. He stood outside a warehouse, the one with the concrete room inside of it, wearing the bottom half of a HAZMAT suit. Behind him, the Ama dei Carabinieri (Military Police) scurried around, most wearing HAZMAT suits. A large crane worked an equally massive, thick, plastic sheeting that they were placing over the warehouse. Some of the Carabinieri escorted people from the area. Others worked on quarantining the area.

"No, I'm afraid not. All dead. I've never seen anything like it." On the other end of the phone, Miller felt the emotion of the moment but tried to hide it.

Amy tried to pull the phone from him. She could see something in his expression. What was it? Fear? Shock?

Miller pulled back. Then, as the horrifying message sunk in, Miller could feel his face flush. His silence was enough.

"What the hell is going on? MILLER!" Amy pushed him. She grabbed the phone.

"Listen to me, Costini, I demand to know right now what the hell is going on."

Costini couldn't tell her. It was hard to believe. They died horribly. What could kill like that and so quickly? And who did this? And why?

"Ah, we don't know much yet," he lied.

"What about my sister?"

"We just don't know. I'll have Miller bring you here. Give him the phone. I'll give him directions."

Amy refused to believe that it was as bad as it sounded. He didn't say she was dead. That was good, right? Slowly, she handed Miller the phone.

"I'm back," he muttered.

"Look, the warehouse is being quarantined. Frankly, no bodies have been identified. So I don't know if her sister is in there."

Miller motioned Amy to follow him. He left the hotel room with Amy at his side, listening to Costini tell him where the warehouse was located. His silence was telling, but she didn't want to acknowledge it. She tried to contain her anxiousness, knowing that Miller wouldn't tell her anything.

Once they got in the car, Amy felt as though they were finally making some progress. She refused to confront the thoughts that wormed their way into her head. Melissa would want her to have hope. That would help. No one could kill her sister. She was too strong to die.

After winding their way through the streets of Naples, the car pulled up to the now completed barricade. Several armed Carabinieri motioned them to stop. Miller pulled over. Amy launched herself out of the car, intent on running to her sister, who she expected to be standing there, waiting for her, but could only stare at the warehouse, partially draped in plastic. It looked as if a giant plastic bag enveloped the building, as 20 or 30 workers worked frantically to complete the process of tenting it. HAZMAT trucks lined the streets. A temporary, large, canvass tent was almost finished. Several workers wearing HAZMAT suits carried a large object from the building, to the canvass tent. What was it? Sort of shaped like a body . . . it couldn't be.

She saw more long objects in plastic bags being carried out of the warehouse into the tent. Plastic bags, like . . . body bags. No, there must be another explanation. But there wasn't. One of the soldiers stood near her but moved over to help the other one determine whether they could pass. She was half aware of Miller arguing with them. She didn't want to know but couldn't avoid the obvious. Melissa.

And then she made a beeline for the tent. One of the startled soldiers called after her, but she focused on one thing: quieting the voice in her head, the voice that told her Melissa was in that building with all those other long things in bags.

Miller and both soldiers ran after her. One of the soldiers pulled his phone out and yelled into it. At the entrance to the warehouse, Costini saw Amy's frantic dash. The poor woman . . .

A Carabiniere stopped her near the tent, saying that she needed a HAZMAT suit. But she pushed past the startled guard with unexpected strength.

The Carabinieri stacked the long objects in bags on the tables positioned around the room. On another table nearby was a pile of what appeared to be personal belongings.

Just then, she saw one of the bags fall to the floor. A bloody torso slipped out. Amy stifled a scream. Well, that did it, she thought. Melissa couldn't be in here.

As she turned to leave, she saw something on the table. She stopped, not wanting to see it. She didn't see it. That's all there was to it. She started to leave when her need for the truth suddenly compelled her to look at the thing she knew was there.

There, on the table, was Melissa's sunshine t-shirt. Slowly, Amy crept closer. It was covered with blood. No, that couldn't be hers. She wouldn't allow it get so dirty. But as she turned to leave, she saw it. The crucifix, just like hers. The one she bought Melissa for her birthday.

She turned back to the room, her eyes flitting back and forth. She was in there. In one of those bags. Dead. "MELISSA!!"

Costini, now wearing a HAZMAT suit, with the top open, put his arms around her and turned her around. "It's too dangerous in here. You have to leave."

Somehow, her feet seemed to move her out of the room. Later, she would remember it as a dream. Costini guided her to just outside the barricade, opened his car door and indicated that she should take a seat. Robotic, Amy complied. Tears ran down her face. She glared at the warehouse, as if it were an animate object that she could blame for what happened. She tried to come to terms with what she knew to be true, but she was numb. She failed to save her. She let her die. What would she do without Melissa?

Satellite Broadcast Station, Naples

Gustav looked at his watch as the van pulled into the broadcast station parking lot. It was getting dark, just about the time the station would be done with their latest news broadcast. He checked his Glock. Five other Trinity members in the van did the same. They didn't have to say anything. They had rehearsed this a hundred times.

They wore business suits. It would get them into the station before anyone knew what had hit them. As they got out of the van, all of them pushed their silenced Glocks into the small of their backs except for Gustav, Bernard, a large, hulking man who walked just in front of Gustav, and Paul, who held the guns at their sides.

Bernard opened the door and immediately focused his attention to the left while Paul focused his attention to the right. Gustav looked straight ahead at a guard who started to get up. But Gustav quickly killed him with a headshot while Bernard and Paul shot the other two guards in the torso. They all hit the ground, dead.

The Trinity group quickly walked past the dead guards and past two office workers, both of whom looked up as they walked by and then looked again, this time startled, realizing that those men shouldn't be there. One of the men got up.

"Hey. You can't go in there . . ."

Bernard shot him in the head before he could finish his sentence, and Paul quickly killed the other one.

Gustav and his men continued down the hallway until they came to a door with a sign over it that read, "Studio." There was a light bar underneath that would be lit up, reading "On Air," when they were broadcasting. For the moment, the "On Air" sign was off.

Gustav opened the door and sauntered in. One of the five men working in the studio jerked his head up when he saw them. He jumped to his feet. All six of the Trinity members had their Glocks drawn. The worker stared at them. One by one, the others in the room stopped what they were doing.

"Do as I say and no one will get hurt," said Gustav. The man closest to them started to protest, but Gustav shoved the Glock in his face, shaking his head from side-to-side. The man quickly relented, raising his hands in supplication.

"Everyone else in this building is dead. I won't tell you twice."

The man sat down, his face ashen. No one else moved. Gustav withdrew the DVD from his coat pocket. He handed it to one of them.

"Broadcast this immediately. Via satellite," said Gustav.

The man walked over to a DVD player, opened it, placed the disc on the platter and then closed it. He turned and nodded at a co-worker who punched some keys. The video screen suddenly displayed Borromean rings, Trinity's symbol.

And then a voice. "We are Trinity. The world, as prophesied in Revelations, is a place of sin and hedonism. We will no longer wait for the cleansing. Seven days from today, we will unleash onto the world, a deadly virus that will cleanse the planet of all the unfaithful. During those seven days, if the unfaithful repent for their sins and if they worship correctly, their faith will save them from the virus. "

Video images showed the tourists first being administered the virus with voice over. "What you are witnessing is the time lapsed death of nineteen people who were exposed to the virus. The virus has a 100 percent kill rate, within ten hours of exposure."

The video continued, now showing the sweaty tourists coughing up blood. On the bottom of the screen scrolled, "after 30 minutes of exposure." Then, a final scene flashed on the screen, showing the dead tourists, their clothing stained with blood. Melissa was visible next to two teenage girls.

"We leave you with a quote from Scripture: 'The souls of every human race will die. But when those who belong to the holy race have completed the time of the kingdom and the spirit separates from them, their bodies will die but their souls will be alive and they will be lifted up.' Only the truly faithful will survive. May God have mercy on your soul."

The video screen went blank. The men in the studio stared at the screen, stunned. No one moved. Bernard removed the DVD from the player, and the Trinity members moved backwards out of the room. Gustav was the last to leave.

The video was quickly picked up all over the world. Every major television network had run the segment by the time Gustav and the others got back to their headquarters.

Back at the hotel, Amy watched the news, not wanting to see the reality of what happened to her sister, but she couldn't deny it, or how it fueled her hate. She watched in horror—Melissa slumped against the wall, her t-shirt covered in blood, her face streaked with blood and sweat. Amy couldn't look away, even though she wanted to. All she could see was the terror in Melissa's frozen face.

And one other thing. She saw anger. Amy was certain that Melissa wasn't mad at the men who killed her. She was mad at Amy for leaving her there and not rescuing her. But it wasn't Amy's fault, it was HIS fault. He failed all those people. Amy spent her life honoring him and this is how he rewarded her?

Just as she rose, her face screwed up in shock, Miller knocked at the door and entered. She pulled at the medallion hanging around her neck and threw it across the room, nearly hitting Miller.

"I HATE you," screamed Amy. Miller wondered if she was referring to him. But she was looking at whatever she threw at the wall.

Amy turned back to the screen. "Melissa, I . . . I am so sorry. I am so sorry," she muttered. Suddenly, all she could feel was grief and anger, so she looked for something to throw. She spotted the phone on a nearby table. She picked it up and threw it at the wall. She kicked the table over. She pulled at her hair and kicked a large recliner-type chair hard enough to move it several feet. Then, she slumped to the floor, her head in her hands, the tears flowing down her cheeks. Miller found the medallion on the floor and picked it up. It was a crucifix.

CHAPTER III

Fear not, for I am with you, and will bless you, and will multiply your seed (Gen. 26:24).

Jesus said to [his disciples], 'Those you have seen receiving the offerings at the altar — that is who you are. That is the god you serve, and you are those twelve men you have seen. The cattle you have seen brought for sacrifice are the many people you lead astray before that altar . . .' (Judas Gospel, 46-47).

DAY ONE

COLUMBIA UNIVERSITY

The audience at the Roone Arledge Auditorium at Columbia University waited patiently for the debate to start. Most were students and were required to attend. A few were locals just interested in listening to a debate between two highly respected intellectuals. Even a reporter was there from the Columbia University press. It wasn't often that the school hosted a debate on Creationism vs. Darwinism. Most of the students were intellectuals, or liked to think they were, not "Bible thumpers," as they called their peers who came from the South.

The crowd murmured and then quieted down when the Dean approached one of the two podiums on the stage.

"Thank you for coming. We are grateful that these two esteemed scientists have agreed to debate Creationism and Darwinism. Father Frank Thomas is a world-renowned archeologist who has participated in the restoration of religious artifacts from all over the world. He is the Dean of Religious Studies at Yale and is in charge of the most recent examination of the Shroud of Turin. Jacob Mathews is a veteran of the United States Navy, specializing in cryptanalysis and is an expert in Middle Eastern affairs. Before entering the Navy, he received a doctorate in religious studies from the University of Chicago . Please welcome Father Frank Thomas and Dr. Jacob Mathews."

The crowd erupted in applause as Jacob and Father Thomas emerged from the right side of the stage, walking side-by-side. They waved at the audience and, after shaking hands with the Dean, took their positions at their podiums.

Father Thomas adjusted the microphone. The audience quieted in anticipation.

"The evidence is clear that not even a single celled microbe could have survived in the slurry that existed millions of years ago without the precise combination of temperature, acidity, chemical—"

"But that doesn't mean that God or a Creator was responsible for that," interrupted Jacob. The audience was instantly mesmerized. It didn't take long for these two to get into it.

Jacob continued. "It is more likely that the explanation is evolution. You cannot discount the evidence that all species have evolved."

"No, I agree, but that doesn't mean that evolution AND Creationism can't coexist. The two are compatible—"

"No, no, they are not compatible, at least not as far as the proponents of each would have you believe. They are presented in a way that makes them mutually exclusive."

"Darwinists, like you, Dr. Mathews, lack faith; that is what draws you to a scientific explanation."

"Faith? Leave it to a Creationist to boil everything down to an esoteric religious concept."

"Faith is not necessarily religious," responded Father Thomas, but he stopped in mid-sentence and focused on the side door to the hall. Two men wearing military uniforms pushed past several ushers and rushed to the stage. The Dean intercepted them just as they alighted onto the stage, and they spoke for a moment in hushed tones. Both Jacob and Father Thomas left their respective podiums and joined in the discussion. The audience was abuzz.

"What the hell is going on?" asked Jacob.

The Dean seemed to be leaning to one side, as if whatever the officers said was enough to topple him over. "You, both of you, have to go with them."

"What? We're in the middle of a debate."

One of the military men, a lieutenant, stepped closer to Father Thomas. "Sir, I have orders to take you and Mr. Mathews immediately to the president."

Jacob reared back. "THE president?"

"Yes, sir. It's a grave matter of national security."

Jacob glanced at Father Thomas and nodded. The two quickly left with the lieutenant and the other officer.

The Dean approached one of the podiums, his legs almost wobbly. He stood there for a moment, trying to gather himself. He didn't know the precise details as the lieutenant had only told him that the national emergency had to do with a deadly virus that would kill everyone. But that was enough.

He adjusted the microphone and then slowly spoke, his voice shaky, halting.

"There's been. . . an international incident. You'd better get back . . . check the news. I, I have to leave. . ." The Dean wandered off the stage as the audience seemed to rise in unison.

The soldiers escorted Jacob and Father Thomas to a waiting Chevy SUV. Once inside, Jacob asked the lieutenant if he could explain the nature of the emergency. He responded that he couldn't give any precise details other than it was a matter of national security, that the president and other members of the National Security Council and the UN needed their presence immediately.

Jacob was glad that he had Father Thomas at his side for whatever they might be facing, not only because he valued his friend's assistance, but also because of Father Thomas's acumen. He had been in special forces in Vietnam, having entered the war nearly at its end. But when he killed a man in combat, he swore that he would devote his life to saving lives and souls. He got out the war as soon as he could and entered the seminary.

One of the things that Jacob loved about him was his integrity. It didn't matter to Father Thomas whom he was beholden to or what the protocol might be in any given situation; he would always speak the truth. He had the talent to soften the truth when he had to, but he was uncompromising in his reaction to dishonesty or unclear thinking. Jacob remembered when Father Thomas was in the seminary and had an argument with one of his instructors, a biblical scholar who was unable to separate the honest, intellectual analysis of text from the organized religion approach, which often was quite different.

Father Thomas challenged the priest when he was teaching the New Testament. The priest talked about Jesus dying for us, for our sins. This, of course, was a popular interpretation of scripture, as Father Thomas said when he challenged the priest. The priest pointed out that it wasn't an "interpretation" at all –those were the words used, for example, by Paul in Corinthians. But Father Thomas pointed out that the life of Jesus didn't match that description of his death, that he never talked about sacrificing himself for "our sins," that he focused on turning people from believing in kings and other leaders as god-like when it is only God who should be worshiped and followed. He told the priest that he believed the life of Jesus was more indicative of someone teaching people who their true religious leader was and to be willing to die for that belief. To prove who he was, he performed miracles.

This debate went on for the entire semester. Jacob had heard about it from Father Thomas himself, who often laughed about it. But it impressed Jacob because it was a testament to Father Thomas' honesty. It was ironic that Father Thomas could debate such a point but in the end, he believed in what the Bible said, even though he didn't always believe in the Church's spin on it.

After seminary, he worked for years in the Vatican, when, during a long lasting and bitter argument with a fellow priest about – what else – honesty in assessing Jesus' message, he became so enraged that he clocked the priest. Knocked him out, with one blow. The Church nearly ex-communicated him. Instead, it cast him adrift in academia where Father Thomas actually flourished.

There, he became a world-renowned expert the language and interpretation of Biblical texts, particularly the New Testament. He was an expert in ancient Hebrew and Aramaic. And he was a crack shot with a gun and was still able to hold his own in a fistfight.

WHITE HOUSE

President Holcomb hustled through the corridors of the White House, trying to put on his tie. Next to him was Carmela Anderson, his Chief of Staff. She carried his sport coat and a file. Frustrated, he pulled the tie off and handed it to her. As she handed him the file, he tried not to stare, which he always found difficult when in her presence. He marveled at her intelligence wrapped in a package that gave most men the willies. And she knew it. No one was as good at disarming a room as Carmela. Women were jealous of her. Men couldn't stop staring. She used her looks and demeanor like a net, snaring everyone in her presence.

Holcomb opened the file and read as he walked. It didn't take him long to digest the gist of their bizarre and frightful message. He stopped.

"Jesus, they said this?"

"It was originally broadcast in Italy and then worldwide."

Holcomb started walking again, still reading. "This is going to be a disaster. Who the hell are these nuts?"

"Religious fanatics."

"Are they here?"

"I assume you mean Jacob and Father Thomas. Yes, Mr. President."

"You must have something on Trinity," said Holcomb.

"Some we know; some is rumor. They started during World War II fighting the Nazis, a sort of clandestine resistance organization, but Vatican-based."

Holcomb's eyebrows rose. "The Vatican? I thought they were more pro-Nazi than they would like to admit."

"That may be, but Trinity was started, we think, by disgruntled priests inside the Vatican, who wanted to make a statement against the Nazi occupation. In part, they protected the Vatican."

"I thought Switzerland agreed to do that."

"No one's heard of them. In Italy, their existence was only a rumor."

"Well, a rumor just threatened to take everyone out."

Holcomb stopped in front of a mirror, while Carmela handed him the tie. He began making the knot.

"Since World War II, Trinity has been involved in religious fanaticism. They're tied to abortion clinic bombings, assassinations of atheist leaders and non-Christians," said Carmela.

"How many and how are they financed?"

"Not sure as to either."

"Our knowledge base has to change, and fast. CIA and Interpol on this?"

"As we speak, operatives are in Italy."

Holcomb made a final adjustment of his tie and Carmela handed him his sport coat. He threw it on as they turned down the hall to the pressroom. He stopped at the door.

"So their leader—"

"Is unknown."

"We need to get on this right away. I want to know everything about them."

"Yes, sir."

"What about the rest of Europe?"

"The expected reaction. Calls from NATO, the Kremlin, the Prime Minister, Italy, the UN."

"And they've all called for a state of emergency and are thinking about declaring martial law. That about cover it?"

Carmela nodded. Holcomb shook his head in disbelief. "You prepare for this and then when it happens…"

Holcomb turned to Carmela. "My family?"

"It's taken care of."

"Have you contacted…"

"Yes, well, Amy is in Italy, but I have an agent bringing her back. The other two will be here shortly, if they're not already here."

Holcomb nodded, feeling better already that he would have the assistance he needed to beat these terrorists. He grabbed the door handle and as he opened it, he muttered, "God help us all."

MILWAUKEE, WISCONSIN, KOHL'S DEPARTMENT STORE

When Jackson Stuart heard the news about the end of the world coming in a week, he was in the middle of shoplifting a shirt and a pair of pants from a Kohl's in Milwaukee, Wisconsin. He had the shirt and pants on underneath the clothing he wore into the store when he walked past the electronics department and noticed a large number of people glued to the TV sets, all playing the same channel.

The president was speaking, something that never interested Jackson. The jerk would put him in prison if he could, so why would Jackson care anything about what he had to say? But the fact that everyone else was glued to the screens and they all looked like death, was enough to get his attention. It never occurred to him that stopping was a bad idea, as it gave the store security guards more time to figure out what he'd done.

He sidled up to a pretty blond girl with a low-cut tank top. He glanced at her, looking for a connection, and when she ignored him, he turned his attention to the event, whatever it was. It certainly had people's attention. The girl seemed to be in a trance. Her mouth hung open, her face both blank and scared at the same time, as if she just found out that she had terminal cancer. Now he wondered if she knew that he was standing there, still stealing glances at her cleavage. He glanced around to the others watching the broadcast and noticed something that gave him the creeps.

Everyone had a similar expression. Hell, thought Jackson, I guess I'd better listen. He looked up at the president, who didn't look very good. He said something about how they were doing everything possible, that people shouldn't give up hope, that they would find Trinity and stop the virus. Then he said something that just floored Jackson–something about the week they'd been given to live. He just couldn't comprehend what the president said.

Instead, he turned to the girl and asked what the president said about a week. She looked at him and said, "The virus will kill us all in a week unless we have faith. The terrorists said anyone with faith would make it."

The words seemed to resonate in his brain. Anyone with faith would survive? What the hell did that mean? Faith in what? God? Jesus? Buddha? Yourself?

It scared him. Not the death part. The faith part. He didn't want to die, that part should be clear. But his mind reeled at the thought of faith saving anyone. He remembered his neighbor, a curly-haired nerd who went to church every Sunday and talked about being good and obeying your parents. It never made any sense to him. It still didn't. It was a waste of time.

But now he wondered. Maybe it wasn't a waste of time. Maybe he would be left behind because he didn't believe. Maybe he could save himself if he worked at it. But he had to think hard about what to do. Who could he ask? Most of his friends were stoned half the time.

This was something he'd have to do on his own. He glanced around; the people were there, still listening. What more did they need to know? It was time for action. He turned and left the group, heading for . . . well, he hadn't figured that out yet.

Jackson tried not to think about where he came from, the man he used to be, the life he used to live, the anger that boiled underneath the surface. The drugs he'd taken over the last five years had dulled his intellect and deeply wounded his body. One bad night had changed his life. He drank too much, got in a car and nearly hit someone crossing the street. He was convicted of a misdemeanor and lost his job. His wife thought he was cheating at the bar–he flirted with a co-worker and probably would have done her if she was willing–and left him.

Jackson was high most of the time. It was the engine that gave him the guts to commit crimes, to care about nothing and to hurt people.

The girl he tried to talk to was Lilly, a 30 year-old, single mother of two, who couldn't imagine the world ending so soon. She never went to church because she didn't believe in God. But the first thing she thought of was that maybe it was time to believe, maybe that would save her and her children.

The thought of her children – Mandy, 13, and Bryan, 11–having to exercise faith to survive, when she wondered if they knew anything about God, scared the crap out of her. Was it possible that faith could save them? She didn't know where to start.

Near her house was St. Anthony's Catholic Church, only 10 miles from the Kohls department store where Lilly and Jackson so fortuitously met. Father John was a young priest with many new ideas about the Catholic Church and the direction it should follow. Lilly knew Father John quite well and wondered if he had a slight crush on her. He had tried to talk her into going to church in the past. She'd resisted, unwilling to explain to him why she didn't want to go. There was a certain element of revenge in her denial of the father's entreaties, as if denying what he wanted would somehow make her pain go away.

Now, while she stared at the TV monitors in that department store, those denials lurked in her mind, causing her to doubt how easily she had dismissed the father and his concerns. She had given her kids the option of going to church and they surprised her by going and becoming involved in youth groups. She had rejected her Catholic upbringing, but now it gnawed on her, as if doubt was eating her from the inside out.

Her mind raced. Should she go to the school and get her kids? What would they do now that they couldn't do tomorrow or the next day? Maybe they should get in the car, pack as much as they could carry and head for the nearest mountain range. That seemed to make some sense. At a high elevation, they might be protected from the virus.

Once she got in her car and headed for home, she called her boyfriend, Jack. He was a stockbroker. When she couldn't get through, she tried again and again, but it was always busy. Then she realized that the news must be destroying the stock market. She turned the radio to a news channel. The reporter said that the stock market had dropped 1000 points since the news from the president. During his broadcast, he said that it had dropped another 500 points in the last five minutes, with no end in sight. Experts predicted the total collapse of the market, unlike anything in the history of the world, making the Great Depression look like a one-day glitch in the market.

She had some money in the market, but at her age, she hadn't saved much. Most of her money she'd sunk into a home she'd purchased last year, made possible in part when she got a job with a large, local counseling agency, her newly minted master's degree in counseling in hand. She enjoyed helping people with their problems, but now, she felt lost. Who would help her? She didn't know what to do.

Without warning, thoughts of her childhood flashed through her mind. It was as if the thought of the end reminded her of the beginning. She hated her father for what he did to her—in those secret meetings they would have at night in her bedroom and for what he didn't do. She never had a real father with real childhood memories and good times to reflect on. All of her memories were about trying to stay away from him, exactly the opposite of how it should have been.

But now, she didn't feel anger as much as sadness. She was intent on providing her children with the memories she didn't have, and now some weirdos were trying to take that away from her. It just didn't make sense.

At St. Anthony's, Father John was in the middle of writing his Sunday sermon when Father Paul busted into his office, his face red and his eyes bulged out, like he'd just been told the world was about to end, which is what he proceeded to describe to Father John. He quickly turned on the LED TV in his office, donated by a man who kept the church in business almost single—handedly. A thousand here, then thousands and thousands more. He was very successful, no doubt, but the man puzzled Father John. He was on his third marriage, having been unfaithful in his prior relationships and revealed in a recent confession that he'd cheated once again. His sons were notorious slumlords, his daughter a spoiled, bigoted woman who couldn't keep a job for more than several months. But he gave and he gave and he gave.

The president was on every channel. He looked propped up, almost robot-like, trying to maintain a level of calm that he clearly was manufacturing for the nation. Who could be calm while announcing that some crazed fanatics had a deadly virus that could be defeated by those with faith? It was ironic, thought Father John, as he listened to the message, that here was something that normally would have attracted any pastor like a bee to flowers. But this was different, or so it seemed, based on the credibility that the president was giving to the threat.

He did talk about the best scientists from all over the world working on an antidote for the virus, assuring everyone that a "cure" was right around the corner. Father John didn't buy it. He didn't know why, but it took him less than a couple of seconds to decide that he would have to get his parish ready for the end. His challenge, he realized immediately, would be to decide how to handle the impending crisis. Would his message be to prepare everyone for the end or would it be that they could beat this thing with faith, as Trinity proclaimed?

He truly believed in the power of the teachings of Jesus, but when the tires hit the asphalt, would he be able to say, with conviction, that faith could cure an illness? He went to the doctor, which didn't mean that he didn't have faith, but there was only so much God could do. Or was there?

He immediately recalled the case of the Grants, a good Catholic family that decided to use faith to heal their sick daughter. It was a difficult situation for him– and the Church–because he couldn't deny the power of faith, but at the same time, the Church didn't have a problem with seeking the care of a physician. The Grants came to him, telling him that their 15-year-old daughter was very sick but that they believed God would save her, unless it was her time. He had a difficult time denying their logic and their commitment, but ultimately, he couldn't give them his blessing. Instead, he took the easy way out–he told them that the Church would not take a position.

He'd felt guilty since he made the decision not to have a voice. Personally, he loved their commitment. The incident caused him to wonder. If they truly believed in the power of God, why wouldn't they rely on his mercy in times of trouble? That's what they preached with regard to almost every other facet of life; why not health? He began to see a certain hypocrisy in the Church, and it burned him to think that he hadn't noticed it before. When he addressed the Vatican about his concerns, he didn't get much of an answer.

Now, the incident stared him in the face. And the result seemed particularly appropriate. The Grants's daughter recovered. Medical experts opined that she'd had some form of intestinal cancer, given her symptoms, but, of course, an accurate diagnosis was impossible without an exam. But her survival may have proven a point. Maybe faith was all they needed.

AMERICAN EMBASSY, ROME, ITALY

Amy sat in an office, her head in her hands and her packed bags next to her. She couldn't wait to go home, though part of her wanted to remain in Italy, to be with Melissa. If she stayed behind, would she be able to get involved in the investigation? Costini and Miller were telling her that they wouldn't let her do anything there. Bull, she thought. I'll be back.

Someone knocked on the door and in walked Costini and a CIA agent.

"Can I help you with your bags?" asked Costini.

Amy picked up her bags and pushed past both of them, but before she left the room, she turned back and got in the CIA agent's face. "You don't know squat about Trinity, do you?"

Neither one answered. Then the agent said, "You know that we can't tell you."

"You're pathetic."

She hurried out of the room. The CIA agent gave Costini a dirty look and then followed Amy.

Once they got outside the embassy, Amy said, "You and I both know that you're here for another reason. What the hell is going on?"

"All I know is that I have orders to get you back to the US as quickly as possible."

WHITE HOUSE PRESS ROOM

With Carmela standing at his side, President Holcomb stood at the podium.

"As of now, we know very little about this virus. The best scientists in the world are working around the clock. What we do know is that the virus appears to kill everyone who has contact with it within 10 hours of exposure. We have not had time to examine the virus ourselves, so I must warn you that I used the word, 'appear,' for a reason. We will determine if the virus is as lethal as Trinity says it is. For now, we are assuming the worst because of our preliminary examination of the bodies of those poor tourists. As for Trinity, they are a fanatical Christian organization. No one knows much about them. For now, we are doing everything we can to contain an outbreak of this virus. So I've ordered that all public events and public forms of transportation be cancelled."

Before Holcomb could continue with his speech, the room exploded with questions. He tried to silence the crowd, but it was useless. He pointed to a reporter near him.

"Is the threat credible?"

"Trinity has been involved in some extremist activities. If we take them at their word, they believe they've been anointed to cleanse the world. What we don't know, yet, is where the virus came from, whether it's as virulent as it appears."

Another reporter got the president's attention. Holcomb quieted the crowd and pointed to the man. "Mr. President, the ban on public transportation is going to create havoc. Millions of people will be affected. I don't understand the reason for—"

"The reason, Mike, is that if we can't contain the virus, it'll spread quickly at large public gatherings. It's airborne, as far as we know. Imagine what it would do at an airport or busy subway terminal. I know people hate this, but inconvenience is better than death."

The room erupted with questions and Holcomb quieted them again. "Look, I know you've got a lot of questions. I implore you to do everything you can to help me diffuse the fear, not instill it. We can beat this, but we all must work together. And I mean everyone—not just United States citizens, but citizens of Russia, France, England, Spain, China. Every country of the world."

For a moment, the room was silent. Holcomb walked out with Carmela and his staff following him.

He turned to Carmela. "How are we coming with Amy and the others?"

"She should be here soon. Father Thomas and Jacob will be here at the start of the UN meeting."

Holcomb nodded his approval. He was particularly glad to have Jacob with him on this. Jacob was an amazing code breaker, a man who loved the challenge of deciphering ancient languages and puzzles. He and Jacob were in the Navy together in their early 20s, nearly getting kicked out because of insubordination. They were both creative and rule breakers–Holcomb because he thought he could do things better than his superiors, and Jacob because he didn't want anyone else telling him what to do. Holcomb remembered an incident in which they were asked to go underwater for 10 minutes with one tank between the two of them. In order to survive, they had to share the air. Jacob couldn't do it. He had to come up for air.

That was how Jacob was–he believed in himself and his ability to turn any situation to his advantage and he couldn't allow anyone else to save him. That strength was needed in a situation like this, when the world was threatened by religious fanatics. Holcomb could rely on him to do what was necessary to save everyone because there were few people who were as strong in their faith as Jacob.

As for Father Thomas, Holcomb didn't know him personally but was well aware of his background and friendship with Jacob. He needed Father Thomas for his expertise in languages and the New Testament, his love of religious archeology and his willingness to take on the Vatican if necessary.

Holcomb didn't know Amy, but he trusted Carmela who knew her well. She was a brilliant scientist, with an expertise in genetics. She had been on several archeological digs because of her love for religious artifacts. She was regarded as an expert in ancient languages and religion. It was a formidable trio to add to the teams of scientists who were gathering at the UN and in the Vatican, a group that Holcomb had a lot of confidence in.

MILWAUKEE, WISCONSIN.

Lilly went to her children's school but because of the worst traffic she'd ever seen, had to park a block away. Walking to the school wasn't any easier. Every parent was there at the same time, picking up his or her kids. Parents parked their cars as if everyone had seven or fewer days to live, bypassing convention and leaving them wherever they could, including the middle of the road. As a result, the road was barely passable.

Some parents sat in their cars, swearing, yelling and honking their horns. Others, like Lilly, got out. She pushed through the throng of parents who pushed through the throng of kids looking for their parents. Kids screamed for their parents, some crying and shaking. Others seemed unable to focus on much of anything, their faces a mirror of the fear and uncertainty they felt.

Parents couldn't find their kids, kids couldn't find their parents. Lilly nearly got pushed to the ground. One woman near her fell down. People walked around her but Lilly helped her up, only to have the women push her aside and forge forward.

Other parents shoved people aside, as if they weren't really people, but inanimate impediments to their children. A father slugged another father who was in his way. A mother kicked another mother in the shin when she got between her and her child.

Once she actually spotted her kids, another parent got in her way, forcing Lilly to push her aside. She never gave it a second thought. When she finally made it to them, she hugged them as if they'd been apart for months. The whole thing was appalling to Lilly. She knew many of these parents. One of them was Julie who she saw in the distance, looking for her daughter, Sydney. Dragging Bryan and Mandy with her, she finally got within shouting distance of Julie.

"Julie." Nothing. "Julie!" She turned to Lilly, a crazed look in her eyes, then she turned back to the task of finding her daughter.

Drawn in by the fanatic parents around her, Lilly couldn't help but lose her composure. She failed to notice how she pushed some parents aside, how she nearly struck them. Then, she noticed that Bryan and Mandy looked stunned. Who was this person? Surely, not their mother.

She pulled and pushed them too as they made their way through the pack of frenzied parents, most of whom looked at her jealously, as if she had broken some code because she had her kids and they did not.

"What's going on?" asked Bryan once they got into the car.

"Did the school make any announcements?"

"Not much. Just something about a virus. Kids starting talking about dying and stuff."

Lilly tried to find a way to soft sell the end of the world, but couldn't come up with anything that made sense, so she just jumped right into it. "Terrorists have a virus that they will release in seven days that will kill all but the faithful."

"What? That doesn't make any sense," said Molly.

"Why would they do that?" asked Bryan.

"They think the world is sinful and that certain people, who are worthwhile, can survive the virus."

"You mean, like them."

"Yes."

"But how do they know they won't die like the rest of us?" asked Mandy.

"They don't. But they have faith. It seems they're challenging the world to save itself by having faith."

"Faith in what?" said Bryan.

Lilly thought for a moment. The president hadn't said. But she assumed it was religious based. "Faith in the Creator, in Jesus, I guess."

"We have faith. Everything will be OK, Mom," said Bryan, trying to will it to be true.

Lilly wanted to believe that, but in the short time that she had to think about this, all she could feel was doubt.

CHAPTER IV

Love your neighbor as yourself (Matt. 19:19).

Jesus said, 'Come, that I may teach you about secrets no person has ever seen. For there exists a great and boundless realm, whose extent no generations of angels has seen in which there is a great invisible Spirit' (Judas Gospel, 86-87).

DAY TWO

UNITED NATIONS SECURITY COUNCIL

President Holcomb stood at the front of the National Security Council, its 14 other members, plus scientists from all over the world, crowding the circular table, with others spilling over into the audience area. He quieted the group. Just to his left sat Carmela, Jacob and Father Thomas. To his right was a PowerPoint set up.

For the last hour, Holcomb couldn't settle them down enough to get through one or two slides of the PowerPoint. It was understandable that people were frantic. No one understood if Trinity was serious, if they really had a virus, how they could be stopped. Some wondered if they might be able to survive if the world had the faith that Trinity talked about.

At the moment, leaders struggled with allowing their enemies to enter their borders, know their secrets, to open up their countries in the ultimate act of cooperation. But Holcomb knew that they had to get this done now, that they didn't have days to consider this. They had hours, minutes. Of the seven days Trinity gave them, there were only five left. A joint resolution had to happen today, in the next hour.

"We would never allow our enemies…" said the Chinese President.

"We cannot allow OUR enemies to—" responded the Russian Federation President.

"It's unthinkable!" yelled the African representative. They were all talking over each other. Holcomb fumed.

"THAT'S ENOUGH!" Holcomb boomed. The room was quiet again.

"We are all afraid. In each country, martial law has been declared, borders closed. This is the time to put our differences aside."

Both the Russian and Chinese presidents rose and started to object, but Holcomb quieted them.

"I cannot overstate the importance of uniting to fight this threat. Our ability to survive is dependent on getting along."

The room was silent as this sunk in. In an effort to follow Holcomb's lead, the Chinese and Russian Presidents stared at each other and then nodded their accession to Holcomb's request. Holcomb let out a sigh of relief. He turned to Father Thomas who got up.

"I would like to introduce Father Thomas, world expert on ancient languages and texts."

Before Father Thomas could take his place at the podium, everyone's attention was drawn to the chamber doorway. The guards were tussling with someone who apparently wanted entry. The person–a woman–pushed them aside and adjusted her clothing. "I've got vital information for this gathering. Now, let me in!"

Her voice was loud enough that it could be heard throughout the assembly. Jacob recognized her and the voice, as did Carmela. Amy.

Jacob felt his back stiffen. He hadn't seen her for years. It all came back to him, the failed relationship, his unwillingness to tell her why he didn't want to be with her then.

He remembered when they met in Qumran, five years prior, when an archeological team had discovered what looked like an ancient catacomb buried in a hillside. The discovery was near the caves where the Dead Sea Scrolls were discovered so there was a great deal of excitement and anticipation. Amy had been teaching Biology and Ancient Studies at Emory University, near Atlanta, Georgia. Jacob was hired by the US government as an "advisor."

Amy didn't know who he was or how he was qualified to do anything with respect to the dig, in contrast to several renowned professors who treated him as an equal. During several discussions she'd had with them, she intentionally used scientific terminology that Jacob wouldn't understand, yet he seemed to follow everything they talked about. Jacob remembered how she chided him for this or that, any chance she got. He found the whole thing amusing, which angered her even more. He was convinced that the more he appeared her equal, the angrier she would get.

Amy reluctantly accepted him as a colleague but never as an equal. At one point, Amy suggested examining a clay jar they'd found for trace DNA. Jacob wondered what she was hoping to find, whether she could determine whether the DNA was human or animal and what she would do with the information. Jacob quipped that all DNA was animal and the base pairs were the same in all animals, including humans. Amy challenged him to see if he knew the difference. He did– although the base pairs are the same, the sequences and the number of genes found were different in humans and other animals. She thought she'd had him. His response was unexpected and just put them in further conflict.

It wasn't long after that they began a short, awkward relationship. Amy had not dated much, but she liked his "in your face" honesty, his brashness and confidence. For Jacob, he knew that there was a fiery woman hiding inside of her, and she was alluringly beautiful. But it soon became apparent that she wouldn't allow that to surface. This became obvious during a planned sexual encounter, as Jacob now called it, in which it became clear that she would not allow herself to open up to him. He interrupted things before they'd had sex. From that moment on, their relationship in the field was forced. Instead of talking about it, Jacob just left. He could tell that she was embarrassed about it, but she didn't know how to let go. He didn't want to deal with it.

All Amy could think of when she saw him was how he'd hurt her. Her sister's face seemed to be everywhere. She couldn't stop thinking about her. So when she saw Jacob up there at the podium, it didn't make her mad or nostalgic. She felt nothing.

As Amy stood at the door, waiting impatiently, Carmela leaned over and whispered into Holcomb's ear that it was Amy, who he had never met. Holcomb bent over the podium.

"Guard, let her in."

Amy rushed past the guard and up to the front where the president stood along with Jacob and Carmela. She pushed past Jacob, moving toward Carmela, making more of an effort than she'd expected to avoid making eye contact. Carmela gave her a hug, whispering in her ear that she was sorry about her sister. Amy tried to muster up a smile but instead choked back her emotion and nodded her appreciation.

Jacob rose and slid in next to Amy. He was surprised at how good she still looked, though her hair was matted and her skin glistened with sweat. Part of him wanted to give her a hug, but instead he drew close to her and whispered in her ear.

"I'm very sorry about your sister." Amy backed away and looked as cold as she could, never once acknowledging that he had spoken to her. She pulled a flash drive out of her pocket and plugged it into the computer sitting on the table. Amy stood in front of the podium. Jacob leaned back, hurt more than he would like to admit by her unwillingness to acknowledge him.

"I've just come from the National Academy. We have isolated the virus."

Everyone in the room cheered.

"We have the RNA replication. The antigen is within our grasp. But there is a problem."

The room grew silent again. Amy turned on the computer, typed in some information, and a picture of a mutating virus flashed on the screen.

"As you can see, we've mapped the virus. But it's mutating backwards, to its original DNA sequence. Some of our scientists think the virus is 2000 years old."

"And this means what?" asked Holcomb.

Both Jacob and Father Thomas joined Amy at the podium. Jacob ignored Amy while she gave him a dirty look.

"It means that finding a cure or even a vaccine is more complicated. Not impossible but difficult," said Jacob.

Amy pushed her way between Father Thomas and Jacob. "As soon as we design a vaccine, it is instantly outdated. Think of it as an airborne version of Ebola. We can't keep up with the mutations."

The room gasped. Someone muttered, "Ebola?"

"It's worse than Ebola, at least we believe it is. This is the most deadly virus the world has ever seen," said Amy.

Father Thomas said, "If we could locate a 2000-year-old cell, we could create an antidote." Father Thomas looked at Amy and Jacob for approval but got only Jacob's nod of approval.

"Where would we find that?" asked President Holcomb.

"People who were alive 2000 years ago had much different immune systems. There may be carriers who were immune to it. Those antibodies could be incorporated into the immune systems of present day man," said Father Thomas.

The room was hushed. Holcomb's attention was riveted to Father Thomas, Amy and Jacob.

"Finding something that old, and intact, is unlikely," said Amy, her voice filled with doubt.

"There are many artifacts around the world that could contain viable DNA," responded Father Thomas.

Amy stepped up and grabbed the microphone, determined to counter the Father's bizarre suggestion. "Like what? Even if you could find viable DNA, which is unlikely, what artifacts could contain DNA that hasn't been disturbed, given the age of these artifacts and the number of people that have handled them over the years?"

Unraveled, Father Thomas took on the challenge. "The Shroud of Turin, Veronica's veil, the true cross, the nails used on the cross – all of these could contain viable DNA. As I understand it, DNA can survive for thousands of years."

Father Thomas turned to Amy and glared. Holcomb didn't like the way the conversation was going so he wormed his way between them. "Father, the quote by Trinity. What does it mean? Do you know the source?"

"Yes, the quote in the broadcast. It is from the Judas Gospel, a Gnostic text. It offers the controversial view of Judas as the savior of Jesus, not his killer. In the Gospel, Judas explains that Jesus was a spirit and wanted to be freed from his earthly ties. I don't know how it's significant except that Trinity quoted from it."

"Is there any significance to it being a Gnostic text?" asked Holcomb.

"Possibly. The Gnostics believed in the existence of a 'gnosis,' or knowledge, that could lead to salvation. They were ostracized by mainstream, organized religion, as interpreted by Emperor Constantine, and declared blasphemous. The Gospel of Judas, along with many other gospels, was sent 'underground,' so-to-speak, never to be spoken of again as being 'Christian,' " explained Father Thomas.

Jacob stepped forward. "So, we can assume that Trinity is Gnostic, which doesn't help us much."

"Except that we know they're not mainstream," said Holcomb. "What does it tell us about their resolve?"

"Well, one can interpret the Judas Gospel as answering the question that they have a hard time putting into words. Judas discusses the knowledge they seek at length."

"Ok. I think each of us should discuss these issues with our religious leaders. We'll meet back here in an hour," said Holcomb as he called the meeting to an end. Secret Service agents quickly escorted him out of the room.

Carmela sidled up to the president. "What was that about?"

Holcomb half-turned to her. "Religious issues are so sensitive. I want to give them some time to work it through. Hopefully, we can cut through the dogma and resolve this without conflict."

Father Thomas, Amy, Jacob and several Secret Service agents left the United Nations Assembly room and were immediately mobbed by a throng reporters. The agents quickly indicated to the press that they weren't welcome. As the reporters moved away, Father Thomas slid in next to Amy. The agents walked in front of them and they followed.

"I'm Father Thomas. Sorry that your sister was involved in this. She is in my prayers."

Amy absent-mindedly extended her hand and the two shook, but she stared past him. She tried to smile. Thoughts of God's failure to protect her sister gave Amy's face a questioning, angry look. There was an uncomfortable tension between the two. No one seemed to know what to say, although Jacob and Carmela knew that her faith, always strong, had been tested.

Carmela caught up to them and said, "The President wants to meet with you."

The group turned around and followed Carmella. Jacob walked next to Amy and tried to come up with the right thing to say. Several things come to mind, but when he replayed them in his head, nothing sounded right. He thought he'd try an apology.

"I, uh, wish . . ." stammered Jacob.

"Save the platitudes," she said with startling force.

Jacob looked for some emotion, but all he saw was Amy's stone cold expression. It was clear that she was incredibly angry–that was understandable, given what happened to her sister, but he couldn't help but feel that some of that anger was saved for him. Not that he didn't deserve some of it. The more he thought about the guilt she must have felt, how he screwed her and the unfairness of it all, he couldn't completely contain his emotions. For a moment, he thought he felt his eyes swell with moisture. But he wouldn't allow that to happen so he thought about something else.

Carmela stopped at a doorway with two large Secret Service agents stationed just outside. They nodded and she opened the door. Inside, Holcomb paced. The large room was a flurry of activity. Computer technicians set up monitors and connected desktops wirelessly to a large server that sat against the far wall. Secret Service agents checked the room for bugs. On one of the walls was a large TV monitor that was playing news stories about the Trinity threat. Opposite the wall was a large desk.

Holcomb looked up when the four entered. "What can you tell me about these nuts?"

"Well," said Father Thomas, "I think more background on Gnosticism might be helpful. Gnostics focused on Jesus' esoteric teachings about the secrets of the kingdom of heaven. According to them, He only taught these 'secrets' to those who had proven themselves to be spiritually mature. Gnostic Christians claimed to offer those 'secrets' to their followers. The source of this knowledge is not terribly clear, although followers claim that some of his disciples did have secret knowledge. Thomas and Mary Magdalene, among others, wrote gospels that were repressed by the Church, in favor of the four that we've become familiar with."

"What makes Gnosticism very confusing is that Gnostics can't tell you what this knowledge is, where to get it, what it means. There are theories but no more," said Jacob.

"And that's what makes these guys so dangerous," added Father Thomas. "The Judas Gospel, I'm willing to bet, answers the question that all Gnostics work a lifetime to get answered: It offers them the secret to salvation."

"Don't we have to know what that secret is to defeat them?" asked Holcomb.

"I think we do," said Father Thomas.

"Given that this is amorphous, what's the next step?" asked Carmela.

"For most Gnostics, that knowledge is individual, not shared by the group. We have to learn what this means to Trinity," said Jacob.

"Jesus. How in the hell are we going to do that?" asked Carmela.

Holcomb turned his attention to Amy. "I understand a vaccine or a cure would contain this thing. What if we can find some ancient DNA to assist in the creation of a vaccine?"

Amy looked hard at him. "With all due respect, sir, I'm not convinced . . ." Her voice trailed off as Holcomb returned the look. She could see that it wasn't the time to question his resolve so she reluctantly nodded in agreement with his suggestion.

"Isn't it theoretically possible? That the Shroud and other artifacts could contain DNA?" asked Holcomb.

Reluctantly, Amy nodded. "It's possible. We've found viable DNA hundreds of years old. But not all DNA sources are good for creating a serum. And even if we find it, we'll never know its origin."

"If it's there, we'll find it," commented Jacob.

"I don't understand how this works. How would the DNA help?" asked Carmela.

"First, the virus is very old, we think from the time of Jesus," said Amy.

"Yes, I remember that. But I still don't understand why that matters," inquired Holcomb.

"Because there's a chance that anyone alive during that time period, who didn't die from the virus, has natural immunity to it."

"Come again?" asked Holcomb, shrugging his shoulders.

Jacob said, "We all build up natural immunities to disease, viruses. If we find someone with that immunity, we might be able to synthesize a serum."

"I get that. But how do we know if a person alive then died from something other than the virus?"

"I'll take that one," said Father Thomas. "We know that Jesus was killed by the Romans. That's why his DNA would be the perfect source for a serum."

"This sounds a little bit like a bad movie," quipped Carmela. "You know, the mad scientists trying to clone Jesus. Besides, how would you know that the sample you find, if you do, belongs to Jesus?"

"Sure. That's true. It's only a guess. It could belong to a guard or someone else who left DNA on the Shroud. But if we assume that Jesus was buried with the Shroud and if we get a sample from it that has blood on it and then cross check it with other parts of the Shroud and we get matching DNA, what are the chances that it could belong to someone other than Jesus?"

Reluctantly, Amy nodded. "He's right. We can match the DNA to other samples and a match would increase the likelihood that they came from the same person. However, you have to assume that the Shroud was used to bury Jesus – a big assumption, is it not?"

"Actually, not. Recent research and experiments prove, I believe, that it is authentic. There is no currently known method for producing on a cloth the marks of a body that we see on that Shroud. Nothing. It's a mystery. If we can't do it today, how could they have manufactured it hundreds of years ago?" said Father Thomas.

Holcomb thought for a moment and started pacing. "I thought the virus was mutating. What if it goes further back than year one, so-to-speak?"

"That's possible, but the mutation was slowing," said Amy.

"But how do we know that it is mutating to the years that Jesus was alive? It isn't possible to know that, is it?"

"Well, not with any accuracy. It's a guess."

"The survival of the human race rests on a guess? Jesus, we need more than that." Holcomb scratched his head and stopped, suddenly realizing that they were missing something.

"How can I be of service?" asked Father Thomas, sensing Holcomb's realization.

Holcomb put his arm around Father Thomas's shoulders. "You're reading my mind, Father. I want you to use your influence with the Vatican to get a copy of the original translation of the Judas Gospel. There's a reason they quoted from it, and we have to tear that thing apart. And it may help us answer the Gnostic, secret knowledge question. So, you go to the Vatican and start in."

"I can do that. I have some knowledge of the Gospel, but I've never read the original translation. I think I can help you with Trinity, as well."

Holcomb's face lit up. "I'm all ears, Father."

"Not a lot is known about them outside of the Vatican, that is true. But inside, it's a different story. The history reputedly goes back to the Vatican's less-than-adequate response to Nazi Germany. Frankly, the Church was deaf to the so-called Jewish question. Instead of condemning the Nazi regime, the Vatican actually signed a concordat with Germany, in 1933, that kept the Church out of the political business, which meant that the Church would not protect the Jews and could not condemn the Nazis. Frankly, it was an amazingly naive cop-out. No one in the Church, so it is claimed, understood how Hitler would use that agreement to advocate for his position.

After Hitler's plans became obvious and the horrible plight of the Jews became apparent, there were those inside the Vatican who couldn't stomach the agreement. Unbeknownst to the Vatican's leaders, an internal organization was formed–Trinity–to secretly support the Jews. A lot of it was subsumed under the leaders of the French underground, but Trinity was responsible for terrorist acts against the Nazis throughout Italy. More importantly, Trinity assisted local Jews to escape from Nazi persecution."

"Nothing wrong with any of that," quipped Jacob.

"I thought the pope, Pius XII, did actively oppose the Holocaust," questioned Holcomb.

"He did, to an extent. Many Jews were protected behind the Vatican's walls. But prior to 1942, the Church was quiet in the face of Nazi atrocities and Pius never spoke out publicly against the Nazis, perhaps in part because of the concordant.

After World War II, Trinity was quiet for many years. Then, about 15 years ago, there were some rumblings that they were involved in political causes, mostly involving radical religious beliefs."

"Any examples?"

"Frankly, I can't remember. They're noted in the Vatican archives, I'm sure. We have a section on Trinity."

"In that case, Father, I would like you to pull those materials for us and get them back here, to the UN, as quickly as possible," said Holcomb.

Father Thomas shrugged his shoulders. "I have no power over the Church, Mr. President. They will do whatever they want. I can ask."

Holcomb thought for a moment and then remembered something that Father Thomas had said. "Father, you said that Trinity was 'reputedly' started in World War II."

"Yes, well, many believe that Trinity has been in existence since the Church was formed. At various times, depending on the needs of the time, Trinity was there to champion causes the Church was too timid to deal with. Some of that has to do with how large the Church has become. There are many inside the Vatican who privately believe that the business of religion has gotten in the way of Jesus' message."

"That could describe many churches and many religions," said Jacob.

Father Thomas nodded. "It didn't take long for very early Church founders to see how quickly the Church misunderstood Jesus' true message. Look at all the violence perpetrated in the name of religion. Jesus preached love, not violence. Trinity was probably born hundreds of years ago in response to the Church's misdirection. But it couldn't proclaim its existence because to do so would be suicide. Instead, it festered inside the Vatican —"

"Waiting for the right time, if there is such a thing," said Holcomb. "Jesus, Father, these guys are really serious, aren't they? I mean, they're not a bunch of crackpots."

Father Thomas lowered his eyes but didn't answer.

Holcomb turned his attention to Jacob and Amy. "I want the two of you to assist with the examination of the Shroud, in Turin. Amy, I'm counting on your knowledge of DNA."

"Yes, Mr. President."

"We're sending teams to examine all the artifacts that might contain trace DNA. Hopefully, the collective effort will enable us to extract the DNA that we need before the day is out."

"What about the release points? Shouldn't I be focused on that?" asked Jacob.

"We're working on it. You really think that Trinity wants us to beat this thing? Or are they just nuts, looking for a way to force the end of the world?"

"In their own way, yes, I do think they want us to beat this. I don't think they believe we can . . ." Jacob stopped in mid-sentence. "You know, I don't know many, except faith healers, who would choose faith over science, but that seems to be their message."

"Do not underestimate the power of faith. 'We walk by faith, not by sight.' II Corinthians," said Father Thomas.

Amy, fuming with anger, stepped in front of Father Thomas. "Faith didn't do a DAMN thing for Melissa or those other innocent people. Science is the only thing that can beat these bastards."

Carmela put her arm around Amy's shuddering shoulders. For a moment, there was an uncomfortable silence in the room.

Holcomb cleared his throat and said, "Okay, well, a car's waiting to take you to Andrew's Air Force Base."

Carmela handed Jacob a cell phone. "You must check in every four hours or a GPS signal will automatically track your location. We've got agents packing your essentials."

"I guess we're not sleeping in," quipped Jacob. Father Thomas smiled but Amy sneered. Carmela led the way out of the makeshift office followed by Amy, Jacob and Father Thomas.

In the United Nation's hallway, Jacob slid in beside Amy, who ignored him once again. He looked at her, waiting for some recognition, but she gave him none. She looks tired, he thought. He wasn't very good at making small talk, much less consoling his ex-girlfriend who just lost someone she was close to. And then there was the matter of how he'd left her. She probably thought he was a jerk. Maybe he was. He had an emergency, or so he told himself, and had to leave the country in a hurry. What made it worse was that he didn't call her, not before he left or when he arrived. When he got back to the States, several months later, he never reached out to her. It was easier to avoid the conflict.

But now they were going to be spending a lot of time together and those bad decisions hung between them like a shroud. He noticed her looking at him and imagined what she must be thinking. It wasn't good.

"What?" he asked.

"Nothing," she said.

"I saw that."

"You see what you need to see. I don't think it's me."

Father Thomas, Carmela and a Secret Service agent looked uncomfortably at each other. Jacob could see the disapproval in their gaze and wished he could be more tactful.

Trying to recover, Jacob said, "Look, I —"

"Admit that you're a jerk. Unless those words pass your lips, don't talk to me."

They walked to the waiting car without saying anything else. For Amy, the memory of their failed relationship was both embarrassing and filled with disappointment. She was attracted to Jacob, but when he abruptly left the dig, off to assist with another find in Jordan, she swore off men. The truth was that Jacob was the only man she'd been with since college, some 15 years ago, and she hadn't been with one since their tryst. She was too busy to bother with a relationship, or so she told herself. Seeing him stirred up her emotions, which, when added to her current emotional state, caused her to feel more on edge than she was used to.

Jacob ran his right hand through his hair and then adjusted himself in his seat. He glanced at his shoes. The GMC SUV pulled away, following a lead car full of fully armed agents, each carrying Glock 19s. Each car also had two M4 carbines secured in a compartment in the back-seat area.

Amy tried not to think of Jacob, but his presence brought back all those memories—some good, some not so good. She remembered when they first met, about five years ago, in Qumran. She was called in as an ancient languages expert, which she found odd, since she was more of a genetics expert. She knew a lot about ancient religions and she knew it, but what she didn't expect was the immediate confrontation she had with Jacob Mathews. After she was dropped off at the busy site, the first thing she noticed was the tall man standing just outside the cave where the artifact had been found, his shirt stuck to his sweaty torso. She was drawn to him. He stared at her as she approached until she stood just in front of him, trying not to give away her schoolgirl attraction.

"Who are you?" he'd asked. She had the impression that he was giving her the once over.

"Amy—"

"—Oh, yeah, the scientist. We'll get in the cave and start helping your colleagues."

"Excuse me? I don't work for you, in case you haven't noticed."

Jacob had smiled, as if he liked her sharp tongue. She actually did what he asked, but not because he told her. From that moment on, all they did was argue. He didn't like the fact that she knew more than he did about many aspects of archeology and that she loved letting him know it. She didn't think she liked the odd combination of swash buckling adventurer and rare intellect. It was quite disarming. But it also made him very different from the men she had hung out with before and that was the attraction.

One incident came to mind. They were arguing about the proper translation of a particular artifact. A "real" ancient languages expert had been reviewing the materials when Amy made a comment that challenged the interpretation. Jacob heard that, looked at the expert's interpretation and sided with him. While Jacob and Amy got into it, the expert stayed silent, wondering why these two seemed intent on manufacturing conflict. Amy remembered how engaged she was during that argument, noticing for the first time that whether they were arguing about the weather or something more serious, she enjoyed being around him. Part of it was his sarcastic attitude. A lot of it was the incredible, creative intellect that lurked beneath his exterior. A lot of it was his never-say-die attitude, his strength and confidence. But that stuff made her crazy, as well. It was a cliché, love-hate relationship.

They finally declared a truce, agreeing not to discuss their opinions about discoveries they made at the dig. That was also when some romance wormed its way in, but Amy couldn't handle the loss of control that came with that. So, she knew that although Jacob left without saying a word, everything that needed to be said had been. But it still angered her.

Carmela lovingly patted Amy's knee, ending the brief memory she had of the events that led to their breakup. "We're all trying to understand what happened. I can't believe she's gone, Amy. We'll get them," said Carmela, trying to change the subject.

For a moment, Amy was still lost in the past and then realized Carmela had referred to her sister. She nodded. "I know we will. It's been a long time. When was it?" said Amy.

Amy thought for a moment, and then answered her own question. "Probably Syria."

Carmela thought for a moment. Then it came to her. "Oh, sure, when we sponsored the Syrian effort to extract DNA from that artifact, what was it…"

"A cloth, from an urn that a local found in a cave."

"Right, right. That was amazing."

Jacob overheard the conversation and said, "I remember that. Wasn't that artifact tied to one of the disciples?" Jacob posed the question as conversation, since he knew the answer.

Amy half turned to him. "You know it was. It was one of the most significant finds in a century." She tried to manufacture an emotionless response, but the anger was apparent in her tone of voice.

Jacob nodded and tried to ignore her again, wondering if she was really angry with him or was deflecting her anger from her sister's death to him. He and Father Thomas exchanged looks as the limo pulled into the airport and parked near the waiting transport. Secret Service agents got out, grabbed several bags of luggage and escorted the three of them to a pair of Learjet C21As. As they got out of the car, Carmela and Amy hugged.

Carmela said, "You take care of yourself. Give him a chance. We need him."

Amy half smiled. "We'll beat this thing, Carmi. Just remember that. My sister didn't die for nothing," said Amy, her voice cracking

as she held back the tears. The two hugged and Amy joined Jacob and
Father Thomas on the gangway.

Jacob and Father Thomas shook hands as Father Thomas got on
one and Amy and Jacob got on the other—Father Thomas headed to
the Vatican, Amy and Jacob to Turin.

On the jet, Jacob leaned back in his chair and closed his eyes.
Amy opened her brief case that had been delivered by Secret Service
agents and stared at a paper she wrote on extracting DNA samples
from ancient artifacts. It wasn't that she didn't know how to do it, but
she never took anything for granted. But all she could do was stare,
the anger and hurt eating her alive.

Milwaukee, Wisconsin

The first thing that Jackson did surprised even him. For a split
second, he thought about going straight right up to the end, then
quickly decided that wasn't any fun. For a week, he would live like
a king. So he stopped at a local Acura dealership to "borrow" an
MDX for the week. It was after hours, but he broke in, found the
keys and drove the car off the lot. The cops didn't even come. He
couldn't believe how easy it had been; then he realized that there were
several other cars missing. The news reported that a large number of
service officials, state workers, government employees and even some
local police officers left as soon as they'd heard the news. Others were
conscripted into the National Guard. That was the reason, said the
president, that he had instituted martial law.

Jackson giggled sitting behind the wheel, taking in the rich, tan
leather seats and marveling at the brightly lit dashboard. He'd never
seen anything like it.

He'd never felt happier.

He drove to his girlfriend Ashley's house. She thought he worked
in construction, seemingly blind to what Jackson really did for a "liv-
ing," which was fine with Jackson, since he was sure she'd leave him
if she knew. She was way too pretty and way too nice for him. He figured that sooner or later, she'd get the drift about who he really was.
Hopefully, it wouldn't be today.

He pulled in front of her condo and jumped out of "his" car. When she didn't come to the door, he used the key she'd given him. She wasn't home. For a moment, he panicked. Then he realized it was only 4:00 p.m. She hadn't gotten off work yet.

He grabbed a beer from the fridge, slumped onto her couch and turned on the TV. Every station had frantic reporters talking about the virus, about Trinity, about the "end." Reporters trained cameras on a massive exodus of humanity, bumper-to-bumper traffic, going . . . well, that was the interesting thing about it. Folks were interviewed and very few knew where they were going or if the did, were too afraid to tell anyone. People wanted to just leave, get away, as if fleeing the city would effectuate an escape from the virus. On one station, religious leaders debated whether the virus fulfilled biblical prophecy, whether Trinity was actually an instrument of Christianity. This notion was quickly discarded, but Jackson was impressed that they considered the possibility.

On another channel, people were lined up, waiting to get into a large building to hear from someone who promised to give them the answers they sought. The signs outside read, "Only $100 per person will get you the keys to salvation."

Jackson wasn't one to shy away from good old American greed. He loved taking advantage of people, using their fear to profit. But even to him, this was a bit below the belt. Yet, people were so desperate, they would spend any amount of money to get answers.

In the middle of the broadcast, someone got up on a ladder and added a "zero" on the end of the $100. No one in the line balked. After all, did salvation have a price?

The whole thing was so depressing he flicked off the TV, and for a moment, actually wondered if he was doing the right thing. But then he remembered what a loser he was. He had no chance. He might as well go out in style. He wished he had some meth left over but he'd run out. He would have to stop by his dealer.

The more he thought about it, Ashley would want to be with her parents and siblings, anyway. She would invite him to go with her, since she believed that his parents were dead. They weren't, but they might as well be. But he didn't want her to slow him down.

He plopped his beer on her end table, nearly knocking over a picture of he and Ashley, hiking in Colorado. It was odd, he thought, how easily he could dismiss her in the midst of almost certain death. He hoped she felt differently about him. He closed his eyes, just for a moment, remembering the good days, before the drugs, drinking and petty crime, when he cared. He dozed and a flash of his family intruded-his wife and kids, smiling at him and playing in the backyard of their home. Then, the house and his family pulled away from him, as if some unseen force was sucking them down a drain. He reached for them but they were gone.

And then he saw it. The bright light and the shimmering figure, slowly moving closer. Just as when he'd seen the figure before, he called out to it, but there was no answer. He hoped that this time it would get closer to him before he woke up so that he could make it out.

It did. The figure stopped about ten feet from him. She was beautiful, with light skin, blond hair, radiant eyes, wearing a white robe of some sort. She'd never spoken before, but this time, she did.

"It will be time soon, time to change your life around, Jackson. He is expecting you to accept your role."

"Who's he?" a voice asked, before Jackson realized that it was his voice.

"You know. It is your destiny. All of these things you've done doesn't change that. He forgives you. But you must help these people. You must regain faith in yourself. In several days, there will be a sign. Don't miss it."

With that, he woke up. For a minute, he sat there, staring at nothing in particular, not sure what to think about the dream. He wasn't sure what to do next. He wasn't going to pay attention to the dream, that was for sure.

He figured that with everyone fleeing the cities, he could have some fun in downtown Milwaukee.

CHAPTER V

We are saved by Hope (Rom. 8:24).

*Jesus said, 'Come, that I may teach you about secrets no person has ever seen.
For there exists a great and boundless realm, whose extent no generation of angels
has seen, in which there is a great invisible Spirit' (Judas Gospel, 86-87).*

DAY THREE

St. John's Cathedral, Turin, Italy

Amy and Jacob hadn't talked at all on the flight from New York
to Turin. Once they landed, the UN team that had come with them
other teams from England, France and Russia. They piled into UN
military vehicles and headed for the cathedral.

Outside the cathedral, people lined the streets. A large barricade
was set up near the street in front of the Cathedral. Armed UN security forces, mostly Italian, prevented anyone who wasn't either a scientist or otherwise on their list of authorized entrants from entering.
Protestors wanted inside, to see the Shroud, hoping to get some solace
from it and the church.

Amy, Jacob and the security team that flew with them, plus other
UN security team members that had picked them up, got out of the
vehicle. The atmosphere was tense. People were yelling and screaming. Jacob assumed they wanted inside. It felt as if they were a hair's
breadth from an all-out riot.

Jacob looked up at the famous church, made out of marble, towering in front of them. As the team escorted them toward the entrance,

people behind barricades yelled at them, as if somehow they were responsible for the virus.

The Cathedral of St. John was a magnificent structure, towering above them, its white façade a testament its sacred contents. All of this was not lost on Amy, but the pending task dimmed her excitement. The Shroud, located in the Guarino Guarini Chapel, was partially damaged in a fire in 1552, when it was in Chambery. The fire would have no effect on their examination, however, as the damage was mostly along the edges of the fabric.

Amy and Jacob stood outside a barricade, waiting for the UN security team to allow their entry. The streets were packed with military vehicles and the Carabineers, Italy's military police who helped hold the hoards of people at bay. Several other scientists were ahead of them, and, while Amy and Jacob waited, the guards checked their ID's and let them pass. Then Amy and Jacob handed over their passes, which consisted of a letter from the UN, which the guards crosschecked with their list. But for some reason, they kept looking at the list and their letter, as if something was wrong.

Amy felt the impatience welling up inside of her, ready to blow up. Didn't these idiots realize that she had her sister's death to avenge? What could be so important? She felt her face get red as she stepped forward, words of anger at the tip of her tongue.

Her thoughts were disrupted when Jacob gently pulled her back. She looked at him and then forward again at the guard, who had his hand on his sidearm. Jacob whispered in her ear, "Relax. We'll get inside."

Jacob saw a questioning look on her face. She looked from him to the officer and realized that she had moved quickly toward the officer, the anger apparent in her movements. He was prepared to draw his weapon, unsure of her intentions. Once she realized what she had done, she nodded to the officer and then backed up even more. Another officer took Amy and Jacob aside, checked their ID again and then led them past a throng of people on the other side of the barricade, who were carrying signs that read, "The End of the World is the Beginning," and "Repent – Jesus Returns."

Amy whispered to Jacob, "Did I really just challenge an armed guard?"

Jacob nodded. "You didn't look like you were here, Amy. What were you thinking?"

She shook her head. "I don't know . . . my sister . . . all of this. Geez."

Once they were allowed inside the cathedral, a priest took them through the ornate church. They passed the remains of Pier Giorgio, who was beatified in May, 1990. Amy glanced at his picture, hanging above the coffin. Jacob knew that the Shroud was usually kept close by, but for now, it was in the basement. As they passed the main altar, Jacob marveled at the amazing tree branches carved in wood, climbing up the right and left sides of the altar, their detail mesmerizing . In the middle was Jesus at the Last Supper. At the front of the church was an unusual depiction of Christ on the cross, with an ornate, red-rimmed baldachin with gold candleholders flanking the tabernacle that undoubtedly held the host.

The majesty of the cathedral tended to induce awe-inspiring silence for most visitors. Amy couldn't feel much, however, as the pending task was on her mind.

After they passed the altar, Jacob asked the priest, "Is the equipment here for our examination?"

" All of the equipment you need is in the basement. And there are many other scientists already here."

Jacob got closer to Amy and whispered into her ear, "So why do you suppose those people want inside?"

"Probably to see the Shroud. To seek salvation. You know, your specialty."

"Perhaps it's more about them wanting to go somewhere the government wants them to stay away from."

Suddenly, a man ran down the hall at them, his eyes wide with fear. Before the UN guards could stop him, he grabbed Amy, his eyes boring through her. "He is returning. How can I be saved?" Amy pulled away from him and then wondered if she should respond, so she gently touched his forearm and patted him on the back.

"You will be saved, if only you believe." Two UN guards grabbed him and dragged him past them, out of the cathedral. Jacob leaned into Amy and whispered, "I didn't know salvation was so easy to earn. Would you throw me a blessing when you have some time?"

"You need a book of blessings to make it. I don't know if there are enough."

Jacob caught her angry expression and whispered in her ear, "Beautiful architecture."

"Renaissance. Built in the late 1400s."

"How are you doing?" Jacob asked, sorry he'd asked her the minute the words left his lips.

Her eyes flicked at him. "You're kidding, right?"

"I . . . you were kind of out it a minute ago. Look, I'm doing my best—"

"You had your chance. You blew it."

Jacob, trying to reformulate what he intended to say, said, "What I mean is that—"

"Just let it go."

Jacob wanted to say something, but nothing seemed to come out right, so he kept his mouth shut. Once they neared the stairs to the basement, the number of technicians, movers, scientists and smock-wearing scientist wannabes, increased significantly. The hall near the stairway was packed with boxes and crates, some of which were empty. Two workers carried a large box of scientific instruments down the stairs. Near the door to the Shroud room were several armed guards. Workers emerged from the room and bounded up the stairs, while a young woman holding a clipboard directed the pair ahead of them to a spot in the room.

Near her stood a 45 year-old Italian scientist, his hair tossed about as if he'd been in a windstorm. He wore loud, white-on-black-striped pants with a white t-shirt underneath his blue lab coat. On his feet were flip-flops. There was something funny and confusing about the man.

"Striped pants?" Jacob whispered into Amy's ear. She pulled back, looking at him askance, putting her finger to her mouth to silence him.

In the background was the Shroud of Turin, lying horizontally on a table, encased in glass with argon gas inside. Several scientists set up a portable electron microscope on the far side of the Shroud. There was a quiet reverence in the room, as if they all assumed they were in the presence of something holy and sacred.

Jacob couldn't help but feel it, too. He glanced at another scientist standing next to him whose eyes were misty. He and Amy walked slowly toward the Shroud, staring at it. The scientist with the weird pants looked up at them as they walked by, seemingly unaffected by the object whose space he shared.

"Yes, well, let's get on with it, shall we? Smocks are over there." He pointed to a spot to their left.

Neither of them paid attention to his direction. Jacob approached the Shroud, anticipating with each step that, in a moment, he might be looking into the eyes that at one time belonged to Jesus. He barely noticed that Amy was already standing there, her eyes fixed on the Shroud as though it was speaking to her. He stopped next to her. Neither of them could speak. Jacob felt his hairs stand on end, as if the image threw off an electrical charge.

It was longer than he had expected and the image of a man was clearer than he had imagined. Fully stretched out, as it was, the linen cloth measured a little over 14 feet long and nearly four feet wide. He had seen pictures of the Shroud, as had Amy, but it was like watching a football game: You could see more of a play on TV, but there was nothing that could compare with being at the game, taking in the action and seeing a play unfold. The Shroud was just like that.

Jacob couldn't take his eyes off the head. Was that Jesus? No scientist could explain how the image was transferred from the body to the cloth. Such an image transfer could not be duplicated with known technology, so believers in the Shroud's authenticity argued that it could have only happened as the result of a miracle or the intervention of a supreme being. The first team of scientists to examine the Shroud, who called themselves the Shroud of Turin Research Project (STRUP), discovered that the image on the cloth was three-dimensional, something that cannot be duplicated with traditional painting or photographic methods. They discovered that the image could not have been painted, or photographed, or imprinted due to body heat or by any natural means that occurred when the cloth was draped over a human body.

Jacob couldn't imagine how this amazing artifact could be anything other than the shroud used to cover the body of Jesus. A DNA sample would be invaluable in trying to manufacture a serum.

Nearby, several scientists worked on the Shroud's container. A worker handed out smocks to those who had ignored Striped Pants, including Amy and Jacob, and the headgear that they each had to wear in order to protect the surface of the Shroud. Amy and Jacob donned the smocks, put on the headgear and secured the masks over their mouths and noses.

"Ok, folks, we're going to open the container. Does everyone have their smocks and masks on?"

Jacob looked up to see who spoke and by the stripped pants sticking out of smock, he knew who it was. The others in the room checked their gear and looked at each other as the container was opened. There was an audible popping noise as the lid came off.

"Ok, you've all been given a map showing where to start your examination. That way we won't duplicate our efforts. Let's get going."

Amy took her spot and grabbed a magnifying glass. Many of the scientists used hand-held, digital microscopes with long USB cords attached to small desktops that lined the edge of the long table.

Jacob stood next to Amy, observing. She was bent over, examining sections of the cloth with the magnifying glass, getting a general idea of its condition. He glanced at her figure, remembering earlier days, and then jerked his head up as though he'd been caught looking at a Playboy magazine. After several moments of examining the Shroud, she shook her head in amazement.

To no one in particular, she said, "This cloth is in amazing condition. It looks almost new."

A male scientist next to her nodded in agreement. "Something isn't right."

Jacob stepped in beside her and held his hand out, palm up. She glanced at him. "Could I borrow your magnifying glass?"

"No. You're not qualified to decide how old this cloth is."

"Is that what you really think?" asked Jacob.

"What are you talking about?"

"You don't believe that Jesus was our savior, do you? Answer me!" Amy spat out the words, her face a picture of anger.

Jacob nodded toward the rest of the scientists, indicating that Amy should look around the room. She did, noticing for the first time that everyone was staring at them.

Trying to recover from their embarrassing argument, Amy put down the magnifying glass and grabbed a hand-held digital microscope and began examining a portion of the cloth, near the edge. She was expecting old, linen cloth that somehow had survived the burial and death of Jesus, along with iron-colored bloodstains. But what she saw was so obviously not old that she couldn't believe her eyes.

She stared at a spot on the cloth, looked up, still not believing what she saw there and said, "I think I found something." This time, Jacob stood off to the side.

The other scientists in the room seemed to all nod in unison. Several audibly agreed, that they too had found something. Little by little, all the scientists looked up from the Shroud. Amy was the first to speak.

"There's no viable DNA here. The relic is a fake."

For just a moment, the room was silent as her revelation sunk in but the others had seen the same thing. Most of them were reluctant to believe what they had seen. The lead scientist—Striped Pants'— looked at the area Amy had been examining and then glanced around at the rest of them.

"Well, it's pretty obvious, isn't it? This cloth is new, artificially worn to make it look reasonably like the Shroud with markings in all the right places. But it's not three-dimensional, there's no blood on it. It looks like paint."

A scientist across from them nodded in agreement. You could hear a pin drop as they tried to assimilate what was staring at them. Who could have done this? The Shroud was heavily guarded. And why? Whoever did it was not trying to attempt even a good forgery; they only wanted to create a copy that would pass muster from a distance. They–it had to be Trinity–were already a step ahead of them.

"They must have known we'd work this angle," said Jacob. The others in the room turned toward him, wondering who had spoken.

"What do you mean?" asked Striped Pants.

"Trinity has been here."

An Italian scientist said, "What? You mean they replaced the Shroud? Why would they do that?"

"For the reason that I said. They don't want us to get a DNA sample from which a serum can be made," answered Jacob.

Amy's head was down, taking it all in. If they were capable of this, they were a lot more powerful than any of them had thought. She looked up. "It's the only thing that makes sense. We'd better call Carmela. The other artifacts may be compromised as well."

Jacob pulled the cell phone from his pocket and pushed the 'call' button. He waited a moment and then heard Carmela's voice. "What have you got?" she asked.

"The Shroud has been replaced. And it's a bad imitation. Assuming Trinity is responsible, they knew we would try this."

"I'm getting similar reports from the other teams. Veronica's Veil, the nails from the cross, they've all been replaced. Do your scientists have any ideas how to deal with this?"

Jacob moved the phone away from his ear while he addressed the room. "It's the same all over. Any idea how to get around this little problem?"

The room seemed to sigh at the same time. There WAS no getting around the problem. If there was any DNA that could be used to create a serum, the possible sources were very limited.

"We're not going to be getting any DNA, that's for sure. Damn," said Amy, as she backed away from the Shroud and began pulling off her smock. The others in the room followed suit.

Jacob put the phone back to his ear. "What do you want us to do?"

On the other end of the line, the president took the phone from Carmela. There had to be other options. "Is there anything else that might have some cells, anything from the same time period?"

"I don't know. Here's Amy." Jacob gave her the and the president asked her the same question.

She thought for a moment. Was there something else that they hadn't thought of? Nothing, except . . . "I've got it. The so-called True Cross. Jesus of Nazareth, King of the Jews. It could have his DNA on it. And there's one other thing. The Sudarium of Ovideo, in the Camara Santa of the Cathedral of San Salvador in Ovideo, Spain."

"I don't know what that is," said Holcomb.

"The Sudarium is the cloth that supposedly was wrapped around the head of Jesus after he died. It's mentioned in John's Gospel," said Amy.

"Where's the True Cross?" asked Holcomb.

"Here, in Rome, at the basilica, Santa Croce, Gerusalemme," said Amy.

"Go there first. On your way to Spain, I want you to stop at the Vatican and assist Father Thomas with the Judas Gospel," said the president.

Amy hung up the phone and joined Jacob and the others, picking up the middle of a conversation. ". . . how they could have done this without being detected. They must have some connections."

"The security for the cathedral is high. I don't know how they could have gotten in," said one of St. John's priests.

"Trinity must have some members in high places," said Amy.

"I agree," said Jacob. Replacing all those artifacts is daunting. Can we track who's been in and out of here?"

Father John, the priest who had spoken earlier, answered. "Yes, anyone who visits the Shroud has to sign in."

"But this would take more than one guy. We're talking about replacing the Shroud," said Jacob.

Suddenly, Father John remembered. "Oh, my. We had a Vatican-sponsored viewing two weeks ago."

"Not sure what that means. Who were they?" asked Amy.

"I don't remember, but I do know it was private. Vatican orders." Father John hesitated, the conclusion obvious but not one that he wanted to recognize.

"No one could get in without Vatican approval, correct?" said Jacob. No one answered. "And I assume that there has been no other breach of security?"

Striped pants shook his head, "no."

"So, whoever did this must have at least tacit Vatican approval," reasoned Amy.

"Well, I don't think it means that at all. It couldn't have been the Vatican. They wouldn't do something like that," answered Father John.

"It's the only logical explanation," said Jacob.

"And that means the Vatican at least has been duped into assisting in the theft," said Amy. Father John nodded and then lowered his eyes.

"I cannot believe, however, that they would participate know-ingly," said Father John.

Striped Pants said, "I agree. Perhaps it is someone operating out-side Vatican authority."

"That's the only possible answer. If I could suggest, pull the records of that visit, see who was here, and we may have our first lead on the identity of Trinity," said Father John.

"Or one of their leaders," said Amy.

"At this point, we can't ignore wherever the clues lead us," said Jacob, as he pulled out cell phone. He opened it and pushed the call button.

"Carmela, hey, we've been talking about this and it's obvious that the only way all these artifacts could have been replaced is if Trinity has some inside help. Most of these are guarded like the Shroud. Security is tightly controlled by the Vatican."

"We agree. The president has ordered a full investigation into access to the artifacts. We should have some answers quickly."

"All right. You want me to look into that before I leave?"

"We'll give you an hour. Then you've got to be at the airport."

———

Jacob, Amy, the Archbishop of Turin and Father John stood in the archbishops office, looking at the security records and a digital recording of the Vatican's recent visit. They watched a large van pull up to the rear of the building. Six guys wearing tan pants and white shirts got out of the van, followed by the driver, who kept his head down as they headed for the rear entrance.

"How long were they inside?" asked Jacob.

"I've got it flagged for when they left," said the archbishop. He entered a number, and the scene displayed the same group leaving, but now they were carrying a long, tubular object.

"That's about the size of the Shroud," said Amy.

The archbishop shook his head from side-to-side and bristled with anger. "They took it from right under our noses. But I can't believe the Vatican knew about it."

"I don't disagree. We don't know that the Vatican took the Shroud. The van and its occupants represented themselves as Vatican; it doesn't mean they were," said Jacob. He glanced at Amy for some confirmation, but she seemed to be somewhere else.

"But it was arranged by my staff directly with the Vatican."

"Let's get them on the phone and find out who they sent, who talked to whom," suggested Jacob. The archbishop was on the phone before Jacob could finish his sentence. A few minutes later, the archbishop had his answer.

"The viewing was arranged by someone from Cardinal Orfeo's office. They have no idea if Orfeo ordered it or if he or anyone in the Vatican knew what the occupants in the van were up to. And they have no idea where the original was taken, assuming that they removed it."

"We don't know for sure the van took the original," said Father John.

"This shouldn't be too tough to track down. How many folks in the Vatican have access to a Cardinal's office?"

No one responded, but it was obvious: It had to be someone who either worked or lived there. "Was that the last time anyone had access to the Shroud?" asked Amy. Father John thought about it for a moment and then nodded.

"It hasn't been touched by anyone in several years. It had to be the guys in the van–no one else has been in to look at it," said Father John.

But the question that hung in the room like a pink elephant was this: why would anyone in the Vatican be involved? It didn't make sense. For millions of Catholics, the Vatican was the window to salvation. Even though Trinity started there during World War II, it wasn't possible that the Vatican could be involved in anything like this, was it? Certainly, neither the archbishop nor Father John thought so, but they couldn't help but see logic in a Vatican connection.

"We're going to have to assume that the Vatican is where we start with this, do you agree?" asked Jacob. The Archbishop fidgeted, trying not to think about it. He sort of half nodded, unwilling to fully commit to the idea.

"How do we broach that subject, without getting kicked out of the Vatican?" asked Jacob.

"Father Thomas would be your best bet. He has a bit of a history with the Vatican, but that might actually help him. He also knows Orfeo," said the archbishop.

"All right. Can you think of anything else?" said Jacob, turning to Amy. She shook her head, "No." He nodded and they left the office as Jacob called Carmela.

Jacob turned to Amy. "We need to leave now for the basilica. What equipment do you need?"

"The UN soldiers have to be good for something."

"They're supposed to save our ass."

"I can save my own ass, thank you," said Amy, the sarcasm clear.

Later, on the C-47 they shared with United Nations security forces, Amy asked Jacob about Father Thomas' relationship with the Vatican.

Jacob said, "Frank's father worked in Rome, where he lived in a rough neighborhood. He got into a lot of fights and turned the skills he learned on the street into a pretty successful boxing stint during his college years. He was in the military for a brief period of time, hated the violence, managed to get out and transferred to a seminary in Rome. He worked at the Vatican and had the fortune, or so he thought, of working for Orfeo, a powerful Cardinal. Not a good experience, from what he told me. He hated the political nature of the Vatican, what he thought was near blasphemy. That's when it happened." Jacob paused for a moment, smiling at the thought of it.

"What happened?" asked Amy.

"He clocked another priest. In the Sistine Chapel."

Amy stifled a laugh, then covered her mouth. "He didn't."

Jacob nodded. "Yeah, he's got a temper."

"Why did he hit him?"

"He's never told me. But in any case, the Vatican forced him out and there was talk of defrocking him. They marooned him instead at the University in Turin where he taught religious archeology. He's quite an expert on the Shroud."

"He taught in Turin? That hardly sounds like marooning him."

"Yup. We butt heads all the time, but he's my best friend. And I agree. They were going to send him to Tunisia, I think, but he talked them out of it."

"What was he doing at Columbia if he's a professor in Italy?"

"He's sort of the unofficial curator of the Shroud. But now, he travels a lot, teaches classes. Not as much in Turin anymore. He was actually supposed to be a guest professor at Columbia, focusing primarily on religious artifacts as they relate to religious archeology."

"I can't believe that the Vatican would welcome him back after all that."

"Well, the urgency of the current situation is what is driving this."

For a moment, whatever stood between them seemed to shrink away. Jacob could see a certain degree of acceptance in Amy's eyes, as if the connection they used to have was restored. But then it quickly faded.

BASILICA, SANTA CROCE

Amy was amazed at how quickly the populace had responded to the threat. The police were everywhere, chasing people who ran from stores with armfuls of clothes, electronics, food–anything they could get their hands on. It was as if people had lost their minds. She thought it particularly ironic that the people were proving Trinity's point: With death almost certain for most of them, many people lost all sense of morality. Around almost every corner was a new form of immoral behavior. Theft was not the only thing on people's minds. They passed some kids smashing the window of a store and the windshield of a car. The police hadn't caught up to them yet. Around another corner, someone had set a car on fire.

"What the hell is wrong with these people?" said Amy.

Most of the churches they passed had lines of people outside, waiting to get in. Police barricaded the streets around the churches, trying to keep the hoards of worshipers at bay. Some people, including children, were pushed aside by anxious adults, intent on getting inside the church where they believed they would be saved. To hell with everyone else, even children. It was an amazing, sad picture of what humanity had come to. Jacob couldn't help but wonder if we deserved the virus. Maybe Trinity was right.

The basilica was a different story, as it was closed to the public. The van carrying Amy, Jacob and several United Nations soldiers and religious scholars and scientists parked in a nearby lot. Before they exited the van, a group of religious zealots approached them. They carried signs that read, "Jesus Will Save You, Not Judas."

The soldiers got out first, then the scientists and their crew, carrying the equipment Amy and the others would need to conduct the extraction. Before they could get into the basilica, they were besieged by a mob of people who had surrounded the church. They were calm and more organized than the others, but clearly, these were people who wanted answers and didn't know where to turn. A young woman grabbed Amy, her eyes wide open but staring through Amy rather than at her.

"What are we going to do? Can anyone help us?" she asked.

Amy pulled back as a man crowded Jacob, asking him if he knew how to save them from death. The UN soldiers tried to push them back. Several other UN soldiers escorted them into the basilica. On the way, Jacob turned to Amy and said, "That was interesting." Amy didn't respond.

They were met at the door by Father Aldo, the curator of the True Cross, who ushered them into the basilica. Behind them, workers rolled in boxes and containers containing chemicals, containers and a strange selection of liquids.

Once inside the basilica, Father Aldo said, "The Vatican has some reservations about allowing an examination of the Cross, but given the urgency of the situation, they are allowing it."

"How nice of them," quipped Jacob.

Ignoring him, Father Aldo said, "We've removed the cross from its case. It is back here." Father Aldo directed them past the sanctuary, replete with stained glass and a soaring ceiling. The sun filtered through the glass, splintering the light into various shades of green, gold, red and blue. There was something prophetic about the light, as many of the rays lit up the previous resting spot of the Cross.

In a small room, near the rear of the basilica, was the Cross. It didn't look like much–a couple of large pieces of old, battered wood– but it might offer salvation for man. The workers placed the boxes in the room and began opening them. In the meantime, Amy grabbed a bag out of one of the boxes and examined the pieces of wood. Jacob sidled up next to her.

"What do you look for?" he asked.

"If you're asking whether I can see the DNA on the wood, the answer is no. I'm hoping I can see some spots of blood."

"Doesn't it strike you as odd that Trinity didn't think of this? It's an obvious source for DNA," said Jacob.

"You asking me?"

"Well, yeah. Something about this doesn't seem right."

"I'm a scientist. I don't deal in speculation or . . ."

"Or what?"

"Never mind."

She extracted a magnifying glass from the bag and carefully looked at the wood. She scanned every inch of it, looking for something that could be blood. She found a spot, rust-colored, and scraped it off the wood. She motioned behind her.

"Bring me that box," she said, pointing at one of the boxes. Jacob grabbed it and set it at her feet. She opened it and pulled out a plastic shaker glass and a sports drink.

"You're drinking that, in here?" asked Jacob, incredulous.

She gave him a questioning look. "Hardly." She poured the drink into the cup and then put the stained piece of wood into the shaker, closed it and shook it.

"Huh? A sports drink?"

"I need something to emulsify it. I could have used water, but this will do. Any more stupid questions?"

Jacob would have responded to that, but for the stress she was under. He watched her reach into the box and extract some dish detergent. Then she took out a small test tube, put the detergent into the test tube and added the sports drink, until it was about half full. She closed the test tube and shook it. With her other hand, she pulled some meat tenderizer out of the box.

"OK, I know a lot about many things, but I have no idea what you're doing. Dish detergent? Meat tenderizer?"

"I had to improvise a bit, but these will work. The dish detergent will break open the cell membranes so that we can extract the DNA. DNA consists mostly of lipids. Dish detergent is particularly good at breaking up clumps of lipids. Think of lipids as grease. When you want to clean something, you reach for a soap and hot water, right?"

Jacob nodded. "You're telling me that the DNA has been released and is now floating around in the test tube?"

"If it's in the sample we extracted, almost. Now, we add a pinch of enzyme to the tube." She opened the top of the tenderizer and took a small amount out with her thumb and forefinger and put it into the tube. Gently, she inverted the tube five times to mix it. Then she put it in a test tube holder on the bench and checked her watch.

"Now we wait a few minutes."

"You want to tell me about the meat tenderizer?"

"DNA strands are quite long. The DNA is wrapped tightly around proteins. The enzyme in the tenderizer is protease, which is an enzyme that cuts the proteins into small pieces. The DNA unwinds as the protease cuts up the proteins."

Amy picked up another test tube and put some alcohol in it. "The alcohol will help to split up the DNA so that the lipids and proteins separate from the DNA. Once we have the DNA strand, then we have to extract it."

"Are you going to be able to tell if it's human or animal?"

"There's a microscope in that box. Yes, I can tell. But what I can't tell you is if it's Jesus' DNA. So even if we extract it, we won't know."

"Isn't that the same problem with DNA from the Shroud or Veronica's Veil?"

"Sure. But we presume it's Jesus' DNA because of where we found it. If we can extract DNA from several sources, we can compare them and see if they match. If they do, it almost certainly belonged to Jesus."

"Jesus never knew who he was, what his mission was."

Amy reared back. "What are you talking about? Of course he did. He asked God to take the cup from him, as he waited for the guards to take him to his death. He repeatedly talked about his role."

"But he never said he was there to die for man's sins."

Amy shook her head from side-to-side. "Where did all this come from?"

Jacob didn't answer. Suddenly, Amy knew. "You're talking about us, aren't you?"

"I don't know what you're talking about."

A priest ran into the room, frantic. "There are men outside, with guns."

"Trinity. Grab the sample. Let's get out of here," said Jacob. Then, he stopped. Amy hurriedly packed up her backpack and saw Jacob standing there.

"We have to get going," he said.

"Yeah, but we won't need the sample. It's fake."

"What?"

"I said earlier that this bothered me. It was a trap all along. They already removed the real true cross," said Amy.

Jacob ignored her and the fact that it was him who said that the situation bothered him. He grabbed the test tube with what he hoped was the separated DNA cells. He also took the flakes that Amy had extracted from the Cross.

"You don't believe me?" she said as she angrily flung the backpack over her shoulder.

"You're not explaining yourself, so no, I don't. This is important, you know?"

"What the hell would you know about what's important? You only care about yourself!"

"Yeah, and that's why I'm cleaning up your mess, because I'm NOT worried about the whole world dying from some bizarre virus."

The priest tapped his foot and wrung his hands. He kept glancing over his shoulder, as the sounds of the shooting seemed to grow nearer by the second. Finally, he spoke. "Ah, excuse me, but we have to get out of here."

Amy and Jacob's eyes were locked on each other, unwavering. The priest grabbed Amy and turned her. "Really, we have to go." Amy didn't say anything, but Jacob looked at him and nodded. The priest motioned toward the rear of the room. They heard gunshots, just outside the room. Jacob hoped the UN soldiers were giving them a run for their money.

They followed the priest down a hallway toward the rear of the basilica. He led them down some stairs until they reached an old, metal door. He pulled a key from his pocket, opened the lock, and pulled on the door. It reluctantly creaked open. A cold breeze, infused with a damp, musty smell hit them in the face.

"Go all the way to the end. It's an old escape tunnel. At the end, you'll exit nearly half a mile from here. God bless."

Jacob pulled a flashlight from his backpack, turned it on and led the way. As soon as they entered, the priest closed the door behind them, the sound of the key turning in the lock a sure sign that there was no turning back. Jacob slowly moved forward, panning the flashlight around the narrow corridor. It was made of old stones, slightly moist. Their feet made a crunching sound on the crushed rock floor.

"This is quaint. What do you suppose it was for?" asked Amy.

"Oh, it was probably an escape route for 18th century clergy. There was a lot of religious turmoil back then."

"Right."

They continued on in silence. The secret passage finally ended at a door. It was locked, fortunately from the inside. Jacob opened the lock and slowly pulled the door open. He and Amy looked up at a steep stairway ending at a gate. Natural sunlight filtered its way down the shaft. They went up the rock stairs, closing the door behind them, until they reached the gate.

———

MILWAUKEE, WISCONSIN

Father John couldn't believe how quickly the church filled up. No more than three hours after the president's announcement, more people than were in the parish crowded the church pews. He watched them from a doorway near the sanctuary. Some talked wildly with exaggerated hand movements, others stared straight ahead, too stunned to know how to act and still others cried. This would be, without a doubt, Father John's most challenging moment.

The Vatican had issued an edict, their official position. The thought of what he was supposed to say churned in his stomach like a bad taco. As if to give him the confidence to deliver the Vatican's message to the waiting throngs of people, Father Samuel, the pastor and his leader, stood at his side. Father John glanced at him, seeking some support. Father Samuel nodded his encouragement. With that, Father John entered the sanctuary.

Instead of quieting down, the people got louder. He heard the muffled crying, the raised voices, the disembodied voices demanding answers. Obviously, these people were scared. How could he quiet their fears?

He approached the lectern and stood there for a moment, waiting for people to quiet down.

"I understand that all of you seek answers, that you're scared and uncertain about how to respond to this threat. The Vatican has an official response that I have been asked to relate to you."

He paused for effect as everyone in the church held their breath. "The Vatican believes that God would not countenance such an edict as a test of one's faith. It is blasphemy to suggest any apocalypse that denies one's faith in catholicism. That is what Trinity asks of you. It is, therefore, prohibited for any Catholic to place their faith in Trinity. Pray for your friends, for you family and for mankind, and you will be saved."

Father John turned around to leave but he stopped. Inside, he was boiling.

He looked out at all the people, wondering what they were thinking, wondering if any of them were thinking what HE was thinking, which was this: The Vatican just punted. Instead of giving people some hope in religious salvation, the almighty leader of the millions of Catholics in the world couldn't, or wouldn't, give them any answers. No messages to help them through this crisis, no words of wisdom, just sit tight. "You're going to be OK." It felt like a sucker punch.

He took a couple steps back to the podium and looked out at the people, who were expectant, who wanted more. He was about to deliver what they wanted.

"What I just told you is the official Vatican message. I, for one, do not agree with it. You need our help, and we have abandoned you at a time that you need us most. The Church is afraid that if it tells you to have faith, it is endorsing the terrorists. If it tells you to oppose the terrorists and to ignore them, it implies that faith is not enough to save you. So, it chooses to do nothing. I will be here for you to counsel you and to help you through these difficult times."

Father John left the pulpit and the sacristy, the parishioners quiet and contemplative. Their serenity was matched by Father Samuel's fury. "You have just bought yourself a ticket out of the Church, you realize that, don't you?" yelled a red-faced Father Samuel, as he met Father John when he left the church. Of course he did, and he didn't care.

After a moment of reflection, Father Samuel said, "You have completely misunderstood the Vatican's message. They're telling everyone not to worry, that their faith will save them."

Really, Father John thought? Their faith will save them? Against a deadly virus? Crap, the Church had never condoned faith healing, but now it did?

"That isn't what the message was, Father, and you know it. The Church didn't give those people any hope and that's exactly what they need."

Father Samuel didn't respond but Father John knew the die was cast, that the Church would ban him from preaching. So, before he even heard from the Vatican, Father John packed up his bags and left for northern Wisconsin, where his brother lived with his wife and two kids. He had tried to call them earlier that day, but he couldn't get through.

Father Samuel told him he should wait for the Vatican to issue its verdict but that he was forbidden to speak with any parishioners, just in case he would poison them further. Without even saying goodbye to the people who relied on him at the parish, he got in his 2008 Ford Focus and headed north.

———

UNITED NATIONS PRESIDENTIAL OFFICE, HALLWAY

President Holcomb stared out the window in the hallway outside the temporary room they'd set up in the UN , wondering how he was going to put a stop to these terrorists. The room was filled with representatives from world powers and some lesser countries. They had split off from the meeting in the UN council chambers, and were in the midst of a break.

For Holcomb, and the rest of the representatives, this was the most difficult and challenging situation they had faced. Holcomb had a hard time believing that anyone could be so rabid as to believe that the answer to what ailed mankind was a virus that only certain people could survive–the faithful, they'd said. He'd discussed this with religious leaders from every country, and no one could agree on its meaning. Faith meant different things to nearly everyone. For Christians, it was faith in Jesus, the savior. For Buddhists, it was harder to describe but ultimately did not revolve around Jesus. The same was true of Muslims. No one could agree on what something as simple as faith meant.

Of course, the more pertinent question was what it meant to Trinity. Based on the various targets they'd hit, their analysts believed they had to be Christian, but even that was murky, given their apparent belief in Gnosticism. Knowing that they had some Christian values didn't help decipher why they were doing this or where the virus would be released, but it might help them figure out the location of their base of operations.

Holcomb had been discussing with his national security advisor and some key Cabinet personnel whether the virus might be released at one or multiple locations. If only the faithful would survive, why would it be necessary to release it at multiple locations? That would be the kind of thing that terrorists would do to achieve maximum results. Here, time would take care of the faithless. If they planned on releasing it at multiple locations, the conclusion they'd reached was that Trinity was in a hurry and maybe afraid of something. Several consulting scientists felt that they could be afraid of someone discovering a serum.

Holcomb and others had countered that if Trinity truly believed that faith could save people, why would it matter if a serum were the manifestation of faith– faith in science to eradicate the disease. Of course, this made good sense, but they were dealing with an organization that didn't think like the rest of them.

During a break in their discussion, Holcomb had left the room and (as always) was escorted through the hallways of the United Nations, stretching his legs, when he almost bumped into Carmela talking on her cell phone. Her face exploded with shock and fear when she saw him and then she tried to wipe it away, but he'd seen it. Odd, he thought, that she would react that way. He meant to ask her but then forgot.

Carmela had given him a background paper on the Gnostic movement, as prepared by Father Thomas, with some references to the Judas Gospel as well. He turned from the window and headed back to the meeting, glancing at the some notes he'd made on the Father's research project. He opened the door to the meeting room and entered.

At the back of the room was a large plasma display. One of Holcomb's computer experts turned on the display, and Father Thomas' face appeared on the screen, via Skype.

"Father, we understand that you have some information about Trinity. What can you tell us?"

"The religious scholars who have been contacted, all of them from your countries, have just arrived at the Vatican. I believe that the background of Gnosticism and Trinity, as related to the Judas Gospel and its message, is the key to understanding Trinity, its origin, leaders and the reasons for its doomsday message. This is what we know about Gnosticism, which is the key to understanding the relationship between The Judas Gospel and Trinity.

"Bishop Irenaeus in Lyons, France, in 180 A.D., preached that there could be only one, united, Catholic church and that all others were heretical. He purged the so-called heretical gospels from the official books, adopted by the Church. These became known as the Gnostic Gospels. It was a crime to possess them, so they were buried in earthenware jars near Nag Hammadi. They remained there until they were discovered in 1945.

"Gnostics do not think they are heretical; Gnosticism means an insight or intuitive process of knowing one's self that allowed the Gnostic believer to know human nature better than a non-believer, which in turn gave them a deeper relationship with Jesus. To truly understand yourself is to know God, which the Gnostics believe unites them with God, in a way that makes the divine and the human self identical.

"An example of this is Mary Magdalene, who claimed to experience the continuing presence of Jesus. She stood up to Peter when she insisted that she saw Jesus. He belittled her. What is significant here is that Peter is considered to be the cornerstone from whom flows the pope's authority. When Mary opposed Peter, she opposed the Church. She espoused views that correspond to the Gnostic view that Jesus spoke to his followers in parables, which he did because they were not equipped to understand his message if he shared the mysteries of the kingdom the way he did with the disciples.

"Gnostics focus on the self," continued Father Thomas. "They believe that the truth is hidden inside of us and that we need the spiritual realm to tell us how to find salvation. The Judas Gospel promises to reveal this truth. Gnostics didn't know where to look for the knowledge that will save them, not until the Judas Gospel.

"During my review of the Judas Gospel, I discovered an unusual reliance on numbers. For example, Judas explains that there are five angels that organize heaven. Do those five angels correspond with the five artifacts that could contain Jesus' DNA (the Shroud, the veil, the true cross, the steps and the thorns)?

"I believe that it is possible that Trinity took the artifacts because they have something tangible that may assist them in their journey to the spirit world. I also think that the Judas Gospel is Judas' message to his followers that what Jesus told him, which is startling by mainstream Christian standards, is that Jesus sacrificed himself so that his spirit could be liberated. All of us, including Judas, of course, can liberate ourselves from our realm of existence by rejecting the "God" who demands sacrifice and instead, invoking the knowledge of the divine. Gnostics have always struggled with what this means until Judas, who is assuring them that they don't have to fear death, that there is life after death. I'm not sure yet what that means, but that's all I know for now. Once the scholars and I consult, hopefully we'll know more."

"It sounds like a lot of speculation, if you ask me," said the Russian representative.

"This is all very anti-Christian, anti-Church and is considered blasphemy," said the Vatican representative. "In fact, the Church does not recognize these suggestions. I am shocked that Father Thomas would make them."

Father Thomas said, "With all due respect, I don't think it's about Church doctrine; it's about interpreting what the Gospel says and what Trinity thinks it all means. Of course, once we thoroughly analyze the original Gospel, which is at the Vatican, we will know more."

"I don't recognize that we have the document," said the Vatican representative.

The others in the room ignored the comment.

Holcomb said, "If you think about it, Father Thomas' view that the Judas Gospel encourages followers to escape this world, Trinity's actions make a bit more sense. I also wonder if Trinity might be after something else. What if this is a rouse? What if they're counting on our response to demonstrate to the world how we react to this kind of threat?"

"But it is all of us, Mr. president, who respond. Not just the U.S.," said the Russian representative.

"There are plenty of examples of extreme violence in the name of religion, throughout the history of the world. It is up to us to respond appropriately," said the Vatican representative.

"But what is appropriate? We can't do nothing," said Holcomb.

"But perhaps that is what we should do. Is it not possible that we are being tested, that our faith is being tested like never before?" answered the Vatican representative.

The room stirred, almost as if everyone responded in unison. Some were shocked at the suggestion, others seemed to be OK with it, but the vast majority wouldn't allow their fate to rest on something so fleeting as faith.

Holcomb quieted the room. "Gentlemen, we needn't respond in one way to the exclusion of the other. In other words, we can respond in a secular and in a religious way. They are not mutually exclusive. Do you agree, Father Thomas?"

"I do. You can be sure, this is about a lot more than just Trinity and its manifesto. It is about the fundamental nature of organized religion and the simple faith in a higher being, without all the hoopla of religion. Trinity is testing us at our basest level."

The room was silent. Holcomb looked from one to the other in the room, willing them to agree. First one nodded, then another until the room seemed to be in agreement. Holcomb turned his attention to the Vatican representative. "Father, I'm counting on you to devise a religious response, and the rest of us will work on a secular one." The priest bowed in agreement. A technician turned off the Skype connection.

Basilica, Santa Croce

At the gate, Amy and Jacob could hear the sounds of cars and people. Amy peered out, trying to see where they were. "Isn't that the piazza we saw near the basilica?"

Jacob looked out as well. "Not sure."

"It's probably the piazza Santa Croce."

Carefully, Jacob unlocked the gate and opened it. They emerged at the bottom of a large building. There were no Trinity soldiers in sight. "We need to get this DNA to a lab where it can be tested. I think we should take this to the Vatican. They've got to have the equipment necessary to examine this," said Jacob.

"What about the United Nations team we left behind?"

"We can't wait for them. Time is short, remember?"

Jacob flagged down a taxi and told the driver to take them to the Vatican. Once inside, Jacob said, "I don't understand why you think the Cross is a fake. Why go through the extraction process if you don't think it's real?"

"I . . . can't say for sure."

"You can't say? What, so now you're making an intelligent guess? Since when do you do that?"

Amy swung her head around toward him. "I don't think it's a fake, OK? I just . . . you're just so exasperating!"

Jacob didn't know what to say so he kept his mouth shut.

After several moments of silence, she said, "I'm not sure. I find it hard to believe that Trinity didn't think of this. They thought of everything else."

"They are hoping we'll take the bait and go on to Spain. It's a diversion."

"But how do we know what's a diversion and what isn't?"

Jacob thought for a moment. "There's always evidence to support a rational and logical decision."

Downtown, Milwaukee, Wisconsin

Jackson wasn't the only one who thought that downtown Milwaukee would be a good target for some fun. By the time he got there, the police were in full force, dressed in riot gear, running through the streets, shooting at and hitting some of the many looters who seemed to think as Jackson did–that the "end of the world" justified a moral free-for-all, the suspension of all laws and common sense in favor of just doing whatever anyone wanted to do. Jackson didn't realize that his morals were corrupt. He never thought about it. All he thought about was what he wanted and whether he could get it.

He had a nice car, but it didn't seem enough. After stopping at the homes of several friends and finding them gone, he decided that he'd have to go it alone. He certainly didn't want to get arrested and had never thought the cops would be out in force. He figured they'd be so busy worrying about the next terrorist attack that he would have the city at his disposal.

He tried to call his friends but the phones weren't working. He wondered if they'd ever be up and running again. He heard that all of the airports were closed. He couldn't get ahold of his brother in Chicago or his parents in Boston. He was on his own.

He thought about driving north, to Canada, but the borders were closed. Perhaps he could head for the Dakotas, where he could get on top of some serious mountains, but the uncertainty of that territory scared him-not that he'd ever admit this to anyone. He'd lived in Wisconsin all his life and somehow, didn't feel good about leaving now, when things weren't looking too good.

Maybe if he went to a remote part of the state, he could avoid the virus. Door County came to mind. It was pretty, not a lot of people there even though it was the middle of summer, and there would be very few cops. He'd need some camping gear, though. He figured he could steal some from a sporting goods store. Maybe the smart thing to do was to lay low until it all passed over. He could camp in the wilderness there, maybe move on to northern Wisconsin and wait for this whole thing to blow over.

After he got back to his car, he headed for Highway 43. Maybe he could break into a store in Green Bay and lift some camping gear. No one who lived there would dare do anything like that. Everyone knew that Green Bay residents were special, uniquely tied to the Packers and the collective morality of the team. Up there, he thought he could find some solace. Maybe he could break into a marina in Sturgeon Bay, steal a speedboat and have some fun.

He turned on the radio, looking for some news. Most of the stations were reporting that all airports were closed, that all communications, whether it be cell phones or land lines, were temporarily down, that martial law had been declared in all states and that the president had imposed a 10:00 p.m. curfew. Officers were authorized to shoot anyone found outside after curfew.

There wasn't much that scared Jackson, but that did. It surprised him, in fact, how much that scared him. Not the shooting part, but the move toward a police state. Jackson wasn't a real smart guy but even he knew that giving the police that kind of power would not lead to anything good. The next thing would be stopping people at random and searching them. It was funny, thought Jackson, what fear did to people.

Lilly tried calling her parents and then her boyfriend but couldn't get through. She knew the phones were probably still down, but she had to give it a try. She stopped by her boyfriend's place, but he wasn't there. The thought of waiting for him or going to his job to see if he was there crossed her mind, but there was an urgency to the situation that she couldn't put her finger on. She felt as though she had to do something now. And, she liked the guy but certainly wasn't in love with him. The thought of death had a certainty and immediacy to it that she found puzzling because it didn't seem real.

It wasn't just Lilly who wanted answers and solace in family members—everyone was frantically trying to get ahold of family. Lilly's parents lived in St. Louis. She thought about driving there, but the freeways, she'd heard, were packed. No one seemed to have any real plans for escaping the virus. They all just hit the road, at the same time. The news she was able to get featured one expert after another talking about how this virus would probably spread (they said it was airborne, which was bad news for everyone), and if there was enough time to create an antidote and whether it was possible to escape its release. A lot of rich folks were trying to get to high ground. In the Rockies and the Cascade Range, the roads and trails were already packed with people trying to escape. The ultra rich were angry because they weren't allowed to fly to Europe or the Far East to build camps in places like Kilimanjaro, were it was believed the virus could not spread.

She needed someone around her that she could rely on, someone to guide her, and her parents seemed like the logical choice. But she couldn't go there because travel was nearly impossible. The children's father was in prison, so she couldn't rely on him. She didn't know what to do.

Several news stations reported many attempts to fly out of the United States that tragically ended in the destruction of the planes defying the president's grounding of all flights. She understood the reasoning–no one could be certain that the virus wasn't going to be released by one of those planes–but the gratuitous loss of life seemed like a bad movie.

By the time she got home, her neighbors were frantically packing their cars with essentials. A friend three doors from her said she and her husband would ride it out, go to church to pray and trust in their faith to save them. She wished she had that kind of faith.

It was her next-door neighbor who told her about getting to high ground. That was hard to come by in Wisconsin, but given the low population of Door County and northern Wisconsin, that might be the best they could do on short notice. Most people, he said, were trying to get out of the state and drive to either the Bad Lands, in South Dakota, or to North Dakota, where there were some remote regions. Besides, she had an aunt up there she hadn't seen in years. She used to live in Egg Harbor.

She wondered what people in the densely populated areas on the East and West Coasts would do to escape. There was probably nothing they could do.

She told Molly and Bryan to pack some essentials while she did the same. Food would be a problem for most people, but they had purchased a large box of emergency food rations and could live on that for a long time.

While Lilly packed some clothes, she worried about her kids. They were as scared as she was. Neither of them spoke much but they had these blank looks on their faces, as they contemplated the possible end of their short lives. She heard them whispering in the next room as they packed. On the way to Door County, she would have to address their concerns. She had been thinking about what to tell them, but nothing made any sense. Was escaping the populated cities the wise thing to do? Her kids had never learned the value of believing in a Creator and in Jesus. Now, she regretted it. She wondered if this was some kind of bizarre test of their faith. From what she knew about the Bible, it certainly didn't fit the paradigm.

She threw the last of the clothes she needed in the suitcase and left her bedroom, entering Molly's room first. She sat on the edge of her bed, with her suitcase behind her, crying. Bryan stood next to her, his arm awkwardly draped over her shoulder.

Lilly sat next to her. Molly leaned into her. They sat like that, next to each other, silent. Somehow, it seemed the only thing to do.

A short time later, they left their house, the car packed with several suitcases, food, tents and supplies. The traffic was unreal, as most of the city seemed to be going somewhere. But once she got on to the back roads, things improved considerably.

It was then that she decided to broach the subject of their survival.

"I know this is difficult, that you have many questions. I don't know if I have the answers, but I'll try."

"Why are we going up north? Shouldn't we be going to church or something?" asked Molly.

"My aunt is up there. I don't know. It just seems right."

"But what if Trinity is right? Aren't they testing us?" asked Bryan.

"What right do they have to test us? Remember, they're terrorists. I think it's better to do what we can to escape the virus. What do you two think?"

Bryan and Molly looked at each other, then looked forward. Bryan spoke for both of them. "We don't know. But we wonder. If they are challenging everyone to beat this with faith, maybe it's possible."

Lilly had always been impressed with Bryan's intelligence. She knew that talking him into whatever she would be doing, even though she wasn't sure what that would be, wouldn't be easy without some kind of logical explanation. Yet, Bryan's question surprised her. Wouldn't the intelligent response be to fight Trinity with science, not faith?

Molly leaned back and looked out the window. She could feel tears coming and tried to hold them back. But she couldn't. Her voice cracked as she spoke.

"Are we going to die?"

Lilly wondered when they were going to ask that question. She'd thought about the answer, but somehow she couldn't come up with one. Frankly, she didn't know how to answer the question for herself. Dying was part of life, but when you know when you will die, then what do you do? Prepare? If there is an afterlife, is it possible to make amends for your mistakes? Is it better to fight the possibility of death at the hands of the terrorists or should they give in?

"I don't know. We will go when it is time."

The answer didn't satisfy Lilly, but she knew it was the best her mom could do. She really couldn't justify going north, either. It just seemed that they had to do something. Other people were doing it. What else could she do? Wait? What would they wait for?

They stopped in Appleton, just outside of Green Bay, for some lunch. Inside the restaurant–a local mom and pop joint–Lilly couldn't help but overhear a middle-age couple discussing the virus. She noticed that the man was nicely dressed, in kakis and a polo, and the woman, tan slacks and a white top. They left the impression that they were wealthy.

"There is no way we can assure our salvation. Our pastor told us that yesterday. I'm going. If you don't want to come, that's up to you," said the man.

"They said all air travel has been canceled. You can't get there," responded the wife.

"I'll find a way."

"What about me?"

"You made your choice. I don't have any confidence in them."

"Them?"

"You know, the religious nuts."

"What about me? You're going to abandon me?"

"No, you've made your choice, and I don't agree with it."

Lilly was surprised how unemotional his wife had been up to that point, but just then, the tears started to run down her cheeks. Her husband was strangely unaffected. After a few moments, he took her hand in his.

"Come with me. We need to get as close as we can to Jerusalem. That's our only chance."

His wife didn't respond. Outside the restaurant, a group of young men were arguing. One of them talked about letting loose and partying until the end. Another said that this was giving in, that he wanted to fight. The third wanted to know what they would fight with and who they would fight. Maybe they should just make peace and accept the inevitable.

When Lilly got in the car with Molly and Bryan, she could tell right away that what they heard was bothering them. As they drove through a residential neighborhood, they saw people fighting. Other households were in disarray, with people running from their houses to overstuffed cars, as if they could take all their "stuff" with them somewhere where they would be safe the virus.

Lilly marveled at how people reacted to the possibility of death turning into a near certainty. They focused on the material things in life, with what really mattered–the way they lived their lives–taking second chair. People fought, argued, sought solace in a place that they believed would save them. Lilly knew that these things would not provide answers, but she didn't have the courage–yet–to make an affirmative decision. The prospect of a concept as fleeting as "faith" saving one from almost certain death made the whole process seem unnaturally personal. Who could tell someone to have faith or what to have faith in?

So, when it was clear that she saw questions in the faces of Bryan and Molly, she didn't know how to answer them. Maybe redemption was unnecessary. Maybe it was and more obvious than they realized.

CHAPTER VI

*"Where there is envy and strife, there is
confusion and the proliferation of evil" (James 3:16).*

THE VATICAN

The pope regally sat at the head of a table with his attendant standing next to him. Seated around him were his most trusted advisors, mostly archbishops and cardinals who represented churches and parishes throughout Europe and the United States. Several seats to the right of the pope sat Father Thomas, looking and feeling a bit out of place. Next to the pope was a vacant chair. The room was quiet as everyone waited in anticipation for the pope to speak. He made the sign of the cross and leaned forward in his chair.

"Since the discovery of the Judas Gospel, Trinity's acts of violence have increased. They've bombed churches, mosques, Buddhist temples. Thousands of lives have been lost. And always they leave behind a quote from the Judas Gospel."

The door to the room opened and everyone glanced around as Orfeo walked in. "My apologies, gentlemen, I had some other business to take care of." Orfeo took his place at the table, next to the pope, who patted Orfeo's hand.

Father Thomas tried to hide his disdain for the man, made all the more difficult by Orfeo's cold stare that bore through him like a bolt of lightening. But Father Thomas threw it off with a half smile and an almost imperceptible nod of recognition.

Father Thomas said, "I don't think the importance of the Judas Gospel can be overstated. Trinity is using it to support its terrorist agenda."

Orfeo retorted, "They are not attacking humanity. Many scholars think that Judas is describing Jesus' wish to die to reach salvation. It is through death that all men will reach the same salvation as Jesus."

"Life is to be taken only by God, not by man," said the pope.

"Trinity doesn't want to wait for God," replied Father Thomas.

"Which means what, Frank?" asked Orfeo, the sarcasm in his voice clear.

"You've studied Gnosticism, Orfeo. Why don't you tell us?"

Orfeo turned to Father Thomas, his face now showing red with anger. "Are you implying that I'm Gnostic?"

"I'm not implying anything. I think it is very clear."

The pope leaned forward again. "Enough. Your bickering isn't helping anything. Make your point."

Father Thomas bowed in supplication. "The Judas Gospel proposes that Jesus was a spirit, not a man. What if this is the faith that Trinity is talking about?"

"The world survives the virus if it believes Jesus was a spirit," replied the pope.

Father Thomas nodded in reverence. "Yes. A reasonable interpretation of the Gospel is that, what we do here, doesn't matter. The only way we can make it to the next realm is to believe as Judas teaches. Die with the knowledge that Jesus was a spirit and you achieve the Gnostic version of everlasting peace."

"This is the special knowledge that Gnostics can never really define," said the pope.

"Right, so in the Judas Gospel, they have, for the first time, a definition of what that knowledge is."

"And they want all of us to join in this knowledge? What's the purpose of that, Frank?" replied Orfeo.

"We take them at their word. The world is a cesspool. Gnostics or those who believe as they do, are the only ones worth saving. Essentially, they are telling us, 'Join us or die,'" said Father Thomas.

"Only Gnostics will survive? Really, Frank, that's a reach even by your standards," said Orfeo as he shook his head in disgust.

Father Thomas started to reply but a look from the pope shut him up. The pope said, "We must carefully analyze the Judas Gospel. Perhaps we will discover clues to who they are, how we can stop them."

The Pope turned to Father Thomas. "I will grant you access to the Gospel."

Father Thomas lowered his head indicating his acceptance of the offer. But then, with his head still lowered, he said, "We will need the original translation."

Father Thomas pulled a list from his pocket and handed it to the pope who glanced at it and then passed it on to Orfeo. "Those are the scholars that I will need to assist me," said Father Thomas.

Just then, there was a knock on the door. A priest entered and whispered into the pope's ear. He nodded and the priest went back to the door and ushered Amy and Jacob inside.

"Welcome to the Vatican. I understand you have some information," said the pope.

"We do, Your Excellency. We feel that finding Trinity's leader is paramount. We might have our first lead," said Jacob. There was an almost imperceptible stir in the room. Jacob felt it and looked directly at Orfeo, not knowing who he was but sensing that it came from him. The two locked eyes for a moment but then Jacob shrugged off the sensation and continued.

"Have you been made aware that many religious artifacts have been replaced?"

That got everyone's attention. Jacob continued. "The Shroud, the Nails, Veronica's Veil." The room was eerily quiet as they tried to assimilate what Jacob had just said. The pope shook his head from side-to-side, his face registering visible distress.

"Those are crucial artifacts for all Christians. The Shroud. My goodness," said the pope, his eyes wet with emotion.

"Why would anyone do such a thing?" asked one of the cardinals.

"Well, it's Trinity. They knew we'd be after the artifacts. They knew we'd try to extract DNA," said Amy.

"I don't understand how they could have thought so far ahead," commented the pope.

"Clearly, they are several steps ahead of us. But there's also some good news that we can take away from this. We are on the right track. The virus must be susceptible to eradication or they wouldn't have removed possible sources for a serum," said Amy.

"And, we may have extracted a DNA sample from the True Cross. We were at Santa Croce before we came here. Trinity got there just after we arrived. We did extract a potential DNA sample that we brought with us. Amy will need a lab to examine it."

"We have all the equipment you'll need here," said the pope. "What do you hope to get from the DNA?"

"We might be able to make a serum out of it. Any DNA from a known source, from someone we know didn't die from the virus, is a potential source for a cure. I must emphasize the word, 'potential.' "

"Why would Trinity leave the True Cross there for you to take?" asked a bishop. "It makes no sense."

"Perhaps they didn't remove it because they know it doesn't have any DNA on it," suggested Jacob.

"Tell me more about your lead," asked the pope.

Jacob said, "We know that the Vatican sent a team to examine the Shroud several weeks ago. . . . The order came from Orfeo's office."

Father Thomas glared at Orfeo, who was unfazed. "I did order an exam. But that is all," said Orfeo.

The pope looked from Father Thomas to Orfeo, sensing the accusation in the priest's eyes and the hatred in Orfeo's. "Certainly, you are not accusing Orfeo of having anything to do with these religious terrorists," said the pope, as he stared at Father Thomas. "He is my most trusted aide."

Father Thomas lowered his gaze. "Certainly not, Your Excellency."

"What was the purpose for the exam?" asked Jacob.

"Educational. It was a group from the seminary," said Orfeo.

"We saw them leave the cathedral with a long tube, the size that one might imagine could hold the Shroud," said Amy. "What do you suppose that was?"

"I don't know. You'll have to ask them."

"I suggest we continue to look at everyone who accessed the Shroud. We have no idea when it was replaced, do we?" asked the pope.

"No, we don't," said Jacob.

"We have a lot to do. Let's get at it," said the pope who ignored the evidence staring him in the face.

Everyone had left the room except the pope, his assistant and Cardinal Alfonso. The cardinal said, "We have another matter to attend to."

"What's that?" responded the pope.

"We are having trouble with many of our congregations in the United States, England, Mexico, Italy–virtually any place there is a Catholic Church."

"Trouble?"

"Many of our priests feel the Church should be more involved in a solution as opposed to doing nothing."

"We're not doing nothing."

"I understand. But many of the priests that I've spoken with want us to give their congregation answers and guidance. "

"Catholics do what we tell them and that will lead to their salvation."

"Yes, I understand. But people want answers, not the old Catholic standby: 'Listen to what we tell you and just do it because we know best.' People are more sophisticated than they used to be."

"What religion actually responds to what people want? We are in the business of telling people how to seek salvation."

Cardinal Alfonso nodded, carefully formulating his next question. "If I may speak plainly?"

The pope nodded.

"All of Christianity is in a quandary. Trinity tells us that to survive, we must have faith in a Gnostic text. These were rejected as heretical hundreds of years ago. So, we are to tell our parishioners that to survive, we must have faith in a Gospel that has never been officially adopted by mainstream Christianity. All we can tell them is NOT to believe. But what if we are wrong? What if believing might save them? What if Christianity should not have excluded certain Gospels based on the whims of the Church and the teachings of Bishop Irenaeus."

The pope dropped his gaze, thinking about what the Cardinal said. By the time he looked at the cardinal, his face was red with anger. He nearly trembled when he spoke. "You will not speak of this again. What are we to do? Ignore hundreds of years of history? It's not just us—it's the Protestants, Lutherans, Baptists, Episcopalians. We CANNOT and WILL NOT tell Catholics that to survive, they must consider the option of having faith in Gnostic teachings. We tell them to pray and let us worry about them."

The cardinal nodded and turned to leave. But before he'd taken three steps, he stopped and half turned around. "But what are we to say in our prayers?"

The pope grunted and dismissed him with a wave of his hand.

VATICAN CATACOMBS

The room was dimly lit with a constant drone, reminding Father Thomas that to keep the valuable artifacts in the room secure and dry, a dehumidifier removed moisture while an HVC unit kept the room at a constant 72 degrees. He was hunched over several texts, including the original translation of the Judas Gospel and several interpretative texts. A desk lamp illuminated the Gospel. To his right was a legal pad he used for notes and observations.

Near the door and just behind Father Thomas, a lone figure stood in the shadows, staring at him from behind. Without lifting his head from the text, Father Thomas said, "You just gonna stand there?"

Orfeo emerged from the shadows and stood next to Father Thomas.

"I figured it was you," said Father Thomas. "Don't look so happy to see me."

"I'm here, believe it or not, to see if you need some help."

"I don't…believe it, that is. Sure as hell didn't help me the last time I was here."

"You struck a priest, Frank. In the Sistine Chapel."

"The ass deserved it."

Father Thomas looked over his materials, grabbed something and slid it across the table. "Start working."

Orfeo glanced at the papers, fingered through them without reading anything. "You realize that it wasn't just the chapel incident that did you in."

"If you're talking about my distaste for our hypocrisy and inability to deal honestly with the horrific crisis regarding the sexual abuse of young men, I have no problem admitting that the Church must be reformed."

"The Church has been around for a long time and is run by humans who make mistakes. Wholesale changes are not necessary. We must trust the process."

"The process is full of lies and obfuscation. It must be changed to maintain integrity. People lose trust if they can't believe in their leaders."

Before Orfeo could answer, the door opened again, and this time, Amy and Jacob walked in. Orfeo turned and left the room, unwilling to say anymore for fear of exposing his true feelings.

"What's with him?" asked Jacob.

"I assume you know. Have a seat."

Jacob and Amy sat down, and Father Thomas handed them chapters of the Judas Gospel. "Dig in," said Father Thomas. Amy wondered what Father Thomas meant by his comment but assumed he was referring to the Sistine Chapel incident.

Six hours later, the room was packed with the religious scholars that Father Thomas had asked for. Nerves were frayed. Most of the men in the room were showing growth of facial hair. Father Thomas had his head in his hands and then dropped his head to the table. They hadn't come up with anything, and the one thing they didn't have was time.

Both Amy and Jacob had been staring at the same text for the last 45 minutes. On the far wall was a projection of one of the chapters of the Judas Gospel. Jacob pushed his chair back, turned around and grabbed the coffee pot and poured another cup. He drank half of it, made a face when he realized that the coffee was cold and plopped the cup on the table. Amy wiped her eyes and then glanced at Jacob.

"This isn't going well. We've got to do something."

"No shit. I don't know what to tell you, but I'm stumped."

The room was now full of religious scholars. Cardinal D'Amato, from the Vatican, was one of the world's best at ancient languages, as was Walter Damp, an English, Biblical scholar. Two experts were from the United States–Professor Thurgood, from Harvard, and a friend of Father Thomas', Doctor Williams, from Yale. One of the scholars, from the University of Rome, Doctore Baglio–the Professor, as Jacob addressed him–scrolled down the pages and stopped. Jacob got up and started pacing.

As he paced, Jacob reviewed what they knew, in an attempt to solve the puzzle. "Look, we know that Trinity's terrorist activities have increased after the Judas Gospel was discovered. We also know that they've quoted passages from it before."

He stopped in front of the Professor. "We need to pull all the previous passages they've quoted to see if there are any clues."

"You mean to the location of Trinity," said the Professor.

Father Thomas raised his head off the table. "Why did it take us so long to think of that? The relationship between the passages could help us find the release points."

"Right. Trinity believes that the Gospel gives them the road map to salvation, and a means to get there," said Jacob.

"You're not telling us anything we don't know," said one of the other scholars –Claudia Bogart, from Columbia—who Jacob referred to as the Brain.

"I'm trying to work this out. One step at a time."

Jacob hesitated for a moment, gathering his thoughts. "Ok, so it's a new beginning for man," said Jacob.

The Professor decided to play along and tried to hide his impatience as he scrolled to the passage in which Judas discussed Adamas (a person, probably 'Adam,' as mentioned in the Old Testament). They all read the passage to themselves:

Then, Saklas said to his angels, 'Let us create a human being according to the likeness and according to the image.' Then they formed Adam and his wife, Eve. But in the cloud, she was called 'Zoe'('Life'). For in this name all the races shall seek after (life), and each one of them calls her by their names.

"So he's talking about Adam and Eve. The beginning." Jacob looked around the room at blank faces. "What?" he asked.

"You state the obvious," said the Professor.

Amy began to see that Jacob was simply forcing them to discuss the obvious, hoping that it would lead them to a conclusion that they were missing, or the only one that was logically possible–classic Sherlock Holmes analysis.

"It's not just that. It's a new beginning, for man and for…"

"…for anyone who has faith," said the Brain.

"Yes, only the faithful will survive, according to Trinity," said Amy, her voice rising in pitch along with her level of excitement.

"But that passage doesn't have anything to do with faith," said the Professor.

"We have to determine what all this means in terms of where the virus will be released and how we can stop Trinity," said the Brain.

"But Trinity could be relying on this not for its literal meaning but as a means to justify what they are doing," said Jacob.

"What's unique about the Judas Gospel that they would rely on it?" asked Amy.

"You're not understanding—" said Jacob.

The door to the room suddenly opened and Orfeo and Gustav entered, distracting Jacob in the middle of his sentence.

"You have to determine what a new beginning would look like," interrupted Orfeo.

"It's a genocide of the faithless. Wiping out the unbelievers," said Father Thomas.

The Brain shook her head and muttered, "I don't see what any of this has to do with the translation."

"You have to remember that the special knowledge that Gnostics seek is not that simple. For Gnostics, this is something that defies description," said Father Thomas.

Orfeo approached the table and dismissively pawed through the stack of papers, tossing some of them aside as if they were garbage.

"I disagree, Father," said Jacob. "I think Trinity is using the Judas Gospel as doctrine, its blueprint. And it's not just the philosophy I'm talking about. I'm talking about a template to force this special knowledge on mankind."

Jacob stopped abruptly. There was something he was missing. He grabbed the Judas Gospel and paged through it. He flipped through, page after page. The others in the room became restless.

"Share, will you?" asked Amy.

"Numbers dominate this text. Many of them have spiritual or symbolic references," said Jacob, as he read the text.

"Yes, I think that is obvious. What does it have to do with anything?" said the Professor.

Even though Jacob's point was obvious, it still had an impact on the group. Numbers did dominate the text. That meant something, but what? Father Thomas paged through the text, confirming what he already knew.

"In the section where Judas talks about the number of angels that order heaven, we see the numbers 12 and 360," said Father Thomas.

Amy slid in next to Jacob, looking at the text. Jacob glanced at her and could see her increased level of curiosity. The scholars, with renewed vigor, stared at the screen and the text where the numbers were referenced.

"OK, so some of these have obvious references. So 12 months in a year, 12 disciples, 360 degrees in a circle…" said Amy.

"…360 lunar days. But in the beginning, what are the number of angels?" asked Jacob.

The Professor pointed to the text as he read it. "'Adamas was in the first luminous cloud that no angel has ever seen among all those called God.'"

Jacob looked at the projection, reading it to himself. He pawed through the papers on the desk, looking for a file. Once he found it, he started reading. He looked up at the screen and saw that the text that he was reviewing was on the screen.

"So, after Eve's sin, there are 19 angels who rule over the chaos. Scroll to the next passage please."

After these things he said, "Let the 12 angels come into being so they might rule over the chaos and the oblivion." And behold an angel appeared from the cloud whose face was pouring forth fire, while his likeness was defiled with blood. And he had one name, "Nebro," which is interpreted as "apostate," but some others call him "Ialdabauth." And again another angel came forth from the cloud called, "Saklas." Nebro then created six angels along with Salkas to attend him.

"So there's 12, then seven more angels for a total of 19."

"But why would these numbers carry any more significance than all of the other numbers in the text?" asked Orfeo.

"Because Trinity is creating a new beginning. The literal beginning is Genesis. Here, in the text, is an association between the number of angels and Genesis," said Jacob.

Amy saw the logic of Jacob's reasoning. "Right, after Eve's sin, Judas is explaining that there are 19 angels who rule over the chaos that resulted from her decision."

Jacob quickly glanced at the text, copied some other numbers onto a piece of paper and then looked through his research until he found a detailed statistical analysis of the locations of Trinity terrorist acts. Had they been using this text to determine the location of their terrorist acts in the past? He found the location of one of these acts and then, using his computer, he Googled a tool to determine longitude and latitude.

"They bombed a Muslim mosque in Halab, Syria. The coordinates of the attack are approximately 36 degrees north, 0 minutes east."

"What? These numbers refer to longitude and latitude?" asked one of the scholars, shaking his head in disagreement. "I can't agree—"

"No, no, this is not literally what Judas meant–this is a Trinity interpretation, a way to use the text as a guidebook," said Amy, now fully grasping what Jacob was talking about.

"Right. The Judas Gospel is a targeting system for Trinity," said Jacob.

Jacob scrolled the text down and stopped. "So after Nebro creates the six angels, there are 12 more and then another five. So the coordinates are 19 degrees longitude, 17 degrees latitude."

"But is it north and east or south and west?" asked Orfeo, the sarcasm in his voice apparent.

"Yes, it is much easier working the problem backwards. Perhaps they must match up exactly as in Halib," said the Professor.

"But here we have four digits to match. In Halib, there were only two," said the Brain.

"You still have to decide which direction to use," said Orfeo.

For a moment, no one said anything. Then, Orfeo said, "The magi used the star in the eastern sky."

"That hardly seems like a good reason to choose east," said Father Thomas.

"Do you have a better idea?" answered Orfeo.

No one responded. Amy pulled her GPS out and entered the coordinates. "19 by 17, assuming 0 minutes… That's in Chad, near Emi Koussi. Trinity has been active in Africa."

"But what do we hope to find there? Even if it's a coordinate that will provide us with some information, what will it be? Their location? The location of the release point?" asked the Professor.

"There are problems, but time isn't on our side. I say we give it a shot," said the Brain. The others nodded their agreement.

Jacob pulled the cell phone from his pocket and hit the 'send' button. Carmela answered. "It's Jacob. We've got a lead. In Emi Koussi."

"Where's that?"

"Chad. Africa."

"How did you determine. . . "

"It's complicated. Number references in the Judas Gospel. We believe they've used it before as a targeting system. The bombing in Halib, for example, corresponds to numbers, used as longitude and latitude, in the Judas Gospel."

"Seems like a long shot."

"Have any of the other teams come up with clues?"

"No. I'll call them all and get them on this. I'll have a military transport ready at Da Vinci International within an hour. I'll take care of the diplomatic issues."

Jacob closed the cell phone and turned to the group. "While we're in Africa, use the same formula and pattern on the other sites they've hit to see if we're right."

"And if we're not?" asked the Professor.

Jacob didn't say anything, shaking his head from side-to-side, unwilling to consider the possibility of not having any leads. On the far wall was a calendar with the days marked off since Trinity's threat. Only four left. God, if this didn't get them any closer, there wasn't anything they could do.

Orfeo and Gustav slipped out, having gotten the information they needed. While they walked through the Vatican, Orfeo grabbed Gustav by the arm and pulled him closer. "I told you they would follow the clues. They are now headed for the trap we've laid for them."

"Yes, Your Excellency, you were correct, as always," said Gustav, trying to sound as though he meant it.

Orfeo smiled as he thought about how his plan to bring an end to everything the Vatican held holy was coming together. He hated them all–the Pope, the Cardinals, the Church–the arrogance of their proclamations to so many who sought salvation. Orfeo would correct the imbalance created by organized religions and lead a new world order of people with true faith, not the junk pushed on them by the Catholic Church.

As soon as he could, Gustav broke off from Orfeo and headed to the catacombs, where he'd set up for the delivery of the serum he'd prepared. Everyone in Trinity wanted to be inoculated. It was hard to keep from Orfeo, but they all knew that if he found out, he would not be happy. He believed in the power of the Gnostic teachings and faith.

Gustav trudged through the catacombs to the outer door, where the scientists would be waiting with the serum. Not much had been produced, but by the end of the week, he was counting on a large supply. He would use it to gather Trinity around him—not Orfeo—after most of the world had died from the virus. By then, it would be clear that Orfeo was wrong.

CHAPTER VII

"Deliver me from the hand of my [enemy]" (Gen. 32.11).

UNITED NATIONS PRESIDENTIAL OFFICE

Holcomb waited expectantly for Carmela to brief him follow-ing the phone call with Jacob. He stood at the table where members of the UN Security Council were seated. Standing nearby were key members of the World Health Organization and NATO, includ-ing representatives from Greece, Hungry, Israel, Italy, Japan, Spain, China, Australia, Canada, Brazil, Sudan, the United Kingdom and the Russian Federation. Other member countries had given proxies to those in attendance.

Their discussions had been sobering and depressing. All the arti-facts were gone, none of their teams had come up with any leads on Trinity's whereabouts or membership, other than the wild lead that Jacob and his team had developed. Trinity was a small, fringe group that no one had paid any attention to. Now, they were on the minds of every country in the world, but their anonymity was the perfect cover. It was as if the world was being held hostage by a remote tribe in Africa.

Holcomb turned to Carmela and asked her, "Could you explain the lead that the Vatican team has developed?"

"I don't know the specifics, but Jacob and the others have uncov-ered a number code buried inside the Judas Gospel that may lead us to Trinity, their base, or perhaps the release points."

France's representative looked relieved but dissatisfied. "Pro-mising, perhaps, but they don't know where they are going or what they will find?" he asked.

"No, no, they do know where they're going. Emi something or other. In Chad."

The representative from England spoke up. "Koussi. It's Emi Koussi."

The Sudanese representative nodded in agreement. "It is a difficult place– dry and unforgiving."

"But they don't know what's there?" asked Holcomb.

"Apparently not. But they should be on their way within the hour," said Carmela.

"That's the best we can do? With all the great minds we have working on this?" said the Russian representative.

"We have so little time. We must trust the experts we've asked to analyze this. The team that the Vatican has put together is comprised of some of the greatest religious scholars in the world. And each of you have experts in your own countries working on this, I'm sure," commented Holcomb as his eyes roamed about the room. Most of the leaders acknowledged him with a nod.

"Do any of you have a lead that we could benefit from?" asked Holcomb. The representatives looked from one to the other for an answer, but all they got from one another was a shake of the head.

"All right then. It's the best we can do for now. If we cooperate, we can do this," said Holcomb.

No one said anything, but there was an overwhelming feeling of dread in the room. The leaders felt helpless, relying on scholars, which for some of them, required a leap of faith that was beyond uncomfortable. Old-fashioned smash-mouth military force is what most of them envisioned as the way to defeat the enemy. This notion of relying on intellectuals to save the world didn't sit right with any of them, including Holcomb. But it was all they had. Hopefully, it would be enough.

Carmela slipped out of the room, walked around a corner in the hallway where she had some privacy, got on her cell phone and spoke rapidly, agitated, worried.

John F. Kennedy Airport

Between the lines of cars waiting to get into the airport, stacked, one behind the other for three miles, and the military trucks and armed soldiers manning barricades, the airport looked like a scene from an end-of-the-world movie. No one was getting into the airport as all flights had been grounded. This had been made clear, but many people didn't listen. They were afraid. Many wanted to be with their families in other cities. Some wanted to escape, not sure where to go but sure that they had to be somewhere else. Still others saw this as Trinity's prophesy–it was the end times and they sought forgiveness and salvation.

A businessman who needed to fly to Chicago for a meeting with the executive of a company his employer was doing business with felt his promotion slipping away. He had to get there. His family's financial future hung in the balance. His boss said he'd try to get him on a private jet. But apparently that hadn't worked out.

A young woman and her three children were packed into a small Kia, hoping to catch a flight to Denver, where her husband had just gotten a job. All she wanted to do was get her family together before the end. A fiercely religious woman, she needed to be with her family. Her parents also lived in Denver. She had no one in New York. How could the government do this to her? Now was a time when people needed their families. There were so many people all over the world who lived apart from their families. It was inhumane to separate her from them.

Her oldest–12 year-old Sandy–tried to comfort her 8 year-old brother and 6 year-old sister, but they could sense the lack of normalcy, the unrest and worry that hung over the people hoping for the lifting of the president's no-flight restrictions. She'd heard a rumor, as had many others, that he was doing just that. But she wondered how he would have time for them when a deadly virus threatened everyone.

She was disappointed in her unwillingness to allow something as amorphous as faith to save her and her family's life–she needed something more tangible to hang onto. Everyone in her family had faith.

They should all be able to survive anything that faith would protect them from. But when faced with an imminent threat, they wanted the government to attack the terrorists head on while they waited for science to solve the puzzle of defeating the virus.

Her husband had told her that she shouldn't worry, that Holcomb was a great president who would get them through this. But she didn't have much hope. No one knew much about this Trinity, and she had heard that the virus they had was unbeatable, something about it mutating.

She looked at her kids and then got out of the car. The line of cars behind her was getting longer; she could no longer see the end. The airport was visible in the distance, and the line was moving very slowly, but the cars coming back the other direction, were a talisman of what she feared would be her fate when she got to the front of the line. She hoped, which is all she could do. She could see a large group of demonstrators near the airport's entrance, carrying signs that she couldn't read. Armed soldiers carrying riot gear tried to keep them out of the airport. She couldn't imagine what they wanted here. Maybe out, like everybody else. She thought she heard a gunshot. Great. Now they were killing each other. Fear was so damn powerful.

Then, she had a thought. Did the need to be with her family signal an assumption that they would not make it? As awful as that thought was, it occurred to her that faith was a personal thing. How could being with your loved ones help anyone discover the faith necessary to survive? Even if one could determine what kind of faith Trinity spoke of, was it the same for everyone, if that was even possible?

VATICAN

In the catacombs, surrounded by valuable Vatican artifacts and historic documents, Gustav closed his cell phone. He glanced at Orfeo, who stood next to him.

"They must be taken care of. Are things in place?" asked Orfeo.

"Yes, Your Eminence. I've been in contact with our mole."

"Good. Get my car ready. We need to beat them there."

Gustav looked surprised. "You should stay out of harm's way."

"This is too important."

Gustav nodded, and the two slipped out of the shadows. For Gustav, this was as difficult as anything he'd done with Trinity. There had to be a way to ensure their survival. He didn't have the kind of faith that Orfeo had in the Judas Gospel and its odd assortment of number-specific prognostications. The virus was scary. He wasn't sure anyone could survive it. But Judas, who was the carrier, or so they believed, obviously did not die from it. That they knew how he died, just as they knew how Jesus died, was the basis of their faith in the power of the virus.

Gustav wondered if Orfeo sensed his un-ease or the questions he had about their actions. Did he really believe as strongly as he professed that they would all be safe from the onslaught of the virus? Gustav wasn't the only one in Trinity who questioned Orfeo's sanity. But he was a forceful leader, one who was easy to follow, one who was at great ease with himself and what he believed in. Gustav and the other members of Trinity hoped he was right. No one would survive if he was wrong.

SOMEWHERE IN NORTHERN WISCONSIN

Jackson managed to drive through most of the State of Wisconsin without committing any real crimes, unless you called stealing gas a crime. Looters had rifled through the station, but they didn't know how to unlock the gas pump. Jackson was proud of how he could steal almost anything and never get caught, how he knew all the tricks necessary to hot wire a car and how easy it was to steal money from little old ladies. He wasn't a very good con man, unbeknownst to him, but he did have some success stories, like the 75-year-old woman whom he talked out of $50,000. He'd convinced her that he was a new kind of stock broker–one that traveled and came to your home–and that he had an inside line on an unbelievable investment that would return–guaranteed–150% on her investment and in only six months. Of course, there was no such thing, except that he did manage to blow through the money she gave him in six months.

Once he got near Green Bay, the traffic picked up considerably. People seemed to be fleeing north, just as he was. He saw some cops here and there, but they were too busy trying to keep order to notice him. His recent success gave him new ideas and emboldened him. He'd never thought about robbing a bank, but now, with success almost guaranteed, he might give it a shot.

With that in mind, he drove through Green Bay, only to be discouraged by the police presence around the banks. It seemed that others had the same idea. It occurred to him that money didn't mean anything since he would probably die in about a week–give or take a couple of days–but the thought of taking things away from others before they could take things from him, just steeled him further, or so he thought.

He didn't like to think about all the jerks out there who took from him all his life and how he would get back at them because it made him even madder. For a moment, he couldn't avoid the memory of his father, who used to lock him in the shed when he disobeyed, or his mother who did nothing. The thought of it made his stomach turn–that shed, whether it was 10 below or in the 90s outside, either baked him or froze him. And the anger inside grew to mammoth proportions. He hated his parents for doing that to him; he hated his older brother for never doing anything to help him and his younger sister because their dad never did any of the stuff to her that he did to him. He hated his boss for ruining his life when he "let him go," as he liked to say, which devastated his family and led to his divorce and his current predicament. He hated his wife for leaving him, his kids for siding with his wife, his parents for failing to bail him out. Come to think of it, he hated everyone.

He drove through Green Bay and headed for Door County. On the way, he remembered that he had an aunt in the area he hadn't seen for years. Maybe he should stop by. It seemed like the right thing to do. But she probably wouldn't give him the time of day because she hated him—or was it that he hated her? He couldn't remember.

For Lilly, the trip to Door County was more stressful than she had imagined. Bryan and Molly peppered her with questions. "Why is this happening? What if there's no God? Why would these people risk their own deaths? What are they trying to prove? Why can't the governments of the world fight this together? Why can't they find the terrorists? Why do we have to run? Why are we going north? Shouldn't we go to church? Wouldn't church have the answers we're after?"

Lilly tried to answer all their questions, but it wasn't easy. She didn't know most of the answers, and Bryan in particular, wouldn't let it go. She got the sense that Bryan wanted to do something, that running didn't seem like the right thing to do, which was something she admired about him. For now, running was the only thing they could do. But the thing that bugged her the most were the religious questions. She wasn't expecting her kids to "get religion" so quickly. She had given them the tools to make decisions about that because she didn't want to tell them how to feel or what to believe. Now they were asking her just that and she didn't believe that Church or Jesus or God would help them. But they seemed to think that he would. She wasn't sure what to do.

The traffic on their way north had been varied. Near Milwaukee, it was bumper-to-bumper. She was glad she had filled up her hybrid Highlander yesterday because gas stations were running out of gas; people were so desperate they'd pulled guns on attendants to force them to sell them gas they didn't have.

Once they got past Whitefish Bay, the traffic let up a bit. Most people seemed to be heading west, probably for the Dakotas, where there were some very remote areas. Others, she heard on the radio, went to church and prayed for the faith to survive.

By now, closer than she liked to think to what might be the end, the crazies were emerging. Jim-Jones-like cults grew overnight. There was a report of a mass suicide near Kenosha. Others were being planned. Local religious leaders encouraged people to have hope. One news commentator talked about how religious leaders struggled with whether to tell people to wait for the government to develop a plan to attack the terrorists or to tell them to rely on their faith for survival.

Lilly was increasingly unsure about how to help herself and her children through this mess. Escaping seemed like the thing to do, but it didn't feel right. Still, it was all she could think of; there was no other answer. It was a matter of just letting it happen because she had no other way of dealing with the crisis. Increasing their chances of survival was the only thing that mattered.

She could tell from their questions that Molly and Bryan didn't completely agree with her. She had feared that when they went out on their own to explore religion, there might be a time when she and her children wouldn't agree. That was inevitable anyway, but religion failed her so badly, when God took her 4 year-old sister from her, that she wondered if the net result would be the loss of her children. It scared her, this issue of faith and belief. She had already decided that she wouldn't fight any decisions her kids made, in light of this crisis, but she hoped she could support them.

Finally, they pulled into her aunt's driveway in Egg Harbor. She knew right away that she wasn't there. No one came to the door and so she peered inside at the empty house, confirming her suspicions. The only option left was staying at a motel, but she'd heard that all credit cards were temporarily cancelled. She left her aunt's house in search for a bank where she could get some cash.

In Egg Harbor she found Baylake Bank. The parking lot was so full that cars were parked on the street; lines of people snaked out the front door. Everyone was in the same boat, apparently.

Lilly had tents and some supplies, so she and her kids headed for Wagon Trail Campground, on the other side of the peninsula. She had camped there when she was a kid.

On the way, after standing in line for an hour, she managed to buy some food at a small grocery store. She had a portable generator that was full of fuel and spare propane tanks for a small, efficient refrigeration unit that would run for days without needing any additional fuel.

Before she left the store, she noticed a man who looked familiar. She couldn't place him but she was sure that he was casing the joint. At the checkout stand, he bought a small amount of food. Outside the store, she watched him get into an Acura MDX, which didn't fit him.

Jackson never noticed Lilly, which was surprising, considering how pretty she was. But Jackson was too busy trying to figure out a way to steal some groceries. What he needed was just too big to hide on his person so he reluctantly used the small amount of money he had to buy some peanut butter and bread. He also bought a six-pack, a Styrofoam cooler and some ice.

He was headed for Wagon Trail Campground, since he couldn't remember his aunt's name. He wasn't sure why he was going there, but he had been there as a kid. He remembered the yurts that they stayed in. That was where he'd committed his first crime. He was only 10 when he stole a radio from someone he befriended.

His parents took it from him, knowing that he must have stolen it, but they never told him to return it. In fact, they used it.

Nearby was Father John. Since the Church had kicked him out, he was headed for his sister's house in Egg Harbor. He didn't regret what he'd said and hoped that the Church might accept him back after all this blew over. They hadn't excommunicated him—that took some time—but for the moment, he was unable to give Mass and do everything that a Priest does. Forbidden from wearing his collar, Father John felt comfortable in shorts and a t-shirt. It wasn't as if he hadn't dressed like that in the past, but he was relieved—not because he didn't want to help people but because he didn't know what to say. It was a strange situation that had no obvious answers.

By the time Lilly got to the campground and they'd pitched their family tent, it was late. Before they went to bed, Lilly turned on the radio and listened for any updates regarding the virus. She wondered how many days they had to live, then chastised herself for not being more positive. She didn't want her kids to think about death—they were too young for that—but the reality of the virus was like a pink elephant in the room.

On the news, reporters talked about a gathering at the local church. She wondered if that's where her sister was. She could see in the looks she got from Bryan and Molly that they wanted to go, so without saying anything, she got up and grabbed a jacket.

"You two want to go to the church, don't you?"

They nodded. It was almost dark out, but she remembered where the church was—St. Anthony's. She didn't want to tell her kids what she was thinking, that going to the church was the last place she wanted to go. Her kids surprised her. She had discussed church with them, and her kids had religious instruction both in school and privately, but Lilly never pushed them because she didn't believe. They knew this, in spite of her attempts to keep it from them. But they didn't know about the pain she endured when her 4-year-old sister drowned. Lilly was 12 when the two of them went for a swim at a pond near their house. Her sister hadn't done anything to deserve such a quick end before she'd barely gotten to the starting line. It didn't make sense. Lilly concluded then that no God would allow such a thing. But she didn't want her kids to be influenced by her beliefs, not to the extent that they didn't feel free to make their own decisions. She didn't understand why her kids wanted to go to church, but she wouldn't fight them, either. So, without discussion, they piled in the car and took off.

CHAPTER VIII

"As you have done to me, it shall be done to you" (Lam. 1:22).

DAY FOUR

LOCKHEED MC-130, OVER CHAD, AFRICA

Along with a UN team of 20 soldiers, Jacob, Amy and Father Thomas had been in the air for several hours when Jacob woke from a nap. Sitting next to him was Father Thomas. Behind him was Amy, her head buried in the Judas Gospel. Next to her on a vacant seat were several of the interpretative texts she'd had at the Vatican.

Jacob dreaded the talk he knew he should have with Amy. When he awoke, the first thing he thought of was her. He wasn't good about discussing his feelings. Of course, she wasn't either. And it wasn't as if they had a long, heavily romantic relationship before he'd left.

And, he'd had an excuse for leaving: He was desperately needed by a good friend who found an ancient cistern—probably from around 100 A.D.—with a strange language on it. His friend had been captured near a remote village in Pakistan by some crazed locals who wanted him to translate the writing on the cistern. They thought the writing led to a stash of gold, which he knew it did not, but they didn't believe him. Somehow, one of the men had heard of Jacob and mistakenly believed that he could tell them what they wanted to know. In what turned out to be a comedy of errors, Jacob flew in and pretended to translate the writing. When they were on the road to the fictitious site, Jacob had dispatched all 10 of them, hardly a fair fight in his mind.

Then he stuck around Pakistan for a month, helping his friend on other digs. They finally located several other artifacts, engraved with the same language, and no one was able to figure out what it was, much less translate it. He actually had returned to the United States with photos of the written language, intending to show them to Amy, hoping she could be of some help, but he never had the guts to approach her. He knew she'd be pissed.

He got up and turned around, trying to put a smile on his face. Amy glanced at him and then returned to her work. He grimaced.

"That seat taken?" he asked, nodding to the aisle seat covered with Amy's research materials. She ignored him.

He picked up the books and sat down, plopping them on his lap. "So, you'd rather steep yourself in this than talk to me?" As soon as he said that, he regretted it. He knew the answer. He tried a different tactic.

"We've got to work together. So, I think we should talk about it."

She continued reading. Jacob carefully slipped the book from her hands. She allowed him to use his forefinger to slowly turn her head toward him. After a couple of seconds, she looked at him.

"OK, agreed. I'm waiting."

"I didn't think we were . . . compatible so I decided to deal with it by not dealing with it. I didn't know what to say."

Amy didn't say anything. She tried looking at Jacob but ended up casting her eyes down, on the fuselage.

"Look, you're a scientist," Jacob continued. "Romance didn't seem to be your cup of tea."

"And I suppose you're an authority on that subject?" replied Amy.

Jacob sure thought he was, but his answer to that question might be the thing that would end this right now, so he said nothing.

"We're going to get these guys, I promise," he said.

She looked him square in the eye, and he saw her face soften, giving way to the kind of person he knew her to be. "I'm doing the best I can. For now, we're professionals working on a problem."

"Agreed. You learning anything new?" asked Jacob, pointing to the Judas Gospel open in Amy's lap.

"No, not really. But I'm even more convinced that we're onto something. The number references in here are odd. I can see how someone could believe that they mean something. Why spend so much time talking about them if they aren't important to the author? What do they symbolize? Is it longitude and latitude or could it be something else?" said Amy.

"Remember, the author wouldn't have known about longitude and latitude," said Jacob. "That's how the numbers are interpreted by Trinity. The authors couldn't have intended that."

"OK, but my question remains. What else could they represent?"

"Like what?"

"Not sure. I'm just asking, keeping an open mind. This isn't exactly my cup of tea. My specialty is in the tangible, reproducible. Not this," said Amy.

"It'll expand your horizons." Amy didn't look as though this thrilled her.

Suddenly, the plane started to descend rapidly, causing them to hold on. For a moment, Amy wanted Jacob to grab onto her, but the thought passed quickly. Jacob turned to her. The plane bounced again and the two shared an unexpected laugh. Amy felt some pressure on her right hand and pulled it back, when she realized that the pressure was Jacob holding on to it. She wasn't sure what to think about that.

"Guess these military planes don't concern themselves with passenger comfort," said Jacob, trying not to let on that he'd enjoyed touching her again.

Amy's eyes grew wide with fear as thoughts of crashing suddenly came to her. "Is everything OK?" she asked. Jacob looked around for the commander of the UN troops who sat quietly near the exit. The plane was headed sharply downward, preparing to land.

"I think so."

Fifteen minutes later, they taxied to a stop at an old, abandoned military base in Chad, Africa, near the city of Emi Koussi. Outside, the landscape was bleak. The land was a brown-gray, with very little vegetation and uninteresting, flat topography, except for Emi Koussi, the only mountain in Chad.

The door opened, and a rush of hot, desert air, hit them like a frying pan in the face. The dusty, parched landscape didn't appear to be hospitable to any form of life.

"Isn't this quaint," said Jacob as he alighted from the plane, just behind Amy. He slung his backpack over his shoulders and rolled up his sleeves.

Father Thomas followed Jacob down the stairs, shaking his head from side to side. "This doesn't feel right."

"It's hotter than hell, that's for sure," said Jacob.

"Why here?" asked Father Thomas but no one answered him.

The UN commander motioned them to military vehicles, and along with some of the troops, they got in. Amy retrieved her GPS and turned it on. In the front seat, the commander used a satellite receiver to locate their position and the direction they'd have to travel to get to the coordinates. Amy looked to her right as the data loaded and the commander, as if on cue, did the same.

"This way," he said to the driver, pointing to the spot Amy had been looking at.

Jacob looked behind them as they left. Of the 20 soldiers that flew in with them, only seven were in the military vehicle. The rest stayed behind at the airport, securing it from possible incursion by the many tribes and guerillas that inundated the region. The UN had promised more troops, but they were running a little thin. And the government of Chad couldn't help because they were dealing with local unrest over Trinity's announcement.

Around the world, people were seeking answers, some in places of worship, others in the street, staging protests, as if that would help. The UN Security Council had sent troops to every major city to quell the unrest. No one realized the urgency of the mission to Chad. Everyone was consumed with the fear of dying. Jacob would have let them riot and do whatever they wanted if that meant giving more attention to thwarting Trinity. Only seven military men. What could they do if they were ambushed by locals or worse yet, ran into a Trinity stronghold?

Jacob reached around and grabbed a Glock and an ammo belt. He strapped it around his middle and handed a Sig Sauer to Father Thomas.

"No thanks. I'll make do with this," he said, fingering his cross. On the plane, Father Thomas had removed his priest collar, but now, he'd put it back on. "You would be surprised at the power this has."

"Can't stop a bullet though."

"Oh, I think it can."

Jacob smiled. He rummaged through his backpack and found a small Glock and some ammo. He handed it to Amy, who sat next to him, looking out the window. She looked surprised when she saw the gun.

"You need to carry this. This is a great gun. Never jams."

He started to show her how it operated, but Amy took it from him, quickly checked the chamber to make sure it was empty and then rammed a clip inside the grip and flipped the lever on the side of the gun, quickly loading a round. Jacob handed her some spare clips.

"Where did you . . . ?"

"Father, remember? Career military. We all know how to shoot. Dear old dad wouldn't have it any other way," she said, the sarcasm clear in her voice.

About an hour later, they drove across a hill toward their destination, came around a bend in the road and suddenly, a small village materialized. They stopped, partially hidden by a berm. Village people wearing colorful wraps, were carrying baskets around, occasionally entering bancos—small, mud-brick homes.

The commander turned around. "This is it."

"Here?" said an incredulous Amy.

"Yup."

The commander turned to the driver and said, "Nice and easy." They drove forward and came into view. The people wandering about noticed them but didn't bat an eye. The vehicle stopped again, and everyone got out. Each soldier, with the exception of the commander, was armed with an M-4 carbine.

Jacob and the UN soldiers immediately scanned their surroundings, making a mental note of the village's layout. The village center, where they stood, reminded Jacob of a Mexican square, as it was covered by compacted clay and stone, forming a rough but usable road surface. At the far end, near a series of bancos, stood a well with a large trough, which the villagers apparently used as a universal source for water. Several women stood around it with large, wooden buckets on their heads, filled with water. Trickles of water leaked out of the buckets, trailing down their heads and faces—a welcome, natural air

conditioner. On either side of where they'd parked were a series of bancos, seemingly placed with no particular overall design in mind. They
looked unorganized, as if someone had plopped a house wherever they
saw fit. On their left, just behind the bancos, was a large, man-made
mud wall that went from one end of the village to the other. Jacob
turned around and saw that behind them, the wall was unfinished.

Jacob stood next to the vehicle with Father Thomas and Amy at
his side, wondering why their intrusion went unnoticed. These people
were most likely not accustomed to visitors, especially white folks. The
area was rife with warring tribes, but Jacob couldn't imagine that they
saw armed soldiers everyday. They should be reacting more to their
presence. Shaking his head from side to side, Jacob said, "Something
isn't right."

"I know what you mean," said Father Thomas.

The people acted as if they weren't there. But Jacob noticed that
some of the villagers had strained expressions on their faces, as if
they were holding something back. Then, he saw something else. Fear.
They were trying to hide it, but he could still sense it.

Amy could see it as well. "They're afraid. But not of us," she said.

The UN commander saw a banco that was larger and more ornate
than the others. Deducing that the village leader must live there, he
headed toward it.

"Commander, wait," said Jacob.

But he didn't wait. The other soldiers spread out near the military
vehicle. Suddenly, the townspeople started moving away from them,
as if they had been told not to get too close. In the distance, near
one of the bancos, Jacob saw furtive movements. Then someone ran
behind a hut, carrying what looked like a gun. And he wasn't dressed
in a wrap.

"Commander!" Jacob yelled. Simultaneously, he pulled a startled
Father Thomas and Amy to the ground. Before the commander could
react, guns roared to life. Bullets flew all around them. In a matter of
seconds, the commander and three of the soldiers fell to the ground,
wounded or dead. The villagers scattered, giving way to a large contingent of thugs, dressed in fatigues, armed with AK-47s.

The UN soldiers still standing aimed their carbines in the direction of the village and the gunfire. They fired indiscriminately. The

thugs were hidden behind and inside bancos. Many of the UN bullets slammed into the bancos, missing their mark. Dried mud went flying. One bullet connected, and a thug fell to the ground.

The UN soldiers were in complete disarray. Jacob quickly realized that the thugs were secreted all around the village and that picking them off would be difficult. They had them pinned down.

Jacob, Amy, Father Thomas and two of the soldiers, huddled on the passenger side of their vehicle. That at least gave them some cover, as the thugs were in front of them and to their left. When the firing started, one UN soldier scattered toward a banco on the driver's side of the vehicle. But he had a bad angle from there and couldn't lay down much useful gunfire.

"Who the hell are these guys!" screamed Amy. Jacob shook his head from side-to-side.

"Whoever they are, they're well armed," said Father Thomas.

Jacob raised his Glock and fired off several shots, but knew that if he connected, it would be a matter of luck. Father Thomas looked under the vehicle, toward the shooting, attempting to count their opponents. The din of gunfire made it hard for him to think. He yelled, "At least 20."

"Maybe they're insurgents," said Amy.

A long burst threw up dirt near them. After ducking, the UN soldiers returned the fire. "They seem awfully well armed for insurgents," commented Jacob.

Jacob and the UN soldiers let off a couple of shots. "We don't stand a chance," he muttered. He looked at the UN soldier who nodded his agreement. He pointed to the banco where the other soldier had fled.

"We can't stay here. This thing is a time bomb," said the soldier, pointing to the military vehicle.

Jacob looked across the way, wondering how they could get over there without being shot. The soldier shimmied his way to him and grabbed his arm. "We'll lay down some heavy fire and you three high-tail it."

Amy grabbed Jacob's other arm and pointed frantically to the other side of the village. "They're moving closer!"

Jacob reached into the vehicle and grabbed his backpack. Several shots ricocheted off the vehicle. He quickly withdrew the backpack and ducked for cover. The UN soldiers got in position to lay down cover fire. They flicked their carbines to automatic and gave Jacob the nod. He got Father Thomas's and Amy's attention.

"On three, run for that banco." He pointed. "Run as fast as you can and don't stop for anything. Clear?"

Amy didn't acknowledge him but could only stare. Jacob grabbed her and turned her toward him. Her face was etched with terror. She looked past him. She flinched when several bullets struck the ground nearby. Very slowly, she nodded her understanding.

Jacob put up one finger, then two and then three. They darted from the cover of the vehicle, and the gunfire increased dramatically. But the UN soldiers were ready. They held down the triggers and swept their guns from side-to-side. Jacob darted across the road, with the others following. It was only 20 yards. He was nearly halfway there when he sensed that something was wrong. He turned around. Amy had stopped moving forward and was frozen with fear, uncertain if she should go toward the banco or back toward the UN vehicle. Father Thomas nearly ran into Jacob when he stopped, but Jacob pushed him forward.

He ran back to Amy. Multiple bullet strikes threw up dust and bits of stone on either side of Amy. She cowered on the ground, burying her head in her hands. He tried to pull her up but she resisted. She screamed something he didn't understand. Bullets peppered the ground around them. Jacob fired his Glock in the direction of the gunfire. He didn't bother to aim.

With his other hand, he tried to pull Amy to her feet. Suddenly, one of the UN soldiers fell to the ground. They'd just lost one-half of their firepower.

Amy wouldn't move. Jacob sensed movement from the banco side of the street. He raised his gun and pulled the trigger, forgetting that he hadn't loaded a fresh clip. It was a good thing that he'd been preoccupied with Amy because the movement was the remaining UN soldiers running from the banco to help him. They fired their M-4s as they crouched in front of Amy and Jacob.

Jacob used the cover of their daring move to pull Amy to her feet and drag her across the street. He threw her into the banco, pushed the button on the Glock that discharged the empty clip and slammed home a new one. He turned and fired.

One of the UN soldiers that came to help them fell forward, killed by the thugs. The other tried to get to the far side of the vehicle, but he was shot in the leg before he could get there. Blood spewed from the wound, as if someone had been holding the end of a hose with his/her thumb, dispersing the water. He yelled and began crawling for safety. The last standing UN soldier kept firing but then he was hit in the chest, his uniform suddenly red from the blood that oozed from the wounds. He looked surprised but then fell backward, unconscious. The one with the leg wound stopped crawling just as he passed the right, front quarter panel. He didn't return any of the gunfire.

Inside the banco, Jacob noticed why the UN soldier hadn't fired. He was dead.

It was over. They were on their own. The three of them against at least 20 well armed thugs.

Somewhere in Northern Wisconsin

By the time Father John got to his sister's house, it was late and he was tired from a long day on the road. He parked his car in her driveway and sat there for a moment, thinking about what had happened. The reality of what he'd done, the decisions he'd made that resulted in his temporary removal from the church, really hadn't sunk in yet. It felt right when he did it and it still felt right, but his resolve was weakening. Maybe he'd been too rash. He already missed the people he'd grown to think of as his extended family, from the church staff to the regulars he saw during church events and on Sundays.

He hadn't been able to tell his sister what happened, because the phone lines were still down. She would be surprised to see him. He hoped she wouldn't be disappointed in him.

It wasn't until he got out of the car that he realized something was amiss. It was so quiet. In fact, the entire neighborhood was eerily quiet. Suddenly, a chill went up and down his spine. It couldn't be that they'd all left, he thought. Where would they go?

By the time he got to the door and knocked, he knew his sense was right. They weren't home. The only place his sister would rather be now than at home was in church. He wanted so badly to see her, and he knew she would want his guidance at a time like this, so he got back in his car and drove to a local Catholic church, in spite of his need for sleep.

Nearby, Jackson decided to stop at a small tattoo parlor that he visited when he was a kid. When he walked in, he was startled to see the same, grizzled old man who ran the shop when he was a kid.

The man–Benny–sat on a large, high-back office chair, his feet propped up on a sink that he used to clean his tools. He was reading a *Time* magazine. The cover read, in extra large print, "Special End of the World Edition." Hundreds of dyes lined the walls, some with lids crusted with old dye. The room was dusty and smelled like old socks. On a table near the door was a large book filled with designs and pictures of clients and their tattoos.

Jackson stopped at the book and paged through it, pretending not to remember Benny.

Without looking up, Benny said, "Haven't seen you in years. You ruined your life. You still a thief?"

Without flinching, Jackson continued his search. He cocked his head sideways, toward the old man. "You talkin' to me, old man?"

"I know all about you. You did time. You had it all and let it go. You disappointed your family," said Benny, never lifting his eyes from the page he was reading.

"How would you know?"

Benny picked up a cigar that he'd been sucking, never having lit it up. He shoved the soggy end between his lips and rolled it around as if it were a sucker. "I know a lot. Always have."

Jackson didn't like being called a thief so he reared up and crossed the room in a couple of steps. But Benny didn't budge. That surprised Jackson. He fully expected Benny to jump away, cowering from him. Jackson stared at him, weighing whether he wanted to punch out an old man.

Benny finally looked at him with his grizzled, wrinkled eyes, surrounded by creased, old skin that looked like sandpaper. "You don't scare me. You're a prick," he said, still sucking on the cigar.

"You don't know nothin' about me."

"I know enough. You come here to die?"

"Die? Nope. I'm going to beat this thing."

Benny laughed so hard that his face looked like it might crack. He dropped his feet to the ground and stood up.

Jackson wagged his finger at him. "You watch me, old man. I can do it."

"With what? Faith?"

"Damn right."

"Ah, shit, Jackson, you've never had faith in anything."

"Did too."

"And you still talk like a 10 year-old."

Jackson turned from Benny in a huff and returned to the picture book. He paged through until he stopped at beautiful picture of Jesus. It was a small tattoo but rich in detail. He grabbed the book and threw it at Benny's feet.

Benny glanced at the book and chuckled. "Oh, that's perfect. Picture of Jesus?"

"Yeah, what's wrong with that?"

"Why would you want a picture of Jesus?"

The truth was, Jackson wasn't sure. It just seemed right. So, he tried to make something up.

"If I'm going down, at least I can go down swinging."

Benny gathered the dyes he would need and put them on a small table that sat next to a large, flat mobile gurney that he'd gotten from a local hospital's trash heap. He pulled the wet cigar from between his lips and laid it on the table.

Benny turned toward Jackson and patted the bed with the palm of his left hand. "Well, get your ass over here so I can do it. Where do you want it?"

Jackson wasn't sure that he wanted it at all but, he decided that if he was going to do this, he might as well make it noticeable. "On my cheek."

"Which side?"

"I don't know." Jackson sat on the edge of the bed.

"Get on your side and face me. This will take awhile and will hurt like hell."

About an hour later, Jackson was sorry he asked for the tattoo. Benny was right—it hurt. But Jackson never let on that he was in pain. He got up and looked at his face in the mirror.

"Looks good." Jackson turned to leave when Benny grabbed his arm.

"You think that will save you?"

Jackson pulled away and stormed out of the shop. He got in the Acura and squealed his tires as he pulled away. After a few moments, he saw a church steeple and a lot of cars parked outside. He wondered what they would be doing at this hour so he stopped and got out of his car. Something drew him inside.

Ironically, Father John walked into the same church that Jackson and Lilly would be in.

Once he entered the church and sat in a pew, he felt oddly out of place sitting there instead of saying Mass. He ought to be preaching to these people. He didn't know the priest who was leading the service but he was doing a good job, explaining that in spite of the potential drastic consequences of the terrorist's act, belief in Jesus and his love would save them. He didn't say anything about faith, which Father John found interesting. Maybe he was avoiding it because he didn't know how to separate Christian faith from any other kind of faith, which may or may not be sanctioned by the church.

But the whole thing made him uncomfortable. He couldn't put a label on it when it suddenly came to him. He was angry. Darn angry. The Church had taken his life away from him. What was he doing here, of all places? The Vatican was more concerned about its institutional power base than helping anyone. The Church had rejected him, and he should reject the Church. But something glued him to the seat. It was the preacher's message. Was this guy a true Catholic, he wondered, because his message didn't sound like the Vatican crap he'd spewed forth several days before.

He said they shouldn't worry about expressing faith to save themselves. They already had faith, or they wouldn't be here. Pray for inner strength and the love of God, and they would be fine.

Here was a guy who, just like him, had been given a message to deliver and who had refused to deliver it. But this was a small parish and there wasn't time for the papal authorities to punish him for his blatant disregard of their edicts.

And what the preacher said weighed on him. Maybe it was that simple. Have faith in yourself and your beliefs and screw anyone else. That was at the root of the message.

Lilly and her kids slid in next to Father John. Then came Jackson, who did a double take when he noticed Lilly sitting next to the good-looking, middle-aged man on his left. She looked familiar, but he couldn't place her.

Jackson listened for a few moments to the propaganda spewing from the minister's mouth, and it was all he could do to sit there and take it. All this talk about love and Jesus was nauseating. He never had anything to do with Jackson's life, that was for sure.

Jackson got up and headed for the door. The man sitting next to him gave him a funny look, undoubtedly wondering why he'd stayed for only a few minutes. Too bad that poor guy has no idea how he was being brainwashed.

As he passed through the crowd in the church, folks stared at the image on his face, some sure it was Jesus, others trying to get a look. Once he got outside, Jackson decided that he should consider going straight. It just came to him. Maybe that tattoo was having a positive impact on him. But if he started now, he could pull himself out of the world of crime and make a new life for himself. All those people in the church were with family or friends. Not him.

As he mulled this over in his damaged brain, his thoughts changed, and he became internally defensive. He didn't need anyone. He could survive on his own. He didn't need church, friends or any of that crap that all of those people had.

Jackson felt a certain amount of relief as he got into his stolen Acura. That was a close call, with him thinking about being like all those folks in the church, like sheep, led around to God knows where.

That settled it. While the people were at church, he would break into their homes. He'd show them who knew what it was all about.

Inside the church, Lilly was mesmerized by the priest's sermon. She noticed how the entire congregation seemed to hang on every word, wishing for words of wisdom that would assist them in surviving the virus, which would hit in about a day-and-a-half. She had lost hope in the US or anyone else finding a way to beat the virus. As the days progressed, she wondered if this was a test for humanity. She hated to give in to the terrorists' plot, but who knew if this wasn't a way, sanctioned by God, or the Creator, or by Buddha, or by Mohammad, or by whomever, to reach salvation? No one could know if it was a test, but she realized, as she listened to the priest, that this was the point. It didn't matter if it was real. What mattered was that they were all being challenged by the threat of death. It was how you responded to the threat that mattered. Yet the priest didn't really give them any answers. He gave them a lot of ways to seek those answers but that frustrated Lilly and her kids and probably most of the people in the church.

Father John was similarly frustrated, but he had his own answer. After listening to the priest, he realized how selfish he'd been in pushing his own agenda and failing to realize that the answers he sought and wanted others to see were more apparent than he realized.

But when he left the church, he still wasn't sure what he should do. If he was forbidden from going back to his church, what could he do?

Nearby, Jackson broke into a house. No one was home, undoubtedly in church. He stole some money, a Glock, ammo and some camping gear. You never knew when you might need any of those. He decided he'd head to northern Wisconsin and maybe into Canada and wait out the virus. He peeled out of the driveway and raced down the street as though he was being chased. But instead of heading north, he made a wrong turn and headed south.

Once in the car, Lilly and her kids talked about what the priest had said. She had a hard time accepting that salvation was so easy to come by if they simply were at ease with who they were and what they believed in.

Bryan said, "Maybe all we're supposed to do is to correct the path we're on, if it's wrong, and we'll be OK."

"I don't know what that means," said Molly.

"If you're a bad person, now's your chance to get it right, I guess," he said.

Lilly listened, uncertain if she should let them hash it out. But before she could say something, Bryan said, "It's time to think about others and not ourselves. That's what the priest was really saying."

Lilly was never prouder of her son. That was the perfect answer to a question that she thought was unanswerable.

"Mom, how do we do that?" asked Molly.

"We should minister to the needy, I guess. Maybe we should go back to Milwaukee. They could use our help there, I'm sure." Lilly eased the car out of the parking lot.

Father John got in his car and headed south. Lilly and her kids pulled in behind him. As he was coming around a blind curve on the highway, in a remote section of Door County, a speeding car couldn't negotiate the curve and headed into the oncoming lane. The Acura came straight at Father John, who instinctively aimed his car left. The Acura clipped the tail end of Father John's car, causing it to spin out of control and off the road, into the woods and a small ravine on the side of the road.

Lilly watched in horror as the accident unfolded in front of her. The Acura flew across the road, right at her. She tried to avoid it but she didn't know which way to turn. Before she could decide, they collided and her momentum forced her car off the road as well, into the same ravine that Father John was in.

The Acura, containing Jackson, ricocheted off a rock wall on the far side of the road and slid into the ravine, about a hundred yards from the other two cars.

Lilly's car ended up next to a large boulder, which pressed against the driver's side of the car. For a moment, she sat there, uncertain what had happened. The sound of Molly's voice brought her back to reality.

"Mom . . . Mom . . ."

With her children's lives potentially in the balance, Lilly quickly assessed the situation. The rock next to her blocked her exit from the car. She was in a lot of pain. There was blood on her leg and her torso. She turned around and saw that Molly was awake and Bryan was coming to. They were bruised and bleeding.

Lilly's mothering instincts continued to push her forward. She unhooked her seat belt and tried to crawl into the back seat. The pain in her chest and lower body prevented her from getting back there with ease, but she did manage to pull out from under the partially collapsed dashboard.

By the time she was turned around, Molly had taken off her seat belt and was trying to get Bryan to wake up. "Bryan, Bryan," she said, shaking him gently by the shoulders. Bryan moaned and then opened his eyes.

"Bryan?" said Lilly. He looked at Molly and then his mother. His face and arms were scratched, with a small amount of blood trickling from the wounds.

"I think I'm OK," he said.

Lilly groaned and held her mid-section. Bryan took off his seatbelt and leaned forward. "Mom? Are you OK?"

Lilly tried to sound convincing when she said, "I'm fine," but both Molly and Bryan could see that she was badly hurt. "We have to get out of here," said Lilly, in a strained voice. Molly struggled to open her door but she managed to force it open enough to crawl out, followed by Bryan.

Father John was awake through the entire accident, up to the point at which his car stopped moving down the ravine. He knew he was badly hurt, as his legs were bloody, his back hurt and his head was throbbing. But he was afraid to stay in the car, so he managed to force the driver's side door open. He stumbled out onto the ground, which sloped down from the car. He was unable to keep his balance. When he hit the ground he could barely keep himself from audibly expressing the pain he felt. It was hard to tell where it was coming from. He hurt all over.

For a moment, he laid on his back and then rolled onto his side. The car was wedged against a tree. The entire hillside was heavily wooded. It came to him that he had hit someone or someone had hit him, he wasn't entirely sure. He managed to get up on his knees and then onto his feet. His legs hurt like hell, but apparently, they weren't broken. He held his left side, which was bloody from a deep cut he received in the accident.

Lilly's car was about 50 yards away. He started to move toward it when he remembered that there'd been another car, the one that had caused the accident. He slowly turned around, grimacing as the movement made his side hurt even more. The other car, the Acura, was badly twisted and upside down, not more than 25 yards to the rear of his car. He decided that whoever was in that car could wait.

By the time he headed slowly toward the other car, he could see some movement. The rear door opened and a girl and then a boy emerged. They struggled to open the passenger door. The car was wedged against a large boulder, precariously balanced, with the car listing forward.

The kids looked at him as he stumbled toward their car. The girl said, "We need help!"

Father John did a double take, realizing that he recognized the children. Lilly must be in the vehicle, probably badly hurt.

He tried to quicken his pace, but all he could do was lurch forward. Bryan saw that he was struggling and went to help him. Father John leaned on him as Bryan tried to support his left side. When the two of them got to the car, Molly had determined what was preventing them from opening the passenger door. It was a tree limb jammed underneath the car, along with a couple of partially buried boulders.

Father John leaned inside the broken passenger window. Lilly, jammed into her seat, was moaning but barely conscious. He pulled on the passenger door, but it wouldn't open. He glanced around, trying to figure out what was jamming it. He couldn't see anything. Everything seemed confusing, in a haze, as he tried to assimilate what he was seeing in a semi-conscious state.

In the meantime, Jackson was upside down in his vehicle, barely hurt. He unclipped the seatbelt and dropped onto his head and then rolled out of the broken window. He glanced at the other two cars and saw a man and two kids near the passenger door of the vehicle farthest from him. Before he turned away from them to head up the hill, he reached inside the Acura and pulled out the backpack and the tent he'd stolen, along with the Glock. He didn't know anything about guns, having never shot one, but it wasn't too late to start. He could use it to steal another car.

He shoved the gun in his waistband and was about to head up the hill when he stopped, wondering whether there might be something in Lilly's car that he could use. He turned back and walked toward it. He saw the man from the other car trying to open the passenger door.

The two kids looked hurt and spooked. They turned to him, and the boy said, "Please help. My mom is stuck inside."

It didn't seem worth his time to help, but he decided there could be something in it for him so he reached down and joined the other guy trying to move the broken limb from just under the bottom door jam.

The man moved very slowly, his face strained, sweat pouring down his face. It was obvious that he was badly injured. Jackson put forth some effort to help him when the boy joined and seemed to take control of the situation. He dug in and moved the limb, using all his strength. Jackson stepped back and looked inside the car. It was pretty messed up. There wasn't anything in there for him.

He backed away. The injured man fell back, onto his butt, exhausted from his efforts. The boy got the door open, reached in and pulled his mom out. She was badly hurt, her legs bloody from injuries suffered when he had struck her car. Blood stained her face and her chest as well. Her daughter and son cradled her head, both crying softly. She started to cough, and then she spit up blood. The other man leaned forward and tried to comfort her and her children.

Jackson didn't know what to do so he started up the hill toward the road. When he was half way up, he heard the girl scream, "NO!" He figured her mother was dead. He never saw the large, unstable rock in the ground. When he stepped on it, he fell forward and the gun went off in his pants, hitting him in the leg. He dropped to the ground, his leg on fire. He lost consciousness. And he saw something strange, just when that happened—a shimmering light. Was there someone in the light? It seemed to be the woman he'd seen in his dreams. What was she doing here? She said something about it being time. Time, for what? He wasn't sure.

About 10 minutes later, the boy, Bryan, was at his side, trying to stop the bleeding in his leg. Jackson woke up. And then the weirdest thing happened. It was as if a light went on inside Jackson—a bright light that, for the first time in his life, made everything come into focus. He was a jerk—he knew that—and had just walked away from the boy's mom like she was so much dead wood. Yet, here he was, taking care of him. He didn't deserve it. It was an act of kindness that hit him in the gut. The Jackson that used to be, the guy who cared, before the drugs robbed him of all the good that remained, suddenly peeked his head out.

Father John leaned over Lilly and pulled his belt through his pants, tying it around the worst of her two legs. Lilly opened her eyes and locked on Father John's face.

"Father," she moaned.

"Just rest. You'll be OK."

Molly sniffled and said, "We're all going to die anyway. What are you talking about?"

Father John shook his head from side to side. "No, we're not."

Bryan came back from helping Jackson and after he heard the priest, he turned away, uncertain he believed that.

For a moment, Lilly could see it, the answer she had been looking for, an instant of unusual clarity that seemed to happen to her. She turned to her family and said, "He means that whether an accident takes you or a virus, life and death is not defined by that moment in your life. It's defined by everything that's not death."

Lilly looked into Father John's eyes and saw that he believed what she said.

Father John nodded his head. He lifted his head slightly and said, "Will you help me up? I have a lot of work to do and only a day to do it."

CHAPTER IX

"Seek and you will find (Luke, 11:9).

Stop struggling with me. Each of you has his own star... (Judas Gospel, 59)."

AIRPORT, NEAR EMI KOUSSI

Six of the remaining UN soldiers stood near the UN plane. The other seven soldiers were unloading the plane. In a concentrated, planned maneuver, one of the six nodded at the other, and they unslung their M-4s and slowly approached the plane. One of them called out and the seven soldiers gathered around, not noticing that the six-armed soldiers had their rifles ready to fire. At the moment that one of the seven realized something wasn't right, the six opened fire, killing them all. The leader of the 6 gestured to his men, and they began dragging the bodies to the vehicle. They would have to hide the bodies so they could ambush Jacob and the others if they returned.

INSIDE BANCO

A family huddled to one side of the banco, shaking with fear. The dead UN soldier was near the door, his blood staining the floor where he laid. Amy tried to console the startled family, which consisted of a mother, father and two little boys and a girl. They were afraid of them, probably unsure if they were friend or foe, but when the mother saw Father Thomas, she pointed to his collar. Father Thomas smiled, and they relaxed. Near the rear of the banco was a wooden door. For the moment, the firing outside had stopped. They could hear the patter of feet. The thugs were getting into position. If they didn't act fast, they would never get out of there alive. Jacob cracked the back door and peered outside. He saw the wall more clearly than he'd seen it from the other side of the banco. It was about five feet high and stood about 15 feet from the rear of the mud house. Father Thomas and Amy came up beside him.

"We go over that wall, " said Jacob, pointing.

"Then what?" asked Father Thomas.

Jacob turned his head to the left. "See that vehicle down there?"

Father Thomas wondered if Jacob meant the broken down supply truck that looked as though it had been there since WWII. The full canvas covering that used to shield the contents of the supply truck's bed was tattered and torn. The lift gate was gone as well. He looked incredulously at Jacob.

Reading his thoughts, Jacob said, "You see any other options?"

Father Thomas didn't respond. Just then, several shots whizzed by, coming from their right. They pulled back inside.

"I don't see them on our left. When I say go, I'll lean out and lay down cover. You run for the wall and hop over. I'll be right behind you." Jacob handed the backpack to Father Thomas. "Don't lose this." Father Thomas gave Jacob a look.

Jacob reached for his Glock, but it was gone. He grabbed the backpack from Father Thomas and reached in, pulling out a spare Glock 19 and three clips. He nodded and quickly half-stepped outside, pulling the trigger as fast as he could, aiming in the general direction of the thugs. In front of him, Father Thomas and Amy fled to the wall. Jacob could see the thugs flying for cover, unprepared for the flurry of bullets. They were closer than he thought, having commandeered the banco next door, not more than 20 feet from their current position.

He kept firing as he left the protection of the banco. He ran blindly for the wall. He could see it out of the corner of his eye. Just before he got there, he stopped firing, launching himself over the wall. But he took off too soon. Instead of landing over the wall, he landed on top of it. The impact knocked the air out of him. Father Thomas pulled him to safety. Just then, the wall was peppered with gunfire, barely missing the lower half of Jacob's body.

On the other side of the wall, Jacob sat against the wall, struggling to gather his breath. He forced himself to move forward. Father

Thomas took the Glock from him, realizing that he didn't have a choice. He grabbed a fresh clip from Jacob's ammo belt. Suddenly, his military training came back to him. With the speed and dexterity of a well-trained soldier, Father Thomas dropped the empty clip from the handle, pushed in the fresh clip and pushed the small lever under the muzzle, causing it to sling forward and load a fresh cartridge into the chamber. He popped up and started firing.

While he fired, Amy helped Jacob along the wall. Father Thomas made his way behind them, alternating between firing and moving down the wall. At one point, when he popped up, he started to fire and then stopped. In his gun sight was Gustav. For a moment, Father Thomas stared at him. The guy looked familiar, but he couldn't place him. Had he seen him at the Vatican? Why was he here?

Gustav smiled and raised his Sig Sauer but didn't fire. They stared at each other. One of the thugs came into view and Father Thomas instinctively moved the gun sight to him, fired two shots, dropping him to the ground, dead. Gustav looked at the dead soldier and then at Father Thomas, who could see that Gustav was at once, surprised and impressed that he had the resolve to defend himself. Father Thomas dropped behind the wall and joined his friends, who had stopped several feet from him, just on the other side of the vehicle. They made their way down the wall, using it for cover, knowing that they had to hop back over the wall to the vehicle on the other side.

When they were even with the vehicle on the other side of the wall, Jacob reached back for the Glock but Father Thomas shook his head from side to side. "You may have to hot wire that thing. I've got you covered."

Jacob grabbed Amy, helping her over the wall, to the vehicle they would escape in. Father Thomas hopped over, crouched down near the rear passenger wheel and started firing. Several thugs were only 20 feet behind them. They scattered. But more were approaching their position. Father Thomas caught some furtive movements near the closest banco and fired some shots in the direction of the movement.

Jacob pulled the wires from under the dash of the old supply truck and found the ones he needed to jump-start the vehicle. Amy crawled into the back seat and found a toolbox. She pulled out a wrench, not knowing what, if anything, Jacob needed. She reached across to hand it to him. At that moment, a thug emerged from the banco to Jacob's left. He leveled the AR-15 at Jacob. Amy saw him before Jacob did. She hurled the wrench at him and smacked him on the side of the head, a million-to-one-shot.

The thug staggered and fired the gun as he fell to the side. Jacob yanked his head up, saw the thug, jumped out of the supply truck and hit him hard, causing him to fall to the ground. He hit his head on a rock and was motionless. Shots rang out around Jacob. He ducked, grabbed the AR from the man's slack grasp and several ammo clips and was about to turn around when he stopped. He looked down at the man's uniform. On the left breast was a symbol: Borromean rings. The symbol of Trinity. He turned and jumped back into the seat and twisted the wires together. The supply truck started up.

Jacob turned around, gave the AR to Amy along with the clips.

"Point and pull the trigger. It's fully automatic so hang on. Release the clip here," he said, pointing to the side of the gun.

Father Thomas, still shooting the Glock, jumped into the supply truck's passenger seat. The thugs were gaining on them. Amy crouched down in the back seat and aimed the gun through the rear of the truck. She pulled the trigger as Jacob hit the accelerator. In a couple of seconds, she nearly emptied the clip. The force of the kick threw her into Jacob's seat back. Bullets flew wildly, hitting the bancos and the ground and the front of a vehicle that just appeared 20 yards behind them. The startled thugs jumped from the vehicle, as the windshield exploded from the impact of the bullets. Father Thomas leaned out of the passenger door and fired as Jacob pulled away. Several thugs hit the ground, dead or wounded.

As Jacob drove away, he saw the shattered windshield behind him. But he couldn't see Amy in his rear view mirror. That's when he realized the 'thud' he'd felt was her hitting the seat back.

"Hey, you OK?" he yelled, trying to outdo the reverberations of Father Thomas's Glock.

Father Thomas reached into the back seat, touching Amy on the shoulder. She sat there, stunned. Looking vacantly at him, she struggled to get up. Finally, with him pulling her up, she sat on the seat. Jacob smiled at her in the rear view mirror.

"Nice shooting," he said.

Amy nodded, a blank stare on her face.

Father Thomas looked at Jacob and the two chuckled. "Sometimes it's better to be lucky," said Father Thomas.

By now, Jacob had cleared the town and was racing back the way they had

come, to the airport. But behind him, the thugs ran to their vehicles and gave chase.

"Keep an eye out. They're not going to let us get away so easily," said Jacob.

"You realize that was Trinity," said Father Thomas.

"I saw Borromean rings on one of their uniforms," said Jacob.

"That's who that was."

Jacob jerked his head around. "Who? "

"It was Gustav. He's Orfeo's right-hand man. I never did trust that jerk. I knew of him, mostly, when I was at the Vatican. He's a sniveling little shit."

"Gee, Father, tell me what you really think."

Amy roused at the mention of Orfeo. "You don't think the Vatican is complicit in this, do you?"

"No, not even the Vatican is that politically stupid. But what a cover. Operate Trinity right under the Vatican's noses," said Father Thomas.

That changed their strategy. Now, they couldn't trust the Vatican. Could they trust the UN teams and the president? It didn't take a genius to figure out that someone tipped off Trinity. Were there any other Trinity members at the Vatican? Presumably, whatever they were doing was being relayed to Gustav who got the troops in place. How could they hope to surprise Trinity if Trinity knew their moves?

In the rear view mirror, Jacob saw Amy flex her right shoulder. "Are you OK?" he asked.

She nodded. Then, Jacob thought he saw the slightest of smiles. She liked the fact that he was concerned about her.

"They'll be waiting for us," said Father Thomas.

"What do we do?" replied Amy, looking in the mirror at Jacob.

"Kind of depends on where we're going next," he said.

"Which was my next question," replied Amy.

Jacob reached for his cell phone, but it was gone. He frantically searched his other pockets. This got the others' attention. "What is it?" asked Father Thomas.

"Cell phone's gone. Crap. That's our only connection."

"That and the UN forces. Back at the plane," said Amy.

"Pretty obvious that was a trap. I wouldn't expect that the plane will be there," said Jacob.

"At some point, we're going to have to speak with Carmela about Gustav's apparent involvement," said Amy.

"If Gustav is there, you can be assured that Orfeo is behind all of this," said Father Thomas, the ire in his voice clear.

"Don't let your personal problems with him color your judgment," said Jacob.

Father Thomas nodded.

"Who ELSE knew we were coming?" asked Jacob.

"The UN, president's staff, pope and his staff," said Father Thomas.

"Way to narrow it down, guys," said Amy.

"Whoever it is, he's got to be a major player," said Father Thomas.

"OK, so that leaves the president, probably Carmela and a few of his Deputies."

"And Orfeo," insisted Father Thomas.

"This guy is an important member of the Pope's staff. I can't imagine that he could operate something as sinister as Trinity right under his nose," said Amy.

"She's got a point," said Jacob.

Up ahead was a small oasis with large boulders scattered around. Jacob pointed to it and pulled around one of the boulders and parked the vehicle. He turned around in his seat, half facing Amy in the rear seat and Father Thomas in the passenger seat.

"We need some time to consider our next step. I think we need to re-examine the clues. Let's pile into the back," said Jacob.

He grabbed the backpack and motioned for the others to join him, as he left the vehicle and crawled into the back of the truck. He reached into the backpack, searching for the research they'd brought with them. A few moments later, the three of them had the maps, Judas Gospel and notes spread out. The diffused sunlight, shining through the ripped canvas covering, cast slivers of light onto their work.

They yanked their heads up when the sound of an approaching vehicle disturbed their concentration. It was Trinity, coming from the village. As they drove past, all Amy could think about is that they would see them there, stop and shoot them. After they passed by, Amy felt Jacob's eyes on her. She returned his gaze.

"What?" she asked.

He motioned down with his eyes. She followed his gaze and saw that her hand was not only on top of Jacob's but that she was strangling it. Immediately, she thought of pulling it back, but she didn't. Instead, she gripped harder. When Jacob smiled, she slowly withdrew her hand. He glanced down at the maps and notes, and it came to him.

"We're on the right track. The numbers 17 and 19 have symbolic meanings as well."

Jacob pulled out a piece of paper, and Amy and Father Thomas slid over next to him. He cleared a place on the bottom of the truck bed and flattened the paper, stretching it to its full size. He drew three interlocking circles on the paper.

"The Holy Trinity," said Father Thomas.

"And Trinity's symbol," said Amy.

Jacob added more circles until he had a total of 17. He sat back and waited for a reaction. For a moment, Father Thomas and Amy stared at the circles. Then, a moment of recognition.

"The tree of life," said Amy, pointing at the drawing. "Seventeen interlocking circles."

Jacob added two more. "Now, it's the flower of life."

"Interesting. Symbols of both Christianity and Judaism," commented Father Thomas.

"Right. And if you subtract 17 rings from the flower of life you end up with the Holy Trinity," said Jacob.

"What? Wouldn't it be . . ." said Amy, as she mentally subtracted the rings.

Jacob counted backwards, from 17, pointing to each ring as he did so. Then he flipped the paper over and re-drew the circles until he ended up with the Holy Trinity.

"Ok, I see where you're going with this. The number references in the Judas Gospel are codes, essentially, to the tree of life, the flower of life, Borromean rings, all symbols of Christianity. But what does it have to do with the virus?" asked Father Thomas.

"Or the release points?" asked Amy.

TRINITY

FLOWER OF LIFE

BORROMEAN RINGS

TREE OF LIFE

COMBINED

Jacob stared at his research, wondering what they were missing. There were all these clues that seemed to fit, but they were lying out there, like a puzzle that couldn't be put together. Frustrated, he threw his pencil on the bed of the truck. What does all of it mean?

"It's not like we have a lot of time here," said Jacob.

"Our next step is crucial. We can't afford another trap," said Father Thomas.

Amy unfurled another map and spread it out on her knees. Jacob glanced at the map and then did a double take. When she opened it up, he saw something on the back of the map that caught his attention. He reached and flipped it over.

On the back was a reproduction of an "old style" map made in the 1600s. The Earth's hemispheres were laid out, one next to the other. And then it came to him.

"How could I have missed it? The Borromean rings."

Jacob pointed to the map and traced the third circle with his index finger, turning the map into a picture of Borromean rings.

"How does that help us? You lost me," said Father Thomas.

The answer seemed to jump off the map for Jacob. He glanced left, right, looking for something that he could use to make a fixed length, so that he could draw what he saw.

"I need a string or something six inches long."

Jacob grabbed his backpack and rummaged through it while Amy and Father Thomas tossed old, deteriorated pieces of a military tarp aside. Amy turned around and saw a faded white piece of nylon netting. She handed it to Jacob.

He yanked his knife out of his pocket and, using the length of his blade—six inches—he measured the netting, holding it out, two inches longer than the blade. He cut it there and then tied the netting to the bottom of the pencil, just above the lead. Then, he took the map from Amy and spread it on the floor of the vehicle. He found the point he was looking for and, using his thumb, he held the free end of the netting to that spot. He pulled the string taut. Then, with the pencil resting on the map, he drew a circle over the map, always keeping the string taut.

When he was done, he had a perfect circle drawn over the map.

"The circle is 12 inches in diameter. Twelve is a key number in the Judas Gospel. The third circle that I just drew transforms the map into Borromean rings," said Jacob.

"How did you determine where to start the circle?" said Amy.

"Five degrees. The number of angels in the beginning. Seth, Harmathoth, Galila, Yobel, Adonaisos."

"You realize of course that you're assuming that Trinity used a map like this to locate their headquarters or the release points," said Father Thomas.

"Or both," said Jacob.

"You said five degrees. North or south?" asked Amy.

He had to make an assumption. His life was based on acting upon empirical evidence. He just didn't operate that way—guessing.

"Jacob, we've only got one shot at this," said Father Thomas.

"Yeah, I know. Thanks for reminding me." Jacob would have paced if the space in the bed allowed him to. Instead, he tapped his foot on the floor of the truck and glanced around, looking at nothing in particular, wondering if he'd get inspiration from somewhere. His gaze landed on Father Thomas.

"You can ask me for his blessing if you think it would help," said Father Thomas.

All Jacob could do was shake his head from side to side. As he spoke, he pointed to his research.

"This . . .this corroborates the coordinates. It's 19 and 17. The rings, the tree of life—Christian symbols, the symbol of Trinity." He pulled out additional research and the Judas Gospel, checking through quickly and randomly, hoping the answer, the one that would save EVERYONE, would somehow leap off the page. If ever there was a time when he needed to simply know that his answer was right, this was it. But he didn't know. He could make guesses. But they were barely "educated guesses." He could find lots of numbers in the Judas Gospel that would add up to other numbers. Given enough time, they could probably find hundreds of clues based on using a series of different calculations. The thought of using any numbers bothered him. Number theory, used to predict the future, the past—all sorts of calamities—had been used many times over the years. He was a little embarrassed that this was all they had to go on, given the disdain he had for things like the Bible code—a bizarre theory that the authors of the Bible had implanted codes to predict the future. Those that studied the "codes" pointed out that historical acts were correctly predicted by deciphering them. He didn't buy it.

There was something in Jacob's eyes that was unfamiliar to him and those who knew him—fear. Father Thomas saw it and so could Amy. While he thumbed through his research, Amy reached across and gently put her hand on his. He stopped and looked at her.

"Jacob, you're going to have to guess."

"I don't guess. There has to be a way . . ." He saw something in her eyes that he'd seen once before, many years ago: trust. She believed in him. He glanced at Father Thomas who nodded.

Father Thomas made the sign of the cross, and said, "Jacob, you can do this. He will guide you."

"But I don't guess. There has to be an answer here..."

" 'For we know in part and we prophesy in part.' First, Corinthians," said Father Thomas.

Jacob pulled his hand from Amy's and broke eye contact. He felt something else he wasn't used to—helplessness. Glancing away from his books and past Father Thomas and Amy, he realized that there was no answer to his question outside of himself. So he took the pencil and started making the calculations on the map.

"Just so you know, you're not witnessing a rebirth," said Jacob.

"I assume that this is directed at me?" asked Father Thomas. "I realize that you only believe in Jacob. Even now, you demonstrate something greater."

Jacob tried to ignore him, but at his core, he knew he was right. "It's 17 degrees north, 19 minutes east . . . starting point is, ahhh, 5 degrees north."

Amy checked her GPS and then the other, more current map, locating the place that corresponded with the coordinates. "It's not far from here. Faya-Largeau."

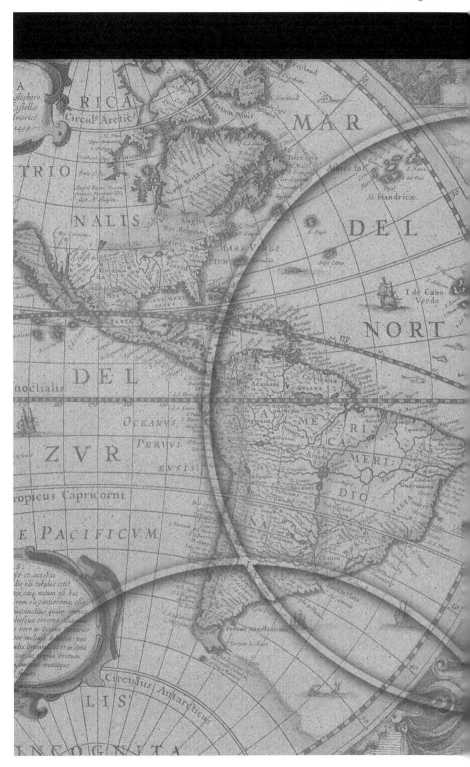

BORROMEAN RINGS

FAYA-LARGEAU

Father Thomas stared at the map and then realized something. He pointed, saying, "Look, the third ring you drew."

Jacob and Amy looked at the map and saw that the third ring passed through Chad. He traced the ring through Chad until he stopped where the line he'd drawn passed almost directly through Faya-Largeau. It was the empirical evidence he needed. But he had to guess to confirm it.

Airport, Emi Koussi

Gustav waited, along with Trinity soldiers, to spring the trap on Jacob and the others, who they presumed would be coming along soon. Orfeo insisted on being present in Africa to deal with Jacob, Amy and Father Thomas, who were following the trap they had laid for them. But, Orfeo was worried that they were getting too close, that they might actually find the true release points. He had a bad feeling about them. So they decided to eliminate them altogether.

It gave Gustav a great opportunity to hatch his plan, the one he'd been planning since they stumbled on the virus several months ago. He remembered that day, on Mount Ararat, where they'd found an ossuary buried in the ice. Actually, they hadn't found it but a group loyal to Trinity and Gnosticism did. He remembered the message from the team, Orfeo's excitement when he heard the news and the overall expectation: they'd found the ossuary containing the bones of Judas Iscariot. The Judas. This was every Gnostic's dream come true. And then, when the ossuary had thawed, they found an unexpected bonus. The ossuary had a small growth inside that when tested, turned out to be a very dangerous virus. Before they contained it, several workers died. But their scientists were sure that the virus that had survived the thousands of years in the ossuary because it had been frozen. This, they were told, was feasible but not often observed in nature. Really, it didn't matter because they had a very deadly virus that no one on Earth would have the ability to fight.

There it was, the virus, screaming to be used. That's when Orfeo came up with his faith-based challenge to the world. The real issue, however, was that the extinction of most of mankind, would force—or so they hoped—the Second Coming. This theory had not been well explained to anyone and really concerned Gustav. He never thought it made any sense. Why would God send his Son to save man after a virus had wiped out almost everyone? This is when Gustav became worried about Orfeo's mental health.

It was not hard to imagine Orfeo losing his mind. When he was a child, his father continually tormented him, both physically and emotionally. It became commonplace to see his father hit his mother, then go after Orfeo. She couldn't protect herself or Orfeo from his drunken rages. When he was 15, he'd had enough and killed his father. But it didn't end there. He planted evidence that implicated his mother in the death. His mother hated him for what he did to her but she couldn't maintain her sanity. She ended up in a mental institution. Those who were aware of his story were impressed that he managed to achieve success in spite of his hatred for the world. In fact, most believed that he overcame that hatred to truly love God and his parishioners.

In reality, as those close to him realized, he never out-grew that hatred. He just redirected it and managed to hide it underneath his black robe. It was interesting, thought Gustav, how Orfeo had so easily convinced everyone that he was really going to kill everyone, except for those with faith. In reality, he was going to release only a very small amount of the virus. Even if it was more virulent than his scientists believed, Orfeo believed that the virus would quickly mutate into something relatively benign. Many of his followers, including Gustav, did not believe this; hence, Gustav's precautions.

But Gustav couldn't back out because momentum had developed, and he couldn't stop it. Orfeo's followers revered him, some saying that HE would be the second coming. So, Gustav came up with a plan to protect himself and a few select Trinity members. One of Trinity's members was a biologist with expertise in infectious diseases. He had actually worked for the CDC for years. At Gustav's direction, he made a serum that would, at least in theory, beat the virus. That was the rub—they didn't know if it worked. He had spent years to perfect the serum, which, of course, worked on rats.

Gustav had kept it from Orfeo, which wasn't easy. But the more he thought about it, Orfeo would be able to use the virus to establish his power base in a new world, one in which people would pay a lot of money to survive. With a cure for the disease, Gustav could do the same thing, only he could control who survived and who died.

The scientist, a geneticist, would be bringing several thousand vials of the serum. It would put Gustav in a position to survive the release of the virus and give him the means to save people who were willing to pay for it.

AIRPORT, EMI KOUSSI

Amy and Father Thomas stood just outside the beaten-down truck, just off the road, hidden behind a berm from any traffic that might pass by, while Jacob looked through his binoculars at the airport.

"We left 13 UN soldiers behind. I count six or seven. Where are the others?"

He lowered the binoculars, not expecting an answer. Amy took the binoculars from Jacob and looked through them.

"Some must be Trinity. They killed the troops. Jesus."

"You mean the ones still alive are Trinity," clarified Father Thomas. "We're back to the same question."

"Who knew we were coming here?" asked Amy.

"The president, cabinet personnel, Carmela. Can't assume the pope knew. We certainly didn't tell him," said Jacob.

Father Thomas was losing his patience. "Right. We've been over that. It's the folks back in the US. It can't be Orfeo, according to Jacob. So, back in the States, one of them . . ."

"Must have warned Trinity," said Amy, finishing Father Thomas's sentence.

"It can't be Carmela," said Amy.

"Who suggested East?" asked Father Thomas.

"Orfeo. He led us to the ambush. He was standing there when we announced the coordinates. Has to be him," reasoned Jacob.

"That's what I've been saying. I knew it was him," said Father Thomas, the frustration in his voice apparent.

"You mean I was in the same room with the bastard that killed my sister?" said Amy, as the realization set in. Without thinking about what she was doing, she grabbed the AR, tried cocking it, as if she was going to use it on Orfeo. Her lips trembled with anger. Jacob gently took the gun from her.

"We'll get him, " he said.

A single tear ran down Amy's cheek. She wiped it aside and sniffled. "When? When are we going to get him, as you say? We don't have much time, and that asshole is running around, free, after killing my sister!" screamed Amy, still trembling with anger.

"Take it easy. We can't rush into things. There is a way to do this correctly," responded Jacob.

"Rush? How can we NOT rush? He has to PAY for what he did!" The reverberations from Amy's outburst hung in the bed of the truck like the blackness of night, in the middle of nowhere. No one spoke for a few moments.

Father Thomas broke the silence. "I understand your anger. But Jacob is right. We have to approach this as calmly as possible. We're all out of our comfort zone a bit."

Amy swallowed and tried to contain her emotions. "What would cause someone–a cardinal, no less–to do something so evil!" asked Amy.

"Well, I know a little about Orfeo. His story is somewhat legendary inside the Vatican. He had a very difficult childhood. When he was 15, he caught his perpetually drunk father beating his mother once again and he blew a gasket. He shot him, dead. His mother literally lost her mind after that."

"So he lashes out now at the world–his mom–for what she did to him," commented Jacob.

Father Thomas shrugged. "Perhaps. He was always revered for how he overcame his origins."

"Maybe he's been hiding his true objectives all along," said Amy.

"I doubt he understands what is behind his actions. I'm sure, as twisted as he is, he believes that he's doing the right thing," said Father Thomas.

"Where did all this understanding come from? I thought you hated this guy," asked Jacob. Father Thomas didn't answer.

Jacob looked through the binoculars again at the airport. He saw more soldiers now—maybe another 15.

"Trinity soldiers from the village are here," said Jacob.

A small plane stood at the far end of the runway, similar to a Cessna. There was a small hangar near that plane and then, of course, the main hangar next to the jet. He estimated that the plane was maybe a quarter-mile from the jet. He looked once again at the UN soldiers, some gathered around the plane, others near the hanger and two guarding the entrance to the airport. He lowered the binoculars again.

"Well, Gustav is there. And, there's a small plane on the other end of the runway. I don't know how we're going to get there without being spotted."

"And the plane helps us how?" said Father Thomas.

"I never told you about my father, the crop duster? I was flying before I was driving," said Jacob.

"I thought you and your father didn't get along?"

"This is getting way too introspective for me. Let's get on with it, shall we?"

"There is the matter of getting past the soldiers," said Father Thomas.

"And if Gustav is there, where is the rest of Trinity from the village?" asked Amy, sounding more like the low-key woman that Jacob knew.

Jacob shrugged. "They're here?" He started the truck.

Father Thomas reached back and took the AR from Amy. "I assume that the plan consists of flooring it and hoping that I can shoot enough of the soldiers so that we can get to the plane in one piece."

Jacob put the truck in gear and sped around the berm. "I can't see any other way in. Surprise is key. I don't think they're expecting us to come back." Once he hit the road, he accelerated quickly.

"Then why are they still here?" asked Amy.

"You ask too many questions. Trust me," said Jacob.

At the entrance to the airport, just ahead, stood two vehicles, their front ends partially on the road, blocking clear access to the airport. On either side of the entrance were old, stone, guard stations and a fence that appeared to border the entire airfield. There was no way around them.

The two Trinity soldiers ran onto the road, raised their AR's and started firing. Father Thomas leaned out with his AR and fired off a couple of bursts. Jacob extended his left hand out the window and fired his Glock in their general direction. One of the soldiers fell to the side, hit by either Jacob's or Father Thomas's bullet. The other scattered for cover.

Jacob blew through the two vehicles, hitting them with such force that they spun around. The other Trinity soldiers ran for cover around the plane and the hanger. Jacob and the others were close enough now that they could make out Gustav, who yelled orders to his men.

"Get them!" he screamed. Gunfire erupted all around the truck. The front windshield was hit several times. Jacob slunk down in his seat, peering over the steering wheel. Father Thomas got off a couple of shots and then used the firewall between the engine compartment and the cabin for protection. It didn't take long for the engine to sputter. It started but made a grinding noise; wafts of smoke curled out from under the hood.

Gustav and the soldiers jumped into their vehicles, started them and mashed their accelerators, causing puffs of sand to filter into the air. Jacob flew past them and headed for the small plane, but he knew they'd never make it. The hangar was about a hundred yards off to his left, the jet to his right. He aimed the truck for the jet and hoped to God he'd make it before the engine blew.

CHAPTER X

"By grace are you saved through faith" (Eph. 2:8).

CIA SATELLITE RECON ROOM

With a computer screen in front of him, an operative pointed to the image on his screen. His supervisor stood behind him.

"There it is. Gunshots near Emmi Koussi."

The supervisor reached over, grabbed a phone and dialed. On the other end was the general, at the Pentagon.

"What is it?" asked the general.

"Sir, unexplained gunshots near Emi Koussi."

"We've got a team there. I'm on it."

The General hung up the phone and dialed another number, ordering the deployment of another team to Emi Koussi. He instructed his subordinate to get the team there within the hour and to keep him posted. Whatever was going on there, he was worried. They'd lost communication with the UN team. He hoped they were still alive.

NORTHERN WISCONSIN

Father John tended to Jackson's wound while Bryan and Molly helped their mother to her feet. Lilly took a tentative step forward, testing the leg. She nodded. It wasn't broken and the bleeding had stopped.

Jackson stared into the sky as Father John finished tying a bandage together around the wound. "Father, I think…something just happened to me. I'm a thief and a liar. But now…"

"…you feel the grace of God."

Jackson vigorously nodded. "Yes, that's it."

Father John glanced at the tattoo of Jesus on Jackson's cheek. "That looks fresh. Why'd you get it?"

"Just got it. Why? I don't know… trying to find my way."

"You were looking for an easy way out. You thought that if you had Jesus on your cheek, you'd be forgiven."

Jackson lazily nodded. "Maybe. But isn't that what happened? I told you. I feel different. It's got me a little shook up."

"What do you mean, 'different?'"

Jackson shook his head from side-to-side. "Can't describe it. Can I tell you something? Promise you won't think I'm crazy."

Without waiting for an answer, Jackson said, "When I was out for a minute there…

"…more like 10 minutes."

"Yeah. I saw something. Sort of a person who spoke to me."

Father John didn't respond but he had the strangest feeling what Jackson was going to tell him. "It was this pretty gal…sort of shimmering…she said this was my only chance to save myself, that if I did, I could pave the path for others." He paused. "I've seen her in my dreams before."

"Sort of like an angel?" quipped Father John.

Jackson's eyes lit up. "No angel's gonna talk to me. But she said something about how I should be leading man out of the shadows of darkness into the light." Jackson sat up, at once shocked that he'd said that, much less believed it. What was happening to him? "Me? I'm nothing. A loser. A criminal. I don't know the first thing about leading men. I can't make my own life work."

Father John had a hard time believing it as well. How could this man be chosen? Could there be a person who was less likely than this guy to lead?

Jackson struggled to his feet. He could see in Father John's face that he didn't believe him. Heck, HE couldn't believe what he'd just said. Just then, Bryan and Molly were close by, helping Lilly. Jackson smiled and limped to help them. Father John reached out to help him but Jackson moved well on his own. The wound on his leg was severe; Father John was surprised that it had stopped bleeding so quickly. He was equally surprised that Jackson moved with barely a limp.

Jackson sidled up to the family and helped them up the hill. Father John followed. By the time they got to the road, a large SUV came by and stopped for them. Seeing that they were hurt, the SUV took them to the hospital in Sturgeon Bay. During the ride, Jackson felt the wound on his leg itching. He pulled the bloody bandage aside and was shocked to see that the wound had closed and was healing rapidly. He reached across the seat and took Lilly's hand in his. She was looking out the window so she jumped when he touched her. Lilly looked at him and saw peace and strength in Jackson's face. In spite of the silly tattoo, there was something about him that was alluring and captivating. She found herself staring at him. Slowly, she withdrew her hand from his. She didn't notice until later that her leg felt a lot better than it had.

AIRPORT NEAR EMI KOUSSI

Jacob sped toward the plane on the far end of the airport. But gunfire erupted from behind, hitting the truck and the dirt on the ground. A truck with several Trinity soldiers suddenly appeared on their right, having caught up from behind. Father Thomas squeezed off several shots but the soldiers opened fire, hitting the engine and one of the tires. Amy crouched behind the front seats as bullets tore up the cabin. She held onto the Glock, waiting for an opportunity to use it.

Father Thomas ducked down, still holding the AR, the barrel resting on top of the passenger window. He fired, blindly, hoping to at least deter Trinity. But they had more severe problems to deal with. The engine was badly damaged. Smoke billowed out from under the hood. The right tire was nearly flat. Jacob struggled to hold onto the truck, all the while losing speed.

At that moment, Jacob decided they wouldn't make it to the plane. A better alternative than getting stuck in the open with a disabled vehicle was to head for the hanger, use that for cover and make a stand there. Of course, Jacob counted on the engine getting them to the hanger. What he didn't count on was the engine seizing up. Father Thomas glanced at him when the engine stopped.

"Do we have enough to make it?"

Jacob shook his head. "Don't know. We're losing speed rapidly." The speedometer hovered at 50 mph.

The hanger was just ahead, no more than 100 yards from their position. Jacob continued to lose speed. He realized there were two vehicles with Trinity soldiers in them—the one that used to be to their right, which was now speeding up, taking advantage of the damaged engine and one from behind, which now sped ahead of him on the left. What were they doing?

They stopped their vehicles, forming an inverted "V" and took positions behind them. Jacob didn't have enough momentum to take their truck around the vehicles and still get to the hanger, which was about 30 feet behind Trinity. Did he have enough to plow through them? He didn't know but he guessed they wouldn't expect him to do that.

As he barreled forward, Father Thomas knew at once what he was doing. "Straight at them," he said. Jacob nodded. By now, Amy had popped up, realizing they were going to ram them.

"You're going to do what?"

"No time for a debate. Take cover. They're going to open up on us in…"

Just then, a wave of bullets hit the front of the truck. Jacob aimed the truck for the point of the "V" formed by the trucks, held onto the steering wheel and ducked down. Bullets ripped through the window and hit the seat he'd just vacated. But the engine block protected all three of them from any fatal shots getting through.

With Trinity firing at least 7 AR's at them, the truck soon had so many holes in it that it started to look like netting. Gustav and his men thought the truck would stop but it didn't. They jumped out of the way as the truck plowed into the vehicles, still pointed directly at the inverted "V" formed by the two trucks. Because the point pointed away from Jacob and the others, the truck didn't need as much momentum to propel it through them and into the hanger.

Unexpectedly, the engine suddenly came to life just as they hit the trucks. Jacob still had his foot on the accelerator, causing the truck to lurch forward and propel them into the hanger, when the engine finally stopped. When the truck came to a halt, Jacob opened the door and scrambled out, yelling, "Everyone out!"

Father Thomas crawled over the seat toward the driver's seat that Jacob had just left. Amy was already out by the time Father Thomas exited. For a moment, the shooting had stopped. They huddled around the exterior of the truck, looking for some cover. Jacob spotted a piece of an old fuselage nearby, pointed to it and the three jumped behind it. Amy carried the backpack, Father Thomas still had the AR with several extra ammo clips and Jacob had the Glock but with only one extra, 15 round clip.

Jacob glanced at Amy. "Any rounds left?"

"Just this clip," she said, patting the Glock. She pushed the release and the clip fell out. Amy counted the rounds left. "Ten left."

They looked around, seeing that the hanger was mostly empty, except for a nearby refueling truck. When Father Thomas glanced back at the truck, he shook his head from side-to-side. Amy's mouth fell open. There were holes everywhere. The grill was gone, the bullets ripping it to shreds. It seemed impossible that the engine had cut in for several seconds, just when they needed it. But it had happened.

Bullets erupted around them again. Trinity had repositioned themselves around the damaged trucks. Jacob glanced around the fuselage, trying to get a look at whether they'd killed or disabled any of them when he rammed the truck through their vehicles. Jacob could see at least two bodies and one soldier who looked as though he favored one of his arms. There were five of them still shooting. He couldn't tell if the vehicles still worked.

"Two men down, one hurt. Father, let them know we're still here."

Father Thomas aimed at the men and fired off several rounds. Several hit the dirt, throwing up debris. Father Thomas stopped firing, turned around and shook his head. Jacob could see it on his face – the pain of killing or hurting another human being.

Jacob reached out and put his hand on Father Thomas' arm. "It's OK. Here, give me the gun."

"No, I was trained for this, remember?"

"But that was before…"

"…it's still part of who I am!" The words came with the denial and anger that still seethed inside of Father Thomas. Jacob reached for the AR and winced from a sharp pain in his shoulder. Amy noticed a large red spot on Jacob's shoulder. "Jacob! You've been shot!"

Jacob glanced at the blood. "Crap. I hate it when I get shot."

"When did that happen?" asked Father Thomas.

"I don't know. Didn't notice it until now." Amy quickly opened Jacob's shirt and moved the fabric aside. She pulled her shirt out and tried to rip off a piece from the bottom. Father Thomas pulled a folding knife out and she used that to make a cut in her shirt and then used the cut to rip through the fabric.

"You'd better keep an eye on those bastards while I get bandaged up by Florence Nightingale," he said to Father Thomas, who turned back toward Trinity and let off another couple of bursts. The gunfire from them was not as heavy as before. Father Thomas wondered if they were conserving ammo.

While Amy fashioned a bandage from her torn shirt, Jacob tried to stem the flow of blood from the wound. Now that he knew he'd been shot, the thing hurt like hell—sort of a hot, burning sensation.

Jacob half turned toward her. She looked at the other side and saw a small exit wound. "Looks like it came out."

She tied the bandage tightly around his arm. For a moment, the closeness to him and his need for her help, coursed through her body, like a brief but barely perceptible electric shock. She didn't want to feel that way. And she could see that Jacob sensed it.

Their eyes met for a moment and Jacob wondered if she was going to kiss him, something they hadn't done much the first go-around. Father Thomas fired off a couple of shots. Trinity was moving toward them, using old parts of airplanes as cover.

"They're coming. One of them is working on a truck. We can't hold 'em back. I'm almost out of ammo."

Jacob stared at the refueling truck and then pointed at it. "That's our way out."

"That? Its' a death trap," said Father Thomas.

"There's no other way we can make it to the plane. The truck can't be more than 20 feet from here. We can make it." Jacob handed Father Thomas the AR.

"How many shots left?"

Father Thomas patted the clip. "Full clip and that's it."

Jacob pulled out his Glock and patted his pocket. "I've got another clip for this. You lay down cover fire as we run for the truck. Once we get there, I'll get the thing started. I'll pass you the Glock when you're empty." Father Thomas nodded.

"Amy, hold onto your Glock. Don't fire it. We may need it later."

All of the Trinity soldiers were at or near the open door to the hanger, with the exception of the soldier who fiddled with one of the trucks. Just as Jacob and the others took off for the re-fueling truck, they heard the Trinity truck start up. Amy sprinted ahead of them, carrying the backpack.

Several Trinity shots hit the truck they'd just abandoned and it erupted into a fireball. The three instinctively ducked as they ran faster for the re-fueling truck. The irony of the truck blowing up now, after resisting anything of the sort while being turned into what looked like a piece of wood full of worm holes, didn't escape any of them.

That distraction was enough to allow them to get halfway to the truck without being noticed. Then, Trinity opened up. Father Thomas took aim at the hanger door and let off several bursts, just enough to cause Trinity to duck for cover. The three jumped into the truck and Jacob was pleasantly surprised when he found a key in the ignition. He fired up the engine and headed for the plane. At that moment, the Trinity truck swung by the hanger doors and picked up the others. Father Thomas could see Gustav hanging out of the passenger door, clinging with one hand to the doorframe and using the other to take wild shots at them with his AR.

Several shots hit the side of the truck. Father Thomas turned around and saw that the re-fueling spigot had been dislodged. Airplane fuel spilled on the ground.

"We've got a problem," said Father Thomas.

"Only one? That's encouraging," replied Jacob.

"We're leaking airplane fuel. I assume you know what it means if a spark happens to hit it."

"Yeah, something about meeting Peter at the pearly gates."

Father Thomas pulled the trigger on his AR, only to find his clip was empty. He reached across for Jacob's gun. Jacob saw his entreaty and handed it to him. Just then, Amy decided that they needed her help.

She stuck her head out of the window and fired off several shots at the Trinity truck, which was slowly gaining on them. One of her shots hit the window, causing the driver to duck. He momentarily lost control of the vehicle, allowing the three to get distance on Gustav and the other thugs. They were still only a football field away from the plane.

As they got closer to the plane, Jacob could see that it was an old Cessna 172. It was the version from the late 50's, with the silver, aluminum belly and a red and blue top. He'd never flown that model but Cessna's were as easy to fly as a homemade paper plane.

Jacob slammed on the brakes, bringing the truck to a sliding halt on top of the overgrown runway. They piled out and ran for the plane. Trinity was gaining on them, almost within effective firing range. Jacob pulled the cockpit door open. It was dusty inside. That meant the fuel might be old, if it had any fuel. The irony is that they had the means to fuel the plane but not enough time.

"Father, pull the blocks. I'll work on getting this thing started."

Amy waited outside the plane, her Glock pointed at Trinity. Father Thomas quickly pulled the wheel blocks out. Just as he came back around the plane, some shots threw up bits of concrete only 3 or 4 feet from the plane. Amy fired back. Father Thomas got in the co-pilot seat, with Amy still firing off some shots as she climbed in the back.

Jacob had his head under the dash pulling the wires out. He picked the two that would start the engine, put them together and started the pre-flight requirements for getting the thing off the ground. He turned the mixture setting to rich, the carburetor heat to cold, the prime was in and locked, the throttle open a half-inch, the master switch on and the ignition switch to "start." The engine coughed, the propellers teased them with a few rotations but nothing happened. He turned off the ignition switch and primed the engine again. Several shots hit the cockpit.

"Hurry, Jacob! They're almost here!" said Amy.

"Working on it!"

Father Thomas made the sign of the cross. Jacob turned on the ignition switch again and the engine coughed but then caught on. The propeller sprang to life. Jacob freed the parking brake and pushed the throttle as far forward as he dared.

The Cessna jolted forward. Jacob swung it around, to his left. Now, Trinity was to his left as well. He picked up speed. The Trinity truck turned so that it could run parallel to the Cessna. Most vehicles could easily outrun a Cessna, since the take off speed of 55 knots—roughly 63 miles per hour—is well within the specs of most, if not all, vehicles.

Knowing this, Jacob could not imagine how they would be able to outrun the Trinity truck. They had hit speeds of only 50 to get to the plane but that was because of the re-refueling truck's limitations.

"Father, we'll never make it. We can't outrun them. You're going to have to shoot out a tire or something."

Father Thomas crawled into the back seat as Amy slid out of the way to make room for him. The vehicle was now parallel to them and quickly gaining. Shots hit the struts and the cabin but so far, nothing had hit flesh. Father Thomas opened the door and took careful aim as the vehicle approached. Jacob kept one eye on the speed indicator. He was traveling at 20 knots—no wonder Trinity was gaining so fast. Whatever lead they had, they were losing at an alarming rate.

Father Thomas saw Gustav with his AR and for a moment, aimed at him. But he turned his attention to the front grill, the largest and most vulnerable part of the vehicle, other than the tires, which he would never be able to hit.

The plane bouncing over the rough runway further challenged his aim. Gustav was smiling. Father Thomas wanted to punch him in the face. Gustav knew they were done. He may not have a lot of ammo left but there was plenty at that close range to ground the plane. What he didn't expect was Father Thomas' prowess with a firearm.

When Gustav saw the gun in Father Thomas' hand, his smile broadened. Father Thomas thought he might be laughing. That's when he fired 7 quick shots into the grill. The truck smoked and lurched to an abrupt halt. One of the bullets had dislodged a piston, forcing the rod to jam through the engine. Before Gustav realized what was happening, the vehicle slowed dramatically. The plane, however, was picking up speed.

The airspeed, indicated by the knots indicated airspeed indicator, showed 40, then 50 then 55. Jacob pulled back on the stick and the plane was airborne. Behind them, Gustav and his men emptied their clips at them but it was too late. They had escaped.

"I need someone up here. There should be an aviation map somewhere."

Father Thomas slid back into the passenger seat and looked for a map. He found an old one under the front seat. It was decayed, looking like it might fall apart if opened. He carefully opened it. A musty, mildew smell wafted through the plane. The map wasn't anything like he'd ever seen—he had no idea how to read it. Jacob would have to tell him how to find Faya-Largeau on the map.

"Oh, God," said Amy.

"What? Are you OK?" said Jacob, looking over his shoulder at Amy.

"I am but we aren't," she said.

Both Jacob and Father Thomas saw her looking down, to their left. They followed her gaze and saw what she was talking about. Hidden behind the hanger where they'd holed up was a Bell helicopter. Gustav and his men were running for it.

"Can they catch us in that thing?" asked Father Thomas.

"It's a lot faster than we are," said Jacob.

Down on the ground, an exhausted Gustav stood near the helicopter while three of his men started it up and took off. The Bell 206 helicopter was modified—it had a very efficient, M60, 7.62 machine gun mounted where the side door used to be. The gun had a 2.3 mile range. The Cessna was armed with a couple of Glocks, nearly out of ammo. They were defenseless.

Gustav dialed his satellite phone as the copter took off. He was not looking forward to this call. Orfeo would not be happy.

"Tell me they've been terminated," said Orfeo.

"They escaped," answered Gustav.

Orfeo didn't say anything. In an instant, the thing that drove him to take the world to the brink of extinction, hit him like a right hook. He flashed back to the pain of his miserable existence, his mother's weakness and failure to protect him from his father, who not only beat her but him as well.

The other teams the UN sent out posed an even greater threat but Orfeo was not worried about them. There was something about Jacob and his friends that threatened him. He couldn't put his finger on it.

"The lab...I think they're heading for the lab," said Gustav, breaking the uncomfortable silence.

"Meet me here," said Orfeo.

CHAPTER XI

"There is no truth in Satan (John, 8:44)."

Jesus said, 'It is not possible to sow seed on rock and harvest its fruit" (Judas Gospel, 69).

OASIS, NEAR FAYA-LARGEAU

Orfeo hung up the phone and surveyed the desert and the oasis around the lab where he and the scientists Trinity had employed created the virus from the remains of Judas's ossuary. Around him, Trinity soldiers finished loading several trucks with equipment they had taken from the lab before they destroyed it. They all hid behind several large boulders where one of his men handed him a digital, remote detonator. He tripped it, and the lab blew. Rock and wooden debris flew into the air, but the bulk of the lab, which was underground, sunk in as the force of the explosion imploded the structure.

Orfeo rose from the safety of the rocks and watched the genius of his creation burn. It was ironic that Judas had provided him with the means to destroy man, just as his traitorous ways paved the way for the death and resurrection of Jesus. How fitting was it that the man who helped saved the sinners of the world thousands of years ago could do it again in the present?

CESSNA OVER AFRICA

While holding onto the wheel of the Cessna, Jacob studied the aviation map. He found the coordinates and adjusted his course. He flew low—just above tree level—on the off chance that Trinity or some other malevolent force might acquire them on radar. They would have been better off flying as high as the Cessna could take them—somewhere around 13,000 feet—where the air was thinner and the gas would go further. The one thing that he had no control over was what he now feared would doom their mission. The Cessna had only a half tank of fuel, and they needed at least three-quarters of a tank. On top of that, the plane's engine jolted and sputtered every once in a while. Jacob couldn't imagine how old the gas might be.

Father Thomas looked at the gas gauge, the concern apparent from the way he furrowed his brow.

Jacob glanced at him. "Yeah, I know," was all he could say.

Suddenly, the helicopter came into view, directly behind him.

Amy saw it first. "They're here . . . Oh my, they've got a big—" She was interrupted by a long burst from the large 7.62 mm gun. A couple of shots hit near the rear of the plane but did no real damage. The helicopter came up alongside the Cessna. Jacob glanced at it and then back again, not believing what he was seeing.

"Never saw a Bell with optional equipment like that." He took the Glock from Father Thomas, opened the window and fired off a couple of shots. None of them connected, but the guy manning the 7.62 ducked. He gathered himself and pointed the gun directly at them.

Jacob went through his options in a split second. He couldn't out-run the chopper. They would most likely blow them out of the air. If they landed, they would be easier targets. The chopper was more maneuverable then they were so he couldn't get away from them. He might be able to out-pilot them, but that was doubtful. He decided to give it a try.

"Hang on!" Jacob yelled as he pointed the nose of the plane on a 45-degree angle. The plane rose quickly. The chopper followed. Amy and Father Thomas were pinned to their seats by the G-forces. Jacob pushed the plane to its limits.

"What are you doing?" asked Father Thomas.

"Trying to save our butts!"

Jacob then dove the plane and hit the rudder hard to the left. The plane dipped toward the trees. Just before they hit them, Jacob pulled up and turned hard right. The chopper was right on their tail. The gunman kept getting off shots. One shattered the side window, drop-ping glass onto Amy. One of the shards embedded itself into her arm. Wincing, she pulled it out.

Jacob jerked the wheel right, then left. Amy slid back and forth across the back seat. "Hey, watch it!" she yelled.

None of it worked. The helicopter kept firing. There was too much firepower. They didn't have a chance. Jacob would have to do some-thing to even the odds. But what? They couldn't outrun them, they sure as heck couldn't out shoot them—they'd have to outsmart them.

Then it came to him. He pointed the Cessna up, at a 45-degree angle, and gunned the throttle. He'd use up a lot of gas, but they had no other choice.

Behind them, the chopper chased. The gunman kept trying to get an angle and would fire shots at them, but the Cessna was almost directly ahead. The pilot saw his error and moved to the side so that they could get a shot at the plane as it rose.

But it was a battle the chopper couldn't win. The Cessna wasn't a fast climber, but the helicopter was even slower. The Bell was much better at lower altitudes. Jacob hoped that the other pilot's hatred would overrule his logic.

Jacob kept his eyes glued to the altimeter. They had just passed 8000 feet. The Bell kept following them. Any moment now . . .

And then it happened. The pilot was so busy trying to catch the Cessna that he wasn't paying attention to his altitude. As they passed 8000 feet, he suddenly felt the chopper get heavy.

"What the hell . . ." he said, glancing at the altimeter. "Oh, shit . . ." he said.

The chopper stopped climbing and started falling. It went into a spin. Inside the Bell, the men yelled at the pilot to get control of the ship, but it was useless. It didn't take long for it to hit the ground and blow up.

Up above, Jacob leveled off and started the slow descent while he feathered back the throttle.

"You knew that was going to happen," said Father Thomas.

"Yup."

"What just happened? Why did the helicopter fall out of the sky like that?" asked Amy.

"They have a ceiling of about 8000 feet. I was counting on the pilot's hatred of us to keep his attention. Once he passed the ceiling, the chopper was no longer able to maintain any stability. A skilled pilot could pull them out, but this guy apparently wasn't very skilled."

"But the toll was heavy, wasn't it?" asked Father Thomas as he pointed to the gas gauge, which now hovered near empty.

"Well, we wouldn't normally burn that much on a climb like that so there must be a hole in the gas tank. But yeah, you burn a lot of fuel when you do what I did."

"Are we going to make it?"

"We'll be on fumes for the last 25 miles or so. I don't know," commented Jacob, his facial expression displaying more fear than his verbal explanation. They descended to 1000 feet. Jacob asked Amy to check her GPS. They were close. Faya-Largeau had to be just up ahead.

"We're close. I don't see anything…"

The engine cut out. Father Thomas signed the cross. "'For we walk by faith, not by sight.'"

"How far can we glide in this thing?" asked Amy.

"I have no idea. Never done it before. Theoretically, it should glide over a long distance. The plane is light, but the wings aren't particularly big either."

They just cleared a set of trees, their rate of descent more severe than Jacob expected. Amy and Father Thomas scanned the horizon, looking for the airfield that they thought would be on their heading.

Then, Father Thomas sat forward abruptly and pointed. "There! Straight ahead!"

Jacob looked and saw it. A landing strip. "Got it." He pulled the nose up slightly as the plane descended past 1000 feet, then 750, then 500. When he got to 100 feet, the airspeed had dropped to 55 knots. He landed the plane on the bumpy landing strip where it glided to a stop at the end of the runway, its wheels embedded in the desert sand. To their left, just inside the hangar, was a small plane; next to the hangar was an office.

Jacob, Amy and Father Thomas piled out of the plane. For a moment, Amy stood still next to the plane, the feeling of the ground under her feet so overwhelming that she couldn't move. The air was hot and dry, just like their last location. And the landscape was just as dreary—sand and large rock outcroppings, with palm trees and plants here and there.

The three headed for the hangar, with Amy still carrying the backpack. They all carried their side arms. When they were almost upon the hangar, a Chad military man exited the office with his side arm drawn. He was a big, burly man who looked very angry.

He had the drop on them, but Jacob figured he could take him down before he shot all three of them, not a particularly great alternative to talking with him. Plus he only had a couple of rounds left. Jacob motioned for the others to stop. He hid his side arm under his shirt and slowly approached the man, his hands held out in front of him, palms down, trying to let the man know that they were not violent.

But the man didn't buy it; he waved the gun at Jacob and grunted something in his native tongue, clearly indicating to Jacob that he did not want him to move toward him. Father Thomas came forward and joined Jacob, leaving Amy standing by herself just behind him. That wasn't apparently a good idea, because the man frowned and walked over to them, the gun pointing at Jacob's head.

Jacob fingered his Glock and was about to whip it out when the man stopped in his tracks, staring at Father Thomas. He lowered his weapon and slowly approached Father Thomas, fixated on him. Then, he stopped, knelt and made the sign of the cross. Although it was dirty, ragged and dented, Father Thomas's priestly collar was partially intact. The guy was Catholic.

Father Thomas made the sign of the cross over the man and then pulled him to his feet. While the man held his hands in front of himself, in prayer, Father Thomas again made the sign of the cross. The man put the gun in his holster.

"Do you speak English?" asked Father Thomas.

The man nodded and cocked his head to the side, as if to say that he spoke a little bit. Then he indicated with his hands a small person. "Man like you, came to village."

Father Thomas smiled. "A missionary?"

The man nodded in recognition.

"We need a jeep. Is there one we could use?" asked Father Thomas.

The man turned around and took them to the side of the hanger and pointed at a jeep. Jacob nodded and started to get in. The man

grabbed him and pulled him out, pointing to an old, dirty tarp behind
the jeep. What Jacob could see—a pitted front fender, with almost
no paint and under-inflated tires sticking out from under the tarp—
didn't exactly inspire confidence. Jacob pulled the tarp off, revealing
more of the same and a second jeep, if you could call it that. The seats
had worn away, with almost no fabric remaining, the windshield was
shattered and all of the tires were under-inflated. The jeep was littered
with leaves, branches and sand. It seemed unlikely that the battery
would have enough left to power a clock, much less turn over a starter.

"Does it work?" asked Amy.

The man shrugged his shoulders.

Jacob sat in the driver's seat and turned the ignition key on.
Amazingly, the starter sputtered a bit and the battery struggled to
turn it over, but it started. The engine puffed and skipped. After it
emitted a loud "pop," a plume of smoke blew out of the exhaust pipe.

Amy pulled out her GPS and entered the coordinates. She pointed.
"It's that way."

Father Thomas shook the man's hand.

"That way is Faya," said the man, pointing the way Amy had
pointed. "Can get more gas there." The man smiled at Father Thomas,
obviously still taken by him.

The three piled into the jeep and pulled away, traveling over the
landing strip until they found an old, crushed stone and sand road
that took them through the desert.

Airport Near Emi Koussi

Soon after Jacob and the others high-tailed it from the airport,
the remaining soldiers, with the exception of Gustav and one other,
stayed behind, cleaning up their tracks. Gustav had to join Orfeo at
the lab site.

It didn't take long for the UN troops to land nearby and storm the
airport. They were too late to help Jacob, Amy and Father Thomas,
but they killed the remaining troops with ease.

The officer leading the assault team called the general to report
the status of the operation. He told him that Trinity had infiltrated

their troops and that Jacob and the others had left. The general ordered them to secure the airport and then got on the phone with the president.

———

United Nations

President Holcomb stood near the large table in a room inside the United Nations with the UN Security Council. They'd been meeting for hours, discussing and monitoring the developments around the world. A large plasma screen on one of the walls was used to track the various UN teams, including Jacob and the others, as they tried to locate Trinity and the release points.

The religious scholars from the Vatican conversed with leaders from the World Health Organization, discussing possible locations for the release points. In addition to what Jacob, Amy, Father Thomas and the other teams were investigating, the scholars and WHO worked on their own leads.

Additional clues put together by the scholars resulted in teams being deployed to Frankfurt, Germany, and another to Sydney, Australia. But the leads turned out to be fruitless. They had nothing. Additional teams had been sent all over the world to pursue other clues, but they were running out of time.

As far as everyone in the conference room knew, Jacob and the others had been killed. They'd lost contact with them a day and a half ago. And then the conference room phone rang.

Holcomb's assistant chief of staff answered and after listening, pushed the speaker button. "I think you're all going to want to hear this," he said.

"Sir, this is General Curtis. We've uncovered a plot by Trinity to infiltrate the UN strike team. When we arrived at the landing strip in Emi Koussi, we discovered that there were only five of the UN troops left, that they were Trinity and that Mr. Matthews and the others were no longer there. We dispatched the remaining Trinity soldiers."

"Did you interrogate any of them?"

"No, they fired on us. Sorry sir, but we had to return their fire."

"Did Jacob and the others make it out alive?" asked Holcomb.

"We don't know."

"How did Trinity know where we were sending the team?" asked Holcomb.

"Sir, there must be a leak."

"You mean someone here is Trinity?" said Holcomb.

"That's the only conclusion that makes any sense. How else could they have known we were going to Emi Koussi?" answered the General.

President Holcomb, brimming with anger, turned to Carmela. "I want this leak found and I want it found now."

The Federation representative piped up, "Mr. President, I assure you that we know nothing."

Holcomb waved him off while at the same time giving him an assuring look. "I'm not concerned about you, Yuri. Let's stretch our legs a bit and return in 15 minutes."

Everyone in the room left, but before Holcomb's Deputy Chief of Staff, Mike Peterson, exited with the rest of them, Holcomb tapped him on the shoulder, indicating with a look that he wanted him to stay behind. As soon as the others left the room, Holcomb turned to Peterson.

"Mike, we've known each other for 15, 20 years. You're the only one I'm sure of. Don't let me down."

Peterson nodded. "I won't, Mr. President."

"Run an investigation, including phone taps, records, everything and anything you need to get this leak stopped. I need an answer by the end of today. We don't have much time left."

"I'll get on it right away."

ROAD IN CHAD, NEAR FAYA-LARGEAU

Jacob had been driving for at least an hour. The landscape, which had been spotted with palm trees and bushes, reminding Jacob and the others of desert sagebrush, had given way to rippling sand and rocks jutting up out of the landscape. Occasionally, they would see an Umbrella Thorn or several clumps of Leopard Orchids, particularly near an oasis. And the temperature had risen, as they descended in the Sahara desert. It was now approaching 105 degrees.

As they rounded a sand dune, Jacob stopped. They got out, and Amy checked her GPS. Father Thomas had removed his black shirt, revealing a white t-shirt underneath, which was now spotted with sweat.

Amy couldn't help but be impressed with the man's physical condition. He still had strong-looking arms and shoulders, his torso tapering onto a small waist.

But she found herself continually drawn to Jacob, who sported a safari-style shirt, with epaulets and long sleeves that he had rolled up. He was a powerful man.

Jacob couldn't help but stare at her clingy t-shirt and her legs, which were now exposed, as she had cut her pants off at the thigh. Jacob told her that she was better off keeping her legs covered, in order to save the lost of moisture and protect herself from the sun. But she couldn't stand the heat on her legs, or at least that's what she told herself.

"It's about 10 miles from here," said Amy, wiping the sweat from her forehead.

Amy handed him the canteen and he took a swig. "Probably be dark soon," he said, as he scanned the desert. The sun was just going below the horizon, and it was still hot as hell and very bright.

"I don't know if I could handle the glare without these sunglasses," said Father Thomas.

"It's surprising how much the sun reflects off the sand," said Jacob, as he removed his sunglasses. He reached into the back seat and withdrew the t-shirt he'd removed several hours before and wiped the sweat from around his eyes and forehead.

Amy took a couple of steps until she was next to Jacob. "So what's your plan once we get to Faya-Largeau?"

"To find Trinity and the release points."

"You sure those answers will present themselves?"

"Jacob is very resourceful," piped in Father Thomas. "He'll find a way for us to locate them."

"I sure as hell hope we'll be able to find a sat phone there," said Amy.

"Not likely, unless the local army has one that we can use," answered Jacob.

"My guess is that they've been briefed on what is occurring around the world. I would bet they will willingly help us," commented Father Thomas.

"I sure as hell hope you're right. There are some scary folks wielding guns around this part of Africa," said Jacob.

The three got back into the truck. Jacob started the truck and glanced at Amy. She could feel his eyes on her and didn't mind.

By the time they got into Faya-Largeau, it was twilight. They parked the truck and got out. Jacob flagged down a soldier. He approached the three some, armed with only a side arm.

"Do you speak English?" asked Father Thomas.

The man shook his head from side to side. A local Kanuri tribe member walked by, covered by his jellaba, a traditional wrap around, tunic-like covering, with a skullcap and turban. He stopped.

"Excuse me," he said, in heavily accented English, "Do you need some help?"

"Yes, please," answered Father Thomas. "We are trying to find . . .well, we're not sure what. We have GPS coordinates. It's probably a structure."

"Yes, well, several years ago, a large group of whites came to the town, used locals to build something in the desert. None of the locals came back," said the Kanuri.

While Father Thomas and the Kanuri were talking, Jacob and Amy got back in the truck, drove to a small gas pump and began filling the tank.

"Where did they go?" asked Father Thomas.

"The oasis," answered the Kanuri.

"Can you take us?"

The Kanuri bowed and shook his head from side to side. "Many of my people are afraid of that place. It is the site of an ancient burial ground. It is forbidden for us to go there."

"We are on a mission to bring the men to justice who hurt your people," said Father Thomas.

The Kanuri looked hard at Father Thomas, his expression changing from fear to anger and resolve.

"Just you?" he said. "Our military did nothing."

Father Thomas pointed toward Amy and Jacob. The Kanuri smiled and nodded in recognition. He closed his eyes for a moment and then opened them.

"You are brave. I can take you. In the morning."

Father Thomas returned to the truck, where Jacob was paying for the gas. "Let's get something to eat. Then, some sleep," said Father Thomas.

OASIS – TRINITY LAB – NEXT MORNING

Orfeo and Gustav walked through the debris of the lab, where they had extracted the virus that would change the world forever. Trinity soldiers checked for anything that might be left that could be used to construct a vaccine or that might reveal their release points. Orfeo had been careful to remove any evidence before they'd blown up the lab, but there was too much at stake to be careless.

Back at the Vatican, Gustav's men were completing the final stages of an antidote for the virus. He simply did not trust that Orfeo was right—that the faithful would survive. In fact, it had become increasingly clear to most of them that Orfeo was not playing with a full deck anymore, that what motivated him was something far different than what had led them to where they were today. Their scientists warned Orfeo that the virus was extremely virulent and that no one could survive it, at least not until antibodies were built up against it or a vaccine was created.

For most of Trinity's small membership, the concept of using faith to survive a human threat was just what the world needed. There was so little in the world that seemed worth saving. Rampant sin pervaded most societies. A biblical, global cleansing was the only thing that could save them. Most of Trinity wondered why such a thing had not occurred in the present day. Orfeo suggested that they had been given the power to bring about their own salvation, that the Judas Gospel and the remains of Judas himself, where the virus had been discovered, still virulent in its preserved state in the ossuary, had given them the means to give man a new beginning.

Orfeo was tired of the abject failures at the hands of traditional Christianity. The Judas Gospel and the teachings of Gnosticism were fresh, untested but more appropriate for modern man.

Orfeo believed—and taught his followers—that, as alluded to in The Judas Gospel, the story of Jesus begins when he dies, that the risen Christ revealed himself to certain disciples, such as Paul. Christ revealed a hidden knowledge and wisdom to those who would listen. It was the mystery of the risen Christ—a man who had survived death—that fascinated Gnostics. Bishop Irenaeus led the charge against the Gnostic movement, and it was primarily because of him that Christianity disdained Gnosticism for the teachings in the canonical gospels. What Christianity had failed at, according to Trinity's teachings, was preparing man to relate to God through the Church. The abject failure of organized religion was obvious. But it held man in its grasp. Men like Orfeo threatened most Christians because he believed, as all of Trinity did, that each man was capable of relating to God, that there was no need for a religious leader. This was pure blasphemy to the Church.

Yet, these beliefs drove Orfeo forward. He couldn't help but see something of his mother in the Church. Just as she had failed him, the Church had failed mankind. But he wouldn't allow the world to suffer as he had. That is why Trinity had to succeed.

As he viewed the debris from his creation, a Trinity soldier got Orfeo's attention and gave him the information he'd been waiting for: Jacob, Amy and Father Thomas were on their way. They had taken the bait, followed all the leads that Orfeo had given them and gone down all the roads leading to nowhere. But he had had a bad feeling about Jacob from the beginning. When they escaped from the airfield in Emi Koussi, that only confirmed his fears.

CHAPTER XII

"In My name shall you cast out devils" (Mark, 16:17).

Serve Him in sincerity and truth" (Josh. 24:14).

STURGEON BAY, HOSPITAL

Jackson sat in the recovery room, what was left of his wound bandaged up. Lilly had a serious muscle sprain and some wounds in her leg from the accident, but she was going to be released.

Outside Jackson's room, Father John spoke with the attending physician. "He doesn't have any family?" asked Father John.

"He told us that his family is all of us," answered the physician.

"What does that mean?"

"That's all he'll say. I can't answer you. Are you sure he was shot?"

"I heard the gun go off, saw a blood stain on the outside of his pant's leg."

"You never actually saw the wound?"

"I saw blood, but no, I didn't actually see the wound. I bandaged him up, just covering the area with the most blood."

The physician shook his head from side to side. "I can't imagine that he was shot in the leg. There's a healing wound on his leg that could be from a gunshot, but it looks like it's been healing for several weeks."

Father John nodded. "I guess it's a miracle."

"We could use a couple of those around here. Well, I suppose I can release him. Can you . . . "

"I will help him, yes. We're going to need a car. Is there a car rental agency here?"

"No. There are several in Green Bay."

"All right. Thank you."

Father John shook the physician's hand. He looked in his eyes and saw the doubt that existed there. He didn't believe in miracles. Father John said, "What's your plan to survive the virus?"

The doctor shrugged his shoulders. "I don't have a plan. If science can't beat the thing, I'll let the chips fall wherever."

"You don't think there might be another way to save yourself?"

"Nope. No offense, Father, but I don't believe in God. I see pain, suffering and death that would put most people flat on their back. What deity would allow such a thing to happen? Faith? I don't have any."

"Sure you do. You have faith in science."

The physician nodded. "Yes, that much is true. I don't think of faith in those terms."

"Maybe you should."

"I can't say that, given the terrorists warning, I haven't thought about it. But of course, the problem is that I don't believe. Without that, I'm doomed."

"I don't think so. Think about it in a different way."

"What do you mean?"

"This doesn't have to be about religious faith. It is for many people, but it doesn't have to be."

The physician looked surprised. Father John could tell from his expression that he was processing what he said. He stuck his hand out again, and the two shook. This time, he looked Father John in the eyes and smiled, if ever so slightly. Father John was pretty sure that he'd gotten through.

By the time Father John got past administration to the exit, Lilly was there, partially propped up by Bryan, on one side, and a single crutch on the other. Jackson looked out the window.

"We might be able to get a car from Green Bay. I don't know if you want to share or where you're going," said Father John.

Jackson turned around. "I need to go to Milwaukee, if you're going there. I'm not sure why . . . but I think I'm needed there."

"That's where I'm headed. How about you three?" said Father John, as he turned to Lilly and her children. "Did the doc give you a clean bill of health?"

"Yeah, other than the sprained ankle, I've got some trauma to my mid-section, but it'll be fine."

"Where to next?" asked Father John.

"I think we're going to stay here. We need to spend some time with each other," said Lilly.

"That's the best place to find answers. Best of luck." Father John shook hands with each of them. He noticed that Jackson wasn't at the window anymore but was outside, speaking with several people. Whatever he was saying seemed to attract attention as nearly anyone who passed by, stopped to listen.

Father John pulled up a chair at the window, watching Jackson. More and more people stopped to listen to him. Soon, there was a group of 10, then 15. Father John smiled. What was happening to this man? There was something about him . . . he couldn't put his finger on it. He remembered what he said but dismissed it. He decided he'd go outside and listen to him.

What he heard was astounding. Jackson spoke of faith, and hope and relying on the teachings of Jesus to help with decisions about fate. He talked about relying on the Word, as originally written, and not as interpreted by religious denominations. Some asked him why they couldn't rely on those with more training to help them understand what the Bible says. He said that they could but to be wary of those that might mislead them.

When he was done speaking, Father John approached him. Jackson looked stunned, almost drugged.

"I had no idea that you knew so much about the Bible."

At first, Jackson just stared at him. Slowly, he turned and said, "Neither did I."

"I don't understand."

"The words I used . . . they just came to me. I've never studied the Bible. But it was all there, as if I had. I . . . I don't know what to think."

But Father John did. He was witness to a prophet being born.

FAYA-LARGEAU
DAY 5

Amy and Jacob slept in the front seat of the jeep while Father Thomas studied their research, which was spread out next to him in the rear of the jeep. The sound of an old, rattling engine approaching jolted both Amy and Jacob awake. It was the Kanuri accompanied by another tribesman. He pulled up in a truck that was missing a fender, had no roof where there should have been one and no windshield.

Jacob glanced at his watch. It was 3 a.m. Father Thomas and Amy pried their eyes open. None of them had slept much, but there wasn't time, at least for the next several days. If they stopped Trinity, they would have plenty of time to sleep; if they didn't, they'd all be dead.

Jacob peered into the rear of the truck and saw a large quantity of arrows and several bows. The Kanuri gave them the thumbs up and drove off, with Jacob following.

"Bows and arrows. Great," said Jacob.

"Are they expecting trouble?" asked Father Thomas, trying to sound very serious.

"I can't imagine why," replied Amy.

With the Kanuri leading the way, they drove through the morning until the Kanuri stopped behind a large boulder. Father Thomas got out of the jeep and went around the other side of the boulder to relieve himself.

He looked up at the slowly rising sun and zipped up his pants. The sweat was already moistening his shirt and exposed skin. He walked back to the jeep, wiping the sweat from his face.

"Does it ever cool off here? It's barely past 6 a.m. and feels like a furnace," said Father Thomas as he folded the bandana and put it back in his pocket.

"Not this time of the year. We are in the Sahara," commented Jacob.

"Where are we?" asked Amy.

The Kanuri pointed to the hill in the distance. "It is on the other side of that hill. I'm afraid that we cannot go any further. It is forbidden."

The three said their goodbyes and walked across the sand, carrying their weapons, water and backpack. Behind them, the Kanuri watched them from their jeep.

At the top of the hill, Jacob and the others saw a very large oasis, including several large ponds. Its starkly contrasting green foliage spread out before them, like a painting on a tan canvas, the palm trees dominating the landscape. For the first time, they noticed a light breeze, welcome relief in the heat of the morning. The effect of the green seemed unnatural, especially with the large boulders on either side of the verdant expanse.

The sunlight reflected on top of the small hills and crests of water that moved in the breeze, giving the water an almost golden hue. Jacob thought he could see several palms loaded with dates.

They walked slowly down the hill, watching for any movement. The whole area was so well protected by sand dunes that an entire army could be hiding behind them. But they didn't have much choice. This is where the GPS led them, and whatever was there, Jacob hoped it gave them the clues they so desperately needed.

"This better be it," muttered Amy.

"Whatever 'it' is," said Father Thomas.

In the distance, on the other side of the pools of water, which looked much smaller now that they were closer to them, Jacob saw what looked like a puff of smoke. "You see that?"

Father Thomas nodded.

"What? See what?" asked Amy.

Jacob pointed. "That puff of smoke?"

Amy looked to where he pointed. It was faint, but it was there. They walked past the palms and the other desert plants, the water and some grass until they could see where the smoke was coming from. It was a building—or what used to be a building—still smoking from whatever destroyed it. Parts of the wall still stood, smoking lightly. They could see what looked like charred wood and a lot of melted cement; the fire must have been extremely hot.

The cement, wood and glass rubble from what used to be the building was strewn about the desert floor. Some nearby palms were burned from the heat of the blaze. The air smelled of burned wood and plastic. Cautiously, they picked their way through the rubble.

Amy stopped when her eye caught something shiny. She moved a piece of warm wood aside.

"You might want to take a look at this," she said.

Father Thomas and Jacob turned toward her and saw what had gotten her attention: two beakers.

"This was a lab?" questioned Jacob.

"It appears so," said Father Thomas. "But a lab out here? It doesn't make sense."

Amy saw something else and moved toward it. Jacob and Father Thomas stood their ground.

"I know. It doesn't make sense," repeated Jacob.

"There's something about the numbers that we got wrong. I can't put it into words. But it doesn't feel right," said Father Thomas.

"You're not getting religious on me now, are you? Besides, those numbers got us here."

"Yeah, but . . . " Father Thomas didn't finish the sentence. He kept running the numbers through his head. Nothing jumped out at him—except for the assumptions they made—but he couldn't shake the feeling that they had made a serious error.

Jacob began to think that finding this site may have been a bit easy. Had Orfeo trapped them into coming here? Even if they had, it didn't much matter. They had to follow every clue, no matter the risk. They didn't have any other choice.

Amy, still focused on something she saw, stopped and pulled several boards aside. Whatever it was, it looked almost white. She pulled one more board aside and dropped it, stifling a scream.

"Oh, my . . . " she said.

Jacob and Father Thomas heard the shock in her voice and joined her. There, on the ground, were several human bones. Father Thomas bent over and touched one.

"These weren't burned in the fire. They've been here for a while."

Jacob pulled some more partially burned boards aside and revealed additional bones. These were clearly skeletal remains. Then he saw a partially burned jelabba.

He pointed to it. "So that's what happened to the townspeople," he said, his voice low and shaky. "They killed them and buried them here, under the lab. Why not bury them in the desert?"

Amy looked away, her face white with fear. Jacob followed her. She half turned, acknowledging his presence.

"It's not that I haven't seen a skeleton before," she said. Her eyes were a bit red and clearly tearing up.

Jacob started to put his arm around her, but something else caught her attention and she moved quickly toward it. Feeling a little defeated, Jacob dropped his arm and followed her.

She stopped and stared at a large object that Jacob couldn't make out until he reached her side. And there it was.

A large wooden door with Borromean rings carved in the wood.

"Father, take a look at this," said Jacob.

Father Thomas joined them. "So this was a Trinity site. But what were they doing here?"

"What were they making?' wondered Jacob.

From behind them, an unexpected voice answered.

"We extracted and made the virus. The prophesies of Judas, and the means to carry them out, were discovered here."

Jacob, Amy and Father Thomas whipped around, drawing their side arms. Orfeo, with Gustav at his side, stood at the edge of the rubble, surrounded by Trinity soldiers. The three had been so caught up in their investigation that they had not heard them approach.

"You will drop your side arms," said Orfeo, in a low, commanding voice. The three obeyed, as they were clearly outgunned.

As soon Jacob saw who it was, he stepped forward but Father Thomas gently moved him aside. He crossed over the remains of the lab until he stood so close to Orfeo he could smell his putrid breath. One of Orfeo's men stepped forward but Orfeo motioned him away. Amy lunged toward Orfeo, her face red and streaked with the tears of her sister. The Trinity soldiers flinched. Jacob reached out and held onto her. She strained against him.

"You did this! To my sister and all those people! And you're a fucking cardinal!" Amy screamed, the venom in her tone surprising to everyone. She leered at him, struggling against Jacob's grip, revenge in her eyes.

"The three of you are most resilient and creative. But we will not be stopped," said Orfeo, his gaze fixing on Father Thomas as he finished his sentence. Father Thomas now stood directly in front of him.

"What did you mean, 'the prophesies of Judas?'" asked Father Thomas.

"You don't know?" Orfeo waited for a response. When he received none, he said, "We found Judas's ossuary."

"His what? Here?" asked Father Thomas.

"No, near Mt. Hermon. It was frozen and badly cracked. The government, in order to keep it in one piece, maintained it in its frozen state. When we heard about it, we sent our scientists to Jerusalem, and we took it."

"That's a significant archeological discovery that I never heard of," commented Jacob.

By now, Amy had calmed down enough that Jacob let go of her. "You never heard about it because the discovery was reported to the Vatican, who kept it a secret," reasoned Father Thomas.

"And this was made known to Orfeo . . ." said Jacob.

"And a select group inside the Vatican, yes," said Orfeo, finishing Jacob's sentence.

"The ossuary is where you found the virus. It was frozen for 2000 years. Jesus," said Jacob, as he finally put the pieces together.

Amy shook her head. "That's not possible. It can't survive that long."

"It can if it's frozen," said Orfeo.

Even Jacob knew it was possible. A virus can live for hundreds of years, if it has a host. Or thousands if it isn't active. The scientists who had analyzed the first samples had been right; the virus was thousands of years old. Jacob wondered if Orfeo and his goons anticipated the mutation of the virus. That had to affect their plans. Maybe they weren't aware of that. Could that be his ace in the hole?

"So what's next?" asked Jacob.

"You have to ask? I, for one, am tired of chasing you," answered Gustav.

"Ah, the servant can speak," said Father Thomas, who by now, had stepped back from Orfeo.

"I must admit," said Orfeo, "there is something in the thrill of the chase, to be exhilarated by your ability to do what no one else has done. Before we end your miserable, faithless lives, I must ask: has it occurred to you that the journey you've been on, the clues that you've followed, were all part of my plan, to distract you from my real objectives, that I wanted you to find the lab?"

"You're not smart enough for that," said Father Thomas.

Orfeo let out an evil laugh. He stepped back, gesturing to his men. "Kill them," he said.

At that moment, there were a series of loud, 'whishing' noises. First one, then another and then two more, in rapid succession. Amy, Jacob and Father Thomas instinctively ducked, looking around for the source of the sound. The Trinity soldiers did the same, until they realized that some of their comrades were falling to the ground, dead.

Jacob, Amy and Father Thomas quickly scattered, seeking cover, trying to figure out what was happening. The Trinity soldiers were too busy ducking to care about what Jacob and the others were doing. Gustav and Orfeo dove behind part of the structure that still stood.

Jacob pointed to another partial wall of the burned structure and Father Thomas and Amy dove behind it. From there, they surveyed the area. Several more soldiers hit the ground. And then Jacob saw it. Arrows. It was the Kanuri.

Jacob, Amy and Father Thomas fled from the ruins of the lab to the oasis, while the Kanuri kept Trinity busy with a flurry of arrows. The two who had brought them must have gotten the help of their entire village. Several shots hit the ground around the three of them as they ran around a large rock outcropping.

On the other side, were the Kanuri.

The two who brought them there were perched on top of the rock, firing down on Trinity. One of them slid down and landed next to Jacob.

"I thought you couldn't enter the oasis."

"You were in trouble."

"Now it is you who are brave," commented Father Thomas.

"I can't believe you were able to find so many Kanuri to assist you," said Jacob.

The Kanuri frowned. "It is just the two of us."

Incredulous, Jacob shook his head. "I don't see how . . ."

Just then, the Kanuri took the large quiver of arrows to the far side of the rock and with speed that didn't seem possible, fired an arrow and then loaded another and fired it. It took him about two seconds.

Jacob, Father Thomas and Amy looked at each other in disbelief and then at the Kanuri, who was now sitting next to them.

"You go. We should have done this a long time ago."

Jacob nodded and reached for the Kanuri's shoulder, trying to pull him away. The Kanuri smiled back but didn't move. Shots hit the ground around them. Trinity was gaining position on them. They ducked. But not the Kanuri. The one next to Jacob crawled up the rock, said something to his friend who pointed to the left and right. One took up a position on the right, the other the left and they fired in rapid succession.

Jacob hesitated. He looked at Father Thomas for guidance. The Kanuri would die here. They had to do something to help them. But they no longer had their weapons.

Father Thomas looked up at the Kanuri who seemed to sense his gaze, as they ducked for a moment. Father Thomas pressed his hands together, said a quick prayer and blessed the Kanuri, who bowed their heads. Then, they got up and resumed firing.

Father Thomas indicated to Jacob and Amy that they should go. Reluctantly, they fled, running back the way they'd come. For the moment, the Kanuri were keeping Trinity occupied. Jacob doubted that their jeep would be working, but it was the only chance they had to get out of there.

When they finally got to their jeep, none of them were terribly surprised that the tires were all flat.

"We need a vehicle," said Father Thomas.

"See any car dealerships?" asked Jacob.

Jacob looked back in the direction they'd come. He couldn't help but think about the Kanuri.

Amy sensed his concern. She put her arm around his shoulder. "It was their decision. There isn't anything you could have done," she said.

Jacob didn't look convinced but lowered his eyes, more in supplication than in agreement.

Father Thomas pointed to some boulders nearby. The area was littered with large boulders, sand and some fauna, such as Palm Trees and desert scrub plants. Dead ahead was a large concentration of boulders that lent themselves to a hiding place. It stood out compared to the barren landscape around them. They ran in that direction, looking back to the oasis, wondering when Trinity would over power the Kanuri.

"You realize that if you're right and their vehicles are there, we may run smack dab into them," said Jacob, as he wiped the sweat from his forehead.

"I have faith in our ability to deal with them," said Father Thomas.

"But they outnumber us. And we're no longer armed."

"I'm willing to chance it," said Amy. "I don't know how we're going to get out of here without transportation."

As the three took off for their destination, Amy tried to get the sand off her arms, where it stuck to the sweat and the SPF 50 sun block she'd put there. She wondered how Jacob and Father Thomas could stand long pants in this heat. They all hoped for a breeze to cool them off.

Carefully, they approached the large boulders, looking for Trinity soldiers. Suddenly, shots rang out. They ducked. Jacob stole a look toward the direction of the Kanuri but couldn't see anyone. If the soldiers were just behind them, they must have gotten past the Kanuri.

Nearby, Orfeo directed his men toward the boulder that Jacob and the others hid behind. They'd lost at least 10 men to the Kanuri, but in addition to Orfeo and Gustav, five Trinity soldiers were still alive.

Jacob, Amy and Father Thomas went around the boulder. More shots hit the ground and splintered rock off around them. Amy and Jacob ran for the far side of the boulder, seeing several other rock outcroppings in that direction that would give them additional cover and give them some time to determine where the shots were coming from.

Father Thomas hesitated. Shots peppered the ground around him. More shots seemed to be hitting in front of him so he retreated, trying to find cover behind them and around the other side of the boulder.

Without intending to do so, Trinity had split them up. Amy and Jacob were so focused on their own escape that neither of them realized that Father Thomas was not right behind Jacob.

Orfeo, perched on top of a large boulder, saw what was happening. He scrambled down the rock and pointed to Gustav, indicating that he should follow him. They were going after Father Thomas.

In the meantime, Amy and Jacob ran through a small trail created by two of the large stone outcroppings and finally found a place to hide, under an overhang. When they got there, they both expected to see Father Thomas right behind, but he wasn't there.

Jacob whispered, "Father Thomas?"

"We lost him."

"Damn him," said Jacob, as he peered out from their hiding place, hoping to get a glimpse of him. Where was he?

Then Jacob saw movement out of the corner of his eye. Was it Father Thomas? The movement came into sight, and it was a pair of Trinity soldiers.

Amy and Jacob crouched down but peered over the rocks. The soldiers were behind them, on top of the rocks, on the other side of the small trail they'd just left, meaning that they were still 40 or 50 feet away. They jumped from rock to rock and then stopped. One of the Trinity soldiers signaled to the other. They too stopped, crouching on top of the rock, surveying the area. They had lost them. At least for the moment. But Amy and Jacob were trapped. The rock overhang they had found was a trap—there was only one way out, and Trinity soldiers now guarded that.

Suddenly, the overhang reverberated with an unmistakable rattle. The sound seemed to come from everywhere. Before Jacob could determine where it was, he knew that no single snake could create what they were hearing. No, this was the Mormon Tabernacle choir of snakes. Amy grabbed onto Jacob's hand, her fingers digging so deeply into his skin that he had to suppress the urge to yelp. They slowly turned around.

As Jacob suspected, it wasn't one rattlesnake. And it wasn't two. Actually, it was hard to tell how many it was because they were everywhere, seemingly staring at them. It didn't take a genius to figure out that they were really pissed. The closest one was no more than five feet away, and it was slithering toward them.

That was all Amy needed. She probably would have jumped off the Grand Canyon to get out of there, which is what running back the way they'd come was similar to. Jacob didn't have much choice but to follow. All he could think about was that getting shot was probably better than getting poisoned.

Their advantage was surprise. And the fact that no one in their right mind would run toward trouble. Amy was 15 feet from their hiding spot before the Trinity soldiers saw her. While firing, they dropped from the rocks onto the trail that Amy ran through. They got only glimpses of her head as it bobbed above the edge of the rock.

Then Jacob was right behind her. Chunks of rock scattered into the air as bullets sped past them and tore into the boulders. Several soldiers scuttled back up the rocks, attaining high ground while the others followed Amy and Jacob down the trail. It only took a moment for three Trinity soldiers to get directly above them, looking down. But Jacob and the others were nowhere in sight. Where were they?

Amy had rounded the far side of the boulder and was making her way behind the soldiers. Jacob joined her. They were covered with sweat, panting. The soldiers had the advantage—they were above them. And Jacob had no idea how much they could see. They had to move.

Just as they started to go around the boulder, the soldiers made a huge mistake. They slid off the boulder, one coming at Jacob clockwise around the huge boulder and the other coming for Amy, counter clockwise.

In the meantime, Father Thomas, who was closer to Amy and Jacob than any of them realized, ran into the teeth of the gunshots but managed to get through unharmed. He stopped behind a rock, trying to get his bearings. Amy and Jacob were out of sight. He wasn't sure where they'd gone. He'd have to make his way in the direction they were running so he could catch up with them.

He moved around the rock and was looking for a way back from the way he'd come when Gustav and Orfeo suddenly appeared. Orfeo smiled wryly. Father Thomas could see a degree of satisfaction in Orfeo's expression.

"So, it's come to this, Frank," said Orfeo.

Father Thomas instinctively backed up, looking on the ground for a weapon, something to defend himself with. Orfeo handed his side arm to Gustav. Then he smiled.

"You're such an ass," said Father Thomas.

"Humanity brought us here. I'm going to balance it out."

"What gives you the right? You are disdaining everything the Church believes in."

Orfeo narrowed his gaze and stepped toward Father Thomas, poking at him with his index finger. "That is not what I ever believed. It is the teaching of an institution that has perverted the true Word of God! It is corrupt and interested only in fostering its version of salvation. And I will bring it down!"

"You may very well, Orfeo, but the ultimate price to pay will be when you meet your Maker."

"You know what is the most satisfying about this? I will bring about the change that the church has needed for decades!"

"By killing everyone?"

"No, Frank, the virus will not kill everyone. Those who congregate, like sheep, will get a rude surprise. They will die, seeking salvation from those who lead them astray."

Father Thomas thought for a moment, taking in what Orfeo had said. And then it came to him. "You're not going to release the virus on the world. You're going to punish those who seek redemption from their religious leaders."

"Yes, instead of seeking salvation from Judas, who speaks the truth about Jesus, or from Jesus himself. Anyone but the Catholic church."

"Or from any other church as well. My God, we've been looking in the wrong place. You've led us down the rabbit hole."

"True, but you have to admit that I am right."

"You can't kill all those people."

"But the church is lost...all of organized religion is lost."

"I would agree that the Catholic church as well as other denominations have perverted some of God's word."

"Some? What would Jesus say about discrimination against homosexuals, or Gnostics, or Hindus, or anyone who is not Christian? Would he condone excluding a class of people because of what they believe?" said Orfeo.

"I don't know, Orfeo. It is the most troubling thing about Christianity. But you can't go about it by killing people. The church has hurt its followers for decades and you are paying them back by doing the same thing. You, Orfeo, have become the thing that you despise."

"He will PRAISE me for my insight!" yelled Orfeo, as he stepped forward. Father Thomas held his ground while Orfeo slapped him, absorbing the blow. Father Thomas stared at him, daring him again to strike out. Orfeo obliged and Father Thomas did not respond.

His anger building, Orfeo balled up his fist and hit Father Thomas hard, dropping him to the ground. Orfeo stood over him, yelling.

"Come on, fight me!"

Father Thomas groaned and slowly got up. He stood in front of Orfeo and calmly moved closer to him. Orfeo flinched. With that, Father Thomas reverted to his military training. With great speed but less flexibility than when he was a young man, Father Thomas got into a *tae kwon do* stance and hit Orfeo with an overhand blow, using his right hand, and then a knife-hand blow with his left.

Orfeo, stunned by the effectiveness of the attack, reared back and lost his balance, falling to the ground. Gustav stepped forward but Orfeo raised his hand, stopping him.

Orfeo grabbed some sand, and as Father Thomas leaned in for another attack, threw it in his face, temporarily blinding him. Orfeo leapt to his feet and hit Father Thomas in the nose. Immediately, blood dripped from his nose onto his shirt. Father Thomas wiped the blood off and lashed out with a kick to Orfeo's chest. The blow landed just below where it should have. A sharp pain to his groin area dropped Father Thomas to the ground, alongside Orfeo, who lay on his stomach.

Father Thomas slowly pulled himself up, holding his groin. He failed to see Orfeo take something from his pocket and hold it to his chest. He stood over Orfeo, who wasn't moving. For a moment, he wondered if he'd killed him. He jostled Orfeo's body. Orfeo's eyes were closed. While he may have hated the man, he didn't want to be the cause of his death.

Unfortunately, Orfeo did not have any such compunction. Sensing Father Thomas stood over him, Orfeo rolled over and plunged the knife he had extracted from his pocket into Father Thomas's chest. Father Thomas, stunned by the blow, reared back, a look of surprise and shock on his face.

Orfeo leered at Father Thomas and jumped to his feet, the joy of his treachery acting like adrenalin. Father Thomas tried to keep his balance as he clawed at the knife, stepping backwards and finally falling to his knees. Orfeo bent over, pulling Father Thomas's face up so that he could look into his eyes.

"I should have done this years ago," said Orfeo, as he pulled the knife from Father Thomas' chest. Blood gushed from the wound. Father Thomas fell forward.

In the meantime, Jacob and Amy worked their way around the boulder, unaware that Trinity soldiers were coming at them from both sides. Jacob led while Amy followed.

Jacob saw the tip of the AR as the soldier rounded the corner. He knew immediately what they were doing. He grabbed the gun, violently shoving it away from them, while yelling, "Behind you!"

Amy spun around and hit the soldier hard, with a couple of overhand shots with her right hand. She surprised herself, using a couple of moves she learned in kickboxing. The soldier was too stunned to hit her back, much less pull the trigger on his gun.

When Jacob grabbed the barrel, he pushed the gun toward the oncoming soldier and away from the boulder. He hoped Amy would do the same thing or they'd both get shot.

She did. The soldier, startled when he heard the rapid fire from his comrade's AR, wasn't expecting a frontal assault. He too fired, but Amy had pushed the gun's barrel to the right, causing the shots to ricochet off the nearby rocks. Using the natural leverage of her weight and momentum, while Amy pushed the gun to the side, she ran right at the soldier. He couldn't hold onto the gun, due to the angle and the force of her attack. She yanked it from the startled soldier and threw it aside, crashing her left shoulder into his chest.

Meanwhile, Jacob did the same thing, except when he hit the soldier, he delivered a strong blow to the man's nose, driving the bone into his skull and killing him instantly. He turned to see the soldier pushing Amy off.

The soldier drew back his balled fist and charged her, his anger palpable. She cringed and went low, driving her shoulder into his knees.

Instead of hitting her, the guy flew over her and hit the rock behind. His body went limp and slid to the ground. Jacob pulled her up. "You OK?" he asked.

She nodded. With alarm in his voice, Jacob said, "Father Thomas."

UNITED NATIONS

Carmela walked down the hallway of a remote part of the UN and ducked into a doorway. She glanced around. She was alone. Quickly, she withdrew her cell phone and dialed.

"It's me. We're made."

She hung up.

MILWAUKEE, WISCONSIN

By the time Jackson and Father John got to Milwaukee, they had discussed Jackson's transformation, which was hard for both of them to believe. Father John hadn't known that Jackson was a thief, a narcissist and a vagabond. He learned how he'd been a respectable business person, how he'd lost everything, including his family, and hated everyone for it, how he'd turned to drugs and focused his anger on the world for what had happened to him. Jackson knew that the dream had changed everything, including his vision of his life and his relationship to those around him. But it was hard for him to pinpoint what the apparition said that gave him assurance that it was real. He knew it was real, that the message was one he could not ignore, even if he wasn't so sure what the message was. But as Father John recognized, if a being spoke to him, he'd probably feel obligated to do its bidding as well.

They went to Father John's church and found it abandoned by the clergy. There were a lot of people waiting in the church, seeking answers. Father John spoke with them briefly, but it was Jackson who immediately got their attention. While Father John waited, Jackson addressed the congregation. It was a completely odd experience for Father John and for Jackson, who told him later that he didn't understand where the words he spoke came from.

"It isn't about any institution or what they might tell you that is important," he was saying. "Those things are not bad, but they are not necessary for you to reach salvation. Even this beautiful church and Father John are not necessary. Faith is individual. It is up to each of us to determine what it means—not based on what others say it is, but on what YOU think it is. You may use texts, such as the Bible, as a guide.

But redemption is individual. This is what God expects from you, not what the Bible says it is. But there are some things that are necessary. Leading a good, moral life, caring for others and, at times, elevating others over yourself, is a pre-requisite to redemption. Whether you are Christian, Jewish, Muslim, Hindu . . . doesn't matter. God wants you to love one another and to understand the importance of preaching redemption through faith. If you do everything you can to survive the virus and fail, you will still achieve redemption if you believe that Jesus was here to guide us toward the light, the light of faith, the light of redemption, the light that is worth dying for. God is very forgiving. If you love him and one another, that is all that is necessary."

"But how do we defeat the terrorists?" asked someone from the congregation. Others in the church murmured their agreement with the question. Father John listened in the wings, just outside the sanctuary, and wondered how he would answer that question.

"We don't. Not directly. They will be defeated by their own arrogance, by their misdeeds and violence and evil ways. You will be rewarded for not bowing to them. Believe in what HE has taught you and in yourselves, and you will survive."

The crowd was quiet, taking in what he said. It occurred to Father John that he made a lot of sense, that the Church would not approve of his message, nor would many organized religions. The beauty of his message was that Jesus provided guidance, but ultimately, it was up to the individual to decide how to live. It was interesting, he thought, that this strange man suddenly had the ability to pronounce simple but brilliant blueprints for faith. He knew that if he asked Jackson where he got "that" from, he wouldn't know. The more he listened to him, the more he heard things that Jesus might say to this audience. Who else would tell people that his death was to help people see that salvation could be achieved if one was prepared to die for God, for the belief that we all will be "OK" if we understand and live by one simple rule: there is but one God, the Father of all of us, and don't let anyone tell you anything differently?

As Father John listened to Jackson, he realized that his destiny was here, with Jackson, ministering to the people along with him, another version of Peter's ministry in Jesus' name. That thought hit him like a brick. Did he really believe that his role was as a disciple to the Word of Jackson? The thought made him giggle. Could it be that Jesus would choose this unlikely, worn out, misdirected and immoral person to communicate his message to the world, at a time when the need for salvation was grave?

He realized that he heard clapping coming from the church. Jackson was done, and the congregation was on its feet. Father John stood over to the side and now, Jackson motioned him to the pulpit and Father John obliged him. When he looked at Jackson, once again, he saw something in his face that was simply mesmerizing—a kind of peace and tranquility, a kindness and wisdom that would inspire a person to follow him anywhere because they would all KNOW that he could save them.

He was right, it was HIM. Here, now. Speaking through Jackson. Holy shit.

———

Oasis

Orfeo, with his back to Father Thomas, hung up his cell phone and started to walk away when he heard Father Thomas moving. He turned around.

His voice harsh as he gasped for air, Father Thomas said, "Why did you do it?"

"We've let people down. The Church has been in the business of telling people what to believe for centuries, and look what it's gotten us. Suffering, sin, a dying world."

Father Thomas fought the onslaught of death. He started to see odd colors and a distant light approaching. He had one more thing to say before he left the bounds of earth. He hoped he had the energy.

"You . . are not fighting the Church. You're fighting your past. It . . . controls . . . you." Father Thomas coughed. He closed his eyes but as he did so, he did something unexpected. He gave Orfeo the finger. Then his arm fell to his side.

Orfeo let out a raucous laugh. "We'd better leave," he said to Gustav. "Our operatives should be nearly in position to release the virus. Make sure they are on high alert."

"They will never find the release points," commented Gustav.

"I agree. There are only two days left."

With that, the two of them ran for their jeep, hidden nearby, and left the desert. When Jacob and Amy heard the sound of the engine, they quickened their pace. After rounding one of the many rock outcroppings, they came upon Father Thomas.

A sick, deep dread pounded inside Jacob when he saw the bloody form of his dear friend. He kneeled by his side, next to his head. Father Thomas barely opened his eyes.

"Hang in there, old man. It's not that bad," said Jacob. Amy took one look at the blood pouring out of the wound and could only conclude that death was seconds away.

Father Thomas gathered his strength, and whispered, "Jacob, you get that son-of-a bitch." Jacob couldn't help but crack a smile.

Father Thomas coughed and spit up blood. Jacob felt tears flowing down his face. He tried to say something, but the words wouldn't come. He grabbed Father Thomas's hand.

"Old friend . . ." muttered Jacob.

Father Thomas reached deep inside himself and found enough strength to reach up and pull Jacob down so that he could whisper in his ear. "St. Peter's . . . Quba Mosque, Belz . . . Jerusalem . . ."

Suddenly, he stopped breathing. Jacob sat there, holding his head in his hands.

For the first time since her sister died, Amy allowed herself to experience the emotion of the moment. She put her arm around Jacob and rubbed his arm. She allowed herself to cry.

"He died for us, Jacob, for everyone," she said, between tears. Suddenly, Amy felt anger. She clenched her fists and rose quickly, the anger etched across her face.

Jacob wondered what Father Thomas had meant to say, those words . . . just words, with no apparent meaning.

A short time later, Jacob and Amy, still stunned from the death of Father Thomas, stood on a large sand dune, looking out into the expanse of the Sahara desert.

"We could wait in the oasis for help. At least we have water there," said Amy.

"What chance do we have to get back in time to defeat Orfeo?"

"We don't have the answers to do that anyway."

Jacob thought for a moment. "We have to find him."

Amy didn't say anything but she didn't move either.

"Orfeo didn't have to kill us. The desert will," said Jacob.

They trudged on, with Jacob carrying the backpack, with no water and certain death ahead of them. They'd checked their jeep for the water canteens they brought with them, but they were gone. Orfeo had thought of everything.

After walking for only an hour, Jacob and Amy had lost at least several quarts of water, through sweat and evaporation. Jacob had given Amy his long sleeve shirt, to help block the sun. He wore only a t-shirt. The hot sun, beating down, sucked the life from them. It hadn't taken long for the sun to split their lips and burn and chap their skin, including anything that was exposed. Jacob pulled a couple of hats out of his backpack, and they each wore one, along with sunglasses, to cut the glare. But this only gave them a little more time with no water nor any shelter in sight.

They felt their limbs grow heavy, and their sight, fuzzy and unfocused. The sun blistered their foreheads. Amy's eyelids felt heavy, as if they were swollen. She didn't want to admit to Jacob that she was ready to give in to death, that she had lost the will to live. Yet, there was nothing about this that felt wrong. Melissa had accused her of being an "ice queen." She denied it, of course, but Melissa was right. Everything that she did in life was designed to avoid emotions. Jacob gave her the opportunity to express herself, but when he had entered her life in the past, she was relieved when he left. Now, she was too busy seeking revenge to think about how lucky she was that he was back.

With the backpack slung over his shoulder and Amy's hand in his, Jacob worked as hard or harder than he'd ever worked just to put one foot in front of the other. When they hiked up a small dune, it felt as though they were trudging up the side of a mountain, gaining several thousand feet of elevation, when in fact, the dune was only 20 feet above where they'd just been.

Amy lost her footing, and Jacob couldn't hold on. She rolled down the hill. Jacob went after her, barely able to maintain his balance. After they stopped, they sat on the sand for a couple of minutes.

"I don't think we're going to make it," said Jacob.

"Bullshit. We're only a couple of miles from the next village."

"We don't have any water. I'm seeing things . . ."

"You're not giving up on me. Now get up."

Jacob stared off into the distance, still not moving. He looked at Amy. "I . . . he was my best friend."

Amy took his arm and caressed it.

"I should have been there for him."

Amy removed her hand from Jacob's arm and tried to act miffed, distant. She felt conflicted, unsure how to act. Her anger over Melissa's death had a new target, and she'd let him get away. She hated to admit it, but she wanted to rekindle her relationship with Jacob. But she wasn't ready to let him know that. Now, in the face of death, she questioned that decision. Maybe she should try to settle things now.

Amy said, "Why did you leave?"

Jacob just stared for a moment, not wanting to answer the question. Then, he said, "Now is not the time."

"That was the problem. It's never the time."

"It's hard to . . ." Jacob's thoughts wandered. He didn't know how to answer her because there was nothing to say that would lessen the wrongness of what he'd done. He should have been a man about it and told her why he was leaving. Instead, he avoided the situation and ran, like a scared kid. It was embarrassing. But he knew what he needed to say. He might not get another chance.

"I don't think you know how to love yourself. But I wanted to love you."

Amy didn't answer. She looked forward as if Jacob had never said anything.

"Your life is work. You can't survive doing that. If we get out of this..."

She still didn't answer, but then again, he hadn't answered her question, either. He shouldn't have left without talking to her. He realized that she only wanted an apology. But he thought he'd done that. Maybe he'd blown it. If he had, at least he told her before they succumbed to the desert.

"I have no idea where we're going," said Jacob.

"I know."

"I told you I did."

"Yeah."

They sat there for a moment, the silence between them filled with unstated feelings and intentions. But there was something different about them, an imperceptible shift in the way they related to each other, as if a breeze carried something in the air that was necessary. They could feel it—this shift—so that when Jacob reached for Amy's hand, she was already reaching for his.

He put his arm around her and pulled her closer. She willingly moved closer. It was ironic, Jacob thought, that the glaring sun bore down on them with such intensity that it would surely kill them, but it was also necessary to sustain life. And it was even more ironic that he was facing certain death with someone who he truly cared about but didn't have the guts to tell her. Shielding his eyes, he looked up.

"What?" Amy asked.

"Nothing. It's just odd—we can't live without sunlight but too much can kill you."

"Kind of like chocolate."

"Oh, believe me, there's no such thing as too much chocolate."

Jacob tried to say the words but he couldn't get them out. It might be the end. He had to say something.

"I don't . . . know how to."

"You'll get us there."

He nodded and looked one last time at the sand. They had considered taking the road back the way they'd come, but that could endanger them further, especially if Orfeo sent some of his men back to the oasis. Jacob and Amy had both seen a small village on the map in their backpack, but they had gotten so confused, they could no longer determine if they were heading in the right direction.

And so, Jacob guessed. The second time in two days. He picked a direction, got up, and with Amy's hand in his, the two stumbled forward.

The next thing Jacob remembered, he could see a large body of water ahead with water skiers and men and women in bikinis having fun on the beach. But something wasn't right. His vision was cloudy, and there was this odd image he had of a presence nearby, something that demanded his attention.

Slowly, Jacob realized that he was face down in the sand. He slowly turned over, managing to use his forearms to push himself up. Where was Amy? She was face up, next to him, her eyes closed. But that wasn't the presence. Suddenly, he realized that something was creating a large shadow. He looked up and saw a huge beast—a camel—and a man with weather-beaten hands who was reaching for him.

Jacob slowly reached for the hands but collapsed before he could make contact.

———

Vatican

Orfeo made his final preparations. Those who would release the virus had been dispatched to locations that so far, no one in the world had been able to deduce. He smiled at his intelligence, at how thoroughly he had dominated his oppressors.

He stood in his office, looking out his window onto St. Peter's square. He had never felt so at peace with himself. He was in complete control, for the first time in his life, over everything and everyone who could hurt him. Even Gustav was controlled, although he didn't know it. And those of his followers who had sought Gustav's serum—they, too, were under his control. He worried that when he agreed to Gustav's request to inoculate Trinity soldiers, that not only Gustav, but other Trinity members would wonder about his resolve, his faith. But his plan to deal with Gustav's deception would be finalized in the next couple of days.

Orfeo knew about the large stash of serum that Gustav had commissioned. He played dumb, of course, because it suited him. And his plans. The poor bastards that had asked for the serum didn't know that the injections contained not the serum but a weak solution of the virus, sure to kill them in the next 72 hours, when the virus would be taking victims all over the world.

Poor Gustav, even he would die from the virus. Or maybe his faith would save him. Maybe they all would prove their faith by surviving. That was the true test, wasn't it? It was faith in Orfeo that he sought. Orfeo, the one and only King.

His plan to unleash the deadly toxin on the world had its origins in the Judas Gospel and Gnosticism. But the truth was that he had the picture of his mother in his mind when he concocted the plan, the mother who had allowed his father to beat him and her and had made his life unbearable. She couldn't do anything to protect either of them. Now, he would get his revenge.

CHAPTER XIII

"Let the wicked fall onto their own nets" (Ps. 141:10).

"I have not spoken these things of myself but from the Father who sent Me" (John 12:49).

DAY SIX

Amy and Jacob slept on cots in a mud banco, their faces red and pocked with burns from the hot sun. Amy was dressed in a tobe—a colorful wrap worn by native Kanuri women. A young black woman, similarly dressed, washed Amy and Jacob's clothes in a sink made out of a large tree trunk. The banco, the size of a large, single car garage, was windowless, letting in, however, slivers of light through the roof.

Amy stirred, opening her eyes to see those slivers of light. Nearby, she saw the young black woman. The scene seemed so surreal that, for a moment, she wondered if she was dead. Then, the woman brought her some water. The woman helped Amy sit up. She dipped a mug, made out of a tree root, into the water and gave it to Amy, who tried to chug it. The woman gently pulled the mug away, indicating that she had to drink more slowly. Then, she rubbed her stomach and shook her head disapprovingly, as if to tell her that drinking the water too quickly would upset her stomach. Amy nodded and slowly drank the water.

Amy glanced over to a cot nearby where Jacob was just pulling himself up into a seated position on the edge of the bed. A black man, dressed in a jellaba, took the water basin from his wife and gave some to Jacob. He drank it slowly and nodded his thanks.

Jacob looked around the banco, marveling at its small but efficient size. The man standing near him smiled broadly, as did his wife. Jacob didn't realize that he was wearing a jellaba until he saw the woman taking his and Amy's clothes outside to dry. He was about ready to get up when he noticed that Amy was starring at him. She had a wry smile on her face.

"What?" he said.

Her smile grew wider. "I never knew," she said.

"Never knew what?"

"That you are a cross dresser."

"Yeah, well, at least they put some clothes on me. You don't look that great either, sister," which was a lie, because she did look great. She sat on the edge of the bed with the wrap open at mid-thigh. Jacob couldn't help but stare at her legs. And they'd washed her hair. Her face had a fresh, vital look to it that he hadn't seen before.

And then reality hit. How long had they been out? How much time did they have left? "Any idea how long we've been out?"

Amy shook her head. The black woman came back inside the banco just as Amy tried unsteadily to get up. She almost lost her balance until the woman helped her but frowned. She didn't speak any English but obviously didn't approve of Amy's decision to get up.

Jacob asked, "How long have we been here?" She shook her head from side to side. The woman pointed to the banco's door and motioned for Jacob to go outside. Jacob did as instructed, followed by Amy.

The bright, hot sun momentarily stunned them. Once their eyes got used to the light, they could see that they were in a small village of similar-looking bancos. On the far end of the village was a larger stone house. Jacob had assumed that the woman was indicating that her husband, who stood outside the house, might understand them. Jacob turned to the man and said, "We need a phone."

The man shook his head from side to side. "Great. The world hangs in the balance and we can't find anyone who speaks English," said Jacob.

"I hate to be the bearer of bad news, but we don't have any leads. We're fresh out," said Amy.

"I'm not done yet."

The man indicated that they should follow him; he took them to the larger, stone structure and using his hands, indicated that they should wait outside. The man went inside and Jacob paced. He was getting more and more agitated, wondering how much time they had left.

"Jacob, none of the things that we've done has gotten us any closer to the bastard that killed my sister."

"So revenge is more important than finding the release points and stopping Trinity? What are we really doing here, trying to defeat these crazy wackos or satisfying you?"

Amy got in his face, her eyes on fire. "What I'm doing here is none of your business!"

"It is if you're not focused on the true objective."

"The objective is Orfeo!"

"It's not just him. It's all of Trinity."

Amy felt the anger rising inside of her. "I WILL kill that son-of-a-bitch!"

Jacob nodded, surprised at her outburst. He actually smiled.

"What the hell are you smiling about?" she asked.

He ignored her, looking across to the other side of the village where some kids were stacking old tires. It looked as though they were trying to make a fort. One of the walls they were building collapsed. The tires hit the ground, and three of them landed in what looked like a replica of Borromean rings.

When the door behind him opened again, the Kanuri was with another man who was dressed in a brighter jellaba than the villager who had helped him and Amy. This man must be the village's leader, thought Jacob.

Jacob put his hand to his ear, as if he was talking on the phone. Amy leaned into him. "You realize that he may have never seen a phone," said Amy.

The man pointed. Both Amy and Jacob followed his outstretched arm and saw a road heading out of the village. The Kanuri spoke to each other in their native language. The Kanuri who had helped them motioned for them to follow him back to his banco. Once they got there, he motioned them down with his hands. Jacob and Amy took a seat on two homemade stools outside the banco.

"So, what are we waiting for?" asked Amy.

"I have no idea. Hopefully, a way to get to the phone."

Amy got up and headed inside the banco.

"Where are you going?" asked Jacob.

"To get our research. Maybe we'll see something we missed."

Jacob turned back toward the tires on the other end of the village and stared at the three tires, still sitting on the ground, still looking a lot like Borromean rings. He couldn't take his eyes off of them, hoping that he would see something. And then it hit him.

Amy came out of the banco, and Jacob grabbed the backpack out of her hand. "Excuse me . . ." she said, sarcastically.

Jacob pulled materials out of the backpack, including the maps and the Judas Gospel. Nearby was a small table. Jacob pulled the table closer and plopped the maps on top of it. He opened the map with the old—fashioned map on one side, the one where he'd drawn the third circle over the other two hemispheres.

"What is it?" asked Amy.

"The rings pointed us to the lab. But we still don't know where they're going to release it. God knows how much time we have. But we're looking at it incorrectly. Those tires over there—see how three of them look like Borromean rings?"

Amy looked at the tires and nodded. "Yeah, sort of."

"The rings ARE the locations, if we look at them a little differently. Like the tires. They're part of a fort until they fall over, then they're Borromean rings."

"I'm not following."

Jacob pointed to the rings on the map. "The ring that I drew is twelve inches in diameter. Where the third ring intersects the others . . ." Jacob traced the ring with his finger and pointed out each place where the rings crossed.

"The release points?" asked Amy.

Jacob flipped the map over to the modern map. He traced the outer edges of the map, where the degrees in longitude and latitude are written. "If you divide the circle into equal parts, you end up with the number 12. The Zodiac."

Jacob was getting her attention. Maybe he was on to something. "Which has its origins as a religious symbol. But, why . . ." she said.

"The modern Zodiac, anyway, has twelve signs, which is the number of disciples. The number 360 is prevalent in the Judas Gospel and there's 360 degrees in a circle."

Jacob, in a flurry of recognition, marked off the outer edges of the map, starting at zero degrees and then every 30 degrees until he had 12 marks on the map. He then drew lines from the edges across the map, from one side to the other. Then he took the pencil with the nylon string attached and placed the apex at 5 degrees north. From there, he drew a perfectly round circle that intersected with the lines he just drew. The circle crossed the lines in the Congo, Africa; Egypt, near Cairo; and off the eastern coast of Florida and the western coast of Ecuador.

Finally, Amy could see what Jacob saw. "We use the points where the lines cross to get the exact minutes and seconds. Jacob, I think you've got the release points."

"We've got to get this to the UN," said Jacob.

Jacob and Amy got up and pulled their clothes off the line, wondering if they'd be dry and somewhat surprised that they were. Amy went inside to change, but Jacob put his pants on underneath the jellaba and then took it off and put his shirt on. Amy came out of the banco, tucking her t-shirt into her shorts. At that moment, they heard the most beautiful thing—the sound of an internal combustion engine. The Kanuri from the stone house drove up in an old jeep. He stopped next the banco, sporting a huge smile. He motioned for them to get into the jeep. Amy and Jacob grabbed their belongings, gave their respects to the Kanuri who saved them and took off.

A short time later, after traveling along the sand-and-stone road from the village, they emerged in the town of Faya-Largeau. By now, it was afternoon, the sun beat down mercilessly and they still had no idea how much time they had left. It was driving Jacob crazy. They might be too late already.

If Faya-Largeau didn't have an embassy, how would they contact the UN? What if it was day seven? Jacob hadn't shaved in a long time so he couldn't use facial hair growth to make an educated guess. They didn't have anything.

The jeep stopped in the middle of town, and the Kanuri waived to them as he drove off. Amy and Jacob look around and were shocked to see that the man had dropped them near the American Embassy. It was amazing how well they had non-verbally communicated with each other.

Inside, the embassy was small and messy. Amy and Jacob stood in front of an empty desk and then paced anxiously. Finally, a man came down a hall. Amy and Jacob rushed toward him. The man reared back, clearly shocked that anyone was there.

"We need your help," said Jacob.

The man gathered himself and motioned to them as he turned. "Follow me." The man took them down the hall to another office. He had barely entered when Amy and Jacob hurriedly followed him inside, their sense of urgency readily apparent.

The man turned to them. "I'm Martin Hathaway, the American Consulate for this region. What can I do for you?"

"We're working with the UN to find Trinity, the release points for the virus," said Jacob, the words stumbling out of his mouth.

"What day is it?" asked Amy. Hathaway started to answer when Amy saw the calendar on the wall and motioned to it. Jacob saw it as well. The day of the week was circled in red, the days gone by, crossed out.

"It's day 6," Jacob lamented.

"Or what's left of it," said Amy.

"I wasn't aware that anyone from the UN was here," said Hathaway.

"Listen, we don't have much time. We found the lab where Trinity made the virus. We lost all of the UN troops that came with us. Trinity thinks we're dead. And we have vital information about the release points. I must speak with the president. NOW!" Jacob implored.

Hathaway stared at them for a moment. Apparently, Jacob's raised voice garnered more attention than he wanted because at that moment, an MP entered the office, his hand resting on his firearm. Both Amy and Jacob whipped their heads around and then returned their attention to Hathaway, who continued to consider his next move.

Hathaway waved off the MP and handed Jacob his satellite phone. "If you're not who you say you are, I'll know in a minute."

Jacob quickly dialed an emergency number that he'd been given. Carmella answered.

"Carmella? It's Jacob."

"My God, Jacob, we thought you were dead."

"I don't have much time. We found the lab. We think we know the locations of the release points. Anything from the Vatican?"

"They've identified 20-30 possible release points."

"Jesus. There's no way you can cover all of those."

"We're trying. With the cooperation of the UN, every country in the world is on this. You realize that day seven is upon us."

"Yeah. Listen, here's the list of the locations we've uncovered."

Jacob took the list from Amy and read them off to Carmela, who acted as if she was writing them down. "Ok, I'll tell the president. He's in a meeting right now. Hang on in case he wants to speak with you."

Carmela hurried from her office into the adjoining room, where Holcomb, his assistant chief of staff, Mike Peterson, the head of Homeland Security, the general and the UN Security Council were staring at a video monitor displaying a large map, containing 20-30 red circles, representing the possible release points the scholars at the Vatican had discovered. They watched the progress of teams who were locating those release points and looking for any evidence of Trinity's presence. The scholars stood behind the Security Council, along with several officials from the World Health Organization (WHO). On another screen played a constant stream of news updates from around the world, mostly focusing on the different ways people dealt with the fear of death.

Carmela gave fake location numbers to Holcomb and whispered in his ear that Amy and Jacob had just called and given her these locations. Holcomb pulled back, surprised that they were still alive. He took her aside.

"Where have they been?"

"I didn't have time to ask."

Holcomb handed the locations to the general's aide who started entering them into the computer. The general tapped the screen and the video display changed, showing not the new coordinates that

Carmela had given him, but rather locations in Russia, Great Britain, South America, the United States and Italy that pulsated red. Holcomb turned his attention to the video monitor.

"Within the last hour, troops have landed at each of these locations."

"Any evidence of Trinity?" asked the British representative.

The General shook his head from side-to-side.

"We're running out of time," said the British representative.

The TV monitor continued to show religious gatherings, some taking place at churches, others at whatever location was handy. The screen flashed to a riot on the streets of Italy, one in Spain and several throughout the United States. Local police and military troops attempted to quell the uprisings, hoping to calm people down without injuring or killing them. But many were unsuccessful.

In a large building outside of Moscow, a reporter stood by while bodies were removed from a mass suicide. Nearly 100 people had killed themselves. A banner on the bottom of the screen reported that the number of suicides had increased worldwide as the seventh day approached. The numbers exceeded 20,000.

Holcomb had instructed officials to warn people to stay indoors and not to panic. But nearly everyone DID panic. How does one prepare for the end when one knows when it is? There was little Holcomb could do, and he knew it. He hated the feeling of utter hopelessness. For a moment, all he could see were the images flashing across the screen. Was it really the end of the world? If it was, that would be sometime soon after tomorrow. What did it mean to die? Would there be something after death? Most mainstream religions taught the existence of an afterlife. It just didn't seem possible that any of this was really happening.

Holcomb turned to the WHO representative. "Have you calculated the death rate?"

The WHO official moved to the computer and hit some keys. The display on the monitor changed and a blue light, near Rome, began to pulsate next to the red light.

"Based on what we know, if the virus were released at the train station . . . as in Trinity's video demonstration, we have to assume it will be released as a gas. That makes it easy to distribute and very difficult to stop. If only 25 people get infected, in 24 hours, the disease will spread tenfold."

The WHO representative hit another button on the keyboard, and the screen displayed a large yellow area near Rome. "That would be the initial spread of the disease." He was about to hit another key but paused. "This is what would happen after 48 hours."

He hit the button and the yellow area tripled in size. Holcomb could sense an almost audible gasp in the room, as if the reality had become more real by seeing the results than simply talking about what could happen.

"What's the bottom line?" asked Holcomb.

"In 3 days, over 1 million people will be infected."

No one in the room said a thing. Holcomb felt tears forming and tried to hold them back. Everyone in the room had the same, vacant, defeated look on their faces.

The Belgium representative managed to gather himself, saying, "Isn't there a way to contain it?"

The WHO official shook his head. "We're still working on it, but as of now, no. It's the most volatile and deadly virus we've ever encountered. It makes the Ebola virus look like the common cold."

Holcomb hated feeling helpless. He moved over to the lone window in the conference room and opened the blinds. On the street below were hundreds of protestors, holding signs, professing the end of the world, encouraging people to confess their sins and to ready themselves to meet their Maker. A speaker on a makeshift stage egged them on. Many of them had gathered at the UN's entrance, trying to storm the building, trying to accomplish what, Holcomb didn't know. He'd heard that many people thought that the government had the cure but was hoarding it for a select few. Well-armed troops kept the hoards at bay, but the result of their violent confrontation was displayed for the world to see. Wrecked cars, some of which were burning, littered the street. The dead and wounded lay ignored on the sidewalks and streets.

With approximately one day left until what might be the end, Holcomb had been inundated with national problems that were duplicated around the world. There were mass suicides all over the United States, looting, massive unrest, demonstrations, religious fanatics claiming to have the answers but demanding people's houses and possessions to provide them, and not enough police or troops to keep order. The thing that bothered him the most were the charlatans taking people's money in exchange for the promise of salvation. People were desperate, uncertain if they could be saved, and if they could, what that "looked" like. So they paid anything to get answers. The problem existed in every country in the world.

In Chicago, New York, Los Angeles and every other major city in the United States, highways were clogged with cars escaping to an imaginary place where people believed they would survive the virus. Many people literally camped in churches. New churches sprang up to deal with the overcrowding. The stock market in every country had completely collapsed. Everyone was broke. Every government, every person was the same. So, even if they survived the virus, everyone had to start over. It was as if the planet had regressed to some time pre- 20th century. Of course, those with cash, did OK. Those whose wealth was tied to other assets had lost everything. Many CEOs had committed suicide. Billion dollar companies were now worth nothing. Holcomb wondered if they survived, how they would recover from the massive worldwide panic.

How in the hell had they come to this? Perhaps this was man's true test– how he dealt with the end. How many of them would prove worthy? Not many, based on what Holcomb saw unfolding.

CHAPTER XIV

"He that is the least among you shall be great" (Luke 9:48).

DAY 7

VATICAN CATACOMBS

Inside a large, darkly lit room in the catacombs underneath the Vatican, 100 Trinity members stood in line, waiting for their injection. At the head of the line stood Gustav. Orfeo was due back within the hour. Gustav hurried the doctors at the front of the line. Even though Orfeo had finally agreed to the inoculations, Gustav was suspicious. Orfeo's reversal surprised Gustav, and now he worried that he had a plan. With these inoculations, all of Trinity would be safe, or so they believed.

As they stood there, Trinity was in place at the release points, ready to deploy the virus. Those members had been inoculated two days ago. Once the inoculation was completed, Gustav had instructed the doctors to store the thousands of vials they had produced in a secret room in the catacombs, in a huge refrigeration unit. Getting the unit into the catacombs had proven to be a bit of a challenge, but he pulled it off, in part because Orfeo had given him so much authority. Orfeo had never authorized the production of more serum than was needed. Gustav wondered if and when Orfeo would discover his deception.

With the serum in storage, he had a stockpile of the cure that would catapult him to the power he dreamed of. The more he thought about the power he could wield as the owner of the serum that could save the world, the more he wanted it. And he appreciated the importance of keeping the makers of the serum close to him. The scientists who worked on the cure were close associates of Gustav's and believed in his vision, muddy though it may have been. Those in the lab he commissioned, using money he stole from the Vatican, had all died in a bizarre accident, one that he devised. Oddly, he did not feel guilty about this. He had become so convinced in the righteousness of his actions that the immorality of it was too blurred to be recognizable.

He hoped he could keep it from Orfeo long enough to give his plan a running start. Then it would have a life of it's own, and Orfeo could do nothing to stop him. But the inoculations that Orfeo had authorized puzzled Gustav. If Orfeo believed as he professed, why would he allow his followers to exhibit what, to him, must appear to be a lack of faith? Was he hedging his bets, or was this a test of faith of another sort—faith in Orfeo, as their leader. Perhaps he never really intended anyone to survive the virus, cleansing the earth of nearly everyone. Perhaps he was just as crazy as the rest of the world viewed him.

All but several of the most devote had been inoculated as well. Certain close followers of Orfeo's teachings truly believed that their faith would save them from anything. When Orfeo had started, there were many like this. But as the day when they would release the virus drew close, some lost their resolve.

None of the scientists who discovered and manufactured the virus had allowed themselves to be exposed to the virus. Their research facility had been carefully constructed to contain any contamination. Many of them wondered about Orfeo's sanity, once he declared his plan. He expected all of them to face the virus without any protection, yet he had insisted on it when they were making more of the virus. In fact, the scientists found Orfeo to be quite delusional with respect to his declaration: faith would save anyone exposed to the virus. Several Trinity members had asked Orfeo what he meant by that, beyond the obvious reference to religious faith. Since their beliefs were rooted in Gnosticism, confusion reigned. Was it faith in that belief system that would save people, or was it some other, more esoteric "faith" that he spoke of? No one knew.

Many in Trinity thought Orfeo might be bluffing. Maybe he wouldn't release the virus. Maybe the release canisters held a non-volatile substance. Maybe he would use the threat to achieve some other goal.

When it appeared that Orfeo had correctly predicted the world's response to their threat, Trinity members were more sure than ever that he really was going to release the virus.

The world's focus would be on the Judas Gospel, he'd said, and that they would never realize that the release points had nothing to do with that document. Their deception was complete.

Northern Wisconsin; Milwaukee

Lilly sat in the pew with Bryan and Molly on either side of her. It was day seven and the church was packed. Most of the people she ran into were very scared. Some were quite confident that they would be saved. She couldn't figure out what she felt. On the one hand, she didn't want to believe that her and her children's lives could be over in the next couple of days. On the other, she had to prepare for it. Prior to the accident, she couldn't come to grips with her faith, or lack of faith, and was worried that she would perish because of it. And she worried about her kids, who seemed to have a better handle on this than she did. Sometimes, being young and inexperienced made things so much simpler. Knowledge wasn't always power.

She looked around at the people in the church. It was interesting how all these people, seemingly seeking salvation in the same manner, failed to realize that being in this place together didn't mean that they all believed the same things. She had overheard many of them talking before they took their seats in this sanctuary. She remembered a young couple with a baby who were hysterical. There wasn't anything that could help them. Fear was too powerful.

An elderly couple was expectedly mature about the whole thing, acting as if the church service was "nice" but not necessary. They were confident, Lilly could tell, in their ability to survive almost anything. The husband had made a comment that was particularly odd. "The virus can't kill us," he'd said. That kind of confidence could take them a long way, but Lilly wondered if it was real or just fear dressed up to look different.

The more Lilly thought about it, the more she believed that for her and her kids, it came down to something much more complicated than faith. It was redemption that most of the people in the church were seeking. Lilly realized that many of them were equating faith with forgiveness and salvation. But for Lilly to have faith, did it require her to believe in a deity or to simply believe something, no matter what it was, without being able to prove it? This is what Lilly now believed she had learned during the week that led up to the seventh day: Trinity had it all wrong. It wasn't faith that would save them—it wasn't lack of faith that would kill them. People killed people; Trinity didn't have the authority to save anyone. Lilly wasn't sure that she could be saved by God, like Bryan and Molly and many of the people in church. She was leaning more toward believing that it was the power of her own convictions and man's inventions that would save her.

And so, while she listened to the pastor talk about Jesus, God, the Bible and all that it stands for, she smiled for the first time in days. Her kids saw the smile and assumed that she had finally gotten the faith necessary to survive the virus. They took her hands in theirs and all three hugged. No matter what happened, they would be fine.

In Milwaukee, Father John couldn't have imagined what was happening. The church had been turned into Jackson's private soapbox. People came from miles to listen to him. The line outside the church went around the block. Many with life long illnesses or disabilities flocked to the church. There had even been some claimed healings. Jackson continued to talk about many of the things that Jesus had discussed during his life. In fact, he sounded like Jesus. His demeanor had changed significantly. He was calm, wise, loving and caring. He had none of those qualities before the accident.

Father John was convinced that very few people would die from the virus. God wouldn't send another prophet only to kill him off in less than a week. They would be all right.

HOTEL, FAYA-LARGEAU

Jacob stood in the shower, the warm water washing away the sweat and grime of the last several days. His thoughts strayed to Amy, wondering what she looked like in the shower, wanting to be there with her in the shower, wanting to be with her before the day was over, wondering if it might be his last chance, worried that the end might be near. It was a strange feeling. He was a strong man, sure in his beliefs and his power to withstand just about anything that the world threw at him. But would he be able to survive the virus? He knew that Father Thomas had wanted him to convert ever since he met him, that he'd worried about him and his inability or unwillingness to give himself to any belief system that didn't begin and end with Jacob Matthews.

Jacob didn't think he'd pass the test if it came to that. Of course, Amy was in a similar predicament. He didn't think that faith would save her either, assuming that there was a snowball's chance in hell that faith could possibly save the world. It was a nice thing to believe in, but for a scientist, it lacked logic; moreover, it wouldn't stand up to intellectual scrutiny of any kind. But that's what faith was like.

Jacob turned off the water and dried himself. He stepped from the shower, and for the first time in days, stared at his naked body. The shoulder wound was healing, but it looked pretty nasty. He had scrapes and gouges all over his chest and arms. He half-turned and looked at his back, finding it in similar condition.

Geez, I look like crap, he thought. When he raised his arms to dry his hair, he became aware of how stiff and sore his entire body was, not just his badly damaged shoulder. He needed a rest. Maybe just for a moment.

He stepped from the bathroom with the towel wrapped around his middle. The bed looked inviting. What more could they do anyway? They'd given the president what he needed to stop the release of the virus.

Before he could flop on the bed, there was a knock on the door. He ignored it. But then there was another knock, this one more urgent.

"Crap," he muttered.

"Jacob, it's me! Open up!"

The thoughts he had in the bathroom came back for a moment but he realized, to his embarrassment, that he was too sore for much of anything. He felt a hell of a lot older than 42.

He trudged to the door and reluctantly opened it. Amy pushed past him, her hair still damp from a shower. She had on a fresh pair of shorts and a t-shirt.

"I don't think Trinity's going to release the virus at the sites we phoned in."

Jacob looked at her with a confused daze. What the hell was she mumbling about? As he stood there, the towel slipped off his hips and fell to the ground. Amy turned to him.

"Jacob, are you listening to me? Jesus, man. This is important." She looked away and then back at him again. "And for Christ sake, put some clothes on. You look like crap."

Surprised at her outburst, Jacob muttered, "Yes ma'am," and saluted her in a mocking fashion. For a moment, he remembered their initial fling, the arranged and planned feeling of their tryst. It was one of the reasons he had left, he now realized. She was too regimented, too unwilling to let go. But there was something spontaneous and different about her now. He couldn't put his finger on it.

Jacob groaned as he bent over, picked up the towel and re-positioned it. "Now, what the hell are you talking about?"

"It's not right. The Zodiac is a Christian symbol. Trinity is Gnostic. They wouldn't use a Christian symbol to determine the release points. It's a ruse. All of this is."

Jacob plopped down on the end of the bed, his head pounded. He put his head in his hands. Amy paced back and forth in front of him. "Look, we've been over this. It fits—the Borromean Rings, the clues in the Judas Gospel. They know we're on to them or they wouldn't have stopped us—we found their lab, for Christ sake!"

Amy stopped in front of him. "Did you consider the possibility that they intended to mislead us? You're not listening to me. The whole thing was designed to get us off the trail. All the while, they've been setting up to release the virus without any threats because WE'VE been barking up the wrong tree!"

Jacob got up from the bed. He felt a new tenseness, something he used to feel in his gut when he was a kid and had screwed up.

"Mislead us?" he said.

"You know I'm right."

Jacob turned to the window in the room and stood in front of it, looking outside. He thought about what she said and felt like an idiot. How could he have missed it? The world's best code breaker had been duped by a bunch of religious fanatics.

He turned toward Amy and reluctantly nodded. "Gnostics wouldn't use a Christian symbol. I can't believe I missed that."

"There's no time for that. We've got to figure this out."

Jacob stared at the far wall, willing himself to re-evaluate everything they'd done. Quoting from the Judas Gospel had been a tactic to get them to follow a lead that would never get them close to the release points or to Trinity. Although, they must have figured that no one would ever get the right number combinations, at least not the ones that would expose their lab. That must have been a surprise to them—a miscalculation. But in spite of Orfeo's chagrin at their discovery, it only delayed Jacob, the scholars, the UN and the world from discovering the real release points. Trinity must have used the Gospel to some extent, as their lab was based on coordinates Jacob and the others had discovered, but he was certain, the more he thought about it, that they never anticipated they would get that close. Still, it took them from their real objective.

He turned the events of the last several days over and over again in his brain until it came to him in a flash. "Just before he died. Father Thomas whispered in my ear."

Jacob walked quickly toward the bed, threw the towel off and put on his underwear and pants. Amy stared at him, waiting for his revelation.

"He named off several churches," said Jacob while he pulled his shirt over his head. "What were they . . . St. Peter's, Quba Mosque, Belz."

"Those are all large places of worship."

"Catholic, Muslim, Jewish . . . "

"—They're going to attack the largest places of worship in the world," said Amy.

"Right. That's where many people will congregate, praying."

"Religious centers! It's the perfect test of faith. In a house of worship."

"And if they worship correctly . . ."

"—They will be saved!" said Amy. Amy thought for a moment. "There are a lot of churches, places of worship. How do we know which ones?"

"Orfeo hates Christianity. But it's all of organized religion he's after. St. Peter's Basilica, Basilica of Our Lady of Peace, the Ivory Coast, Belz, Israel . . ."

"Basilica of the National Shrine of the Immaculate Conception, D.C., Taj Mahal. The list is huge," said Amy, finishing Jacob's sentence.

"No, it's only the major religious centers. There can't be more than a dozen. We've got to call this in," said Jacob.

As Jacob tied his shoes, he said, "Orfeo had us pegged from the beginning. He knew we'd follow the false clues in the Judas Gospel. He's after people who follow church teachings without thinking for themselves. He gets them into their place of worship and kills them. It's sick but it's genius."

"He's getting back at those who endorse the sins of the church by seeking out church guidance in times of need. If you stay away, you might not die," said Amy.

He got up and grabbed the backpack, and the two rushed from the room.

"I thought this virus was so lethal. Won't it still spread beyond the places of worship?" asked Jacob.

They ran to the elevator, pushed the down button and waited anxiously. "Well, it depends on the virus. We believe it's very deadly but they probably know more about it than we do. Maybe they have evidence that we have yet to uncover," answered Amy.

Amy spotted the down stairs sign and motioned toward it. She and Jacob ran for the door, opened it and raced down the stairs.

Once outside, they raced down the street, heading for the American Embassy. It didn't take them more than a couple of minutes to get there. They rushed through the door, almost knocking Hathaway on his butt, and demanded the satellite phone. They both talked at once, in hurried, excited voices. Hathaway could tell it was very serious but wasn't sure what they were talking about. He led them back to his office and handed the satellite phone to Jacob, who dialed.

"Carmela?"

"Jacob, it's President Holcomb."

"Mr. President. Those coordinates I gave to Carmela. You know, one is on the coast of Florida. They're wrong."

"What are you talking about?"

"The ones I gave Carmela."

"She never told me about Florida." Thoughts raced through Holcomb's mind. Why didn't she give him this vital information? She told him that Jacob didn't have anything new to report, that the list she'd created was simply another dead end. She wrote them down just in case the president wanted to investigate them . . . that's what she said. And that's what he'd done. They had so little. They jumped at any lead that seemed plausible. She'd known they would do that. Holcomb held the phone away from his mouth for a moment and motioned to his chief of staff.

"Mike, I've got our mole. It's Carmela."

Mike reared back, the disbelief written all over his face.

"I'm sure. Get her. Now."

Holcomb put the phone back to his ear. On the other end, Jacob shook his head, not sure he heard correctly. "Jacob, it's Carmela."

"I know. I heard."

Amy stared at Jacob, seeing the color drain from his face. She finished the list of religious centers and handed it to him. "What is it?" she asked. Jacob glanced at her.

"Carmela never gave the president the locations we called in."

"What?"

On the phone, the president said, "I'm having her arrested right now. Do you have anything new for me?"

Amy crowded Jacob, her eyes beseeching him. She could see that whatever he knew, it wasn't good. He mouthed to her to wait a moment. "Mr. President, it's major religious centers of worship they're after," said Jacob.

"Have you identified which ones?"

"Yes. Amy's got it. The most obvious ones: Quba Mosque, Belz in Jerusalem, Taj Mahal."

"I assume the Vatican is a target."

"The primary one."

Mike returned and whispered that they had some men searching for Carmela right now. Holcomb told him to get the Vatican on the line.

"Mr. President, Orfeo won't be stopped," said Jacob.

"Orfeo?"

"He's Trinity's leader."

"Jesus. I'll relay that to the Pope. I need the rest of the locations." Holcomb grabbed a pen and a piece of paper.

"Okay, here they are." Jacob read them off and hung up the phone.

Amy looked as though she'd been hit in the face with a baseball bat. "It's Carmela, isn't it?"

Jacob nodded. "I'm sorry. I know you were friends."

"I just can't believe it. How could she?"

"Religion is a powerful force. So is faith."

"But to believe blindly . . ." Amy stopped herself, realizing her error. "Why wouldn't she have given the president the release points? She had to know they were false. It led them right to her."

Jacob shrugged. "Not sure, but it's possible not all of Trinity knows exactly where the virus will be released. That's how I'd do it if I were in control. In any case, we need a plane to Da Vinci International. I've got a pressing appointment with Orfeo."

———

CONFERENCE ROOM AT UN

Holcomb waited as the last person—the head of Homeland Security—entered the room. The general was there, as were all the members of the UN Security Council, WHO, the scholars and NATO officials.

"Your most sacred and prized mosques, temples, churches. Those are the release points," said Holcomb, who was concerned that this proclamation would not go over well.

The room was silent as this sunk in. Then, the Belgium representative pointed to the video monitor. "But what of those? This is getting a bit ridiculous. We're chasing all over the world. And still nothing."

"And the end date is today," said the British representative. "We've got to make a decision and stick with it."

"I understand and I agree," responded Holcomb. "But we've been duped. Besides, we've got enough manpower to check out every lead."

The representatives mumbled and protested, but in the end, they didn't have a lot of choice. Nothing had worked yet—they might as well try something else. The leaders opened their cell phones.

"The United Nations will cooperate with each of you," said the president. "Mobilize your forces and we'll coordinate a UN presence in every country that's affected."

At that moment, Carmela entered the room. She saw the members of the Security Council on their cell phones, some taking notes as they spoke.

"What's going on?" asked Carmela.

Holcomb grabbed her by the arm. "Why don't we step outside for a moment?"

She could tell that something wasn't right and for a moment, considered resisting. But there was nowhere for her to go. She followed him out of the room and noticed the Secret Service agents following them. While they walked down the hall, the Chief of Staff joined the agents, unbeknownst to Carmela.

Holcomb steeled himself for what was about to happen. "I trusted you. How could you deceive me?"

"What are you talking . . ."

Holcomb turned to her, and she glanced at him. His eyes bored into her, and her face registered resignation. She adopted a tough exterior as she prepared to go on the offensive.

"The world is a vile place, Mr. President. Cleansing it of the filth would be doing all of us a favor."

"At least have the decency to tell me if he's right."

"Right about what?"

"About the release points."

Carmela didn't answer. She wasn't about to tell him anything.

Looking disgusted, Holcomb motioned to his agents. "Get her out of my sight."

The agents took her away. Although he was glad to catch the mole, Carmela's deception was unexpected. She was one of his most trusted aides. She'd been with him since he was elected. She'd run his campaign. He couldn't fathom how this had happened, much less how she had managed to fool all of them. How could he have missed it? She must have been in constant contact with Trinity over the last six days. He tried to think of when she could have done that, but he realized that because he trusted her, he didn't need to keep track of her. That hurt more than anything . He wouldn't trust so easily the next time.

———

AMERICAN EMBASSY, FAYA-LARGEAU

Amy and Jacob sat still for a minute, after Jacob had given the information to the president. Amy hung her head, trying to control the tears. She'd lost her sister and now a friend. How could she have missed it? Amy couldn't help but think that this was partly her fault. Since they'd hung up the phone, she'd replayed in her mind the time she had spent with Carmela, racking her brain for the clues to her deceit. The only thing she could remember was the time when they were talking about a project Amy had been working on in Jerusalem. Carmela made an odd comment about how screwed up all religions were, that we could all have a personal relationship with God and that no organized religion had a corner on telling us how to worship. Then she'd said something about the world being a cesspool of sin and debauchery, that if necessary, man might have to force the issue. The comments were completely out of character for Carmela, as she never talked about religion. In fact, Amy believed that she was probably agnostic. But now, she wondered, if for a moment, she'd let her guard down, indicating how she truly felt. It sure sounded a lot like what Trinity was saying.

While Jacob continued to comfort her, Amy's resolve grew. Orfeo had killed her sister, he had corrupted her friend and he was holding the world hostage. She felt anger that she didn't know she was capable of. She hated him. She'd wanted to personally take him out. They were almost out of time. She turned to Jacob.

"Let's get the son-of-a-bitch."

CHAPTER XV

"The elder shall serve the younger" (Rom. 9:12).

VATICAN CATACOMBS

Gustav stood in the serum room, as he liked to call it, admiring his cache. Along the walls stood six huge commercial refrigerators, full of the serum. He was assured that it was enough to inoculate at least 50,000 people. And, he had the technology to produce more serum. He was feeling very pleased with himself when he sensed a presence at the door. He flipped his head around. Orfeo.

"What have you done?" said Orfeo.

"Done? I haven't done anything. Most of Trinity has been inoculated. But you knew that. There are a couple of true believers but not many."

Orfeo bristled at the thought that Gustav had defied him behind his back, that the faith he had in Trinity had been breached. He worked for years to develop Trinity into a world power, secretly attacking the morally challenged, organizations and individuals who killed unborn babies, tortured citizens in foreign countries and made life miserable for others. He never considered Trinity's acts terrorist in nature. The mysterious attacks, which Trinity never took credit for, had been debated in the press as being vigilante and outside the boundaries of a civilized society versus the kind of moral righteousness that the world was lacking. Orfeo loved the attention Trinity had gotten, even though no one knew that he was responsible for the deaths.

He thought about who they had killed. There was the abortion doctor, there was the leader in Somalia who had killed thousands of his countrymen, there was the genocidal maniac, Mariam, in

Ethiopia, who was tried in absentia for his atrocities because Trinity had killed him and several other, lesser-known evil people. Who could complain about Trinity getting rid of these people?

All of this was threatened by Gustav's actions, not because there was anyway to undo the good they had done, but because the dedication and faith in their actions was diminished by his lack of faith. But as was typical for Orfeo, he was always one step ahead of Gustav. The serum that Trinity had been given had actually been tainted with the virus—time delayed—so that it wouldn't kick in until day eight. But Orfeo never expected Gustav to outsmart him and create an untainted version.

Orfeo slammed the door behind him. "You are not going to leave here alive!" Orfeo stared at Gustav and smiled.

"What are you smiling about?"

"I must admit, I'm impressed that you had the resolve to create your own batch. You realize, of course, that the serum used to inoculate Trinity is actually tainted."

Gustav looked puzzled. Then it came to him. "You son-of-a-bitch. We've all got it, don't we?"

"It's time delayed. But yes, you have it. You won't have to worry about it, Gustav, because you're going to die today."

"I've got you by 10 years, old man."

"As if that will help you," said Orfeo as he lunged at Gustav, who stepped aside as Orfeo went by him.

Gustav looked around for a weapon and reached for a beaker sitting on a table near the far wall. He picked it up, turned and faced Orfeo, who had taken off his robe. Gustav had never seen him without his robe and was shocked at how muscular he looked.

"I work out—a lot," said Orfeo.

Maybe, but he was no match for sharp glass. Gustav cracked the beaker on the table and it shattered. Out of the corner of his eye, he saw movement. By the time he half-turned around, Orfeo was on top of him. Orfeo swung hard and hit Gustav on the side of his head, propelling him sideways, onto the table. He fell onto some of the glass that lay there, its sharp edges embedding themselves into his face and arms. Gustav yelled out and pawed at his face, trying to dislodge the glass.

Orfeo took the opportunity to hit him again, this time knocking him into one of the refrigeration units. Gustav hit his head, nearly knocking him out. He managed to get up and took a swing at Orfeo, who simply stepped aside as Gustav's momentum took him past Orfeo. He swung hard enough to nearly lose his balance.

Orfeo came at him, grabbed him around the neck from the rear. Gustav tried hitting him as he stood there, desperately trying anything to break free. But Orfeo's arms were strong. They kept squeezing. Gustav trembled, his eyes bulged. He knew he would die at any moment if he couldn't free the muscular arms from around his neck. In a moment, it was all over. Gustav was limp. Orfeo disgustedly threw him to the floor.

Orfeo dragged the body to one of the refrigeration units and opened the door. He pulled the shelves out and angrily threw the vials of serum to the floor. Most of them broke, sending thin slivers of life-saving liquid across the floor. He shoved Gustav into the unit and closed the door. He saw a lock hanging from the handle and latched it. He then went to the closest unit and pulled on the lever, but it was locked. He looked around at all the other units and realized that they were all locked. He needed a key to get in. He glanced back at the unit that he'd put Gustav into, wondering why that one had been left open. Perhaps some of the serum had been released. As he re-processed what he'd seen when he opened the unit that now contained Gustav, he tried to remember if it was full.

He grew increasingly anxious as he ran back to the unit that now contained Gustav, pulling on the handle, swearing and yelling to no one in particular, "The key is in your pocket! Traitor! You will ROT in hell for your lies!"

He hit the unit with the palm of his hand, once, twice, three times, each time, harder than the last, until his hand was red and sore.

VATICAN, ROME, ITALY – DUSK

Just inside the balcony overlooking St. Peter's Square, stood the pope. He put his arms over his head as his assistants helped him don his vestments. This was a big moment for him, for his followers, for all of Christianity, for that matter. What was he going to say? He took a couple of steps to the balcony and looked out onto the square. Thousands of people were still gathering while workers set up a stage with large speakers, designed to carry his sermon to not only everyone in attendance, but to all Catholics throughout the world. It was the middle of the seventh day and they were still looking for Trinity and the release points.

The pope struggled with his role in this mess. Everyone assumed that Trinity had to be stopped, that they were evil, their goals misguided and their means barbaric. But part of him wondered if he was witnessing something ordained. Maybe the end was supposed to look like this; maybe Revelation was simply a parable for the end times.

Since Trinity's announcement, the Vatican directed all priests to tell their congregations that this was a test of their faith, that focusing on what made them Catholics would be enough to save everyone. Many seemed to believe this, but a large number of Catholics simply panicked, as did thousands and thousands of people all over the globe. The pope tried to calm people, telling them to prepare themselves by praying and focusing on doing good, not evil. There were some who listened and some who did not. The lawless outbreaks in every major city in the world were a testament to how bad people really were. Maybe this was a long time coming, maybe the virus was just what the world needed to make everyone see how truly screwed up we were.

The pope's assistant put the last of the vestments over the pope's outstretched arms. Still watching the crowd gather in the square, he knew this might be his last sermon. It seemed unlikely everything would end like this. But nothing was certain, except what they expected in the after life.

After the vestments were fully adjusted, the pope stepped closer to the balcony and peered out, looking toward the door to the basilica. Swiss Guards stood by the door preventing people from entering.

His assistant tapped him on the shoulder. The pope turned to him and noticed the satellite phone in his hand. But more than that, he could see a new kind of shock in his face, the kind one experiences when they they've been duped or when a loved one has died.

"Sorry to interrupt you but you'd better take this."

"What is it?" asked the pope.

"It's the president."

The pope took the phone from the assistant and listened to the president. His face registered shock. He didn't say much. He handed the phone back to the assistant.

"It's Orfeo. He's the leader of Trinity," said the pope.

As he heard his own words, he couldn't believe it could be him. Of all people. He was his most trusted aide.

The pope turned to his aide, muttering, "Find Orfeo. I need to speak with him at once."

Outside St. Peter's Basilica, the Swiss Guard eventually let people inside. Everyone was anxious to hear the pope and what they hoped would be answers to the questions they all had. Would he give them the secret to surviving the coming plague? Would he tell them how to muster the faith necessary? They wanted some hope—someone to tell them that it would be all right.

With several assistants at his side, the pope made his way through the Vatican to the rear of the basilica, where he would make his grand entrance. Outside the basilica, St. Peter's Square was packed. A Vatican priest stood on the stage, speaking to the throngs of people, reading scripture and trying to quell the anxious crowd. Next to him were several massive speakers, set up to broadcast the pope from inside the basilica.

Once the pope made it to the rear entrance of the basilica, he was surprised to see it guarded by several Swiss Guards. He waived them aside but they did not move. He gave them a questioning look.

"Move aside," he said. But they didn't move. He turned to his assistants, but in an instant, he could see that they were with the guards. Orfeo came out of the shadows, but the pope didn't see him.

"What is going on with these guards? I have Mass."

Orfeo stepped in front of him. The pope's jaw dropped. Orfeo smiled.

"I ordered him detained," said the pope, pointing at Orfeo, expecting the guards to obey him.

His assistants ignored him. The pope took several steps toward Orfeo and stopped inches from his face. "So, it is you. I still can't believe it."

"It is indeed," answered Orfeo.

Orfeo turned to the Swiss Guards. "Take him away."

"You have the Swiss Guard?"

"I am more powerful than you, Your Highness," said Orfeo, with a mocking tone of voice.

The Swiss Guards—in reality, Trinity soldiers—led the pope away.

DA VINCI AIRPORT, DUSK

By the time Jacob and Amy landed at Da Vinci Airport, several military vehicles waited for them. Amy and Jacob flew off the plane, their feet barely touching the stairs. Once in one of the military vehicles, they took off, headed for St. Peter's Square.

Several local police vehicles met them at the exit to the airport and escorted them to the square. When they were about a half mile away, the traffic became increasingly heavy, the streets clogged with a combination of vehicles and locals. It looked as though everyone in the city was on the streets. Most of the people were anxiously marching toward the Vatican. Some carried signs that read, "The End is Upon Us: Repent!" One read, "Jesus will Return," another read, "Save us."

They were in an impossible bottleneck, a confluence of people, vehicles and the Carabinieri. The officers tried to corral the massive hoards of people, but they didn't have any luck. The will of the people was more powerful than any police agency could contain so they simply allowed the people to push forward, heading toward the Vatican, the only place many of them felt safe.

"What's going on?" asked Amy. She leaned over the back seat of the military vehicle.

"Everyone is getting as close as they can to the basilica. They want answers. The end could be around the corner," said one of the soldiers.

"Did they get Orfeo?" asked Jacob.

"We lost communication with the Vatican 30 minutes ago."

"All those people have no idea … we can't wait." Jacob opened the car door and exited. The commander started to object but instead sent several UN soldiers with them. The UN soldiers pushed ahead, trying to make a path for them, but all they could do was allow the natural movement of the people to push them forward, toward St. Peter's Square. Soon, Amy and Jacob became separated from the UN soldiers.

Amy clung to Jacob's hand, nearly squeezing the blood from it.

Inside the Vatican, Orfeo stood staring at himself in the mirror, as an aide helped him don his vestments. Orfeo couldn't help but smile. Everything now fit into place. All that he had planned for, the extraction of the virus and the coming test for the world, had coalesced perfectly. It was as if God himself ordained what he had done.

STREETS OF ROME, NEAR VATICAN

Amy and Jacob held on to each other, trying not to allow the crowd to separate them, as they moved closer to St. Peter's Square. People chanted about not wanting to die; some were more encouraging, telling people to adhere to Trinity's mantra: have faith and you will be saved. But it was obvious to Jacob and Amy that most of the people in the streets were desperate. Tension hung in the air, like the fumes from gasoline, ready to ignite. Jacob heard someone yell out that the government had a serum and only a select few were being saved. Amy heard someone yell for his mother. People carried all sorts of signs, ranging from, "Repent, the End is Near," to "Damn the Establishment." She knew that this scene was being replayed around the world, with anxious, scared people looking for some solace before what they believed could be the end.

She was surprised that more people didn't seem engaged by the concept of faith saving them. Perhaps those folks were housed in the various religious centers around the city.

At the entrance to St. Peter's Square, the number of people seemed to increase. The streets were so packed, that it was difficult to move at all.

Jacob had not allowed himself to think much about Trinity's demands and threat, in terms of what it meant to him. But as the final hour drew near, he wondered if believing in himself was enough.

Certainly, Amy didn't ascribe to religious faith—at least not since the death of Melissa—but at the same time Jacob knew that her anger controlled her. She had no logical reason to blame herself, yet, he knew that this was what drove her. What would they find in St. Peter's? Would it be Orfeo and the virus, or was there something more that lurked behind the shadows of that amazing structure?

Finally, they found themselves opposite the entrance to St. Peter's Square. The square was a mass of humanity. In the distance, near the entrance to the basilica, Amy saw the stage. Someone was on the stage, speaking to the masses, but she couldn't hear what he was saying. Jacob looked around the square, trying to find a way past the throngs of people, but couldn't see any way to get past them. Amy poked Jacob in the side, and he turned to her.

"I wonder what the speaker is saying?"

Jacob shook his head and yelled, "What?" The din of people drowned out anything they said.

Amy yelled, "There's a speaker! See, on the stage!"

Jacob heard most of what she said and followed her gaze. He nodded, trying to show her that he'd heard what she said. He guessed the speaker was warming up the audience for the sermon from inside the basilica.

Out of nowhere, the UN soldiers appeared and nodded at them as they led the way through the square. Amy and Jacob followed. Their uniforms seemed to open a pathway through the crowd. They passed by the 25-meter-tall obelisk, dating to the 13th century B.C. Soon, they were close enough to the stage to hear the speaker who had just finished.

Jacob checked his watch. It was 11:30 p.m. He had always assumed the virus would be released, at least here, at midnight. It was stunning, the cruel trick that was being played on these people. They were here for solace and comfort, and they were being drawn in for the kill, as if they were no more than wild animals reacting instinctively to a stimulus.

Once inside the square, several more soldiers appeared, some wearing UN uniforms, others the Swiss Guard. A group moved toward the Sistine Chapel. Just opposite the stage, Jacob stopped, getting the UN soldier's attention. Jacob turned to Amy.

"Orfeo's got to be inside the basilica."

"But where?" asked Amy.

"Who knows?"

Jacob headed for the front door to the basilica with the two UN soldiers in front of them. For a moment, Amy was transfixed by the colossal statutes of Saints Peter and Paul, on either side of the stairs leading to the basilica. Jacob counted 10 heavily armed Swiss Guards standing outside the structure, keeping the crowds at bay. He assumed that the UN soldiers would not assist them in getting past the Guards. They'd have to find another way in. He wished that his old friend Father Thomas was there to help them. His presence would have been invaluable.

Suddenly, the speakers—now behind them—sprang to life. Jacob stopped in his tracks. So did Amy.

In Italian, a voice through the speaker said, "Lord God, Lamb of God, you take away the sin of the world . . ."

"What's he saying?" asked Jacob.

Amy shrugged her shoulders but didn't answer.

"Where the hell is Orfeo?" said Jacob.

Amy continued to listen to the speaker. There was something about his voice. It sounded familiar. She tried to decipher WHAT he was saying, her understanding of Italian not what it once was.

"Can someone please tell me what he's saying?" asked Jacob again. The UN soldiers shook their heads. Jacob decided to see if the Swiss Guards would tell him. Just as he started up the stairs, it came to Amy. The voice.

"Jesus, Jacob!" Jacob turned back to Amy. "It's Orfeo!"

"Christ. He's saying Mass, isn't he?"

Jacob looked to the Swiss Guards for confirmation, and one of them nodded in agreement.

"He's going to release it—" said Amy.

"During Mass!" said Jacob, finishing her sentence.

At the door to the basilica, the Guards blocked their entrance.

Jacob and Amy looked at each other and then at the Guards, worry etched in their expressions. "We're from the UN. These soldiers are with us. We have to get inside! The virus is going to be released during Mass!" implored Jacob.

The Guards remained stoic, barely acknowledging Jacob's entreaty. "Listen, the fate of this city depends on us getting in there!" said Jacob. One of the UN soldiers, the highest-ranking officer among them, stepped forward.

Jacob stood his ground. "Let us past," he said, his voice firm. Still, the Swiss Guard barely acknowledged them.

Finally, the guard said, "I do not have that authority."

"Look, we've got a crisis here. I'm ordering you aside," responded the UN officer. The Guard did not move. Instead, he nodded to the Guards nearby who joined him, their guns now raised in front of them.

"We're wasting time. This isn't going to work. What are we going to do, shoot them?" said Amy.

Jacob thought for a moment, when the voice of Father Thomas seemed to speak to him. It told him about a secret passage . . . and suddenly, Jacob remembered.

He grabbed Amy. "Follow me."

"Where are we going?"

"I know another way in."

"How?"

"Father Thomas."

While the UN soldiers argued with the Swiss Guards, Jacob led Amy to the far side of the basilica. The old, weathered, marble façade of the basilica barely got their attention as Jacob walked around to the far left of the entrance. There were several Swiss Guards near there as well, but there was no visible entrance.

Amy followed Jacob past the Guards, who didn't seem to care that they were there. The massive wall of the basilica loomed to their right, and Jacob took them to the rear, looking for something on the wall. Jacob studied the travertine surface, running his hands over it.

"It's got to be here," he said.

"What are you looking for?"

"An entrance to a secret passage."

"How—"

"Father Thomas. He told me about it. He used it when he worked here. He and other young priests would leave past curfew. They discovered a hidden door."

They finally got to the end of the wall. Amy stared at the rear of the structure. Jacob counted from the end of the wall. The surface was smooth, except for the joints where the massive travertine stones fit together. It seemed impossible that there would be a hidden door anywhere on the wall.

One of the UN soldiers joined them, and after Jacob told him to look for a vertical crack, he joined in the search. Amy stared at the surface, wondering if Jacob had finally lost it. And then, she saw it. A faint, vertical crack in the wall, only it was straighter than a crack would be.

"Jacob, what's this?"

He moved over to her and examined the crack, following the length of the wall. He found the top edge and then followed it around. Amy watched him and was amazed when she saw that the crack stopped at a point to the right, and then went down. It framed what could be a door.

Jacob started talking to himself. "He told me that you had to push on the left side and it would pop open." Jacob leaned on the left side but nothing happened. The UN soldier pushed as well. There was a pop and the 'door' cracked open on the right side, as the left side depressed.

"I bet this hasn't been opened in years," said Jacob. He pulled on the right side and the door opened. The architects who had created this door had done an amazing job hiding it in the wall. The passageway floor was made out of crushed travertine, the walls, unfinished travertine. It smelled musty but not damp. Jacob, Amy and the UN soldier pulled out small flashlights and entered the darkness.

BASILICA OF OUR LADY OF PEACE, IVORY COAST

At the largest church in the world, 7000 people gathered for what they hoped would give them some assurance that they would survive the wrath of Trinity. An additional 11,000 people stood near the nave. Outside, on the massive grounds around the church modeled after St. Peter's Basilica, were an additional 10,000 people, some carrying signs, proclaiming the end of the world, others holding signs with more positive messages focusing on the role that religious faith has in the world.

But the over-arching theme was positive. Not many thought that death was imminent, that their beliefs would get them through this challenge.

Had they known about the four Trinity men, carrying the virus in a backpack and making their way through the crowd, the reality of what was about to happen might have deadened their enthusiasm.

There were so many people there that Trinity members couldn't help but fit in. The virus they carried in the backpack had been put into aerosol form and would be sprayed into the air, infecting everyone there and then carried back to their homes and into the surrounding countryside, where it would easily spread. Certain death would hit almost everyone within 100 miles in 24 hours. It would take a little longer to wipe out the rest of Africa, but, of course, that all depended on the prevailing wind.

One of the Trinity soldiers thought it was odd that they were tasked with testing faith in such an obscene way. Most of them were confused about what Orfeo expected. Did he anticipate that many would survive the virus? Orfeo had convinced them that they were stronger than any virus, that this was a test that everyone but the most evil would pass. He wondered if it occurred to Orfeo or any of the other Trinity members that their actions might have the opposite effect: what if everyone died? What if this was all a cruel joke and nothing could save them from an ugly death?

These thoughts were hard to ignore, but he'd been trained to obey and he wouldn't falter now. Soon, the four of them were at the rear of the basilica where they entered the church. The man carrying the backpack put it down and then extracted four small canisters holding the virus. He handed them out and each of the soldiers took their places on opposite sides of the basilica, waiting for the moment when they would release the virus.

St. Peter's Basilica, Catacombs

Seven Trinity soldiers made their way through the catacombs, one carrying a large duffle bag holding the canisters they would release on the unsuspecting crowd gathering upstairs. They all carried Uzis. The plan was to hide these under their long trench coats and to use them if necessary to prevent people from leaving, once they realized what was happening. The expected stampede of people didn't concern them— they had orders to mow down anyone who tried to leave the basilica.

Nearby, in the secret passageway, Jacob and Amy, with the UN soldier leading the way, walked over the crushed stone passageway, looking for a way out. On the walls, they passed sconces every 10 feet, presumably containing oil that could be ignited. They ignored these, as they didn't have time to light them.

The air had become damper as they walked along. Jacob noticed that they seemed to be descending slightly, which would account for the increase in moisture. Soon, the passageway ended at a door. The UN soldier turned the handle and opened the door. Dust and cob- webs descended in front of the soldier, some of them draping across his head and shoulders. He reached up and wiped them off.

"Guess no one expected any unexpected guests," said Jacob.

"It's pretty obvious that this hasn't been used for many years," commented the soldier.

On the other side of the door, they had only one way to go—up. The stairs, also made of travertine, were covered in a heavy layer of dust that hadn't been disturbed in years. The stairs went up and to the left.

At the top, before they turned to the left, was a landing. The stairs went up from there, another 15 feet to a door. As they ascended this part of the stairs, some light filtered into the stairwell from above. And they could hear a voice get louder the closer they got to the door.

Once they reached the door, the UN soldier very carefully turned the handle and tried to open it. It wouldn't budge.

Jacob took several small tools from his pocket, and using those and his flashlight, he was able to easily open the old lock.

He carefully opened the door. When he did so, the voice became very clear.

"Alleluia!"

The congregation responded, "Alleluia!"

"May The Lord be With You."

"And Also with You," replied the congregation.

They stepped into the magnificent basilica, under a sheltered alcove, near the back. Even now, with a knot in the pit of her stomach like nothing she had ever experienced, Amy couldn't help but be momentarily stirred by the amazing architecture, the tall ceilings, the statues and mosaics, with the famous Bernini canopy rising above in the dome. It was stunning. The last time she'd seen it, the magnificence of it, something that almost seemed to be the work of God, brought her to tears. It had that same effect now, even as they faced the evil that Orfeo brought to this holy place.

CHAPTER XVI

"He shall cry and roar; he shall prevail against his enemies" (Isa. 42:13).

BELZ WORLD CENTER, JERUSALEM

Worshipers lined the streets outside of the center, waiting to get inside to listen to the rabbi who would lead them past the Trinity threat. Inside, the pews were packed. Dressed like the other Jewish men, with skullcaps and white shirts and black pants, four Trinity soldiers lined the upper balcony that ran the length of the synagogue. Like the other teams, they carried the virus in canisters that they would release once the service had begun. And, as in the other locations, they didn't have any trouble getting into the synagogue or in securing their place. No one had any idea what was about to happen.

Particularly not Ben Elkin, his wife Eden and their two children, Liron and Ben-David. Ben was not particularly devout, but in times like this, one couldn't be too careful, at least that's what he told himself. He was a banker, from a long line of Elkins who were involved in the financial industry, and had a difficult time admitting that he didn't believe in what he was doing. For years, he had been told who to lend money to, whose notes to foreclose and even which debtors needed a heavy-handed reminder to pay their bills. While some degree of violence (the "reminder") was rare, it had happened a couple of times, and he simply tried to ignore it.

But just last week, one of the bank's collectors severely assaulted a man and his wife, putting both of them in the hospital and leaving their son and daughter at least temporarily without parents. And he had been the one to order the collection. When he heard what had happened, he was angry, but there was nothing he could do about it. He never told anyone what he'd done, but it was well known in the bank that this behavior was accepted. No one talked about it, but these medieval collection methods were widely practiced. A man of deep convictions, the thought of what he'd done weighed heavily on him. He blamed this for the coming of the Trinity virus. It was his fault—he had put his family in danger, and they would have to pay for his transgressions. He didn't believe there was anything he could do to fix what he'd done except to try to appease the Creator. What that would look like, he didn't know.

And now, as they headed for the synagogue , a place they hadn't visited in years, he wondered if anything could save him, much less his family. They had talked about fleeing for the mountains, maybe in France or Italy, thinking that the elevation might protect them from the virus.

In fact, a contingent of his friends talked this over as soon as they heard about the Trinity threat. It was interesting to see the variety of reactions from people at the bank and the people of Jerusalem. Some co-workers did just what he had thought about doing: they ran. One went to Africa, seeking refuge in the foothills around Kilimanjaro, in Tanzania. Another friend went to a small village near the Amazon in South America. As remote as possible was the thought. No one knew if this would work. But a friend of his, an epidemiologist who had studied the virus with the physicians at the United Nations, was sure of only one thing: the virus was very dangerous and very deadly. And, as Amy had reported to the UN, it was in a state of seemingly constant mutation. No matter what they tried to create a serum, the virus would mutate and make the discovery useless. Many scientists believed that because of this rapid mutation, the virus might very well burn itself out. Once in the air, some felt that it would mutate into something harmless. Others felt that it would wipe out most life forms, faith be damned.

So Ben didn't know what to do. Would escaping do anything to save them, or would it prolong the inevitable? Something about the threat had given him the willpower to fight back. Eden felt the same way. For her, this was a test that they had to pass and that was presented to them as a way to redeem themselves. But Ben had long ago abandoned any notion that a Supreme Being might have an impact on his life. Now, he wondered if he was right. For him, it had always been a matter of atoning for what he'd done. If he could do it, he wanted to give himself up to save his family. He didn't know how he would do that, but he knew he had to.

ST. PETER'S BASILICA

Orfeo sat at the front of the sanctuary, in the celebrant's chair, a red hood covering most of his head. The rest of the red vestment covered his shoulders, arms and legs where he sat, giving some the impression that he wanted to hide his face from the congregation. No one had ever seen any priest wear a hood during Mass.

On one side of Orfeo was a server. In the chair next to him, on the other side, sat a body, slumped over and still, wearing a black robe with a black hood. Orfeo looked menacing, his face barely visible in the shadows created by the hood covering his head. Orfeo rose and walked slowly. The person next to him still did not move. Parishioners tried to see who it was, but the face was shrouded in darkness. If anyone had been close enough to see the left side of the black robe, they would have discovered that it was wet and sticky with blood.

Once Orfeo reached the pulpit, his head bent over slightly and he opened the Bible, never removing his hood. The church, packed beyond capacity, waited in complete silence for Orfeo to enlighten them. Some wept quietly; many had their heads bowed in respect. But some looked directly at Orfeo and then at the still figure. There was something wrong, almost an imperceptible smell of revulsion present in the basilica. What was that? Where did it come from? For those who sensed this came the feeling of fear. And a feeling that they were somehow trapped.

Orfeo slowly pushed the hood back. An almost imperceptible gasp could be heard in the basilica, an expression of shock, maybe fear. Orfeo heard it and, for a moment, he smiled an expression of evil dominance, not respect.

Slowly, savoring his moment of power, he turned to II Corinthians (5:1-7).

He read from the passage, "For we know that if the earthly tent which is our house is torn down, we have a building from God, a house not made with hands, eternal in the heavens . . ."

Amy, Jacob and the UN soldier were too busy trying to figure out where the virus would be released and what mechanism would be used to release it, to listen to Orfeo. But he read the entire passage as they walked along the left wall of the basilica and stopped halfway to the front of the church.

Amy whispered, "What are we going to do?"

Jacob turned to the UN soldier. "Come with me."

The soldier looked across the aisle to the other side of the basilica, where he saw some of the soldiers who had been outside. He got their attention and indicated with his hands that they should move toward the front of the basilica, toward the altar, where Orfeo waited to release the evil virus.

In St. Peter's Square, the UN contingent grew to 20 soldiers. Another military vehicle had arrived and delivered the rest of the soldiers, who now gathered near the makeshift stage, listening to Orfeo and contemplating their next move. The UN commander ordered them to various locations in the square. Once they were there, he got on his mic, and received his orders. He motioned to two of his men, mounted the stage and whispered something to the technicians working the equipment. Suddenly, the speakers cut out. The crowd groaned. The commander reached for a bullhorn and turned it on. He happened to be Italian and so he spoke to the crowd in their native language.

"I have an important announcement. We must clear the square. Please follow the directions of the soldiers who are nearby. They will direct you out of the square."

The crowd murmured and someone yelled, "We are here to worship, to seek salvation. We do not want to leave!" The crowd collectively yelled in agreement with the man. Another voice nearby yelled, "It's the virus!"

At that instant, as the possibility sunk in, everyone in the square hightailed it for the street. One mass of humanity moving in a single direction, without any order, is exactly what the UN commander had hoped to avoid. But it hadn't worked.

People pushed others aside; some fell to the ground, trampled by the hoard of people. It was pandemonium. Fearful that the virus would be unleashed on them, most abandoned their desire for religious leadership and salvation. The reality of certain death melted their resolve. If Orfeo had seen the stampeding crowd, he'd have smiled and thought that they had no faith. Indeed, fear was all most of them could feel.

It was a horrific scene, people pushing anyone in their way, running over people on the ground, so certain that death was near that they thought nothing of killing their fellow man to save themselves.

Inside the basilica, in the utility room, several Trinity soldiers worked on the metal heating duct, cutting an opening so they could insert the aerosolized version of the virus. They used a simple hacksaw to cut through the ductwork. Once they were through, one of the men withdrew the canister release devices—two of them, to be exact—and set the timers for 10 minutes and placed them in the holes. They then sealed the duct with duct tape. As an ultra precaution, they put on gas masks and left the utility room.

In the sanctuary, Amy, Jacob and the UN soldiers—one on either side of the church pews—were now almost to the front of the basilica. The parishioners didn't seem to notice them. They were glued to Orfeo, hanging on every word. Orfeo had just about finished the reading.

". . . knowing that while we are at home in the body we are absent from the Lord, for we walk by faith, not by sight, the word of the Lord."

Orfeo turned to leave, but as he did so, his eyes met Jacob's. Surprised to see him, Orfeo did a double take. For a moment, he couldn't move. He couldn't help but feel threatened by the presence of Jacob and Amy, at least for a moment.

Amy, for one, savored the moment. She smiled back, knowing that they would defeat him.

Orfeo could see her resolve and it threw him. Why did she have such confidence? Did she know something that he didn't ? Maybe they had discovered the serum that Gustav had created.

Near the back of the basilica, eight parishioners got up and took their place at all of the possible exit points. They were Trinity soldiers, ready to kill to prevent people from leaving the basilica, ready to die for their cause, if faith did not save them. They tried to hide their Uzis under their long trench coats, but the butts pushed through the front of the coats on several of the soldiers. Yet the people in the basilica were too focused on the speakers, hoping for some solace, to notice what was happening around them. The Trinity soldiers from the catacombs made their way up to the rear of the church, blending in with the rest of the people, their Uzis ready to be deployed.

Orfeo returned to the Celebrant's chair and sat down. He waited for a moment, milking the drama of the moment to its full effect. He could almost taste the anticipation in the room, the power he held over these people who expected him to save them.

Before Orfeo got up, he looked once again at Jacob and Amy. An evil smile creased his face. This was perfect. He would kill them here, in the basilica, in front of their God, in their Church, where the deception started and today, would end.

Instead of rising, Orfeo nodded to the unmoving figure next to him. Normally, this person—someone more exalted than Orfeo— would give the sermon. But today, Orfeo had a surprise for the congregation, something no one could anticipate. He wouldn't spring it on them yet, because he needed their trust, their attention. The fun would start when he locked the doors and spread the virus. He rose and slowly walked to the pulpit, his hood in place.

BELZ CENTER, JERUSALEM

Liron and Ben-David anxiously awaited the start of the service. Neither of them was particularly excited to be there. The synagogue was as full as they'd ever seen it. People stood near the exits and around the perimeter of the pews. How could the service do any good? They were too young to appreciate the possibility of death. They had talked about faith as a family when the terrorists made their threat a week ago. But they couldn't agree on what they were asked to do. If it was faith in Jesus as their savior, there wasn't much hope for them. The terrorists never said what they meant by "faith." As their father had told them, they should not assume anything. Even though

Trinity had quoted from a religious text, it didn't mean that the solution was to profess faith in a deity.

Ben leaned over and whispered, "I have a bad feeling about this."

Eden gave him an odd look, as if she thought he was imagining things.

"You don't feel it?" asked Ben, to no one in particular. Ben looked for some confirmation that he was right. Others around him seemed content, ready for the rabbi to console them, to give them answers. Ben wondered how other, non-Christian religions were dealing with this. Trinity's message, if it could be believed, didn't focus on any specific belief system, yet the rabbis had been telling them for the past week, that even non-Christians had faith and could be saved.

The discussion, for Ben, soon bordered on the ridiculous. The notion of everyone dying except those with "faith," when the instrument of death was a virus, was preposterous. How could something unseen save anyone from a deadly virus? One of the rabbis said that we act on faith every day of our lives. We have faith that the people in the cars around us will obey the law, that they won't run into us, that the people working on skyscrapers won't drop stuff on our heads, we have faith in our spouse that he/she will be faithful. The list goes on and on.

And, of course, there was religious faith. But what did that mean? Faith in a Creator, faith in Jesus, for Christians, who came to save us from ourselves—that was what fellow Jews wanted to talk about. But it truly was more complicated than that.

The crowd stirred when the rabbi came in to start the service. In the rafters above, Ben noticed some movement. He saw some men moving around, seemingly pushing for a position near the railing. For a moment, he wondered. He had no reason to be suspicious, but a single thought flitted through his brain. Could Trinity release the virus here?

———

St. Peter's Basilica

Orfeo slowly removed the hood. The crowd was quiet, anticipating a clear, hopeful message, already transfixed by one of the Vatican's most important leaders, before he'd opened his mouth.

"We are all here to seek answers. What will happen to us if we die? Will there be, as Christ teaches us, life after death? As Christians, we believe that Christ died for our sins, that the path to salvation is through Jesus, the man. But what if that was wrong?"

The crowd murmured, not expecting Orfeo to blast a hole in Church teachings.

"Here, in this glorious place, we seek protection from the virus. But I assure you, Christianity will not protect you. Over the course of history, mainstream Christianity has been responsible for wars, famine, disease, countless deaths. No other religion would protect you. Not Muslim, Islam, Judaism."

The murmur grew in intensity. People glanced at each other, their confused expressions a measure of what the entirety of the congregation felt.

"The Church continues to drag us through the mess they've created."

Several people, shocked at the priest's blasphemous message, rose and walked to the rear of the basilica to leave, but Trinity soldiers, who guarded the doors, wouldn't let them leave. They had been ordered not to display their firearms unless it was necessary to prevent the congregation from escaping. Bewildered, the people stood there, uncertain what was happening.

In the square, the UN commander tried to get the massive crowd in the square to leave in an orderly manner, but he was only able to slow down the stampede. After frustration set in, he turned his attention to the basilica. He motioned to several soldiers, who joined him as he approached the doors. He told them that he'd gotten orders to prevent the Swiss Guards from blocking entry to the church. He motioned to his men to approach the guards from either side. He went to the center door and told the guard that he was ordering them to relinquish their command to him. The guard ignored him. The commander motioned to his men, and they quickly took the guards into custody. He did the same with the man opposing him. It was obvious to him that their lack of resistance indicated that they couldn't, because of their orders, relinquish control without putting up the façade of resistance. The commander tried the door to the basilica but it was locked. The Swiss Guard saw this and offered to help. The commander indicated that he should be released. The guard jostled the handle as well with no luck.

"Any other entrance?" asked the commander.

The Swiss Guard shook his head, "no." The UN commander ordered some of his men to ram the front doors until they opened.

Inside the basilica, Jacob and Amy continued to move forward until they reached the altar rail. Orfeo continued to talk about the traditional path to salvation and a different path, one more aligned with the Gnostic Gospels.

"You want to know the path to salvation." Orfeo looked down, directly at Amy and Jacob and he smiled.

"It is THIS." He pulled the Judas Gospel out from a shelf inside the podium and waved it above his head. Jacob wanted to jump him, right then and there, be damned that he was in St. Peter's Basilica. But he restrained himself.

At the rear of the church, the Swiss Guard and the remaining UN soldiers pounded on the doors, still heavily guarded from the inside by Trinity. By now, most of the congregation was on their feet, pushing toward the exits, while still listening to Orfeo.

Orfeo puffed his chest out, reveling in the power that he possessed at that moment, feeling the virus flowing from inside of himself, as if it was his virus. He hurried toward the chair that held the prone figure and yanked the hood back. The crowd let out a collective scream—it was the pope, his neck a bloody mess.

Parishioners jumped up and started for the door, then stopped, yelling out things like, "Oh my God, he killed the pope!; he's dead, he's dead!; he's crazy, he killed him!" Orfeo glowed, standing next to the body like a hunter standing over his prey.

Jacob and Amy started to move forward, past the altar rail, toward Orfeo, not as shocked as the rest of the people, in part because they knew who he really was. Jacob could see that Orfeo held something at his side, but he couldn't see what it was. But it was someone standing near the exit who finally saw a gun butt sticking out of a Trinity soldier's long coat.

He pointed at the soldier and yelled, "HE'S GOT A GUN!"

Just about everyone in the church, jumped up and ran for the exits. But Trinity had them blocked, and no one could leave. And now, the Trinity soldiers had their Uzis out, a strong incentive for the congregation not to challenge their authority.

Orfeo yelled into the microphone, over the sounds of terrified screaming, "To truly test your faith, you must believe as Judas teaches! Jesus was a spirit, not a man, who sought death to free him from the evil of the world! It is time for you to see if your faith is strong enough to save you. It was NOT enough to save the pope!"

With that, Orfeo turned from the pulpit and fled through a side door, followed closely by two large Trinity soldiers. Four Trinity soldiers stepped out of the shadows in the rear of the sanctuary. All were armed with Uzis.

If people were anxious before because of Orfeo's strange message and the presence of implied force inside the basilica, what happened now was motivated by terror. Horrific screams echoed throughout the expansive interior, and people ran for the exits, plowing others over, giving the basilica an unfamiliar look and feel, more like a debauchery filled college stadium than a revered place of worship. Trinity was prepared for this. The men guarding the exits raised their Uzis and fired some warning shots into the air.

That stopped everyone in their tracks. The UN soldiers tried to shoot back at Trinity but there was too much danger that they would hit innocent parishioners. Trinity soldiers withdrew gas masks and additional canisters from underneath their coats.

Before the Trinity soldier near the front of the basilica could open his canister, one of the UN soldiers killed him with one shot to the head. His canister fell to the floor. No one in the basilica blinked—they were all too focused on getting out of the room to notice a gunshot.

People screamed for God, for life. As the people in the basilica forced their way toward the exits, they confronted the Trinity soldiers, who killed many of them.

The UN soldiers once again tried to defend the parishioners, but for most, it was difficult for them to get a clear shot. One of the soldiers managed to gain some high ground when he jumped on a pew and was able to get a couple of shots off.

Some parishioners had been trampled, but most were still upright, having a difficult time moving because the mass of humanity pushing toward the exit was packed together like a school of fish fleeing from a predator.

But the UN soldier got a shot off and killed one of Trinity's best. It didn't do much good, as another one fired with his Uzi and dropped a half dozen parishioners with a three second burst.

By now, everyone was pushing toward an exit. The middle of the basilica was strangely empty. In the midst of this turmoil, Amy and Jacob pushed through the people and toward the sanctuary. Several parishioners tried to escape through the side door, but they were promptly shot by two Trinity soldiers. Jacob fired one shot after another at the soldiers, surprising them, as he and Amy headed for the door. The element of surprise was enough to give Jacob the advantage. Both soldiers hit the ground, dead. Jacob and Amy dragged the two dead worshipers from in front of the door, opened it and entered the hallway.

The sheer mass of humanity inside the basilica was more than Trinity could handle. At the doors on the side of the basilica, it didn't take long for some brave parishioners to successfully subdue some Trinity soldiers. But these doors were also locked from the outside, just as the rear doors were. This was where most of the people tried to escape and where Trinity had three heavily armed soldiers. After it was clear that Trinity had no problem killing them, people backed off.

In the basement, the canisters released their deadly toxin through the exhaust pipes, into St. Peter's Square.

In the meantime, Amy headed for the exterior door at the end of the hallway. Before she could open it, Jacob grabbed her from behind.

"No, he's still here. Look for another door."

They were in the anterior chamber used by the priests to change into their vestments and for storage of holy water, wafers used in Communion and robes worn by priests and servers. Amy and Jacob rocketed through the cabinet drawers and closets. Jacob yanked vestments out of the closets and threw them on the floor. He pounded on the wall behind the vestments and found a spot that sounded hollow.

Amy joined him. On the rear wall were several clothes hooks. Amy pulled on one and then another, and a door popped open to Jacob's left. Jacob pushed it open wider. It was dark and musty inside, but Jacob could see evidence that the door had been recently used. There were tracks in the dust, and several cobwebs hung over the entry as if they had been recently disturbed. Jacob and Amy drew out their flashlights and entered the secret passageway.

CHAPTER XVII

"By faith you shall survive; no one can defeat you if you believe, whether it is in Me that you believe or in My teachings" (Mark, 20:12).

BELZ CENTER

Ben knew now that something was wrong, but it didn't seem that anyone else noticed it. He stared at the balcony that ran around the perimeter of the synagogue, unable to take his eyes off of several men who clearly did not belong there. They wore traditional Jewish clothing, including the skullcap, but the caps didn't fit right and the clothes looked as though they were thrown on without any concern for whether they fit. Not everyone in the synagogue was dressed smartly, either.

Ben didn't know what or why they seemed to stick out. Why were these men here? He counted at least four that seemed out of place. Maybe they were anxious to seek whatever help they could get and tried to fit in. He'd heard religious leaders talking about being more open to non-Jews in this time of trouble. Maybe they'd decided to allow in anyone who sought the grace of God. That seemed like a feasible explanation until Ben noticed that the men had backpacks on the floor near their feet. Each pulled something from the backpacks and held it over the congregation. By now, everyone was seated, waiting for the service to start. At that instant, Ben knew why they were there.

He stood, pointed at them and yelled, "Everybody run! They are here to kill us!"

People first turned to him, giving him the stink eye, but several followed his outstretched hand and saw the men, who were obviously up to something. At that moment, two of the Trinity soldiers released the canisters, spewing forth the deadly virus. At once, everyone flew to their feet, running and screaming, as the peaceful congregation turned into a throbbing, moving mass of humanity, desperate to get out and save themselves.

Ben tried to shepherd his family down the aisle, but others pushed past them, knocking him and Liron back into the seats they'd just gotten out of. People from the front of the synagogue jumped over the seats to get out, pushing others aside. Many fell on the ground, their bodies now steppingstones for the leaping, heaving hordes of humanity. The last thing Ben remembered was trying to grab ahold of Liron while at the same time keeping an eye on the rest of his family. He reached for Liron, who had fallen in front of him, when someone else knocked him to the ground. As he fell, he caught a glimpse of Eden catapulting over the seat back. He called out to her but then he felt a sharp pain to his middle and then his head. From under the pew, he could only catch fleeting glimpses of people's feet. The air was filled with the sounds of screams, calls for help, and the rush of humanity reverting to the primitive escape instinct. And then, something hit his head. He felt for Liron, grabbed ahold of her shaking hand, and everything went blank.

CATACOMBS, ST. PETER'S BASILICA

Inside the dusty, limestone hallway, Amy and Jacob made slow progress, their small flashlights barely giving them enough light to see their way. The stale, damp air was unsettled, as if the dust on the floor had recently been disturbed. That gave Amy and Jacob some solace—they were following Orfeo's escape route.

Amy couldn't help but think about the chaos unfolding in the basilica. As they got deeper under the basilica, the sounds of rapid-fire machine bursts dissipated, but they were still there.

They hoped to catch Orfeo and force him to reveal the identity of the agents who were in the other religious centers preparing to release the deadly virus. It was almost certain that they were too late, for some worshipers. But because they didn't know much about the dissipation rate, it was possible that by containing the outbreak, they could stop the spread of the virus.

Jacob had a feeling, however, that Trinity had an antidote. It didn't seem likely that all of them would believe that faith could save them. Orfeo was a power monger, believing in his version of faith enough to trust his survival to it. But did he have the charisma to persuade all of Trinity that the path to salvation was through him and the Judas Gospel? That had bugged Jacob since the beginning, although history was not without some truly bizarre religious figures leading to their believers horrific results—Jim Jones came to mind.

Jacob's flashlight caught a wire hanging from the ceiling. He pointed his light up and saw a series of wires with light bulbs at various intervals. Using his flashlight, he scanned the walls. He found a light switch near the entrance but didn't flip it.

He put his index finger to his mouth, indicating to Amy that she should whisper. "Too risky to flip the switch," he whispered. "They'll know we're coming."

"You don't think they're waiting for us?" Jacob shrugged his shoulders, then nodded reluctantly.

They turned back and headed down the corridor. Up ahead, they could see light emitting from their right and left—an intersection in the corridor. They turned off their flashlights. Jacob put his hand out, stopping Amy before the intersection. They stood there, listening. There was an indefinite sound coming from somewhere, but it was unclear whether it was from down there or from the church. Jacob peered around and saw that just on the other side of the intersection were doors—one opening to the left, the other to the right. Artificial light was visible through the small windows near the top of the doors. The hallway they had been walking down seemed to have some sort of lighting 20 feet or so ahead of them.

Jacob pointed to the door on the left while he took the door on the right. "Be careful," he whispered. Amy nodded. They each tried a door, but they were locked. The two huddled for a moment.

"How do we know which way to go?" said Amy.

"They could have gone through either one of these doors and locked them."

"Or they could have gone straight. We don't have a lot of time, Jacob."

Jacob nodded, thinking. He tried to think it through. Why would they lock the door behind them? The most obvious reason was to prevent anyone from following them. Or did they expect the two of them to follow so they could set up an ambush? It wasn't a secret they were in the church. Orfeo knew they would follow. Maybe he wanted them to keep going—that's why the doors were locked.

"Jacob, you have to make a decision."

For at least the second time that week, he had to guess. He was getting pretty good at it, but he still hated it. He motioned down the hallway and took off, with Amy following.

They ended up at another intersection and turned down the hall—right into the two Trinity soldiers who went with Orfeo. Their eyes locked on Jacob and Amy. It was clear that they were not expecting the two of them, as they had just exited from a room on their left, carrying large boxes, which was fortunate because they couldn't carry boxes and guns.

Jacob immediately threw himself at the guard closest to them, driving him into the other soldier. The force of the blow, combined with the surprise of the attack, was enough to propel them awkwardly onto the floor. Jacob landed on the top of one of them, and Amy attacked the other. By the time she reached the soldier, he had already gotten halfway up. These guys were well trained. Amy was in trouble. She lashed out with a side-kick, but the soldier was ready. He blocked the kick and threw her aside—and he was still on his knees.

Jacob saw her out of the corner of his left eye. He would have to get this guy fast or she was going to be crunched. As the soldier got up, Jacob hit him hard in the head, knocking him back against the wall. He turned to the other soldier and hit him as he went after Amy, who was just getting up from the first blow. He turned back to the other soldier, who had gotten up, and hit him hard in the gut and then the face as he turned to face him. It doubled the soldier over. He struggled to get a breath.

Amy was on her feet, attacking the soldier with several knife hand blows to the neck. He was still reeling from Jacob's blow so it didn't take much to knock him down. But the guy on Jacob kept coming, hitting him again and again. Blood trickled from Jacob's nose and mouth. He started to feel light headed. His assailant was more of a fuzzy apparition than a real person.

The soldier sensed that it was time for the kill. He unsheathed his knife and raised it above his head. Before he could plunge it into Jacob, Amy came at him from behind, grabbing the knife and pulling the soldier backwards. It caught him by surprise, and he fell back. Still in a haze, Jacob fumbled for his Glock and fired two shots at the soldier, hitting him in the chest. He fell to the floor, dead. He then fired one more shot at the other soldier, killing him. It was a good thing because the gun jammed when he tried to take another shot.

Amy helped him to his feet and they slowly opened the door the soldiers had come from. They peeked in.

"He's not there," said a frustrated Amy. She barely noticed Jacob, who was holding his stomach.

"Well, let's find them," muttered Jacob. They closed the door and continued down the hallway. Jacob limped badly and worked on un-jamming the Glock.

After a few moments, the hallway ended at another door. Jacob grabbed the doorknob and opened it. The two rushed past the threshold.

They emerged in another, smaller room in the catacombs. Orfeo stood in the middle of the room, facing them, smiling wryly. Both Amy and Jacob glanced quickly around the room, trying to take it all in. The room was full of religious artifacts—ceremonial flags, urns, display cases full of old chalices and religious symbols, such as stars and crosses.

Orfeo lazily raised his arms and gestured, sweeping them around the room. Amy continued to look around and then focused to the rear of Jacob. She narrowed her gaze, waiting for her eyes adjust to the lack of light in the room. On the far wall, behind Jacob, was a large container, at least four feet wide and over six feet high. The Shroud. "Jacob. Behind you."

Jacob turned around, his jaw dropping as he stared at the large box. "That would be about the size of the Shroud, right Orfeo?" he said as he turned back to face Orfeo.

Orfeo was now holding a gun at waist height, aimed at Amy and Jacob. Before Jacob could react, a shot rang out. At the instant he was hit in the right leg, all he could think about was how stupid he was for not realizing that Orfeo was armed and would readily shoot them. He'd been trapped by the oldest trick in the book—simple misdirection. Jacob crumpled to the ground, rolled over and pulled his Glock out of his waistband when Orfeo fired again, this time hitting him in the gun shoulder. Jacob let out a grunt, dropped the gun and grabbed his wounded shoulder with his left hand.

Amy tended to Jacob's leg and then his shoulder. The bullet had grazed his outer, right thigh but it bled heavily. The shoulder wound went through but it too was a bleeder. She looked for something to stop the bleeding.

Jacob, who lay on his back, tried to get up but moaned and then plopped back to the ground. "Oh, God." he moaned.

Amy ripped some fabric from her shirt and wrapped it around his leg. The bottom of her t-shirt was now just below her breasts. When she saw how much the shoulder wound bled, she took her t-shirt off and used it to press on the wound. She heard the click of the gun and looked up. Orfeo had the gun aimed at her but it had jammed. He worked the slide until the jammed bullet came loose.

Orfeo now stood at Jacob's feet. "You son-of-a-bitch," said Amy. She felt her face turn red as she jumped to her feet and pushed Orfeo in the chest. "You coward! How dare you use your crap to justify the deaths of those innocent people." The spit flew from her mouth as the words came faster than she could process what she was saying.

She pushed him again. He raised the gun. She took a fighter's stance.

"You think I'm afraid of you! Come on! You killed my sister!"

"I've got a gun."

"Come on. FIGHT ME!"

Jacob, who watched the situation, couldn't believe Amy's courage, even if it didn't make a lot of sense. He knew what would happen next. Orfeo slowly raised his handgun until it was pointed at Amy. Jacob looked for something to grab. Outside of his reach was an old statue, about a foot-and-a-half high. He tried grabbing for it. Orfeo, who just wanted to kill them and see the execution of his plan without these meddlers around, moved around Amy, intent on killing Jacob before he could grab the statue.

Amy used this opportunity to lurch out at him with a side-kick that she'd learned in Tae Kwon Do. It connected but didn't do much more than stagger Orfeo, who managed to get off several shots before he regained his balance. But she re-grouped and hit his gun hand with another well placed side-kick. The gun went clattering on the stone floor.

Behind her, Jacob flew backward when one of the wayward bullets glanced off his left leg, below his knee. He grabbed his leg where the blood ran down his pants and seeped through his fingers. He grimaced as the pain seemed to radiate up and down his leg.

Orfeo recovered from Amy's last blow and turned to face her. She lashed out again at him, this time trying a palm heal strike—shoving her hand, palm leading, just under Orfeo's jaw. Orfeo blocked it and hit her hard with a forefist blow to her right cheek. Amy flew back and hit the ground, groggy from the force of the blow. Orfeo turned his attention to Jacob. But first, he found the gun and picked it up.

Standing over Jacob's good leg, Orfeo slowly raised the gun, a goofy smile on his face. Jacob pulled back his leg and as quickly as possible, pounded Orfeo in his groin. He reared back, yelling in pain. The gun flew out of his hand, hitting the floor once again. Jacob felt a new, stabbing pain in his injured leg as if he'd hit him with the wounded leg.

By now, Amy had turned around. She saw that Orfeo had dropped his gun and Jacob was struggling to his feet. He made some progress and then the pain overwhelmed him. He gathered himself and then fell to his left knee, trying to protect his right leg.

Out of the corner of her eye, Amy saw Orfeo moving quickly. She turned back to Orfeo and launched herself at him. She got him around his ankles. He lost his balance and crashed head first into a glass display case.

He tried to break his fall by reflexively raising his hands in front of his head, but it did no good. Various religious artifacts—crucifixes, decorative crosses and religious stars—fell out of the display case and clattered onto the stone floor.

The impact of Orfeo's body striking the display case caused half
of it to collapse on the ground, while the other half balanced itself on
the two remaining, unbroken table legs. Orfeo tried to push himself
up and out of the case, but he was in more pain than he knew possible.

After Amy hit Orfeo, her head hit the stone floor, causing her
to nearly pass out. As Amy slowly regained her sense of place and
time, Orfeo managed to stagger to his feet. She got to her feet. For a
moment, she thought about helping Jacob. But something inside of
her told her that Orfeo was not finished. He wasn't.

Orfeo slowly turned toward her, his arms still partially above his
head, with his elbows at shoulder height, his palms facing outward.
Nothing prepared her for the grisly sight of Orfeo's face and hands.

Shards of glass punctured his hands, face, arms and upper body.
There were several long shards that were still stuck in his hands. Small
pieces littered his face like confetti. Blood was everywhere, oozing
from his face and running down his arms, hands and torso.

Orfeo slowly moved his left arm down and toward his face. For
every movement, Orfeo experienced a new level of pain. But all Amy
could see was a maniacal grin on his face, as if he relished the pain.
He tried to pick the glass from his face but his hands were so full of
glass themselves that he couldn't bend his fingers.

Orfeo almost glowed, enjoying his own agony.

Behind her, Jacob struggled to regain his balance. He was still
bent over at the waist, massaging his damaged groin. Jacob was now
on his knees. He could barely stand the sharp, shooting pains in his
leg and shoulder that only got worse every time he moved.

Jacob slowly pushed himself onto his right leg, then his damaged
left leg. Bolts of lightning, hot pain, radiated up his leg, through his
shoulder. Suddenly, a Trinity soldier came into the room, quickly
assessed the situation and came at Jacob, his arm raised ready to strike
out. With the last bit of tenacity he could muster, Jacob launched his
body at the soldier. The two hit the hard, stone floor. Somehow, the
soldier ended up on top of Jacob. He hit Jacob with a thud. The hard
stone floor and the soldier's body sandwiched Jacob's wracked body in
multiple layers of pain. He moaned and willed himself not to scream
out in pain but then things got very foggy. After a few moments, the
fog in Jacob's had cleared a bit. The soldier was no longer on top of

him but was looking for something. The gun—the one that Orfeo had dropped. Jacob followed the soldier's gaze. He had just located it and lunged at it.

St. Peter's Basilica

Several brave parishioners attacked the remaining Trinity soldiers, managing to secure the remaining virus release devices. None of the parishioners realized that they had already been exposed to the virus, as it had been released by two of the four devices brought into the church, nor did they appreciate that everyone outside the basilica had been exposed to it through the exhaust pipes that vented into St. Peter's Square.

The parishioners finally seized the exits from Trinity and opened the doors. Hoards of people fled the church. Trinity soldiers on the outside had since abandoned their posts, as their job was finished.

Catacombs

Orfeo lurched forward. Using his right hand like a mace, he swung it at Amy. Still startled by his appearance, she was slow to react. A shard of glass sliced through the skin on Amy's cheek, the pain instantly registering on her face. She fell back. Her right hand flew up and over the wound. Orfeo, stiff and robot-like, moved toward her, his other arm raised and ready to strike. He swung it at her. This time, she moved back, but he still clipped her with a shard of glass sticking out of his hand.

He hit her right arm, near her bicep. It sliced into her skin. But instead of reacting to the sharp pain, Amy took action. Using one of the Tae Kwon Do kicks she learned years ago, she hit Orfeo in the mid-section. The blow staggered him, but it wasn't hard enough to knock him to the ground.

She advanced, taking a wild swing with her left arm, connecting with the right side of his face. The impact drove a large shard of glass further into his face and into the fingers of her left hand. Then she kicked him in the gut, throwing him across the room. But he quickly gathered his balance.

The wound in Orfeo's face widened. Blood now gushed from the wound. She came at him again, taking a wild swing. She hit him in the face with her left hand, driving even more glass into his skin. Blood flowed from the wound, dripping onto the floor.

Amy quickly grabbed her left hand, massaging it where it was cut by the glass. She looked up at Orfeo, expecting the blow to slow him down, but the increased blood flow seemed to invigorate him. Their eyes met for a moment. It was obvious to her that pain had no impact on him.

Orfeo reached out with both hands, and before Amy could react, he closed his hands around her shoulders, embedding the shards of glass into her flesh. She screamed when the shards cut through her like a hundred tiny razor blades. He pushed her back. Then, he head-butted her, and she felt another piece of glass cutting her. Staggered by these blows, she was unable to resist when Orfeo threw her to the ground. Any hit the stone hard.

Behind her, the Trinity soldier reached for the gun, but Jacob, now on his feet, pounced on him from behind. The force of Jacob's body against him was enough to push him past the gun, nearly into the far wall. But the soldier kicked Jacob in the right shoulder. The blow was right at his shoulder wound. The pain nearly caused him to collapse; he teetered. He fought it, tried to regain his balance.

It gave the soldier the upper hand. He crawled like a crab toward the gun. But what he didn't expect was Jacob's resolve. Using his left hand, Jacob grabbed him as he went past him. With all the strength he could muster, Jacob threw the unsuspecting soldier against the wall. His head hit hard. He wasn't moving.

Jacob hit the floor, his strength sapped. For a moment, Jacob thought it was over. Then, he remembered Amy. He swung around has he staggered once again to his feet. And he stopped in his tracks, staring into the face of a monster—Orfeo.

He couldn't imagine how Amy had done that to him. His face was studded with glass shards, sparkling in the dim light with the red of his blood. The sight of him froze Jacob. He didn't look real. Who could survive such pain and blood loss?

Orfeo came at him and hit Jacob hard in the face with the palm of his hand. Jacob never knew what hit him but could feel something cutting and gouging his face. He fell to the ground, his face bleeding from the wounds inflicted by Orfeo's hand. What the hell was that? How could he cut Jacob like that?

With both Amy and Jacob prone, Orfeo glanced around the room, looking for something to finish them off. In the corner, near the smashed display case, were various flags, some with pointed, spear like tips. He picked up one of these.

Amy staggered to her feet, staring at Orfeo and the spear-like weapon he held in his hands, wondering how in the hell she was going to kill someone who seemed impervious to pain. She had to have a weapon of her own, something to use against him. Another flag would be good. But it was across the room—and Orfeo was between her and the flag. Orfeo was now poised to attack Jacob, who was still on his back, writhing in pain.

Amy frantically searched for something to use as a weapon. Out of the corner of her eye, she saw a sparkle. It was a religious star, very pointy, sharp looking. She reached for it and then realized that if she shoved this into Orfeo, one end would impale the palm of her hand. Nearby, was half of a star, one end seemingly broken off. She discarded the first one and picked up the broken one.

Orfeo raised the flag and balanced it like a spear, his eyes gleaming with purpose. Jacob turned over and got on his knees, then hoisted himself up, using the edge of another display case to pull himself upright. He tried to ignore the pain in his leg and shoulder, but it seared through him with every movement. Each twinge was like re-experiencing the initial torrent of agony that racked his body. Although his back faced Orfeo, he knew he was bearing down either on him or Amy. For the moment, he forgot about the soldier. He sensed that Amy was in trouble. And he wanted Orfeo—badly.

With blood oozing from his shoulder and leg, Jacob turned around to face Orfeo, taking a fighter's stance. His wounded leg throbbed with pain—he could barely maintain his balance. Orfeo thrust the flag toward Jacob.

Jacob saw it coming and hoped he had enough left to side step and grab the flag. Just as he prepared to make his move, there was a flurry of movement from behind Orfeo. Amy. She lurched forward, screaming.

"You fucking bastard!" She plunged the star into Orfeo's back, then pulled it out and plunged it in again. The blow took Orfeo by surprise. He tried to slow his lunge, to attack the greater threat behind him. But instead, he dropped the flag and turned around, grabbing Amy as he fell forward.

The two crashed to the ground, with Orfeo on top of Amy. He grabbed her around the neck. The shards of glass embedded themselves into her flesh. He was too heavy. Where was Jacob?

With the pain in her neck increasing, Amy glanced frantically around her. She saw an object close by. She gasped for air. She reached for the object, uncertain what it was. It was just outside her reach. She stretched as far as she could.

Orfeo growled. "You are mine, my dear. No one can kill me."

Just then, Jacob came from behind, grabbed Orfeo around the neck with one hand and drove the star further into Orfeo's back with the other. Orfeo let go of Amy's neck and reared back, trying to throw Jacob off, his bloody face finally twisted in pain. There was something comical about him—the shards of glass sticking in his face, like stick pins on a cork board, the blood dribbling down his face, the new look of pain that seemed to animate the glass, as if it was moving on its own. He violently twisted around, clawing at his back, throwing Jacob to the ground. For a moment, Amy thought she could see in Orfeo's face some recognition of the agony caused by the numerous wounds that littered his body.

With Orfeo temporarily distracted by Jacob, Amy scooted across the floor and finally saw what glimmered in the light—a metal cross with sharp ends. She grabbed it but then felt the weight of Orfeo's hands around her neck and the sharp pain of the glass cutting her skin. The pain gave her a surge of energy. She whipped her hand up and plunged the cross into Orfeo's neck with surprising force. Blood squirted from the wound. The edge of the cross was deeply embedded into Orfeo's neck. He clawed at the cross, trying to pull it out. He fell back, his eyes wide with pain. Blood streamed from the wound.

Struggling to his feet, he kept clawing at it, desperate to pull it out, his eyes full of the knowledge that he wouldn't survive this wound.

Finally, he lost his balance and fell to his knees. Amy was now standing, her face torn with anger and revenge.

"Die, you son-of-a-bitch!" she said as she kicked him from behind. He sprawled to the ground, flinched and then lay still.

She looked around for Jacob. To her left, she saw movement—Jacob, struggling to get up, his back to her. But there was someone behind Jacob. She looked around him. The soldier. He had the gun. Pointed at Jacob. Frantic, she looked to her right and left. There was a chalice on the floor. She grabbed it.

"Jacob!" she yelled.

She threw the chalice to him. Amy lost her balance and fell to the floor. With a burst of energy, he caught the chalice, got up and swung it behind him, hitting a surprised soldier in the head. It was a 100 to 1 shot.

It drove the soldier to the side with enough force that he hit the wall. He slid down the wall, limp. The gun fell harmlessly to the floor.

Jacob didn't have enough strength left to stop his momentum. He fell to the ground, so exhausted that he was limp. His shoulder and leg were soaked with blood. Amy crawled to him and lifted his head, cradling it in her lap. He opened his eyes and looked up at her, trying to crack a smile.

"We . . . did we . . . ?" he muttered, barely able to speak.

She nodded, tears streaming down her face. She laid there with him, when she heard a rustle at the door—several UN soldiers appeared. One got on his radio and asked for the medic.

St. Peter's Basilica

The UN soldiers had finally gained the upper hand. Most of the Trinity soldiers were dead. The worshipers streamed from the rear of the church, the UN soldiers trying to calm them down. It was a difficult task. Most of the people believed that they had a chance to live if they could get out of the church. That wasn't true, of course, but they wouldn't listen to the soldiers. Once the soldiers had secured the door, their task was to calm the stampede enough so that no one would be trampled. That much they had accomplished.

Outside the basilica, the UN soldiers led three captured Trinity soldiers from the church. By now, nearly half of the people who had been in St. Peter's Square had fled, hoping to escape the virus. Some never made it, however. Bodies littered the square like discarded mannequins. People assumed it was the virus, but these people had died during the mass exodus, many of them trampled to death.

No one who left the basilica seemed to notice. Once out, they fled. Some cheered, but all were oblivious to the virus that had been released outside as well as inside the basilica. Everyone was subject to the death grip of the virus. It was the ultimate of ironies: if faith could save these people, they didn't know it. In some ways, Orfeo couldn't have asked for more, even in death, for the true test of faith comes when the subject doesn't know he's being tested.

Jacob and Amy exited the basilica on stretchers. Walking next to Jacob's stretcher was the medic, holding an IV drip. Amy kept glancing at Jacob, hoping to see some signs of life. She was worried that he wouldn't make it. The medic said that he'd lost a lot of blood but would be OK. The look on his face told a different story.

The ambulance the medic called ahead for drove across St. Peter's Square, the people from the basilica moving aside to let it through. The driver stopped and two men got out, opened the rear door and guided Jacob's stretcher inside.

Amy pulled on the arm of one of the soldiers carrying her out. He looked down at her. "Put me in the ambulance."

He nodded. Another soldier said that they were only supposed to take Jacob, but Amy rolled off the stretcher before it reached the truck. She teetered when she tried to stand up; one of the soldiers helped her regain her balance, but she pushed him aside, intent on standing on her own. She limped to the rear of the ambulance and pulled herself inside. Another medic listened to Jacob's heart and another placed an oxygen mask over his face.

Amy sat at his feet, tears in her eyes. He wasn't moving.

BASILICA OF OUR LADY OF PEACE, IVORY COAST

The service had just started, the doors had closed and the basilica was packed. The four men carefully removed the canisters, put them against the wall and turned them on. The deadly virus spread silently. One of the men was too scared to trust his fate to faith or to the inoculation so when he activated the canister, he quickly exited the church. Once he reached the exterior of the church, he pushed his way through the crowd. If he was going to die, it wouldn't be today.

Inside the basilica, people worshiped, unaware of the specter of death spreading through the church. The three Trinity soldiers who remained were sure that they would be three of the few who would survive. One of the men believed that most people would survive if they only believed as he did, in the power of Jesus as explained by Judas.

BASILICA OF THE NATIONAL SHRINE OF THE IMMACULATE CONCEPTION, WASHINGTON D.C.

As in other major religious centers around the world, the church was packed with people hoping for salvation. Four Trinity soldiers entered the church with backpacks, containing the virus in canisters. They took their places inside the church, waiting for the moment when they would release the virus.

Once everyone was inside, 10 priests, wearing colorful, ornamental cassocks, walked down the center aisle of the church, as the congregation sang, "Amazing Grace." When they reached the altar, the lead priest started to pray, his voice booming through the sound system.

Many people in the church were regular churchgoers, sure that they would be saved. But quite a few hadn't been to church in years and in fact, had practically abandoned their faith. In times like these, everyone wanted some guidance. On that day, many of the people carried guilt for failing to live a life that could lead to salvation. If they were lucky, the UN soldiers would save them.

In the midst of the guilt and the worship, all four Trinity soldiers made their way to the balcony, seeking the highest point in the church to release the virus.

Soon after the service started, 10 UN soldiers entered the church as quietly as they could. They split up, looking for Trinity soldiers. The worshipers were so engrossed in the service that the presence of armed soldiers didn't seem out of order. But soon after they arrived, people exchanged glances, whispering about them, wondering what they were doing there.

The soldiers walked rapidly around rows, hugging the supporting walls of the structure. Several priests noticed their presence but tried to ignore it.

The Trinity soldiers noticed the UN soldiers right away. Each of them removed the canisters from the backpacks, but one was quicker than the others. He held it over the congregation, ready to deploy it. One of the UN soldiers saw him; he stopped and pointed to the balcony.

"UP THERE!" he yelled.

The church was suddenly quiet, as everyone jerked his or her head up. The Trinity soldier froze for a moment, his gaze fixed on the thousands of people staring at him.

"It's the VIRUS!" someone yelled. With that, the church turned into a mass of human bodies all trying to run from the church at the same time. The church had been transformed, in an instant, from a place that people sought solace to a place of fear and death.

UNITED NATIONS

President Holcomb, the chiefs of staff and the key leaders of every member nation were glued to a series of video and audio feeds. One showed the calamity outside the Belz World Center, where some people were trampled in the mass exodus from the synagogue. The UN soldiers had still not arrived and the virus had been released.

On another screen, they watched a live feed at the National Shrine in DC as a UN soldier fired at the thug holding the canister, hitting him squarely in the chest. Holcomb and the others in the room tensed up as the canister fell from his hand. Had he released it before he dropped it? Would it release on its own once it hit the floor? They all seemed to hold their breath.

People in the church who saw the dropping canister ran from it, except for a 75 year-old man who stood under it, his hands outstretched, as if he were an outfielder waiting to basket catch a fly ball.

The canister fell into his hands. He bobbled it. Everyone moaned. Then, the old man secured the canister. The room seemed to sigh in unison. But the old man couldn't prevent the canister from emitting its poison. When the gas came out, the old man smiled, confident that he wouldn't succumb to the virus. He fiddled with the emitter on one end of it, trying to stem the flow of gas.

Another camera showed UN soldiers running up the stairs and after one of the remaining Trinity soldiers who still held a canister. On the other side of the church, a Trinity thug stopped and withdrew the canister, ready to disperse it. Behind him, two UN soldiers pushed their way through exiting parishioners. First one, and then the other, tried to get a shot at the Trinity soldier, but people kept bumping into them, too afraid of death to realize that the means to survive the virus was there, waiting to vanquish the misguided soldiers of Trinity.

In order to get a shot, one of the UN soldiers slugged a parishioner in his way, quickly brought the gun to bear and fired three shots at the Trinity thug. Two bullets hit him in the head, throwing him backward, into the wall, spraying blood. This time, the canister fell to the floor of the balcony, intact.

The old man had succeeded in turning the canister off. Only a small amount of the toxin had been released. It was at least better than the whole thing pouring out into the congregation.

On the other side, they watched a UN soldier shoot the remaining Trinity thug. The threat in the National Shrine was eliminated, at least for the moment.

Holcomb wiped beads of sweat from his forehead. He turned to his new chief aide.

"Tell me what's going on at the other release points."

"Sir, UN troops have been sent to all the churches on the list. We've been unsuccessful in Brazil, Africa, Jerusalem, the Vatican… there's at least a dozen."

Holcomb's mouth dropped open. How could they possibly survive if the virus had been released in all those locations? He looked around the room at the others, and their faces registered what he was feeling—dread.

The phone rang and Deputy Chief of Staff Mike Peterson answered it. Every eye in the room was on him. He listened, not saying anything. Then, he hung up the phone. He looked as if he'd just found out that he had a day to live.

"Trinity has been stopped in Belgium, Spain and London. But the virus was released at St. John's in New York. We're trying to contain the area."

Holcomb slumped into his chair. Then, the phone rang again and everyone jumped.

CHAPTER XVIII

"He will not fail or forsake you; fear not, you will be [saved]" (Deut. 31:8).

TWO DAYS LATER

WHITE HOUSE PRESS ROOM

President Holcomb stood at the podium, having just started his third press conference in the last 48 hours. His face was drawn and haggard. He'd gotten very little sleep in the last several days as the world waited to see if there would be any people left. He tried to be as honest as he could, but there were things that he knew, or suspected, that he didn't want to say. There were times, such as now, that he hated his job.

"We don't know why the virus didn't spread after the initial outbreak."

A dozen or so reporters stood up and spoke at once. Holcomb pointed to one of them. "Mr. President, our understanding is that the virus was 100 percent lethal and was easily spread. But it killed only several thousand people. Then nothing. What's the explanation?"

Holcomb paused, wondering if this was one of those times when giving a truthful response was ill advised. There had been a lot of political-speak the last week. It would open the floodgates, to say what he really thought, but frankly, he didn't care.

The room was hushed, waiting for his response. He started very softly.

"We'll probably never know for sure what happened. It seems unlikely to me that the virus dissipated on its own, not with what we knew about its virility. What other possibility exits? It's the one that politicians want to avoid. It's the one that relies on exactly how the terrorists challenged us; it's the religious explanation. It's ironic, don't you think, that we beat them at their own game, using world faith, from every religion in the world, to destroy them and their virus?"

The room was still hushed, as if the reporters couldn't believe what they heard. Holcomb felt at peace for the first time in a week.

ONE WEEK LATER

Jacob didn't want to admit it, but he wished he could have attended the president's press conference a week earlier. He heard it on TV at the hospital in Rome, where he was recovering from the surgery for the many wounds he'd suffered "saving the world," as one of the more attractive nurses had said. It was funny, he thought, that he longed to see Amy again and barely noticed the nurse. He asked for her several times. She finally came into his room, with bandages all over her body, evidence of the horrible struggle she'd survived.

When she entered, Jacob noticed something different about her. He couldn't put his finger on it, but she carried herself with more confidence, purpose. In spite of all they'd been through, when she walked into the room, she smiled.

She grimaced as she sat down on the bed next to him. She took his hand gently in hers. "You don't look too good."

"You should talk."

"The doc says he put you back together, just as good as new. So when are we getting out of here, anyway?"

Jacob smiled. "I hear that I may be able to leave in a couple of days. How about you?"

"I'm waiting for you."

"I figured."

"Oh, you did? Getting cocky, are we?"

"I just know what I want."

Jacob pulled her gently forward and they kissed lightly. Then they kissed again, harder this time, but Amy pulled back, holding her lip. Then, they laughed together, their wounds and pain joining them, in a way that just seemed to fit, as if it was meant to be.

WASHINGTON DC, ONE WEEK LATER

Holcomb stood outside the press room, not wanting to discuss once again the fateful events of the last several weeks but relenting to the public pressure to beat what he thought was a dead horse. His speech would be about the growing worldwide belief that faith had defeated the virus. Religious leaders all over the world, no matter who they were, were witnesses to a faith-based resurgence that could not be equaled by anything they'd ever witnessed or read about. Nearly everyone, even atheists, turned to God. Who could argue against what appeared to be empirical evidence of a Creator?

The spread of religious fervor was so pervasive that many governments were being pushed into non-secular based leadership. Countries such as France, Greece and Spain had been thrust, by the new religious movement, into sharing some of the country's political leadership with religious leaders. Holcomb hadn't been pressured in the United States and didn't care if he was, but he understood the need. People used the eradication of the virus as proof that there was a deity. It was undeniable, or so they wanted to believe. It was the first evidence of a Supreme Deity, God, whatever you wanted to call him.

The evidence was not nearly as strong as people believed. Sure, it was possible that faith had defeated the virus, but it was equally possible that the virus dissipated on its own. But Holcomb knew that it didn't matter.

Interestingly, some religious institutions were threatened by people's renewed faith. Instead of turning to them for the answers, people now had confidence to handle the responsibility of faith on their own, as if the death of the virus had given them a manifesto to salvation. Holcomb was worried about how institutionalized religion would react to this new challenge. They needed people to look to them for answers. Now, people seemed to have fewer questions and less need for someone to tell them what faith was, or what to have faith in.

There wasn't much Holcomb could do about this, at least publicly. He waited at the door to the pressroom, waiting for him to be announced. When he heard his name, or rather, his alias—"The President of the United States"—he cringed and entered the pressroom.

OUTSIDE THE WHITE HOUSE

"We're late," said Amy, the irritation in her voice grating through the air of the Explorer. Jacob jerked the car around a corner into the White House parking lot and slammed the brakes on.

"Yeah, well, my leg aches, my shoulders feel like crap, it takes me five times as long to do everything." Jacob opened the door and tried to hop out of the car but grimaced when he was unable to throw his left leg out of the car the way he was accustomed to doing.

"Oh, crap." Jacob moved himself slowly out of the car and then realized that Amy was still in her seat. As he glanced at her, he felt the tightness in his face, the anger palpable. She was half-smiling at him.

"So this is funny? You enjoy this?"

Amy hesitated before answering. Then, she shook her head, "no." But the smile remained on her face. Slowly, she opened the door and watched Jacob try to pull himself out of the car. For a moment, the pain in his leg was too much for him. He slumped back into the driver's seat while Amy opened the rear door and extracted his crutch. She leaned it against the car and turned to Jacob.

She extended her hand. Jacob still looked as though he wanted to take a bite out of her, but his expression softened to one of resignation. He allowed her to take ahold of his arm and then his shoulder, helping him out of the car. When he got to his feet, she pulled him forward.

His face now inches from her, his grimace turned into a half-smile. "We'd better get going," he whispered.

They pulled apart, and Amy grabbed the crutch. Jacob pulled it from her and slammed the car door behind them. Using the crutch for assistance, he started into the White House. Amy walked next to him.

Once inside, Jacob put his crutch on the metal detector and began taking his shoes off. Amy offered to support him, but he gently pushed her arm away. As she walked through to the other side of the machine, Jacob noticed for the first time that Amy looked different, more feminine. She wore a short, black skirt, and a white blouse, with the top buttons open just enough to show some cleavage. Why hadn't he noticed that before they'd left for the press conference?

Jacob stood there, staring at the metal detector, wondering if he'd be able to make it through without falling. As soon as he put weight on his leg, he pursed his lips and tried to ignore the ripping pain that seemed to extend throughout his body. He took one step and nearly fell. Amy started to rush through the metal detector but stopped when she saw Jacob glaring at her.

Intent on getting through this without any help, Jacob dragged himself through the metal detector, a little at a time, only to have the machine beep. He cursed in frustration. Using one hand to prop himself up against the machine, he patted his pockets, trying to find whatever it was that had set the machine off. But he struggled to put his hand inside his pants pocket.

By this time, Amy was standing next to him. Without hesitation, she put her hand in his pocket and fished around. Jacob tried to give her that same disapproving glare that she was so used to, but his expression softened. She looked into his eyes as she located the objects—a couple of coins in the bottom of his pocket—and slowly pulled them out. She could tell that Jacob not only had given in but that he was actually enjoying all the attention. It was about time, she thought.

The guard pulled out a metal detector wand. "You don't have to go back through. Can you lift your arms up?"

Jacob nodded and lifted his arms as the guard ran the wand over his body. Nothing. Jacob grabbed for the crutch, but Amy had already latched onto it. She handed it to him and then propped herself under his other side.

With her help, he headed toward the pressroom. He and Amy had the same, silly smiles on their faces.

THE END

BIOGRAPHY

Mark Geiger was born in Milwaukee, Wisconsin, and currently resides in Salem, Oregon. An attorney who has specialized in criminal law for the past 25 years; he has had a passion for writing his whole life. *The Trinity Effect* marks his first major work. He is currently working on a sequel, The Water Bearer.

Made in the USA
San Bernardino, CA
05 April 2014